The Virgin's Lover

Philippa Gregory

Doubleday Large Print Home Library Edition

A Touchstone Book

Published by Simon & Schuster

New York   London   Toronto   Sydney

This Large Print Edition, prepared especially for
Doubleday Large Print Home Library, contains
the complete, unabridged text of the original
Publisher's Edition.

TOUCHSTONE
Rockefeller Center
1230 Avenue of the Americas
New York, NY 10020

TOUCHSTONE and colophon are registered trademarks
of Simon & Schuster, Inc.

Manufactured in the United States of America

ISBN 0-7394-4864-1

This Large Print Book carries the
Seal of Approval of N.A.V.H.

For Anthony

Autumn 1558

All the bells in Norfolk were ringing for Elizabeth, pounding the peal into Amy's head, first the treble bell screaming out like a mad woman, and then the whole agonizing, jangling sob till the great bell boomed a warning that the whole discordant carillon was about to shriek out again. She pulled the pillow over her head to shut out the sound, and yet still it went on, until the rooks abandoned their nests and went streaming into the skies, tossing and turning in the wind like a banner of ill omen, and the bats left the belfry like a plume of black smoke as if to say that the world was upside down now, and day should be forever night.

Amy did not need to ask what the racket

was for; she already knew. At last, poor sick Queen Mary had died, and Princess Elizabeth was the uncontested heir. Praise be. Everyone in England should rejoice. The Protestant princess had come to the throne and would be England's queen. All over the country people would be ringing bells for joy, striking kegs of ale, dancing in the streets, and throwing open prison doors. The English had their Elizabeth at last, and the fear-filled days of Mary Tudor could be forgotten. Everyone in England was celebrating.

Everyone but Amy.

The peals, pounding Amy into wakefulness, did not bring her to joy. Amy, alone in all of England, could not celebrate Elizabeth's upward leap to the throne. The chimes did not even sound on key, they sounded like the beat of jealousy, the scream of rage, the sobbing shout of a deserted woman.

"God strike her dead," she swore into her pillow as her head rang with the pound of Elizabeth's bells. "God strike her down in her youth and her pride and her beauty. God blast her looks, and thin her hair, and rot her teeth, and let her die lonely and alone. Deserted, like me."

*   *   *

Amy had no word from her absent husband: she did not expect one. Another day went by and then it was a week. Amy guessed that he would have ridden at breakneck pace to Hatfield Palace from London at the first news that Queen Mary was dead. He would have been the first, as he had planned, the very first to kneel before the princess and tell her she was queen.

Amy guessed that Elizabeth would already have a speech prepared, some practiced pose to strike, and for his part Robert would already have his reward in mind. Perhaps even now he was celebrating his own rise to greatness as the princess celebrated hers. Amy, walking down to the river to fetch in the cows for milking because the lad was sick and they were shorthanded at Stanfield Hall, her family's farm, stopped to stare at the brown leaves unraveling from an oak tree and whirling like a snowstorm, southwest to Hatfield where her husband had blown, like the wind itself, to Elizabeth.

She knew that she should be glad that a queen had come to the throne who would favor him. She knew she should be glad for her family, whose wealth and position would rise with Robert's. She knew that she should be glad to be Lady Dudley once more: restored to her lands, given a place at court, perhaps even made a countess.

But she was not. She would rather have had him at her side as an attainted traitor, with her in the drudgery of the day and in the warm silence of the night; anything rather than than ennobled as the handsome favorite at another woman's court. She knew from this that she was a jealous wife; and jealousy was a sin in the eyes of God.

She put her head down and trudged on to the meadows where the cows grazed on the thin grass, churning up sepia earth and flints beneath their clumsy hooves.

How could we end up like this? she whispered to the stormy sky piling up a brooding castle of clouds over Norfolk. *Since I love him so much, and since he loves me? Since there is no one for us but each other? How could he leave me to struggle here, and dash off to her? How could it start so well, in such wealth and glory as it did, and end in hardship and loneliness like this?*

One Year Earlier: Summer 1557

In his dream he saw once again the rough floorboards of the empty room, the sandstone mantelpiece over the big fireplace with their names carved into it, and the leaded window, set high in the stone wall. By dragging the big refectory table over to the window, climbing up, and craning their necks to look downward, the five young men could see the green below where their father came slowly out to the scaffold and mounted the steps.

He was accompanied by a priest of the newly restored Roman Catholic church; he had repented of his sins and recanted his principles. He had begged for forgiveness and slavishly apologized. He had thrown away all fidelity for the chance of forgive-

ness, and by the anxious turning of his head as he searched the faces of the small crowd, he was hoping for the arrival of his pardon at this late, this theatrical moment.

He had every reason to hope. The new monarch was a Tudor and the Tudors knew the power of appearances. She was devout, and surely would not reject a contrite heart. But more than anything else, she was a woman, a soft-hearted, thick-headed woman. She would never have the courage to take the decision to execute such a great man, she would never have the stamina to hold to her decision.

"Stand up, Father," Robert urged him silently. "The pardon must come at any moment; don't lower yourself by looking for it."

The door behind Robert opened, and a jailer came in and laughed raucously to see the four young men up at the window, shading their eyes against the brilliant midsummer sun. "Don't jump," he said. "Don't rob the axeman, bonny lads. It'll be you four next, and the pretty maid."

"I will remember you for this, after our pardons have come, and we are released," Robert promised him, and turned his attention back to the green. The jailer checked the thick bars on the window and saw that the men had nothing that could break the glass, and then went out, still chuckling, and locked the door.

Below on the scaffold, the priest stepped up to the condemned man, and read him prayers from his Latin Bible. Robert noticed how the wind caught the rich vestments and made them billow like the sails of an invading Armada. Abruptly, the priest finished, held up a crucifix for the man to kiss, and stepped back.

Robert found he was suddenly cold, chilled to ice by the glass of the window where he was resting his forehead and the palms of his hands, as if the warmth of his body was bleeding out of him, sucked out by the scene below. On the scaffold, his father knelt humbly before the block. The axeman stepped forward and tied the blindfold over his eyes; he spoke to him. The prisoner turned his bound head to reply. Then, dreadfully, it seemed as if that movement had disoriented him. He had taken his hands from the executioner's block, and he could not find it again. He started to feel for it, hands outstretched. The executioner had turned to pick up his axe, and when he turned back, his prisoner was near to falling, scrabbling about.

Alarmed, the hooded executioner shouted at the struggling prisoner, and the prisoner plucked at the bandage over his eyes, calling that he was not ready, that he could not find the block, that the axe must wait for him.

"Be still!" Robert hollered, hammering against the thick glass of the window. "Father, be still! For God's sake, be still!"

"Not yet!" cried the little figure on the green to the axeman behind him. "I can't find the block! I am not ready! I am not prepared! Not yet! Not yet!"

He was crawling in the straw, one hand outstretched before him, trying to find the block, the other hand plucking at the tight bandage over his head. "Don't touch me! She will pardon me! I'm not ready!" he screamed, and was still screaming, as the axeman swung his blade and the axe thudded into the exposed neck. A gout of blood spurted upward, and the man was thrown to one side with the blow.

"Father!" Robert shouted. "My father!"

The blood was pumping from the wound but the man still scrabbled like a dying pig in *the straw, still trying to get to his feet with boots that could get no purchase, still searching blindly for the block, with hands that were growing numb. The executioner, cursing his own inaccuracy, raised the great axe again.*

"Father!" Robert cried out in agony as the axe came down. "Father!"

"Robert? My lord?" A hand was gently shaking him. He opened his eyes and there was Amy before him, her brown hair plaited for sleep, her brown eyes wide, solidly real in the candlelight of the bedroom.

"Good God! What a nightmare! What a dream. God keep me from it. God keep me from it!"

"Was it the same dream?" she asked. "The dream of your father's death?"

He could not even bear that she should mention it. "Just a dream," he said shortly, trying to recover his wits. "Just a terrible dream."

"But the same dream?" she persisted.

He shrugged. "It's hardly surprising that it should come back to me. Do we have some ale?"

Amy threw back the covers and rose from the bed, pulling her nightgown around her shoulders. But she was not to be diverted. "It's an omen," she said flatly, as she poured him a mug of ale. "Shall I heat this up?"

"I'll take it cold," he said.

She passed him the mug and he drank it down, feeling his night sweat cooling on his naked back, ashamed of his own terror.

"It's a warning," she said.

He tried to find a careless smile, but the horror of his father's death, and all the failure and sadness that had ridden at his heels since that black day, was too much for him. "Don't," he said simply.

"You should not go tomorrow."

Robert took a draught of ale, burying his face in the mug to avoid her accusing gaze.

"A bad dream like that is a warning. You should not sail with King Philip."

"We've been through this a thousand times. You know I have to go."

"Not now! Not after you dreamed of your father's death. What else could it mean but a warning to you: not to overreach yourself? He died a traitor's death after trying to put his son on the throne of England. Now you ride out in your pride once more."

He tried to smile. "Not much pride," he

said. "All I have is my horse and my brother. I could not even raise my own battalion."

"Your father himself is warning you from beyond the grave."

Wearily, he shook his head. "Amy, this is too painful. Don't cite him to me. You don't know what he was like. He would have wanted me to restore the Dudleys. He would never have discouraged me in anything I wanted to do. He always wanted us to rise. Be a good wife to me, Amy-love. Don't you discourage me—he would not."

"You be a good husband," she retorted. "And don't leave me. Where am I to go when you have sailed for the Netherlands? What is to become of me?"

"You will go to the Philipses, at Chichester, as we agreed," he said steadily. "And if the campaign goes on, and I don't come home soon—you will go home, to your stepmother's at Stanfield Hall."

"I want to go home to my own house at Syderstone," she said. "I want us to make a house together. I want to live with you as your wife."

Even after two years of shame he still had to grit his teeth to refuse her. "You know the

Crown has taken Syderstone. You know there's no money. You know we can't."

"We could ask my stepmother to rent Syderstone from the Crown for us," she said stubbornly. "We could work the land. You know I would work. I'm not afraid of working hard. You know we could rise by hard work, not by some gamble for a foreign king. Not by going into danger for no certain reward!"

"I know you would work," Robert acknowledged. "I know you would rise at dawn and be in the fields before the sun. But I don't want my wife to work like a peasant on the land. I was born for greater things than that, and I promised your father greater things for you. I don't want half a dozen acres and a cow, I want half of England."

"They will think you have left me because you are tired of me," she said reproachfully. "Anyone would think so. You have only just come home to me and you are leaving me again."

"I have been home with you for two years!" he exclaimed. "Two years!" Then he checked himself, trying to take the irritation from his voice. "Amy, forgive me, but it is no life for me. These months have been like a lifetime. With my name attainted by treason I can own nothing in my own right, I cannot trade or sell or buy. Everything my family had was seized by the Crown—I know!— and everything you had too: your father's legacy, your mother's fortune. Everything that you had has been lost by me. I have to get it back for you. I have to get it back for us."

"I don't want it at this price," she said flatly. "You always say that you are doing this for us, but it is not what I want, it's no good for me. I want you at home with me, I don't care if we have nothing. I don't care if we have to live with my stepmother and depend on her charity. I don't care for anything but that we are together and you are safe at last."

"Amy, I cannot live on that woman's charity. It is a shoe which pinches me every day. When you married me, I was the son of the greatest man in England. It was his plan, and mine, that my brother would be king and Jane Grey would be queen, and we came within inches of achieving that. I would have been of the royal family of England. I expected that, I rode out to fight for it. I would have laid down my life for it. And why not? We had as great a claim to the throne as the Tudors, who had done the self-same thing only three generations before. The Dudleys could have been the next royal family of England. Even though we failed and were defeated . . ."

"And humbled," she supplemented.

"And humbled to dust," he agreed. "Yet I am still a Dudley. I was born for greatness, and I have to claim it. I was born to serve my family and my country. You don't want a little farmer on a hundred acres. You don't want a man who sits at home all day in the cinders."

"But I do," she said in a strangled voice. "What you don't see, Robert, is that to be a little farmer in a hundred acres is to make a better England—and in a better way—than any courtier struggling for his own power at court."

He almost laughed. "Perhaps to you. But I have never been such a man. Not even defeat, not even fear of death itself, could make me into such a man. I was born and bred to be one of the great men in the land, if not the greatest. I was brought up alongside the children of the king as their equal— I cannot molder in a damp field in Norfolk. I have to clear my name, I have to be noticed by King Philip, I have to be restored by Queen Mary. I have to rise."

"You will be killed in battle, and then what?"

Robert blinked. "Sweetheart, this is to curse me, on our last night together. I will sail tomorrow, whatever you say. Don't ill wish me."

"You have had a dream!" Amy climbed on the bed and took the empty mug from him, and put it down, holding his hands in hers, as if she were teaching a child. "My lord, it is a warning. I am warning you. You should not go."

"I have to go," he said flatly. "I would rather be dead and my name cleared by my death, than live like this, an undischarged traitor from a disgraced family, in Mary's England."

"Why? Would you rather have Elizabeth's England?" She hissed the treasonous challenge in a whisper.

"With all my heart," he answered truthfully.

Abruptly, she released his hands and, without another word, blew out the candle, pulled the covers over her shoulders, and turned her back to him. The two of them lay sleepless, wide-eyed in the darkness.

"It will never happen," Amy stared. "She will never have the throne. The queen could conceive another child tomorrow, Philip of Spain's son, a boy who would be Emperor of Spain and King of England, and she will be a princess that no one wants, married off to a foreign prince and forgotten."

"Or she might not," he replied. "Mary might die without issue and then my princess is Queen of England, and she will not forget me."

*   *   *

In the morning, she would not speak to him. They breakfasted in the tap room in silence and then Amy went back upstairs to their room in the inn to pack the last of Robert's clothes in his bag. Robert called up the stairs that he would see her down at the quayside, and went out into the noise and the bustle of the streets.

The village of Dover was in chaos as King Philip of Spain's expedition made ready to set sail to the Netherlands. Produce sellers with every sort of food and wares bawled their prices into the hubbub. Wise women screeched the value of charms and amulets for departing soldiers. Pedlars showed trays of trinkets for farewell gifts, barbers and tooth-drawers were working on the side of the street, men having their head shaved almost bare for fear of lice. A couple of priests had even set up makeshift confessionals to shrive men who feared going to their deaths with sins on their consciences, and dozens of whores mingled with the crowds of soldiers, screeching with laughter and promising all sorts of quick pleasures.

Women crowded to the quayside to say good-bye to their husbands and lovers; carts and cannon were hauled perilously up the sides and stowed in the little ships; horses jibbed and fought on the gangplanks, with swearing lumpers pushing them from behind, the grooms pulling them from before. As Robert came out of the door of his inn, his young brother caught him by the arm.

"Henry! Well met!" Robert cried, enveloping the nineteen-year-old youth in a great bear hug. "I was wondering how we would ever find each other. I expected you here last night."

"I was delayed. Ambrose would not let me go until he had my horse reshod. You know what he's like. He suddenly became a most authoritative older brother and I had to swear to keep safe, and to keep you out of danger as well."

Robert laughed. "I wish you well with that."

"I got here this morning and I have been looking for you all over." Henry stepped back and scrutinized his older brother's dark good looks. He was still only twenty-three and was strikingly handsome, but the spoiled gloss of a rich youth had been burned off him by suffering. He was lean now; he had the look of a man to be reckoned with. He grinned at Henry and the hardness in his face melted in the warmth of his loving smile. "Good God! I am glad to see you, lad! What an adventure we shall have!"

"The court has arrived already," Henry told him. "King Philip is on board his ship, and the queen is here, and the princess."

"Elizabeth? Is she here? Did you speak to her?"

"They're on the new ship, the *Philip and Mary*," Henry said. "The queen looking very sour."

Robert laughed. "Elizabeth will be merry then?"

"Happy as a haymaker at her sister's distress," Henry replied cheerfully. "Is it true, d'you know, that she is King Philip's lover?"

"Not her," Robert said with the certainty of a childhood playmate. "But she'll keep him dancing to her tune because he guarantees her safety. Half the Privy Council would have her beheaded tomorrow if it were not for the king's favor. She's no lovesick fool. She'll use him, not be had by him. She's a formidable girl. I'd so like to see her if we can."

"She always had a tender heart for you." Henry grinned. "Shall you eclipse the king himself?"

"Not while I have nothing to offer her," Robert said. "She's a calculating wench, God bless her. Are they ready to load us?"

"My horse is already aboard," Henry said. "I was coming for yours."

"I'll walk him down with you," Robert said. The two men went through the stone archway to where the horse was stabled in the yard at the back of the inn.

"When did you last see her? The princess?" Henry asked his brother.

"When I was in my pomp and she in hers." Robert smiled ruefully. "It must have been the last Christmas at court. When King Edward was failing, and Father was king in everything but name alone. She was the Protestant princess and the favorite sister. We were twins in the smugness of our triumph and Mary was nowhere to be seen. D'you remember?"

Henry frowned. "Dimly. You know I was never very good at the shifts in favor."

"You would have learned," Robert said drily. "In a family such as ours was then, you would have had to."

"I remember she was imprisoned for treason in the Tower, while we were still in there," Henry recalled.

"I was glad when I learned she was free," Robert said. "Elizabeth always had the luck of the devil."

The big black horse whinnied at the sight of Robert and Robert went forward and stroked his soft nose. "Come on then, my lovely," he said softly. "Come on, First Step."

"What d'you call him?" Henry inquired.

"First Step," Robert said. "When we were released from the Tower and I came home to Amy and found myself a pauper in her stepmother's house, the woman told me that I could neither buy nor borrow a horse to ride on."

Henry gave a low whistle. "I thought they kept a good house at Stanfield?"

"Not for a son-in-law who had just come home an undischarged traitor," Robert said ruefully. "I had no choice but to walk in my riding boots to a horse fair, and I won him in a bet. I called him First Step. He is my first step back to my rightful place."

"And this expedition will be our next step," Henry said gleefully.

Robert nodded. "If we can rise in King Philip's favor we can be returned to court," he said. "Anything will be forgiven the man who holds the Netherlands for Spain."

"Dudley! A Dudley!" Henry sung out the family battle cry, and opened the door to the loosebox.

The two of them led the nervous horse down the cobbled street to the quayside, and waited behind the other men leading their horses on board. The little waves lapped at the jetty and First Step flared his nostrils and shifted uneasily. When it was his turn to go up the gangplank he put his forefeet on the bridge and then froze in fear.

One of the lumpers came behind with a whip raised to strike.

"Stay your hand!" Robert rapped out, loud above the noise.

"I tell you, he won't go on without," the man swore.

Robert turned his back on the horse, dropped the reins, and went ahead of him, into the darkness of the hold. The horse fretted, shifting from one foot to another, his ears flickering forward and back, his head up, looking for Robert. From the belly of the ship came Robert's whistle, and the horse turned his ears forward and went trustingly in.

Robert came out, having petted and tethered his horse, and saw Amy with his bags on the quayside. "All loaded and shipshape," he said cheerfully to her. He took her cold little hand and pressed it to his lips. "Forgive me," he said quietly. "I was disturbed by my dream last night, and it made me short-tempered. Let us have no more wrangling, but part as friends."

The tears welled up in her brown eyes. "Oh, Robert, please don't go," she breathed.

"Now, Amy," he said firmly. "You know that I have to go. And when I am gone I shall send you all my pay and I expect you to invest it wisely, and look about for a farm for us to buy. We must rise, my wife, and I am counting on you to mind our fortune and help us rise."

She tried to smile. "You know I'll never fail you. But it's just . . ."

"The royal barge!" Henry exclaimed as every man along the quayside pulled off his hat and bowed his head.

"Excuse us," Robert said swiftly to Amy, and he and Henry went up to the deck of the King of Spain's ship so that he could look down on the royal barge as it came by. The queen was seated in the stern of the barge, under the canopy of state, but the twenty-two-year-old Princess Elizabeth, radiant in the Tudor colors of green and white, was standing in the prow like a bold figurehead where everyone could see her, smiling and waving her hand at the people.

The oarsmen held the barge steady, the ships were side by side, the two brothers looked down from the waist of the warship to the barge that rode lower in the water beside them.

Elizabeth looked up. "A Dudley!" Her voice rang out clearly and her smile gleamed up at Robert.

He bowed his head. "Princess!" He looked toward the queen, who did not acknowledge him. "Your Majesty."

Coldly, she raised her hand. She was draped in ropes of pearls, she had diamonds in her ears and a hood encrusted with emeralds, but her eyes were dull with grief, and the lines around her mouth made her look as if she had forgotten how to smile.

Elizabeth stepped forward to the side rail of the royal barge. "Are you off to war, Robert?" she called up to the ship. "Are you to be a hero?"

"I hope so!" he shouted back clearly. "I hope to serve the queen in her husband's dominions and win her gracious favor again."

Elizabeth's eyes danced. "I am sure she has no more loyal soldier than you!" She was nearly laughing aloud.

"And no sweeter subject than you!" he returned.

She gritted her teeth so that she did not

burst out. He could see her struggling to control herself.

"And are you well, Princess?" he called more softly. She knew what he meant: *Are you in good health?* For he knew that when she was frightened she contracted a dropsy that swelled her fingers and ankles and forced her to her bed. *And are you safe?* For there she was, beside the queen in the royal barge, when proximity to the throne always meant proximity to the block, and her only ally on the Privy Council, King Philip, was sailing away to war. And most of all: *Are you waiting, as I am waiting, for better times, and praying they come soon?*

"I am well," she shouted back. "As ever. Constant. And you?"

He grinned down at her. "Constant too."

They needed to say no more. "God bless you and keep you, Robert Dudley," she said.

"And you, Princess." *And God speed you to your own again that I may come to mine,* was his unspoken reply. By the cheeky gleam in her eyes he knew that she knew what he was thinking. They had always known exactly what the other was thinking.

Winter 1558

Only six months later, Amy, accompanied by her friend, Lizzie Oddingsell, stood on the quay at Gravesend, watching the ships limp into harbor, wounded men laid out with the dead on their decks, deckrails scorched, mainsails holed, all the survivors with their heads bowed, shamefaced in defeat.

Robert's ship was the very last to come in. Amy had been waiting for three hours, increasingly certain that she would never see him again. But slowly, the little vessel approached was taken into tow, and drawn up at the quayside as if it were unwilling to come back to England in disgrace.

Amy shaded her eyes and looked up at the rail. At this moment, which she had feared so intensely, at this moment, which she had been so sure would come, she did not whimper or cry out, she looked steadily and carefully at the crowded deck for Robert, knowing that if she could not see him he had either been taken prisoner, or was dead.

Then she saw him. He was standing beside the mast, as if he were in no hurry to be at the rail for the first sight of England, in no rush to get to the gangplank to disembark, with no urgent need. There were a couple of civilians beside him, and a woman with a dark-haired baby on her hip; but his brother Henry was not there.

They rattled up the gangplank to the deck and she started to go toward it, to run up it and fold him in her arms, but Lizzie Oddingsell held her back. "Wait," she advised the younger woman. "See how he is first."

Amy pushed the woman's restraining hand aside; but she waited as he came down the gangplank so slowly that she thought he was wounded.

"Robert?"

"Amy."

"Thank God you are safe!" she burst out. "We heard there was a terrible siege, and that Calais is lost. We knew it couldn't be true, but . . ."

"It is true."

"Calais is lost?"

It was unimaginable. Calais was the jewel of England overseas. They spoke English in the streets, they paid English taxes and traded the valuable wool and finished cloth to and from England. Calais was the reason that English kings styled themselves "King of England and France." Calais was the outward show that England was a world power, on French soil, it was as much an English port as Bristol. It was impossible to imagine it had fallen to the French.

"It is lost."

"And where is your brother?" Amy asked fearfully. "Robert? Where is Henry?"

"Dead," he said shortly. "He took a shot to the leg in St. Quentin, and died later, in my arms." He gave a short, bitter laugh. "I was noticed by Philip of Spain at St. Quentin," he said. "I had an honorable mention in despatches to the queen. It was my first step, as I hoped it would be; but it cost me my brother: the one thing in life I could least afford to lose. And now I am at the head of a defeated army and I doubt that the queen will remember that I did rather well at St. Quentin, given that I did rather badly at Calais."

"Oh, what does it matter?" she exclaimed. "As long as you are safe, and we can be together again? Come home with me, Robert, and who cares about the queen or even about Calais? You don't need Calais, we can buy Syderstone back now. Come home with me and see how happy we will be!"

He shook his head. "I have to take despatches to the queen," he said stubbornly.

"You're a fool!" she flared at him. "Let someone else tell her the bad news."

His dark eyes went very bright at the public insult from his wife. "I am sorry you think me a fool," he said levelly. "But King Philip ordered me by name and I must do my duty. You can go and stay with the Philipses at Chichester till I come for you. You will oblige me by taking this woman and her baby to stay with them too. She has lost her home in Calais and she needs a refuge in England for a while."

"I will not," Amy said, instantly resentful. "What is she to me? What is she to you?"

"She was once the Queen's Fool," he said. "Hannah Green. And she was a loyal and obedient servant to me, and a friend when I had few friends. Be kind, Amy. Take her with you to Chichester. In the meantime I shall have to commandeer a horse and go to court."

"Oh, have you lost your horse as well as your plan?" Amy taunted him bitterly. "You have come home without your brother, without your horse, you have come home no richer, you have come home poorer in every way, as my stepmother Lady Robsart warned me that you would?"

"Yes," he said steadily. "My beautiful horse was shot out from under me by a cannon ball. I fell under him as he went down, and his body shielded me and saved my life. He died in my service. I promised him that I'd be a kind master to him, and yet I took him to his death. I called him First Step, but I have stumbled and fallen on my first step. I have lost my horse, and lost my campaign money, and lost my brother, and lost all hope. You will be pleased to hear that this is the end of the Dudleys. I cannot see that we will ever rise again."

*

Robert and Amy went their separate ways—him to court, where he was sourly greeted as the bringer of bad news, and her to their friends at Chichester for a long visit; but then they returned unwillingly to her stepmother's house of Stanfield Hall. There was nowhere else for them to go.

"We're shorthanded on the farm," Lady Robsart declared bluntly on his first evening.

Robert raised his head from the contemplation of his empty bowl and said: "What?"

"We're plowing up the meadow," she said. "For what little hay it gives us, it's no use. And we are shorthanded. You can help out in the field tomorrow."

He looked at her as if she were speaking Greek. "You want me to work in the fields?"

"I am sure that Stepmother means that you should supervise the men," Amy interposed. "Don't you?"

"How can he supervise plowing? I doubt he knows how it is done. I thought he could drive the cart; he's good with horses, at least."

Amy turned to her husband. "That wouldn't be so bad."

Robert could not speak, he was so appalled. "You want me to labor in the field? Like some peasant?"

"What else can you do for your keep?" Lady Robsart asked. "You are a lily of the field, man. You neither sow nor reap."

The color was draining from his face till he was as pale as the lily she called him. "I cannot work in the field like a common man," he said quietly.

"Why should I keep you like a lord?" she demanded crudely. "Your title, your fortune, and your luck have all gone."

He stammered slightly. "Because even if I never rise again, I cannot sink to the dunghill, I cannot demean myself."

"You are as low as a man can get," she declared. "King Philip will never come home; the queen, God save her, has turned against you. Your name is blackened, your credit has gone, and all you have in your favor is Amy's love and my patronage."

"Your patronage!" he exclaimed.

"I keep you. For nothing. And it has come to my mind that you might as well work your passage here. Everyone else works. Amy has her hens and her sewing, and her work in the house. I run the place, my sons care for the livestock and the crops."

"They order the shepherd and the plow-man," he burst out.

"Because they know what orders to give. You know nothing so you will have to take orders."

Slowly, he rose from the table. "Lady Robsart," he said quietly, "I warn you not to push me too far. I am defeated now but you should not seek to humiliate me further."

"Oh, why not?" She was enjoying herself. "I hardly fear the mightiness of your revenge."

"Because it is petty of you," he said with dignity. "I am very low, as you say. I am a defeated man and I am grieving for the loss of my brother, of three beloved brothers lost in the last two years by my fault. Think of what that means to a man! You could show a little charity even if you have no kindness. When I was Lord Robert, neither you nor Amy's father wanted for anything."

She did not answer, and he rose to his feet. "Come, Amy."

Amy did not obey. "I will come in a minute."

Lady Robsart turned her head to hide her smile.

"Come," Robert said irritably, and held out his hand.

"I have to clear the plates, and sweep the board." Amy excused herself.

He would not ask her again. He turned on his heel at once and went to the door.

"You will be in the stable yard at dawn, ready for work," Lady Robsart called after him.

He closed the door on her triumphant voice.

Amy waited till they heard him walk away and then she rounded on her stepmother. "How could you?"

"Why should I not?"

"Because you will drive him away from here."

"I don't want him here."

"Well, I do! If you drive him away then I will go too."

"Ah, Amy," her stepmother counseled. "See sense. He is a defeated man, he is good for nothing. Let him go. He will go back to Philip of Spain or on some other adventure and in some battle or another he will be killed and you will be free. Your marriage was a mistake from start to finish, and now you can let it finish."

"Never!" Amy spat at her. "You are mad to even dream it. If he goes out with the plow then I will go out with the plow. If you make him your enemy then you make me your enemy too. I love him, I am his, and he is mine, and nothing will come between us."

Lady Robsart was taken aback. "Amy, this is not like you."

"No. This *is* me. I cannot be quiet and obedient when you abuse him. You try to divide us because you think I love my home so much that I will never leave here. Well, hear this: I will go! There is nothing in the world more important to me than Lord Robert. Not even my love for my home, not even my love for you. And even if you will not respect him for himself, you should respect him for me."

"Toll loll," Lady Robsart said with reluctant admiration. "Here's a thunderstorm for nothing."

"It is not nothing," Amy said stubbornly.

"It can be nothing." Her stepmother offered a truce. "You have saved him from the fields, but you will have to find him some occupation. He has to do something, Amy."

"We'll get him a horse," she decided. "A cheap young horse, and he can break it and train it and we will sell it on and he can buy another. He is a master of horses, he can almost speak to them."

"And what will you use to buy his horse?" Lady Robsart demanded. "You'll have nothing from me."

"I will sell my father's locket," Amy said staunchly.

"You'd never sell that!"

"For Robert, I would."

The older woman hesitated. "I'll lend you the money," she said. "Don't sell the locket."

Amy smiled at her victory. "Thank you," she said.

*   *   *

She left Robert alone for an hour to cool his temper and then she went upstairs to the cramped back bedroom, expecting to find him in their little rope bed, eager to tell him that she had won their battle, that he would not go to the fields, and that he should have a horse to train, perhaps the first of many. But the plain linen sheets were turned down, the headboards undisturbed, the room was empty. Robert was gone.

Summer 1558

Robert Dudley came to court with a grim determination. He had faced the abuse of his wife's family, and thought he could not fall much lower. But now, in Richmond, the new-built beautiful palace that he loved as his own home, he discovered what it was to be humbled every day. Now he joined the crowd of petitioners that he had once walked past, wondering idly that they could find nothing better to do than beg for favors. Now he joined the ranks of the men who had to wait for the attention of their betters, in the hopes of being introduced to someone higher up the stair of ambition. Everything at the Tudor court came from the throne as the fountainhead of money, position, and place. Power flowed into the lesser tributaries of the great positions of the court and from there was divided and subdivided. Torrents of wealth cascaded from the badly managed treasury; but you had to be in favor with a man who was already in favor to tap a little of the flow for yourself.

Robert, who had once been the greatest man at court, second only to his father who ruled the king, knew only too well how the system worked from the top. Now he had to learn how it worked at the very bottom.

He spent days at court, staying in the household of a friend of his brother-in-law, Henry Sidney, seeking preferment: anything, a place or a pension, or even service in the household of a minor lord. But no one would employ him. Some men would not even be seen speaking with him. He was overeducated for any lowly place; how could you ask a man who could speak three languages to write a list of goods that needed to be fetched from another house? He was despised by the ruling class of Catholic lords, who had seen him and his father drive through the Protestant Reformation in King Edward's years. He was far too glamorous and bold and colorful for anyone to seat below the salt at their table, or use as a junior equerry. No petty lord gained an advantage with the eye-catching Robert Dudley standing behind his chair. No one would take the risk of being outshone by their own servant. No lady of any reputation could take a man who exuded such powerful sexual charm into her household; no man would employ him near his wife or daughters. No one wanted Robert Dudley, with his dazzling dark looks and his sharp wit, in any personal office, and no one would trust him out of their sight.

He hung around court like a handsome leper and learned to the last chilly note the voice of rejection. Many men who had been glad to be his friend and his follower when he had been Lord Robert now denied that they had ever known him. He found that memories were extraordinarily short. He was outcast in his own country.

Philip of Spain's favor now counted for nothing. He seemed to have abandoned England and her queen. He was living in his glamorous court in the Netherlands and was said to have taken a beautiful mistress. Everyone said he would never come to England again. His deserted wife, Queen

Mary, confessed that she had been mistaken for a second time—she had failed to conceive his child, she would never now give England an heir. She shrank inside her clothes, and hid inside her private rooms, more like a widow than a ruling queen.

Robert, unable to trade in his own dishonored name, sign a legal bond, or join a company of merchants, knew that he would never progress until the slur of treason was lifted from his name, and only Queen Mary could restore him. He borrowed a new hat and a new cape from his brother-in-law Henry Sidney and stood in the queen's presence chamber one damp, misty morning, waiting for her to come out of her rooms on the way to her chapel. Half a dozen other petitioners waited nearby, and they stirred as the door opened and the queen, head down and dressed in black, came out, accompanied only by a couple of women.

Robert feared she would go past him without looking up, but she glanced at him, recognized him, and paused. "Robert Dudley?"

He bowed. "Your Grace."

"You wanted something of me?" she asked wearily.

He thought he would have to be as blunt as her. "I wanted to ask you to lift the attainder for treason against my name," he said frankly. "I served your husband at St. Quentin and Calais and it cost me what was left of my fortune, and also my young brother's life, Your Grace. With this mark against my name I cannot enter into business nor hold my head up. My wife has lost her inheritance, a little farm in Norfolk, and you know I have lost all my father's gifts to me. I would not have my wife demeaned and in poverty for marrying me."

"Women always share in their husband's fortune," she said flatly. "Good and bad. And a bad husband is a wife's despair."

"Yes," he said. "But she has never admired my fortunes. She only wanted to live quietly in the country and I would have done better for her if I had done as she wished. We cannot even live together now; I cannot endure her family, and I cannot buy her a roof to put over her head. I have failed her, Your Grace, and it is wrong of me."

"You were at the fall of Calais," she remembered.

Robert met her eyes with a look that was as bleak as her own. "I never forget it," he said. "It was an ill-managed business. The canals should have been flooded to serve as a moat, but they did not open the sea-gates. The forts were not maintained and manned as we were promised. I did the best I could with my troop, but the French out-numbered and outmastered us. I did not fail you for lack of trying, Your Grace. Your husband himself commended my fighting at St. Quentin."

"You always were silver-tongued," she said with a little ghost of a smile. "Your whole family could charm their way to Paradise."

"I hope so," he said. "For too many of them are there already. Those of us who are left are brought very low in these days. I had seven brothers and five sisters in the nursery with me, twelve bonny children; and now there are only four of us left."

"I too am very low," she confessed. "When I came to the throne, Robert, when I defeated you and your father, I thought that all my troubles would be over. But they were just beginning."

"I am sorry it brought you so little joy," he

said gently. "The crown is not a light burden, especially for a woman."

To his horror he saw her dark eyes fill with tears, which spilled down the tired skin of her cheeks. "Especially a woman alone," she said softly. "Elizabeth may yet find that out for herself; though she is such a proud spinster now. It is unbearable to rule alone, and yet how can one share a throne? What man could be trusted with such power? What man can take the throne, and take a wife, and yet let her rule?"

He dropped to his knee and took her hand and kissed it. "Before God, Queen Mary, I am sorry for your sadness. I never thought it would come to this."

She stood for a moment, comforted by his touch. "Thank you, Robert."

He looked up at her and she was struck with what a handsome young man he was: as dark as a Spaniard, but with a new hard line of suffering drawn deeply between his black eyebrows.

"But you have everything ahead of you," she said wryly. "You have your youth, and good health, and good looks, and you will believe that Elizabeth will have the throne after me, and restore your fortunes. But you must love your wife, Robert Dudley. It is very hard for a woman if her husband neglects her."

He rose to his feet. "I will do," he promised easily.

She nodded. "And do not plot against me, or my throne."

This was an oath he took more seriously. He met her eyes without flinching. "Those days are gone," he said. "I know you are my rightful queen. I bend the knee, Queen Mary, I have repented of my pride."

"So," she said wearily. "I grant you the lifting of your attainder for treason. You can have your wife's lands back, and your own title. You shall have rooms at court. And I wish you well."

He had to hide the leap of his delight. "Thank you," he said, bowing low. "I shall pray for you."

"Then come with me to my chapel now," she said.

Without hesitation, Robert Dudley, the man whose father had powered the Protestant reformation in England, followed the queen into the Catholic Mass and bent his knee to the blaze of icons behind the altar. A moment's hesitation, even a sideways glance, and he would have been questioned for heresy. But Robert did not glance sideways nor hesitate. He crossed himself and bobbed to the altar, up and down like a puppet, knowing that he was betraying his own faith, and betraying the faith of his father. But bad judgment and bad luck had brought Robert Dudley to his knees at last; and he knew it.

Autumn 1558

All the bells in Hertfordshire, all the bells in England were ringing for Elizabeth, pounding the peal into her head, first the treble bell screaming out like a mad woman, and then the whole agonizing, jangling sob till the great bell boomed a warning that the whole discordant carillon was about to shriek out again. Elizabeth threw open the shutters of Hatfield Palace, flung open the window, wanting to be drowned in the noise, deafened by her own triumph, and yet still it went on, until the rooks abandoned their nests and went streaming into the dawn skies, tossing and turning in the wind like a banner of ill omen, and the bats left the belfry like a plume of black smoke as if to say that the world was upside down now, and day should be forever night.

Elizabeth laughed out loud at the racket which hammered out the news to the unresponsive gray skies: poor sick Queen Mary was dead at last, and Princess Elizabeth was the uncontested heir.

"Thank God," she shouted up at the whirling clouds. "For now I can be the queen that my mother intended me to be, the queen that Mary could not be, the queen I was born to be."

*   *   *

"And what are you thinking?" Elizabeth asked archly.

Amy's husband smiled down at the provocative young face at his shoulder as they walked in the cold garden of Hatfield Palace.

"I was thinking that you should never marry."

The princess blinked in surprise. "Indeed? Everyone else seems to think I should marry at once."

"You should only marry a very, very old man, then," he amended.

A delighted giggle escaped her. "Why ever?"

"So that he would die at once. Because you look so enchanting in black velvet. You should really never wear anything else."

It was the rounding off of the jest, it was the turning of a pretty compliment. It was what Robert Dudley did best in the world, along with horse-riding, politics, and merciless ambition.

Elizabeth was wrapped from her pink nose to her leather boots in mourning black, blowing on the tips of her leather-gloved fingers for warmth, a black velvet hat at a rakish angle on her mass of red-gold hair. A train of chilled petitioners trailed away behind the two. Only William Cecil, her longtime advisor, was sure enough of his welcome to interrupt the intimate talk between the two childhood friends.

"Ah, Spirit," she said fondly to the older man who came toward them, dressed in clerkly black. "What news d'you have for me?"

"Good news, Your Grace," he said to the queen, with a nod to Robert Dudley. "I have heard from Sir Francis Knollys. I knew you would want to be told at once. He and his wife and family have left Germany and should be with us by the New Year."

"She won't be here in time for my coronation?" Elizabeth asked. She was missing her cousin Catherine, in self-imposed exile for her fierce Protestant faith.

"I am sorry," Cecil said. "They cannot possibly get here in time. And we cannot possibly wait."

"But she has agreed to be my lady-in-waiting? And her daughter—what's her name?—Laetitia, a maid of honor?"

"She will be delighted," Cecil said. "Sir Francis wrote me a note to accept, and Lady Knollys's letter to you is following. Sir Francis told me that she had so many things that she wanted to say, that she could not finish her letter before my messenger had to leave."

Elizabeth's radiant smile warmed her face. "We'll have so much to talk about when I see her!"

"We will have to clear the court so that you two can chatter," Dudley said. "I remember Catherine when we had 'Be Silent" tournaments. D'you remember? She always lost."

"And she always blinked first when we had a staring joust."

"Except for that time when Ambrose put his mouse in her sewing bag. Then she screamed the house down."

"I miss her," Elizabeth said simply. "She is almost all the family I have."

Neither of the men reminded her of her flint-hearted Howard relations who had all but disowned her when she was disgraced, and now were swarming around her emerging court claiming her as their own once more.

"You have me," Robert said gently. "And my sister could not love you more if she were your own."

"But Catherine will scold me for my crucifix and the candles in the Royal Chapel," Elizabeth said sulkily, returning to the uppermost difficulty.

"How you choose to worship in the Royal Chapel is not her choice," Cecil reminded her. "It is yours."

"No, but she chose to leave England rather than live under the Pope, and now that she and all the other Protestants are coming home, they will be expecting a reformed country."

"As do we all, I am sure."

Robert Dudley threw a quizzical look at him as if to suggest that not everyone shared Cecil's clarity of vision. Blandly, the older man ignored him. Cecil had been a faithful Protestant since the earliest days and had suffered years of neglect from the Catholic court because of his loyalty to his faith and his service of the Protestant princess. Before that, he had served the great Protestant lords, the Dudleys themselves, and advised Robert's father on the advance of the Reformation. Robert and Cecil were old allies, if never friends.

"There is nothing Papist about a crucifix on the altar," Elizabeth specified. "They cannot object to that."

Cecil smiled indulgently. Elizabeth loved jewels and gold in church, the priests in their vestments, embroidered altar cloths, bright colors on the walls, candles and all the panoply of the Catholic faith. But he was confident that he could keep her in the reformed church that was her first and earliest practice.

"I will not tolerate the raising of the Host and worshipping it as if it were God Himself," she said firmly. "That is Popish idolatry indeed. I won't have it, Cecil. I won't have it done before me and I won't have it held up to confuse and mislead my people. It is a sin, I know it. It is a graven idol, it is bearing false witness; I cannot tolerate it."

He nodded. Half the country would agree with her. Unfortunately the other half would as passionately disagree. To them the communion wafer was the living God and should be worshipped as a true presence; to do anything less was a foul heresy that only last week would have been punishable by death by burning.

"So, who have you found to preach at Queen Mary's funeral?" she asked suddenly.

"The Bishop of Winchester, John White," he said. "He wanted to do it, he loved her dearly, and he is well regarded." He hesitated. "Any one of them would have done it. The whole church was devoted to her."

"They had to be," Robert rejoined. "They were appointed by her for their Catholic sympathies; she gave them a license to persecute. They won't welcome a Protestant princess. But they'll have to learn."

Cecil only bowed, diplomatically saying

nothing, but painfully aware that the church was determined to hold its faith against any reforms proposed by the Protestant princess, and half the country would support it. The battle of the Supreme Church against the young queen was one that he hoped to avoid.

"Let Winchester do the funeral sermon then," she said. "But make sure he is reminded that he must be temperate. I want nothing said to stir people up. Let's keep the peace before we reform it, Cecil."

"He's a convinced Roman Catholic," Robert reminded her. "His views are known well enough, whether he speaks them out loud or not."

She rounded on him. "Then if you know so much, get me someone else!"

Dudley shrugged and was silent.

"That's the very heart of it," Cecil said gently to her. "There is no one else. They're *all* convinced Roman Catholics. They're all ordained Roman Catholic bishops, they've been burning Protestants for heresy for the last five years. Half of them would find your beliefs heretical. They can't change overnight."

She kept her temper with difficulty but

Dudley knew she was fighting the desire to stamp her foot and stride away.

"No one wants anyone to change anything overnight," she said finally. "All I want is for them to do the job to which God has called them, as the old queen did hers by her lights, and as I will do mine."

"I will warn the bishop to be discreet," Cecil said pessimistically. "But I cannot order him what to say from his own pulpit."

"Then you had better learn to do so," she said ungraciously. "I won't have my own church making trouble for me."

*   *   *

"'I praised the dead more than the living,'" the Bishop of Winchester started, his voice booming out with unambiguous defiance. "That is my text for today, for this tragic day, the funeral day of our great Queen Mary. 'I praised the dead more than the living.' Now, what are we to learn from this: God's own word? Surely, a living dog is better than a dead lion? Or is the lion, even in death, still more noble, still a higher being than the most spritely, the most engaging young mongrel puppy?"

Leaning forward in his closed pew, mercifully concealed from the rest of the astounded congregation, William Cecil groaned softly, dropped his head into his hands, and listened with his eyes closed as the Bishop of Winchester preached himself into house arrest.

Winter 1558–59

The court always held Christmas at Whitehall Palace, and Cecil and Elizabeth were anxious that the traditions of Tudor rule should be seen as continuous. The people should see that Elizabeth was a monarch just as Mary had been, just as Edward had been, just as their father had been: the glorious Henry VIII.

"I know there should be a Lord of Misrule," Cecil said uncertainly. "And a Christmas masque, and there should be the king's choristers, and a series of banquets." He broke off. He had been a senior administrator to the Dudley family and thus served their masters the Tudors; but he had never been part of the inner circle of the Tudor court. He had been present at business meetings, reporting to the Dudley household, not at entertainments, and he had never taken part in any of the organization or planning of a great court.

"I last came to Edward's court when he was sick," Elizabeth said, worried. "There was no feasting or masquing then. And Mary's court went to Mass three times a day, even in the Christmas season, and was terribly gloomy. They had one good Christmas, I think, when Philip first came over and she thought she was with child, but I was under house arrest then, I didn't see what was done."

"We shall have to make new traditions," Cecil said, trying to cheer her.

"I don't want new traditions," she replied. "There has been too much change. People must see that things have been restored, that my court is as good as my father's."

Half a dozen household servants went past carrying a cartload of tapestries. One group turned in one direction, the others turned in the other, and the tapestries dropped between the six of them. They did not know where things were to go, the rooms had not been properly allocated. No one knew the rules of precedence in this new court; it was not yet established where the great lords would be housed. The traditional Catholic lords who had been in power under Queen Mary were staying away from the upstart princess; the Protestant arrivistes had not yet returned in their rush from foreign exile; the court officers, essential servants to run the great traveling business which was the royal court, were not yet commanded by an experienced Lord Chamberlain. It was all confused and new.

Robert Dudley stepped around the tumbled tapestries, strolled up and gave Elizabeth a smiling bow, doffing his scarlet cap with his usual flair. "Your Grace."

"Sir Robert. You're Master of Horse. Doesn't that mean that you will take care of all the ceremonies and celebrations as well?"

"Of course," he said easily. "I will bring you a list of entertainments that you might enjoy."

She hesitated. "You have new ideas for entertainments?"

He shrugged, glancing at Cecil, as if he wondered what the question might mean. "I have some new ideas, Your Grace. You are a princess new-come to her throne, you might like some new celebrations. But the Christmas masque usually follows tradition. We usually have a Christmas banquet, and, if it is cold enough, an ice fair. I thought you might like a Russian masque, with bear baiting and savage dancing; and of course all the ambassadors will come to be presented, so we will need dinners and hunting parties and picnics to welcome them."

Elizabeth was taken aback. "And you know how to do all this?"

He smiled, still not understanding. "Well, I know how to give the orders."

Cecil had a sudden uncomfortable sense, very rare for him, of being out of his depth, faced with issues he did not understand. He felt poor, he felt provincial. He felt that he was his father's son, a servant in the royal household, a profiteer from the sale of the monasteries, and a man who earned his fortune by marrying an heiress. The gulf between himself and Robert Dudley, always a great one, felt all at once wider. Robert Dudley's grandfather had been a grandee at the court of Henry VII, his son the greatest man at the court of Henry VIII; he had been a kingmaker; he had even been, for six heady days, father-in-law to the Queen of England.

Young Robert Dudley had been running in and out of the halls of the royal palaces of England as his home, while Elizabeth had been in disgrace, alone in the country. Of the three of them it was Dudley who was most accustomed to power and position. Cecil glanced at the young queen and saw, mirrored in her face, his own uncertainty and sense of inadequacy.

"Robert, I don't know how to do this," she said in a small voice. "I can't even remember how to get from the king's rooms to the great hall. If someone doesn't walk before me I'll get lost. I don't know how to get to the gardens from the picture gallery, or from the stable to my rooms, I . . . I'm lost here."

Cecil saw, he could not be mistaken, the sudden leap of something in the younger man's face—hope? ambition?—as Dudley realized why the young queen and her principal advisor were standing outside her premier London palace, looking almost as if they did not dare to go in.

Sweetly, he offered her his arm. "Your Majesty, let me welcome you to my old home, your new palace. These walks and

these walls will be as familiar to you as Hatfield was, and you will be happier here than
you have ever been before, I guarantee it.
Everyone gets lost in Whitehall Palace; it is
a village, not a house. Let me be your
guide."

It was generously and elegantly done,
and Elizabeth's face warmed. She took his
arm and glanced back at Cecil.

"I will follow, Your Grace," he said quickly,
thinking that he could not bear to have
Robert Dudley show him his own rooms as
if he owned the place. *Aye,* Cecil thought.
*Go on, take your advantage. You just had
the two of us at a loss. We stood here, the
newcomers, not even knowing where our
bedrooms are; and you know this place like
the back of your hand. It's as if you are more
royal than her, as if you were the rightful
prince here, and now, graciously enough,
you show her round your home.*

*   *   *

But it was not all as easy as Elizabeth learning her way round the corridors and back
stairs of the warren that was Whitehall
Palace. When they went out in the streets
there were many who doffed their caps and
cried hurrah for the Protestant princess, but

there were many also who did not want another woman on the throne, seeing what the last one had done. Many would have preferred Elizabeth to declare her betrothal to a good Protestant prince and get a sensible man's hand on the reins of England at once. There were many others who remarked that surely Lord Henry Hastings, nephew to King Henry, and married to Robert Dudley's sister, had nearly as good a claim as Elizabeth, and he was an honorable young man and fit to rule. There were even more who whispered in secret or said nothing at all but who longed for the coming of Mary, Queen of Scots and Princess of France, who would bring peace to the kingdom, a lasting alliance with France, and an end to religious change. She was younger than Elizabeth, for sure, a sixteen-year-old girl but a real little beauty, and married to the heir to the French throne with all that power behind her.

Elizabeth, new-come to her throne, not yet crowned or anointed, had to find her way round her palace, had to put her friends in high places and that quickly, had to act like a confident Tudor heir, and had somehow to deal at once with her church which was in open and determined opposition to her and which would, unless it was swiftly controlled, bring her down.

There had to be a compromise and the Privy Council, still staffed with Mary's advisors but leavened by Elizabeth's new friends, came up with it. The church was to be restored to the condition in which Henry VIII had left it at the time of his death. An English church, commanded by Englishmen and headed by the monarch, that obeyed English laws and paid its tithes into the English treasury, where the litany, homilies, and prayers were often read in English; but where the shape and content of the service were all but identical to the Catholic Mass.

It made sense to everyone who was desperate to see Elizabeth take the throne without the horror of a civil war. It made sense to everyone who longed for a peaceful transition of power. Indeed, it made sense to everyone but to the church itself, whose bishops would not countenance one step toward the mortal heresy of Protestantism, and, worst of all, it made no sense to the queen, who was suddenly, at this inopportune moment, stubborn.

"I won't have the Host raised in the Royal

Chapel," Elizabeth specified for the twentieth time. "When we have Christmas Mass, I will not have the Host raised as an object of worship."

"Absolutely not," Cecil agreed wearily. It was Christmas Eve and he had been hoping that he might have got to his own home for Christmas. He had been thinking, rather fondly, that he might have been there to take Christmas communion in his own chapel, the Protestant way, without drama, as God had intended it, and then stayed with his family for the rest of the days of Christmas, returning to court only for the great feast of present-giving on Twelfth Night.

It had been a struggle to find a bishop who would celebrate Mass in the Royal Chapel before the Protestant princess at all, and now Elizabeth was trying to rewrite the service.

"He will let the congregation take communion?" she confirmed. "Whatever his name is? Bishop Oglesham?"

"Owen Oglethorpe," Cecil corrected her. "Bishop of Carlisle. Yes, he understands your feelings. Everything will be done as you wish. He will serve at the Christmas

Mass in your chapel, and he won't elevate the Host."

*   *   *

Next day, Cecil cradled his head once more as the bishop defiantly held the pyx above his head for the congregation to worship the body of Christ at the magical moment of transubstantiation.

A clear voice rang out from the royal pew. "Bishop! Lower the pyx."

It was as if he had not heard her. Indeed, since his eyes were closed and his lips moving in prayer, perhaps he had not heard her. The bishop believed with all his heart that God was coming down to earth, that he held the real presence of the living God between his hands, that he was holding it up for the faithful to worship, as they must, as faithful Christians, do.

"Bishop! I said, Bishop! Lower that pyx."

The wooden fretwork shutter of the royal pew banged open like a thunderclap. Bishop Oglethorpe turned slightly from the altar, and glanced over his shoulder to meet the furious gaze of his queen, leaning out from the royal pew like a fishwife over a market stall, her cheeks flaming red with temper, her eyes black as an angry cat's. He took in her stance—up from her knees, standing at her full height, her finger pointing at him, her voice commanding.

"This is my own chapel. You are serving as my chaplain. I am the queen. You will do as I order. Lower that pyx."

As if she did not matter at all, he turned back to the altar, closed his eyes again, and gave himself up to his God.

He felt, as much as he heard, the swish of her gown as she strode out of the door of the pew and the bang as she slammed it shut, like a child running from a room in temper. His shoulders prickled, his arms burned; but still he kept his back resolutely turned to the congregation, celebrating the Mass not with them, but for them: a process private between the priest and his God, which the faithful might observe, but could not join. The bishop put the pyx gently down on the altar and folded his hands together in the gesture for prayer, secretly pressing them hard against his thudding heart, as the queen stormed from her own chapel, on Christmas Day, driven from the place of God on His very day, by her own muddled, heretical thinking.

*

Two days later, Cecil, still not home for Christmas, faced with a royal temper tantrum on one hand and a stubborn bishop on the other, was forced to issue a royal proclamation that the litany, Lord's Prayer, lessons, and the ten commandments would all be read in English, in every church of the land, and the Host would not be raised. This was the new law of the land. Elizabeth had declared war on her church before she was even crowned.

*   *   *

"So who *is* going to crown her?" Dudley asked him. It was the day before Twelfth Night. Neither Cecil nor Dudley had yet managed to get home to their wives for so much as a single night during the Christmas season.

Does he not have enough to do in planning the Twelfth Night feast, that now he must devise religious policy? Cecil demanded of himself irritably, as he got down from his horse in the stable yard and tossed the reins to a waiting groom. He saw Dudley's eyes run over the animal and felt a second pang of irritation at the knowledge that the younger man would see at once that it was too short in the back.

"I thank you for your concern but why do you wish to know, Sir Robert?" The politeness of Cecil's tone almost took the ice from his reply.

Dudley's smile was placatory. "Because she will worry, and this is a woman who is capable of worrying herself sick. She will ask me for my advice, and I want to be able to reassure her. You'll have a plan, sir, you always do. I am only asking you what it is. You can tell me to mind my horses and leave policy to you, if you wish. But if you want her mind at rest you should tell me what answer I should give her. You know she will consult me."

Cecil sighed. "No one has offered to crown her," he said heavily. "And between you and me, no one will crown her. They are all opposed, I swear that they are in collusion. I cannot trace a conspiracy but they all know that if they do not crown her, she is not queen. They think they can force her to restore the Mass. It's a desperate position. The Queen of England, and not one bishop recognizes her! Winchester is under house arrest for his sermon at the late queen's funeral, Oglethorpe in all but the same case for his ridiculous defiance on Christmas

Day. He says he will go to the stake before he gives way to her. She wouldn't let Bishop Bonner so much as touch her hand when she came into London, so he is her sworn enemy too. The Archbishop of York told her to her face that he regards her as a heretic damned. She's got the Bishop of Chichester under house arrest, although he is sick as a dog. They are all unanimously against her, not a shadow of doubt among them. Not even a tiny crack where one might seed division."

"Surely a scattering of bribes?"

Cecil shook his head. "They have become amazingly principled," he said. "They will not have Protestantism restored to England. They will not have a Protestant queen."

Dudley's face darkened. "Sir, if we do not have a care, they will make a rebellion against the queen from inside the church itself. It is a very small step from calling her a heretic to open treason, and a rebellion by the princes of the church would hardly be a rebellion at all. They are the Prince Bishops; they can make her look like a usurper. There are enough Catholic candidates for the throne who would be quick to take her place. If they declare war on her, she is finished."

"Yes, I *know* that," Cecil said, keeping his irritation in check with some difficulty. "I am aware of the danger she is in. It's never been worse. No one can ever remember a monarch in such uncertainty. King Henry never had more than one bishop openly against him, the late queen, at her very worst of times, had two; but Princess Elizabeth has every single one of them as her open and declared enemy. I know things are as bad as they can be, and the princess clinging to her prospects by her fingertips. What I *don't* know is how to make an absolutely solid Roman Catholic church crown a Protestant princess."

"Queen," Dudley prompted.

"What?"

"Queen Elizabeth. You said 'princess.'"

"She's on the throne but not anointed," Cecil said grimly. "I pray that the day comes when I can say 'queen' and know it is nothing more nor less than the truth. But how can I get her anointed, if no one will do it?"

"She can hardly burn them all," Dudley said with unwarranted cheerfulness.

"Quite so."

"But what if they thought she might convert?"

"They'll hardly believe that, after she stormed out of her own chapel on Christmas Day."

"If they thought that she would marry Philip of Spain, they would crown her," Dudley suggested slyly. "They would trust him to forge a compromise. They saw him handle Queen Mary. They'd trust Elizabeth under his control."

Cecil hesitated. "Actually, they might."

"You could tell those men, in the strictest confidence, that she is considering him," Dudley advised. That's the best way to make sure everyone hears it. Suggest that he will come over for the wedding and create a new settlement for the church in England. He liked her before, and she encouraged him enough, God knows. Everyone thought they would make a match of it as soon as her sister was cold. You could say they are all but betrothed. She's attended Mass almost every day for the last five years, they all know that well enough. She is accommodating when she has to be. Remind them of it."

"You want me to use the old scandals

of the princess as a mask for policy?" Cecil demanded sarcastically. "Hold her up to shame as a woman who bedded her brother-in-law as her own sister lay dying?"

"Elizabeth? Shame?" Dudley laughed in Cecil's face. "She's not been troubled by shame since she was a girl. She learned then that you can ride out shame if you keep your nerve and admit nothing. And she's not troubled by lust either. Her "scandals" as you call them—excepting the one with Thomas Seymour, which got out of hand—are never accidental. Since her romping with Seymour led him to the scaffold, she has learned her lesson. Now she deploys her desires; they do not drive her. She's not a fool, you know. She's survived this far. We have to learn from her, learn to use everything we have: just as she has always done. Her marriage is our greatest weapon. Of course we have to use it. What d'you think she was doing all the time that she was flirting with Philip of Spain? She wasn't driven by desire, God knows. She was playing the only card she had."

Cecil was about to argue but then he stopped himself. Something in Dudley's hard eyes reminded him of Elizabeth's when he had once warned her of falling in love with Philip. Then she had shot him the same bright, cynical look. The two of them might be young people, only in their mid-twenties, but they had been taught in a hard school. Neither of them had any time for sentiment.

"Carlisle might do it," Cecil said thoughtfully. "If he thought she was seriously considering Philip as a husband, and if I could assure him that by doing it, he would save her from heresy."

Dudley put a hand on his shoulder. "Someone has to do it or she's not queen," he pointed out. "We have to get her crowned by a bishop in Westminster Abbey or all this is just mummery and wishful thinking. Jane Grey was queen as much as this, and Jane Grey's rule was ten days long, and Jane Grey is dead."

Cecil shrugged involuntarily, and moved away from Dudley's touch.

"All right," Dudley said, understanding the older man's diffidence. "I know! Jane died for my father's ambition. I know that you steered your course out of it at the time. You were wiser than most. But I'm no plotter, Sir William. I will do my job and I know that you can do yours without my advice!"

"I am sure you are a true friend to her, and the best Master of Horse she could have appointed," Cecil offered with his faint smile.

"I thank you," Dudley said with courtesy. "And so you force me to tell you that that animal of yours is too short in the back. Next time you are buying a saddle horse, come to me."

Cecil laughed at the incorrigible young man; he could not help himself. "You are shameless like her!" he said.

"It is a consequence of our greatness," Dudley said easily. "Modesty is the first thing to go."

*   *   *

Amy Dudley was seated in the window of her bedroom at Stanfield Hall in Norfolk. At her feet were three parcels tied with ribbon, bearing labels that read "To my dearest husband from your loving wife." The writing on the labels was in fat irregular capitals, like a child might write. It had taken Amy some time and trouble to copy the words from the sheet of paper that Lady Robsart had written for her, but she had thought that Robert would be pleased to see that she was learning her letters at last.

She had bought him a handsome Spanish leather saddle, emblazoned with his initials on the saddle flap, and studded with gold nails. His second present was three linen shirts, sewn by Amy herself, white on white embroidery on the cuffs and down the front band. Her third present to him was a set of hawking gloves, made of the softest, smoothest leather, as cool and as flexible as silk, with his initials embroidered in gold thread by Amy, using an awl to pierce the leather.

She had never sewn leather before and even with a cobbler's glove to guard her hand she had pricked her palm all over with little red painful dots of blood.

"You could have embroidered his gloves with your own blood!" her stepmother laughed at her.

Amy said nothing but waited for Robert, secure that she had beautiful gifts for him, and that he would see the love that had gone into every stitch, into every letter. She waited and she waited through the twelve days of the Christmas feast; and when finally she sat at the window, and looked south down the gray road to London on the evening of Twelfth Night, she acknowledged at last that he was not coming, that he had sent her no gifts, that he had not even sent a message to say he would not come.

She felt shamed by his neglect, too ashamed even to go down to the hall where the rest of her family was gathered: Lady Robsart, merry with her four children and their husbands and wives, their young children, screaming with laughter at the mummers and dancing to the music. Amy could not face their secret amusement at the depth and completeness of her fall from a brilliant marriage into the greatest family in England, to being the neglected wife of a former criminal.

Amy was too grieved to be angry with Robert for promising to come and then failing her. Worst of all—she felt in her heart that it was no surprise he did not come to her. Robert Dudley was already being spoken of as the most handsome man at court, the queen's most glamorous servant, her most able friend. Why should he leave such a court, all of them attuned to joy, ringing with their own good luck, where he was Master of the Revels and lord of every ceremony, to come to Norfolk in midwinter to be with Amy and her stepmother, at a house where he had never been welcome, that he had always despised?

With this question unanswered, Amy spent Twelfth Night with his presents at her cold feet, and her eyes on the empty road, wondering if she would see her husband ever again.

*   *   *

It had been Dudley's Christmas Feast as much as Elizabeth's; everyone agreed it. It had been Dudley's triumphant return to court, as much as Elizabeth's. Dudley had been at the heart of every festivity, planning every entertainment, first up on his horse for hunting, first on the floor for dancing. He was a prince come to his own again in the palace where his father had ruled.

"My father used to have it so . . ." he would say negligently, choosing one style or another, and everyone was reminded that all the most recent successful Christmas feasts had been ordered by the Lord Protector Dudley, and Elizabeth's brother, the young King Edward, had been a passive spectator, never the commander.

Elizabeth was happy to let Dudley order the celebrations as he thought best. Like everyone else she was dazzled by his confidence and his easy happiness in his restoration. To see Dudley at the center of attention, in a glittering room while a masque unfolded to his choreography, and the choir sang his lyrics, was to see a man utterly in his element, in his moment of glory, in his pride. Thanks to him the court glittered as if the decorations were gold and not tinsel. Thanks to him the greatest entertainers in Europe flocked to the English court, paid in notes of promise, or sweetened with little gifts. Thanks to him the court went from one entertainment to another until Elizabeth's court was a byword for elegance, style, merriment, and flirtation. Robert Dudley knew, better than any man in England, how to give a party that lasted a long, glorious fortnight, and Elizabeth knew, better than any woman in England, how to enjoy a sudden leap into freedom and pleasure. He was her partner in dancing, her lead on the hunting field, her conspirator in the silly practical jokes that she loved to play, and her equal when she wanted to talk of politics, or theology, or poetry. He was her trusted ally, her advisor, her best friend, and her best-matched companion. He was the favorite: he was stunning.

As Master of Horse, Robert took responsibility for the coronation procession and entertainment, and shortly after the final great celebration of Twelfth Night he turned his attention to planning what must be the greatest day of her reign.

Working alone in the beautiful apartment at Whitehall Palace that he had generously allocated to himself, he had a scroll of manuscript paper unrolling down a table big enough to seat twelve men. From the top to the bottom the paper was covered with names: names of men and their titles, names of their horses, names of the servants who would accompany them, details of their clothing, of the color of the livery, of the arms they would bear, of the special pennants their standard-bearers would carry.

Either side of the list of the procession marched two more lists of those who would be spectators: the guilds, the companies, the waits from the hospitals, the mayors and councillors from the provinces, the organizations who had to have special places. The ambassadors, envoys, emissaries, and foreign visitors would watch the parade go past, and must have a good view so that their reports to their homes would be enthusiastically in favor of the new Queen of England.

A clerk danced from one end of the table scratching out and amending the scroll to Robert's rapid fire of dictation from the lists in his hand. Every now and then he glanced up and said, "Purple, sir," or "Saffron, nearby," and Robert would swear a fearful oath. "Move him back one then, I can't have the colors clashing."

On a second table, equally as long as the first, was a map of the streets of London from the Tower to Westminster Palace, drawn like a snake along a vellum roll. The palace was marked with the time that the procession should arrive, and the time that it would take to walk from one place to another was marked along the way. A clerk had painted in, as prettily as an illuminated manuscript, the various stopping places and the tableaux that would be presented at each of the five main points. They would be the work and responsibility of the City of London, but they would be masterminded by Robert Dudley. He was not taking the chance of anything going wrong on the queen's coronation procession.

"This one, sir," a clerk said tentatively. Robert leaned over.

"Gracechurch Street," he read. "Uniting of the two houses of Lancaster and York pageant. What of it?"

"It's the painter, sir. He asked was he to do the Boleyn family too?"

"The queen's mother?"

The clerk did not blink. He named the woman who had been beheaded for treason, witchcraft, and incestuous adultery against the king, and whose name had been banned ever since. "The Lady Anne Boleyn, sir."

Robert pushed back his jeweled velvet cap and scratched his thick, dark hair, looking in his anxiety much younger than his twenty-five years.

"Yes," he said finally. "She's the queen's mother. She can't just be a gap. We can't just ignore her. She has to be our honorable Lady Anne Boleyn, Queen of England, and mother of the queen."

The clerk raised his eyebrows as if to indicate that it was Robert's decision and would fall on his shoulders and no one else's; but that he, personally, preferred a quieter life. Robert let out a crack of laughter and cuffed him gently on the shoulder. "The Princess Elizabeth is from good English stock, God bless her," he said. "And it was a better marriage for the king than others he made, God knows. A pretty, honest Howard maid."

The clerk still looked uneasy. "The other honest Howard maid was also executed for adultery," he pointed out.

"Good English stock," Robert insisted unblinkingly. "And God Save the Queen."

"Amen," the clerk said smartly, and crossed himself.

Robert noted the habitual gesture and checked himself before he mirrored it. "Now," he said. "Are all the other pageants clear?"

"Except for the Little Conduit, Cheapside."

"What of it?"

"It shows a Bible. Question is: should it be in English or Latin?"

It was a question that went to the very heart of the debate currently raging in the church. Elizabeth's father had authorized the Bible in English and then changed his mind and taken it back into Latin again. His young son Edward had put an English Bible into every parish church, Queen Mary had banned them; it was for the priest to read and to explain; the English people were to listen, not to study for themselves. What Elizabeth would want to do, nobody knew. What she would be able to do, with the church full square against her, nobody could guess.

Robert snatched his cap from his head and flung it across the room. "For God's sake!" he shouted. "This is state policy! I'm trying to plan a pageant and you keep asking me questions about policy! I don't know what she will decide. The Privy Council will advise her, the bishops will advise her. Parliament will advise her, they will argue over it for months and then make it law. Pray God people will obey it and not rise up against her. It is not for me to decide it here and now!"

There was an awkward silence. "But in the meantime?" the clerk asked tentatively. "The cover of the Bible for the pageant? Should it be English or Latin? We could put a Latin copy inside an English cover if she preferred it. Or an English copy. Or one of both."

"On the cover write BIBLE in English,"

Robert decided. "Then everyone knows what it is. Write it in big letters so it is clear it is part of the pageant: a prop, not the real thing. It is a symbol."

The clerk made a note. The man-at-arms at the door walked delicately over to the corner, picked up the expensive cap, and handed it to his master. Robert took it without acknowledgment. Other people had been picking up for him since he was a child of two.

"When we've finished this, I'll see the other procession," he said irritably. "Whitehall to Westminster Abbey. And I want a list of horses, and check that the mules are sound." He snapped his fingers for another clerk to step forward.

"And I want some people," he said suddenly.

The second clerk was ready with a writing tablet and a quill in a little pot of ink.

"People, sir?"

"A little girl with a posy of flowers, an old lady, some sort of peasant up from the Midlands or somewhere. Make a note and send Gerard out to find me half a dozen people. Note this: one old lady, frail-looking but strong enough to stand, and with a strong voice, loud enough to be heard. One pretty girl, about six or seven, must be bold enough to cry out and take a posy of flowers to the queen. One bright apprentice boy to scatter some rose petals under her horse's feet. One old peasant from somewhere in the country to cry out, "God bless Your Grace." I'll have a couple of pretty merchants' wives as well and an unemployed soldier, no, rather, a wounded soldier. I'll have two wounded soldiers. And I'll have a couple of sailors from Plymouth or Portsmouth or Bristol, somewhere like that. Not London. And they are to say that this is a queen to take the country's fortunes overseas, that there is great wealth for the taking, for a country strong enough to take it, that this country can be a great one in the world, and this queen will venture for it."

The clerk was scribbling furiously.

"And I'll have a couple of old men, scattered about," Robert went on, warming to the plan. "One to cry for joy, he's to be near the front so they all see him, and the other one to call out from the back that she's her father's daughter, a true heir. Get them all spaced out: here . . ." Robert marked the map. "Here, and here. I don't mind what order. They are to be told to call out different things. They are to tell no one they were hired. They are to tell anyone who asks that they came to see the queen out of love for her. The soldiers in particular must say that she will bring peace and prosperity. And tell the women to behave with propriety. No bawds. The children had better come with their mothers and their mothers should be told to make sure that they behave. I want people to see that the queen is beloved by all sorts of people. They are to call out to her. Blessings, that sort of thing."

"What if she doesn't hear them, sir?" the clerk asked. "Over the noise of the crowd?"

"I'll tell her where she is to stop," Robert said firmly. "She'll hear them, because I'll tell her to."

The door opened behind him and the clerk stepped swiftly back and bowed. William Cecil came into the room and took a sweeping glance at the two tables covered with plans and the sheets of paper in the clerks' hands.

"You seem to be going to much trouble, Sir Robert," he remarked mildly.

"I would hope so. Her processions are

entrusted to me. I would hope that no one found me wanting."

The older man hesitated. "I only meant that you seem to be going into much detail. As I remember, Queen Mary had no need of great lists and plans. I think she just went to the Abbey with her court following."

"They had carriages and horses," Robert observed. "And an order of procession. Lady Mary's Master of Horse made a list. I have his notes, actually. The great skill of these things is to make them appear that they have simply happened."

"Triumphal arches and tableaux?" William Cecil inquired, reading the words upside down from the plan.

"Spontaneous demonstrations of loyalty," Robert said firmly. "The City Fathers insisted on it."

He stepped between Cecil and the table, obscuring his view. "My Lord Secretary, this is a very young woman whose right to the throne has been contested almost since the day of her birth. The last young woman whose right to the throne of England was contested had a crown crammed on her head in secret and lost it in hiding. I think it important that this young woman is seen as the true heir, is seen as the people's delight, and is seen to take her crown as publicly and as gloriously as possible."

"Lady Jane was not the true heir," Cecil pointed out to Lady Jane's brother-in-law, not mincing his words. "And the crown was crammed on her head by a traitor, also beheaded for treason. Your father, actually."

Dudley's gaze did not waver. "He paid the price for that treason," he said simply. "And I paid for my part in it. I paid in full. There's not a man in her court that has not had to loosen his collar and turn his coat once or twice in recent years. Even you, sir, I imagine, though you kept yourself clear of our disgrace."

Cecil, whose hands were cleaner than most, let it go. "Perhaps. But there is one thing I should tell you."

Dudley waited. Cecil leaned toward him and kept his voice low. "There is no money for this," he said heavily. "The treasury is all but empty. Queen Mary and her Spanish husband have drained England dry. We cannot pay for tableaux and fountains running with wine, and cloth of gold to drape around arches. There is no gold in the treasury; there is barely enough plate for a banquet."

"It's as bad as that?"

Cecil nodded. "Worse."

"Then we will have to borrow it," Robert declared grandly. "For I will have her crowned in state. Not for my vanity, which I know is not of the smallest, not for hers, and you will find she is no shy violet either; but because this puts her more firmly on the throne than a standing army. You will see. She will make them hers. But she has to come out from the Tower on a great white horse and with her hair spread over her shoulders and she has to look every inch a queen."

Cecil would have argued but Robert went on. "She has to have people crying out for her; she has to have tableaux declaring her as the true and only heir: pictures for the people who cannot read your proclamations, who have no knowledge of the law. She has to be surrounded by a beautiful court and a cheering, prosperous crowd. This is how we make her a queen indeed: now, and for the rest of her life."

Cecil was struck by the vividness of the

younger man's vision. "You really believe it makes her safer?"

"She can make herself safe," Robert said earnestly. "Give her a stage and she will be the only sight anyone can see. This coronation gives her a platform that will put her head and shoulders above anyone else in England, her cousins, rival heirs, anyone. This gives her men's hearts and souls. You have to get the money so that I can build her the stage, and she will do the rest. She will enact the part of queen."

Cecil took a turn to the window and looked out over the wintry gardens of Whitehall Palace. Robert drew closer, scanning the older man's profile. Cecil was nearing forty, a family man, a quiet Protestant through the Catholic years of Mary Tudor, a man with an affection for his wife and for accruing land. He had served the young Protestant king, he had refused to be a part of the Jane Grey plot, and then he had been steadily and discreetly loyal to Princess Elizabeth, taking the inferior job of surveyor so that he might keep her small estates in good heart, and have an excuse for seeing her often. It was Cecil's advice that had kept her out of trouble during the years of plotting and the uprisings against her sister Mary. It would be Cecil's advice that would keep her steady on this new throne. Robert Dudley might not like him, in truth, he would never like any rival; but he knew that this man would be making the decisions for the young queen.

"And so?" he said finally.

Cecil nodded. "We'll raise the money from somewhere," he said. "We'll have to borrow. But for God's sake, for her sake, keep it as cheap as possible."

Robert Dudley shook his head in instinctive rejection. "This cannot be cheap!" he declared.

"It cannot look cheap," Cecil corrected him. "But it can be affordable. Do you know her fortune?"

He knew that Robert did not know. Nobody had known, until the clerk of the Privy Council Armagil Waad, had emerged from the royal treasury, which he had last seen filled with gold, with the most rudimentary of inventories shaking in his hand, and whispered, aghast: "Nothing. There is nothing left. Queen Mary has spent all King Henry's gold."

Robert shook his head.

"She is sixty thousand pounds in debt," Cecil said quietly. "Sixty thousand pounds in debt, nothing to sell, nothing to offer against a loan, and no way to raise taxes. We shall find the money for her coronation but we will serve her best if we keep it cheap."

*   *   *

Elizabeth's triumphal procession from the Tower of London to Westminster Palace went just as Dudley had planned. She paused and smiled before the pageant representing her mother, the Lady Anne, she took the Bible offered her by a little girl and kissed it and held it to her breast. She drew rein at the points he had marked for her.

From the crowd came a small child with a posy of flowers. Elizabeth bent low in the saddle and took the posy, kissed the flowers and smiled at the cheers. Farther on she happened to hear two wounded soldiers call out her name, and she paused to thank them for their wishes and the crowd near them heard them predict that peace and prosperity would come to England now that Harry's daughter was on the throne. A little later an old lady called out a blessing for her and Elizabeth miraculously heard the thin old voice above the cheers of the crowd, and pulled up her horse to acknowledge the good wishes.

They thought more of her for responding to the sailors, to the apprentice boys, to the old peasant from the Midlands, than for all the glory of her harness and the pace of her horse. When she stopped for the pregnant merchant's wife and asked her to call the baby Henry if it was a boy, they cheered her till she pretended to be deafened by applause. She kissed her hand to the wounded soldiers, noticed an old man turn his face aside to hide his tears, and she called out that she knew they were tears of joy.

She never asked Robert, neither then nor later, if these people had been paid to cry out her name or if they were doing it for love. For all that she had spent her life in the wings, Elizabeth belonged to the center of the stage. She did not really care whether the rest of them were players or groundlings. All she desired was their acclaim.

And she was enough of a Tudor to put on a good show. She had the knack of smiling at a crowd as if each and every one had her attention, and the individuals who cried out to her—placed so that all corners of the route would have their own special experience of her—made a succession of apparently natural stopping places for Elizabeth's procession, so that everyone could see her and everyone would have their own private memory of the princess's radiant smile on her most glorious day.

*   *   *

The next day, Sunday, was the day of her coronation, and Dudley had ruled that she would go to the Abbey high on a litter drawn by four white mules, so that she appeared to the crowd as if she were floating at shoulder height. Either side of the litter marched her gentlemen pensioners in crimson damask, before her went her trumpeters in scarlet, behind her walked Dudley himself, the first man in the procession, leading her white palfrey, and the crowd that cheered her gasped when they saw him: the richness of the jewels in his hat, his dark, saturnine, handsome face, and the high-bred, high-stepping horse that curvetted so prettily with his hand steady on the bridle.

He smiled, turning his head this way and

that, his heavy-lidded eyes running over the crowd, continually alert. This was a man who had ridden before a cheering crowd and known that they adored him; and had later marched to the Tower amid a storm of booing, knowing himself to be the second worst-hated man in England, and the son of the worst. He knew that this crowd could be courted as sweetly as a willing girl one day, and yet turn as spiteful as a neglected woman the next.

Today, they adored him; he was Elizabeth's favorite, he was the most handsome man in England. He had been their bonny darling when a boy; he had gone into the Tower as a traitor and come out again as a hero. He was a survivor like her; he was a survivor like them.

*   *   *

It was a perfect procession and a perfect service. Elizabeth took the crown on her head, the oil on her forehead, and the orb and scepter of England into her hand. The Bishop of Carlisle officiated in the pleasing conviction that within a few months he would be celebrating her marriage to the most devout Catholic king in the whole of Christendom. And after the coronation service the queen's own chaplain celebrated Mass without uplifting the Host.

Elizabeth came out of the dark Abbey into a blaze of light and heard the roar of the crowd welcome her. She walked through the people so that they could all see her— this was a queen who would pander to anyone, their love for her was a balm for the years of neglect.

At her coronation dinner her voice was lost in her tightening throat, the blush in her cheeks was from a rising fever, but nothing would have made her leave early. The queen's champion rode into the hall and challenged all comers and the new queen smiled on him, smiled on Robert Dudley, the most loyal ex-traitor of them all, smiled on her new council—half of them constitutionally unfaithful—and smiled on her family who were suddenly recollecting the bonds and obligations of kinship now that their niece was no longer a suspect criminal, but the very lawmaker herself.

She stayed up till three in the morning until the trusted Kat Ashley, presuming on the intimacy of having been governess when Elizabeth was a girl and not a great queen, whispered in her ear that she must go to bed now or be dead on her feet in the morning.

*   *   *

God strike her dead on her feet in the morning, thought Amy Dudley, sleepless, waiting through the long, dark winter night for the cold dawn, in far-away Norfolk.

*   *   *

Robert Dudley, rising like a young Adonis from the bed of one of the court ladies, giving her a nonchalant parting kiss while he unclasped her hands from about his neck, and coming into the queen's presence chamber at Whitehall smartly enough next day, was still too late to catch Elizabeth alone. He found her already in close-headed conference with William Cecil, seated over a little table with papers before them. She glanced up and smiled at him but she did not wave him to approach, and he was forced to stand against the wood-paneled walls with the dozen or so other men who had risen early to pay their compliments and found that Cecil had got in first.

Dudley scowled and tried to overhear the low-voiced conversation. Cecil was dressed in dark clothes: *like a clerk,* Dudley sniffed;

but his wealth showed in the quality of the rich velvet and in the expense of the cut. His ruff was of the finest lace, lying in soft folds around his neck, his hair long and lustrous, spread on his collar. His eyes, warm and compassionate, never wavered from Elizabeth's animated face, answering her remarks about the great kingdom with the same steady quietness that he had used when he was advising her how best to run her country estates. Then it had been Cecil alone who had kept the princess from folly, and now it was Cecil alone who had the reward for those years of service.

She trusted him as she trusted no other; he could advise her against her own desires and she would listen. Indeed, when she appointed him to be her Secretary of State she had made him swear that he would tell her the truth without fear or favor, and sworn to him a pledge in return: that she would always listen to his words and never blame him if his advice was not to her liking. No other member of the Privy Council had exchanged such an oath with the new queen; there was no one else who mattered.

Elizabeth had seen her father dismiss advisors whose counsel was against his wishes; she had seen him arraign members of his own council for treason because they brought him bad news. She did not care that her father had become a tyrant, hated by his closest advisors; she believed that was the very nature of kingship; but she was warned by the fact that he lost the best minds of the kingdom because he could not bear to take advice.

And she was not yet old enough to want to rule alone. The crown was unsteady on her head, the country was filled with her enemies. She was a young woman, only twenty-five years old, with neither mother nor father nor a beloved family to advise her. She needed to be surrounded by friends whom she could trust: Cecil, her teacher Roger Ascham, her former governess Kat Ashley, and her plump, gossipy cofferrer Thomas Parry with his wife Blanche, who had been Elizabeth's nanny. Now that Elizabeth was queen she did not forget those who had been faithful to her when she had been princess, and there was not one old friend who was not now enjoying a small fortune in rich repayment for the years of waiting.

Why, she actually prefers the company of

inferiors, Dudley thought, looking from Cecil at the table to Kat Ashley at the window. *She was brought up by servants and people of the middling sort and she prefers their values. She understands trade and good housekeeping and the value of a well-run estate because that is what they care about. While I was walking around the royal palaces and spending my time with my father commanding the court, she was fussing over the price of bacon and staying out of debt.*

She is small scale, not a queen at all yet. She will stick at the raising of the Host because she can see it; that is real, it happens before her nose. But the great debates of the church she would rather avoid. Elizabeth has no vision; she has never had time to see beyond her own survival.

At the table, Cecil beckoned to one of his clerks and the man stepped forward and showed the young queen a page of writing.

If a man wanted to dominate this queen, he would have to separate her from Cecil, Robert thought to himself, watching the two heads so companionably close together as she read his paper. *If a man wanted to rule England through this queen he would have to be rid of Cecil first. And she would have to lose faith in Cecil before anything else could be done.*

Elizabeth pointed to something on the page; Cecil answered her question, and then she nodded her agreement. She looked up and, seeing Dudley's eyes upon her, beckoned him forward.

Dudley, head up, a little swagger in his stride at stepping forward before the whole court, came up to the throne and swept a deep, elegant bow.

"Good day, Your Grace," he said. "And God bless you in this first day of your rule."

Elizabeth beamed at him. "We have been preparing the list of my emissaries to go to the courts of Europe to announce my coronation," she said. "Cecil suggests that I send you to Philip of Spain in Brussels. Shall you like to tell your old master that I am now anointed queen?"

"As you wish," he agreed at once, hiding his irritation. "But are you going to stay indoors at work all day today, Your Grace? Your hunter is waiting, the weather is fine."

He caught her longing glance toward the window and her hesitation.

"The French ambassador . . ." Cecil remarked for her ear only.

She shrugged. "The ambassador can wait, I suppose."

"And I have a new hunter that I thought you might try," Dudley said temptingly. "From Ireland. A bright bay, a handsome horse, and strong."

"Not too strong, I hope," Cecil said.

"The queen rides like a Diana." Dudley flattered her to her face, not even glancing at the older man. "There is no one to match her. I would put her on any horse in the stables and it would know its master. She rides like her father did, quite without fear."

Elizabeth glowed a little at the praise. "I will come in an hour," she said. "First, I have to see what these people want." She glanced around the room and the men and women stirred like spring barley when the breeze passes over it. Her very glance could make them ripple with longing for her attention.

Dudley laughed quietly. "Oh, I can tell you that," he said cynically. "It needn't take an hour."

She tipped her head to one side to listen, and he stepped up to the throne so that he could whisper in her ear. Cecil saw her eyes dance and how she put her hand to her mouth to hold in her laughter.

"Shush, you are a slanderer," she said, and slapped the back of his hand with her gloves.

At once, Dudley turned his hand over, palm up, as if to invite another smack. Elizabeth averted her head and veiled her eyes with her dark lashes.

Dudley bent his head again, and whispered to her once more. A giggle escaped from the queen.

"Master Secretary," she said. "You must send Sir Robert away, he is too distracting."

Cecil smiled pleasantly at the younger man. "You are most welcome to divert Her Grace," he said warmly. "If anything, she works too hard. The kingdom cannot be transformed in a week; there is much to do but it will have to be done over time. And . . ." He hesitated. "Many things we will have to consider carefully; they are new to us."

And you are at a loss half the time, Robert remarked to himself. *I would know what should be done. But you are her advisor and*

*I am merely Master of Horse. Well, so be it
for today. So I will take her riding.*

Aloud he said with a smile: "There you are
then! Your Grace, come out and ride with
me. We need not hunt, we'll just take a couple of grooms and you can try the paces of
this bay horse."

"Within the hour," she promised him.

"And the French ambassador can ride
with you," Cecil suggested.

A swift glance from Robert Dudley
showed that he realized he had been burdened with chaperones but Cecil's face remained serene.

"Don't you have a horse he can use in the
stables?" he asked, challenging Robert's
competence, without seeming to challenge
him at all.

"Of course," Robert said urbanely. "He
can have his pick from a dozen."

The queen scanned the room. "Ah, my
lord," she said pleasantly to one of the waiting men. "How glad I am to see you at
court."

It was his cue for her attention and at
once he stepped forward. "I have brought
Your Grace a gift to celebrate your coming
to the throne," he said.

Elizabeth brightened; she loved gifts of any sort, she was as acquisitive as a magpie. Robert, knowing that what would follow would be some request for the right to cut wood or enclose common land, to avoid a tax or persecute a neighbor, stepped down from the dais, bowed, walked backward from the throne, bowed again at the door, and went out to the stables.

*   *   *

Despite the French ambassador, a couple of lords, some small-fry gentry, a couple of ladies-in-waiting, and half a dozen guards that Cecil had collected to accompany the queen, Dudley managed to ride by her side and they were left alone for most of the ride. At least two men muttered that Dudley was shown more favor than he deserved, but Robert ignored them, and the queen did not hear.

They rode westerly, slowly at first through the streets and then lengthening the pace of the horses as they entered the yellowing winter grassland of St. James's Park. Beyond the park, the houses gave way to market gardens to feed the insatiable city, and then to open fields, and then to wilder country. The queen was absorbed in managing the new horse, who fretted at too tight a rein but would take advantage and toss his head if she let him ride too loose.

"He needs schooling," she said critically to Robert.

"I thought you should try him as he is," he said easily. "And then we can decide what is to be done with him. He could be a hunter for you, he is strong enough and he jumps like a bird, or he could be a horse you use in processions, he is so handsome and his color is so good. If you want him for that, I have a mind to have him specially trained, taught to stand and to tolerate crowds. I thought your gray fretted a little when people pushed very close."

"You can't blame him for that!" she retorted. "They were waving flags in his face and throwing rose petals at him!"

He smiled at her. "I know. But this will happen again and again. England loves her princess. You will need a horse that can stand and watch a tableau, and let you bend down and take a posy from a child without shifting for a moment, and then trot with his head up looking proud."

She was struck by his advice. "You're

right," she said. "And it is hard to pay attention to the crowd and to manage a horse."

"I don't want you to be led by a groom either," he said decidedly. "Or to ride in a carriage. I want them to see you mastering your own horse. I don't want anything taken away from you. Every procession should add to you; they should see you higher, stronger, grander even than life."

Elizabeth nodded. "I have to be seen as strong; my sister was always saying she was a weak woman, and she was always ill, all the time."

"And he is your color," he said impertinently. "You are a bright chestnut yourself."

She was not offended; she threw back her head and laughed. "Oh, d'you think he is a Tudor?" she asked.

"For sure, he has the temper of one," Robert said. He and his brothers and sisters had been playmates in the royal nursery at Hatfield, and all the Dudley children had felt the ringing slap of the Tudor temper. "Doesn't like the bridle, doesn't like to be commanded, but can be gentled into almost anything."

She gleamed at him. "If you are so wise

with a dumb beast, let's hope you don't try to train me," she said provocatively.

"Who could train a queen?" he replied. "All I could do would be to implore you to be kind to me."

"Have I not been very kind already?" she said, thinking of the best post which she had given him, Master of Horse, with a massive annual income and the right to set up his own table at court and to take the best rooms in whichever palace the court might visit.

He shrugged as if it were next to nothing. "Ah, Elizabeth," he said intimately. "That is not what I mean when I desire you to be kind to me."

"You may not call me Elizabeth anymore," she reminded him quietly, but he thought she was not displeased.

"I forgot," he said, his voice very low. "I take such pleasure in your company that sometimes I think we are still just friends as we used to be. I forgot for a moment that you have risen to such greatness."

"I was always a princess," she said defensively. "I have risen to nothing but my birthright."

"And I always loved you for nothing but yourself," he replied cleverly.

He could see her hands loosen slightly on the reins and knew that he had struck the right note with her. He played her as every favorite plays every ruler; he had to know what charmed and what cooled her.

"Edward was always very fond of you," she said softly, remembering her brother.

He nodded, looking grave. "God bless him. I miss him every day, as much as my own brothers."

"But he was not so warm to your father," she said rather pointedly.

Robert smiled down at Elizabeth as if nothing of their past lives could be counted against them: his family's terrible treason against her family, her own betrayal of her half-sister. "Bad times," he said generally. "And long ago. You and I have both been misjudged, and God knows, we have been punished enough. We have both served our time in the Tower, accused of treason. I used to think of you then; when I was al-lowed out to walk on the leads, I used to go to the very threshold of the gated door of your tower, and know that you were just on the other side. I'd have given much to be able to see you. I used to have news of you from Hannah the Fool. I can't tell you what a comfort it was to know you were there. They were dark days for us both; but I am glad now that we shared them together. You on one side of that gate and me the other."

"Nobody else can ever understand," she said with suppressed energy. "Nobody can ever know unless you have been there: what it's like to be in there! To know that below you, out of sight, is the green where the scaffold will be built, and not to know whether they are building it, sending to ask, and not trusting the answer, wondering if it will be today or tomorrow."

"D'you dream of it?" he asked, his voice low. "Some nights I still wake up in terror."

A glance from her dark eyes told him that she too was haunted. "I have a dream that I hear hammering," she said quietly. "It was the sound I dreaded most in the world. To hear hammering and sawing and to know that they are building my own scaffold right underneath my window."

"Thank God those days are done and we can bring justice to England, Elizabeth," he said warmly.

This time she did not correct him for using her name.

"We should turn for home, sir," one of the grooms rode up to remind him.

"It is your wish?" he asked the queen.

She gave him a little inviting sideways smile. "D'you know, I should like to ride out all day. I am sick of Whitehall and the people who come, and every one of them wanting something. And Cecil with all the business that needs doing."

"Why don't we ride early tomorrow?" he suggested. "Ride out by the river, we can cross over to the south bank and gallop out through Lambeth marshes and not come home till dinner time?"

"Why, what ever will they say?" she asked, instantly attracted.

"They will say that the queen is doing as she wishes, as she should do," he said. "And I shall say that I am hers to command. And tomorrow evening I shall plan a great feast for you with dancing and players and a special masque."

Her face lit up. "For what reason?"

"Because you are young, and beautiful, and you should not go from schoolroom to lawmaking without taking some pleasure.

You are queen now, Elizabeth, you can do as you wish. And no one can refuse you."

She laughed at the thought of it. "Shall I be a tyrant?"

"If you wish," he said, denying the many forces of the kingdom, which inevitably would dominate her: a young woman alone amidst the most unscrupulous families in Christendom. "Why not? Who should say "no" to you? The French princess, your cousin Mary, takes her pleasures, why should you not take yours?"

"Oh, her," Elizabeth said irritably, a scowl crossing her face at the mention of Mary, Queen of Scots, the sixteen-year-old princess of the French court. "She lives a life of nothing but pleasure."

Robert hid a smile at the predictable jealousy of Elizabeth for a prettier, luckier princess. "You will have a court that will make her sick with envy," he assured her. "A young, unmarried, beautiful queen, in a handsome, merry court? There's no comparison with Queen Mary, who is burdened with a husband, the Dauphin, and ruled by the Guise family, and spends all her life doing as they wish."

They turned their horses for home.

"I shall devote myself to bringing you amusements. This is your time, Elizabeth; this is your golden season."

"I did not have a very merry girlhood," she conceded.

"We must make up for that now," he said. "You shall be the pearl at the center of a golden court. The French princess will hear every day of your happiness. The court will dance to your bidding, this summer will be filled with pleasure. They will call you the golden princess of all of Christendom! The most fortunate, the most beautiful, and the most loved."

He saw the color rise in her cheeks. "Oh, yes," she breathed.

"But how you will miss me when I am at Brussels!" he slyly predicted. "All these plans will have to wait."

He saw her consider it. "You must come home quickly."

"Why not send someone else? Anyone can tell Philip you are crowned; it does not need to be me. And if I am not here, who will organize your banquets and parties?"

"Cecil thought you should go," she said. "He thought it a pleasant compliment to

Philip, to send him a man who had served in his armies."

Robert shrugged. "Who cares what the King of Spain thinks now? Who cares what Cecil thinks? What d'you think, Elizabeth? Shall I go away for a month to another court at Brussels, or shall you keep me here to ride and dance with you, and keep you merry?"

He saw her little white teeth nip her lips to hide her pleased smile. "You can stay," she said carelessly. "I'll tell Cecil he has to send someone else."

*   *   *

It was the dreariest month of the year in the English countryside, and Norfolk one of the dreariest counties of England. The brief flurry of snow in January had melted, leaving the lane to Norwich impassable by cart and disagreeable on horseback, and besides, there was nothing at Norwich to be seen except the cathedral; and now that was a place of anxious silences, not peace. The candles had been extinguished under the statue of the Madonna, the crucifix was on the altar still but the tapestries and the paintings had been taken down. The little messages and prayers which had been pinned to the Virgin's gown had disappeared. No one knew if they were allowed to pray to Her anymore.

Amy did not want to see the church she had loved stripped bare of everything she knew was holy. Other churches in the city had been desanctified and were being used as stables, or converted into handsome town houses. Amy could not imagine how anyone could dare to put his bed where the altar had once stood; but the new men of this reign were bold in their own interests. The shrine at Walsingham had not yet been destroyed, but Amy knew that the iconoclasts would come against it some day soon, and then where would a woman pray who wanted to conceive a child? Who wanted to win back her husband from the sin of ambition? Who wanted to win him home once more?

Amy Dudley practiced her writing, but there seemed little point. Even if she could have managed a letter to her husband there was no news to give him, except what he would know already: that she missed him, that the weather was bad and the company dull, the evenings dark and the mornings cold.

On days such as this, and Amy had many days such as this, she wondered if she would have been better never to have married him. Her father, who adored her, had been against it from the start. The very week before her wedding he had gone down on his knee before her in the hall of Syderstone farmhouse, his big, round face flushed scarlet with emotion, and begged her with a quaver in his voice to think again. "I know he's handsome, my bird," he had said tenderly. "And I know he'll be a great man, and his father is a great man, and the royal court itself is coming to see you wed at Sheen next week, an honor I never dreamed of, not even for my girl. But are you certain sure you want a great man when you could marry a nice lad from Norfolk and live near me, in a pretty little house I would build for you, and have my grandsons brought up as my own, and stay as my girl?"

Amy had put her little hands on his shoulders and raised him up, she had cried with her face tucked against his warm homespun jacket, and then she had looked up, all smiles, and said: "But I love him, Father, and you said that I should marry him if I was sure; and before God, I am sure."

He had not pressed her—she was his only child from his first marriage, his beloved daughter, and he could never gainsay her. And she had been used to getting her own way. She had never thought that her judgment could be wrong.

She had been sure then that she loved Robert Dudley; indeed, she was sure now. It was not lack of love that made her cry at night as if she would never stop. It was excess of it. She loved him, and every day without him was a long, empty day. She had endured many days without him when he had been a prisoner and could not come to her. Now, bitterly, at the very moment of his freedom and his rise to power, it was a thousand times worse, because now he could come to her, but he chose not to.

Her stepmother asked her, would she join him at court when the roads were fit for travel? Amy stammered in her reply, and felt like a fool, not knowing what was to happen next, nor where she was supposed to go.

"You must write to him for me," she said to Lady Robsart. "He will tell me what I am to do."

"Do you not want to write yourself?" her

stepmother prompted. "I could write it out for you and you could copy it."

Amy turned her head away. "What's the use?" she asked. "He has a clerk read it to him anyway."

Lady Robsart, seeing that Amy was not to be tempted out of bad temper, took a pen and a piece of paper, and waited.

"My lord," Amy started, the smallest quaver in her voice.

"We can't write 'my lord,'" her stepmother expostulated. "Not when he lost the title for treason, and it has not been restored him."

"I call him my lord!" Amy flared up. "He was Lord Robert when he came to me, and he has always been Lord Robert to me, whatever anyone else calls him."

Lady Robsart raised her eyebrows as if to say that he was a poor job when he came to her, and was a poor job still, but she wrote the words, and then paused, while the ink dried on the sharpened quill.

"I do not know where you would wish me to stay. Shall I come to London?" Amy said in a voice as small as a child's. "Shall I join you in London, my lord?"

*

All day Elizabeth had been on tenterhooks, sending her ladies to see if her cousin had entered the great hall, sending pageboys to freeze in the stable yard so that her cousin could be greeted and brought to her presence chamber at once. Catherine Knollys was the daughter of Elizabeth's aunt, Mary Boleyn, and had spent much time with her young cousin Elizabeth. The girls had formed a faithful bond through the uncertain years of Elizabeth's childhood. Catherine, nine years Elizabeth's senior, an occasional member of the informal court of children and young people who had gathered around the nursery of the young royals at Hatfield, had been a kindly and generous playmate when the lonely little girl had sought her out, and as Elizabeth became older, they found they had much in common. Catherine was a highly educated girl, a Protestant by utter conviction. Elizabeth, less convinced and with much more to lose, had always had a sneaking admiration for her cousin's uncompromising clarity.

Catherine had been with Elizabeth's mother, Anne Boleyn, in the last dreadful days in the Tower. She held, from that day on, an utter conviction of her aunt's innocence. Her quiet assertion that Elizabeth's mother was neither whore nor witch, but the victim of a court plot, was a secret comfort to the little girl whose childhood had been haunted by slanders against her mother. The day that Catherine and her family had left England, driven out by Queen Mary's anti-heresy laws, Elizabeth had declared that her heart was broken.

"Peace. She will be here soon," Dudley assured her, finding Elizabeth pacing from one window in Whitehall Palace to another.

"I know. But I thought she would be here yesterday, and now I am worrying that it will not be till tomorrow."

"The roads are bad; but she will surely come today."

Elizabeth twisted the fringe of the curtain in her fingers and did not notice that she was shredding the hem of the old fabric. Dudley went beside her and gently took her hand. There was a swiftly silenced intake of breath from the watching court at his temerity. To take the queen's hand without invitation, to disentangle her fingers, to take both her hands firmly in his own, and give her a little shake!

"Now, calm down," Dudley said. "Either today or tomorrow, she will be here. D'you want to ride out on the chance of meeting her?"

Elizabeth looked at the iron-gray sky that was darkening with the early twilight of winter. "Not really," she admitted unwillingly. "If I miss her on the way then it will only make the wait longer. I want to be here to greet her."

"Then sit down," he commanded. "And call for some cards and we can play until she gets here. And if she does not get here today we can play until you have won fifty pounds off me."

"Fifty!" she exclaimed, instantly diverted.

"And you need stake nothing more than a dance after dinner," he said agreeably.

"I remember men saying that they lost fortunes to entertain your father," William Cecil remarked, coming up to the table as the cards were brought.

"Now *he* was a gambler indeed," Dudley concurred amiably. "Who shall we have for a fourth?"

"Sir Nicholas." The queen looked around and smiled at her councillor. "Will you join us for a game of cards?"

Sir Nicholas Bacon, Cecil's corpulent brother-in-law, swelled like a mainsail at the compliment from the queen, and he stepped up to the table. The pageboy brought a fresh pack, Elizabeth dealt the stiff cards with their threatening faces, cut the deal to Robert Dudley, and they started to play.

There was a flurry in the hall outside the presence chamber, and then Catherine and Francis Knollys were in the doorway, a handsome couple: Catherine a woman in her mid-thirties, plainly dressed and smiling in anticipation, her husband an elegant man in his mid-forties. Elizabeth sprang to her feet, scattering her cards, and ran across the presence chamber to her cousin.

Catherine dropped into a curtsy but Elizabeth plunged into her arms and the two women hugged each other, both of them in tears. Sir Francis, standing back, smiled benignly at the welcome given to his wife.

Aye, well might you smile, Robert Dudley remarked to himself, remembering that he had always disliked the smug radiance of the man. *You think you will have the high road to power and influence with this friendship; but you will find you are wrong. This young queen is no fool, she won't put her purse where her heart is, unless it serves her interest. She will love you but not advance you unless it is for her own good.*

As if he sensed Robert's eyes on him, Sir Francis looked up, and swept him a bow.

"You are heartily welcome back to England," Dudley said pleasantly.

Sir Francis glanced around, took in the court of old allies, conspirators, reformed enemies, and a very few new faces, and came back to Robert Dudley.

"Well, here we are at last," he said. "A Protestant queen on the throne, me back from Germany and you out of the Tower. Who'd ever have thought it?"

"A long and dangerous journey for all us pilgrims," Robert said, keeping his smile.

"Some danger still in the air for some of us, I think," Sir Francis said cheerfully. "I'd not been in England five minutes before someone asked me if I thought you had too much influence and should be curbed."

"Indeed," Robert said. "And you replied?"

"That I had not been in England five minutes and I had yet to form an opinion. But you should be warned, Sir Robert. You have enemies."

Robert Dudley smiled. "They come with success," he said easily. "And so I am glad of them."

Elizabeth reached out her hand to Sir Francis, still holding Catherine tight by the waist.

Sir Francis stepped forward and dropped to his knee and kissed her hand. "Your Grace," he said.

Robert, a connoisseur in these matters, admired the sweep down to his knee and then the style with which he rose. *Aye, but it will do you little good,* he said to himself. *This is a court full of dancing-master-tutored puppies. A graceful bow will get you nothing.*

"Sir Francis, I have been waiting and waiting for your arrival," Elizabeth said, glowing with happiness. "Will you accept a post on my Privy Council? I am in great need of your sound advice."

Privy Council! Good God! Robert exclaimed to himself, shaken with envy.

"I shall be honored," Sir Francis said, with a bow.

"And I should like you to serve as Vice Chamberlain of my household, and Captain of the Guard," Elizabeth continued, naming two plum jobs that would bring with them a small fortune in bribes from people wanting access to the queen.

Robert Dudley's smile never wavered; he seemed delighted at the shower of good fortune on the new arrival. Sir Francis bowed his obedience, and Dudley and Cecil made their way over to him.

"Welcome home!" Cecil said warmly. "And welcome to the queen's service."

"Indeed!" Robert Dudley agreed. "A warm welcome for you indeed! You too will be making your own enemies, I see."

Catherine, who had been in rapid conversation with her cousin, wanted to introduce her daughter who was to be Elizabeth's maid of honor. "And may I present my daughter Laetitia?" she asked. She beckoned toward the doorway; and the girl, who had been standing back, half hidden by the arras, came forward.

William Cecil, not a man to be overwhelmed by female charms, took a sharp breath at the beauty of the seventeen-year-old girl and shot an astounded look at Sir Francis. The older man was smiling, a quirky corner upturned at his mouth as if he knew exactly what Cecil was thinking.

"By God, this is a girl in the very image of the queen," Cecil whispered to him. "Except . . ." He broke off before he made the mistake of saying "finer," or "prettier." "You might as well declare your wife to be Henry VIII's bastard, and have done with it."

"She has never claimed it, I have never claimed it, and we don't do so now," Sir Francis said limpidly, as if the whole court were not nudging each other and whispering, as the young girl's color steadily rose but the dark eyes fixed on the queen never wavered. "Indeed, I find her very like my side of the family."

"Your side!" Cecil choked on a laugh. "She is a Tudor through and through, except she has all the allure of the Howard women."

"I do not claim it," Sir Francis repeated. "And I imagine, in this court and at these times, it would be better for her if no one remarked on it."

Dudley, who had seen the likeness at once, was watching Elizabeth intently. Firstly she held out her hand for the girl to kiss, with her usual pleasant manners, hardly seeing her as the girl's head was bent in her curtsy, her bright copper hair hidden by her hood. But then, as the girl rose up and Elizabeth took her in, Robert saw the queen's smile slowly die away. Laetitia was like a younger, more delicate copy of the queen, as if a piece of Chinese porcelain had been refined from an earthenware mold. Beside her, Elizabeth's face was too broad, her nose, the horsy Boleyn nose, too long, her eyes too protruding, her mouth narrow. Laetitia, seven years her junior, was rounded like a child, her nose a perfect tilt, her hair a darker copper to the queen's bronze.

Robert Dudley, looking at the girl, thought that a younger man, a more foolish man than himself, might have thought that the odd sensation he was feeling in his chest was his heart turning over.

"You are welcome to my court, Cousin Laetitia," the queen said coolly. She threw a quick, irritated glance at Catherine as if she should somehow be blamed for raising such a piece of perfection.

"She is very glad to be in your service," Catherine interposed smoothly. "And you will find she is a good girl. A little rough and ready as yet, Your Grace, but she will learn your elegance very quickly. She reminds me very much of the portraits of my father, William Carey. There is a striking similarity."

William Cecil, who knew that William Carey was as dark as Henry VIII and this girl were matching copper, concealed another indrawn breath by clearing his throat.

"And now you shall sit, and you can take a glass of wine and tell me all about your travels." Elizabeth turned from the young beauty before her. Catherine took a stool beside her cousin's throne, and gestured that her daughter should retire. The first difficult step had been achieved; Elizabeth had faced a younger, far prettier version of her own striking looks, and managed to smile pleasantly enough. Catherine set about telling her traveler's tales and thought that her family had managed their return to England rather well, considering all the circumstances.

*   *   *

Amy was waiting for a reply from Robert, telling her what she should do. Every midday she walked from the house half a mile down the drive to the road to Norwich, where a messenger would ride, if he was coming at all that day. She waited for a few minutes, looking over the cold landscape, her cloak gathered around her against the achingly cold February wind.

"It is too bad of him," Lady Robsart complained at dinner. "He sent me some money for your keep with a note from his clerk, not even a word from himself. A fine way to treat your stepmother."

"He knows you don't like him," Amy returned spiritedly. "Since you never wanted a word from him when he was out of favor, why should he honor you with his attention now that half the world wants to be his friend?"

"Well enough," the older woman said, "if you are contented to be neglected too?"

"I am not neglected," Amy maintained staunchly. "Because it is for me and for us that he is working all this time."

"Dancing attendance on the queen is work, is it? And her a young woman as lustful as her mother? With a Boleyn conscience to match? Well, you surprise me, Amy. There are not many women who would be happy being left at home while their husbands wait on the word of such a woman."

"Every wife in England would be delighted," Amy said bluntly. "Because every woman in England knows that it is only at court that there is money to be made, offices to be won, and positions to be granted. As soon as Robert has his fortune he will come home and we will buy our house."

"Syderstone will not be good enough for you then," her stepmother taunted her.

"I will always love it as my home, and admire my father for the work he did there, and I will always be grateful to him for leaving it to me in his will," Amy said with restraint. "But no, Syderstone will not be good enough for Robert now he is high at court, and it will not be good enough for me."

"And don't you mind?" her stepmother suggested slyly. "Don't you mind that he dashed off to Elizabeth at her accession and you have not seen him since? And everyone says that she favors him above all other men, and that he is never out of her company?"

"He is a courtier," Amy replied stoutly. "He was always at King Edward's side, his father was always beside King Henry. He is supposed to be at her side. That is what a courtier does."

"You are not afraid that he will fall in love with her?" the older woman tormented her, knowing that she was pressing Amy at the very sorest point.

"He is my husband," Amy said steadily. "And she is the Queen of England. She knows that as well as he does. She was a guest at my wedding. We all know what can be and what cannot be. I will be happy to see him when he comes, but until that day I shall wait for him patiently."

"Then you are a saint!" her stepmother declared lightheartedly. "For I would be so jealous that I would go to London and demand that he take a house for me there and then."

Amy raised her eyebrows, the very picture of scorn. "Then you would be much mistaken in how a courtier's wife behaves," she said coldly. "Dozens of women are in just such a situation as mine and they know how they must behave if they want their husband to further his fortune at court."

Lady Robsart left the argument there, but later that night, when Amy was in bed asleep, she took up her pen and wrote to her unsatisfactory stepson-in-law.

Sir Robert,

If you are now indeed as great a man as I hear it is not suitable that your wife should be left at home without good horses or new clothes. Also, she needs diversion and company and a genteel lady to bear her company. If you will not bid her to court, please command your noble friends (I assume that you now have many once more) to have her to stay at their houses while you find a suitable house for her in London. She will need an escort to go to them and a lady companion as I cannot go with her, being much concerned with the business of the farm, which is still doing badly. Mrs. Oddingsell would be glad to be asked, I daresay. I should be glad of your immediate reply (since I lack the sweetness and patience of your wife), and also of a full settlement of your debt to me, which is £22.

Sarah Robsart.

Cecil was at his heavy desk with the many locked drawers in his rooms at Whitehall Palace, in the first week of February, reading a letter in code from his agent in Rome.

His first act on Elizabeth's accession to the throne was to put as many trusted friends, kin, and servants in as many key courts in Europe as he could afford, and instruct them to keep him informed of any word, of any rumor, of any ghost of a rumor, which mentioned England and her new fragile monarch.

He was glad he had got Master Thomas Dempsey into the papal court at Rome. Master Thomas was better known to his colleagues in Rome as Brother Thomas, a priest of the Catholic church. Cecil's network had captured him coming to England in the first weeks of the new queen's reign, with a knife hidden in his bags and a plan to assassinate her. Cecil's man in the Tower had first tortured Brother Thomas, and then turned him. Now he was a spy against his former masters, serving the Protestants, against the faith of his fathers. Cecil knew that it had been a change of heart forced by the man's desire to survive, and that very shortly the priest would turn again. But in the meantime, his material was invaluable, and he was scholar enough to write his reports and then translate them into Latin and then translate the Latin into code.

Master Secretary, His Holiness is considering a ruling that will say that heretical monarchs can be justly defied by their subjects, and that such a defiance, even to armed rebellion, is no sin.

Cecil leaned back in his padded chair and reread the letter, making sure that he had made no error in the double translation, out of code and then out of Latin. It was a message of such enormity that he could not believe it, even when it was in plain English before him.

It was a death sentence for the queen. It assured any disgruntled Catholic that they could plot against her with impunity, actually with the blessing of the Holy Father. It was a veritable crusade against the young queen, as potent and unpredictable as a Knights Templar attack on the Moors. It licensed the deranged assassin, the man with a grudge, indeed, it put the dagger into his hands. It broke the eternal promise that an anointed monarch commanded the obedience of all his subjects, even those who disagreed with him. It broke the harmony of the universe that placed God above the angels, angels above kings, kings above mortal men. A man could no more attack a king than a king could attack an angel, than an angel could attack God. This madness of the Pope broke the unwritten agreement that one earthly monarch would never encourage the subjects of another earthly monarch to rise up against him.

The assumption had always been that kings should stick together, that nothing was more dangerous than the people with a license. Now the Pope was to give the people a license to rise up against Elizabeth, and who knew how many might avail themselves of this permission?

Cecil tried to draw a sheet of paper toward him and found that his hands were shaking. For the first time in these anxious months, he truly thought that they would be defeated. He thought that he had aligned himself to a doomed cause. He did not think that Elizabeth could survive this. There were too many who had opposed her from the start; once they knew that their treasonous plotting was no longer a sin, they would multiply like head lice. It was enough that she had to struggle with the church, with her council, with her parliament, none of which were in full support, some of which were in open opposition. If the people themselves were turned against her she could not last long.

He thought for a moment, for only a moment, that he might have done better to have supported Henry Hastings as the best Protestant claimant for the throne, since the Pope would surely not have dared to summon a rebellion against a king. He thought for another moment that perhaps he should have urged Elizabeth to accept the raising of the Host, to have kept the church in England as Papist for a year or so, to ease the transition of Reform.

He gritted his teeth. What was done had been done, and they would all have to live with their mistakes, and some would die for them. He was fairly certain that Elizabeth would die, to name only one. He clasped his hands together until they were steady again, and then started to plan ways to try to ensure that an assassin did not reach Elizabeth at court, when she was out hunting, when she was on the river, when she was visiting.

It was a nightmare task. Cecil stayed up all night writing lists of men he could trust, preparing plans to see her guarded, and knew at the end that if the Catholics of England obeyed the Pope, as they must do, then Elizabeth was a dead woman, and all that Cecil could do for her was to delay her funeral.

*   *   *

Amy Dudley had no letter from her husband to invite her to court, not even one to tell her where she should go. Instead she received a very pleasant invitation from his cousins at Bury St. Edmunds.

"See? He has sent for me!" she said delightedly to her stepmother. "I told you that he would send for me, as soon as he was able to do so. I must leave as soon as his men arrive to escort me."

"I am so happy for you," Lady Robsart said. "Did he send any money?"

*   *   *

Robert's work, as Master of the Queen's Horse was to order her horses, to run the royal stables, to care for the health and welfare of every animal from the great hunters to the lowliest pack animals of the baggage train. Visiting noblemen, with their hundreds of men in livery, had to have their horses accommodated in the stables, guests of the queen had to be supplied with horses so that they could ride out with her. Ladies of her court had to have sweet-tempered palfreys. The queen's champions had to stable their warhorses for jousting tournaments. The hounds for the hunt came under his jurisdiction, the falcons for falconry, the hawks for hawking, the leather and harness, the wagons and carts for the enormous royal progresses from one castle to another, the orders and delivery of hay and feed, all were the responsibility of Sir Robert.

So why then, Cecil asked himself, *did the man have so much time on his hands? Why was he forever at the queen's side? Since when was Robert Dudley interested in the coin of the realm and the deteriorating value?*

"We have to mint new coins," Sir Robert announced. He had inserted himself into the queen's morning conference with her advisor by the simple technique of bringing a sprig of greening leaves and laying them on her state papers. *As if he had gone a-Maying,* Cecil thought bitterly. Elizabeth had smiled and made a gesture that he might stay, and now he was joining the conference.

"The smaller coins are shaved and spoiled till they are almost worthless."

Cecil did not reply. This much was self-evident. Sir Thomas Gresham in his huge mercantile house at Antwerp had been studying the problem for years as his own business fluctuated catastrophically with the unreliable value of English coin, and as his loan business to the monarchs of England became more and more precarious. *But now apparently, far superior to Gresham's opinions, we are to be blessed with the insights of Sir Robert Dudley.*

"We have to call in the old coins and replace them with full-weight good coins."

The queen looked worried. "But the old coins have been so clipped and shaved that we will not get half our gold back."

"It has to be done," Dudley declared. "No one knows the value of a penny, no one trusts the value of a groat. If you try to collect an old debt, as I have done, you find that you are repaid in coins that are half the value of your original loan. When our merchants go abroad to pay for their purchases, they have to stand by while the foreign traders bring out scales to weigh the coins and laugh at them. They don't even bother to look at the value stamped on the face; they only buy by weight. No one trusts English coin anymore. And the greatest danger is that if we issue new coins, of full value gold, then they are just treated as bad, we gain nothing unless we call all the old ones in first. Otherwise we throw our wealth away."

Elizabeth turned to Cecil.

"He is right," he conceded unwillingly. "This is just as Sir Thomas Gresham believes."

"Bad coin drives out good," Sir Robert ruled.

There was something about the ring of his tone that attracted Cecil's attention. "I did not know you had studied mercantile matters," he remarked gently.

Only Cecil could have seen the swiftly hidden amusement on the younger man's face.

But only Cecil was waiting for it.

"A good servant of the queen must consider all her needs," Sir Robert said calmly.

Good God, he has intercepted Gresham's letters to me, Cecil observed. For a moment he was so stunned by the younger man's impertinence, to spy on the queen's spymaster, that he could hardly speak. *He must have got hold of the messenger, copied the letter, and resealed it. But how? And at what point on its journey from Antwerp? And if he can get hold of my letters from Gresham, what other information does he have of mine?*

"The base drives out the good?" the queen repeated.

Robert Dudley turned to her. "In coinage as in life," he said intimately, as if for her ears alone. "The lesser joys, the more ignoble pleasures, are those that take a man or a woman's time, make demands. The finer things, true love or a spiritual life between a man and his God, these are the things that are driven out by the day to day. Don't you think that is true?"

For a moment she looked quite entranced. "It is so," she said. "It is always harder to make time for the truly precious experiences; there is always the ordinary to do."

"To be an extraordinary queen, you have to choose," he said quietly. "You have to choose the best, every day, without compromise, without listening to your advisors, guided by your own true heart and highest ambition."

She took a little breath and looked at him as if he could unfold the secrets of the universe, as if he were his tutor, John Dee, and could speak with angels and foretell the future.

"I want to choose the best," she said.

Robert smiled. "I know you do. It is one of the many things that we share. We both want nothing but the best. And now we have a chance to achieve it."

"Good coin?" she whispered.

"Good coin and true love."

With an effort she took her eyes from him. "What d'you think, Spirit?"

"The troubles with the coinage are well known," Cecil said dampeningly. "Every merchant in London would tell you the same. But the remedy is not so generally certain. I think we all agree that a pound coin is no longer worth a pound of gold, but how we restore it is going to be difficult. It's not as if we have the gold to spare to mint new coins."

"Have you prepared a plan of how to revalue the coin?" Dudley demanded briskly of the Secretary of State.

"I have been considering it with the queen's advisors," Cecil said stiffly. "Men who have been thinking on this problem for many years."

Dudley gave his irrepressible grin. "Better tell them to hurry up then," he recommended cheerfully.

"I am drawing up a plan."

"Well, while you are doing that we will walk in the garden," Dudley offered, deliberately misunderstanding.

"I can't draw it up now!" Cecil exclaimed. "It will take weeks to plan properly."

But already the queen was on her feet; Dudley had offered his arm, the two of them fled from the presence chamber with the speed of scholars escaping a class. Cecil turned to her ladies-in-waiting who were scrambling to curtsy.

"Go with the queen," he said.

"Did she ask for us?" one of the ladies queried.

Cecil nodded. "Walk with them, and take her shawl, it is cold out today."

*   *   *

In the garden Dudley retained the queen's hand, and tucked it under his elbow.

"I can walk on my own, you know," she said pertly.

"I know," he said. "But I like to hold your hand; I like to walk at your side. May I?"

She said neither yes nor no, but she left her hand on his arm. As always with Elizabeth, it was one step forward and then one step back. As soon as she allowed him to keep her little hand warm on his arm she chose to raise the question of his wife.

"You do not ask me if you may bring Lady Dudley to court," she began provocatively. "Do you not wish her to attend? Do you not ask for her to have a place in my service? I am surprised that you have not mentioned her to me for one of my ladies-in-waiting. You were quick enough to recommend your sister."

"She prefers to live in the country," Robert said smoothly.

"You have a country house now?"

He shook his head. "She has a house that she inherited from her father in Norfolk but it is too small and too inconvenient. She lives with her stepmother at Stanfield Hall, nearby; but she is going to stay with my cousins at Bury St. Edmunds this week."

"Shall you buy a house now? Or build a new one?"

He shrugged. "I shall find some good land and build a good house, but I am going to spend most of my time at court."

"Oh, are you, indeed?" she asked flirtatiously.

"Does a man walk away from sunlight to shadow? Does he leave gold for gilt? Does he taste good wine and then want bad?" His voice was deliberately seductive. "I shall stay at court forever, if I am allowed, basking in the sunshine, enriched by the gold, drunk on the perfume of the headiest wine I could imagine. What were we saying: that we would not let the base drive out the best? That we should have, both of us, the very best?"

She absorbed the compliment for a long, delicious moment. "And your wife must surely be very old now?"

Dudley smiled down at her, knowing that she was teasing him. "She is thirty, just five years older than me," he said. "As I think you know. You were at my wedding."

Elizabeth made a little face. "It was years and years ago; I had quite forgotten it."

"Nearly ten years," he said quietly.

"And I thought even then that she was a very great age."

"She was only twenty-one."

"Well, a great age to me, I was only sixteen." She gave an affected little start of surprise. "Oh! As were you. Were you not surprised to be marrying a woman so much older than you?"

"I was not surprised," he said levelly. "I knew her age and her position."

"And still no children?"

"God has not blessed us as yet."

"I think that I heard a little whisper that you had married her for love, for a passionate love, and against the wishes of your father," she prompted him.

He shook his head. "He was opposed only because I was so young; I was not yet seventeen and she just twenty-one. And I imagine he would have picked a better match for me if I had given him the chance. But he did not refuse his permission once I asked, and Amy brought a good dowry. They had good lands in Norfolk laid down to sheep, and in those days, my father needed to increase our friends and influence in the east of the country. She was her father's only heir, and he was happy enough with the match."

"I should think he was!" she exclaimed. "The Duke of Northumberland's son for a girl who had never been to court, who could barely write her own name, and who did nothing but stay home and weep the moment that her husband encountered trouble?"

"It must have been a fairly detailed little whisper that came to your ears," Robert remarked. "You seem to know my entire marital history."

Elizabeth's gurgle of guilty laughter was checked when the lady-in-waiting appeared behind them. "Your Grace, I have brought your shawl."

"I didn't ask for one," Elizabeth said, surprised. She turned back to Robert. "Yes, of course, I heard talk of your marriage. And what sort of woman your wife was. But I forgot it until now."

He bowed, his smile lurking around his mouth. "Can I assist your memory any further?"

"Well," she said engagingly. "What I still don't know for sure is why you married her in the first place, and, if it was love, as I heard, whether you still love her."

"I married her because I was sixteen, a young man with hot blood and she had a pretty face and she was willing," he said, careful not to let it sound too romantic to this most critical audience, though he remembered well enough how it had been, and that he had been mad for Amy, defying his father and insisting on having her as his wife. "I was eager to be a married man and grown up, as I thought. We had a few years when we were contented together, but she was her father's favorite child and in the habit of being spoiled. In fairness, I suppose I was a favored son and I had been richly blessed. A pair of spoiled brats together, in fact. We did not deal very well together after the newness had worn off. I was at court in my father's train, as you know, and she stayed in the country. She had no desire for court life and—God bless her—she has no airs and graces. She has no courtly skills and no wish to learn them.

"Then, if I must tell the truth, when I was in the Tower and in terror for my life, I fell out of the way of thinking of her at all. She visited me once or twice when my brothers' wives visited them; but she brought no comfort to me. It was like hearing of another world: her telling me of the hay crop and the sheep, and arguments with the house-maids. I just felt, wrongly, I am sure, as if she was taunting me with the world going on without me. She sounded to me as if she was happier without me. She had returned to her father's house, she was free of the stain of my family's disgrace, she had taken up her childhood life again and I almost felt that she preferred me to be locked up, safely out of the way of trouble. She would rather I was a prisoner, than a great man at court and son of the greatest."

He paused for a moment. "You know what it's like," he said. "When you are a prisoner, after a while your world shrinks to the stone walls of your chamber, your walk is to the window and back again. Your life is only memories. And then you start longing for your dinner. You know then that you are a prisoner indeed. You are thinking of nothing but what is inside. You have forgotten to desire the outside world."

Instantly Elizabeth squeezed her hand on his arm. "Yes," she said, for once without coquetry. "God knows that I know what it is like. And it spoils your love for anything on the outside."

He nodded. "Aye. We two know.

"Then, when I was released I came out of the Tower a ruined man. All our family's wealth and property had been forfeited. I was a pauper."

"A sturdy beggar?" she suggested with a little smile.

"Not even very sturdy," he said. "I was broken down low, Elizabeth; I was as low as a man could go. My mother had died begging for our freedom. My father had recanted before us all, had said that our faith had been a plague upon the realm. It bit into my soul; I was so ashamed. Then, even though he had knelt before them to make his peace, they still executed him for a traitor, and, God keep him, he made a bad death that shamed us all.

"My dearest brother John took sick in the Tower with me and I could not save him; I could not even nurse him; I didn't know what to do. They let him go to my sister Mary but he died of his sickness. He was only twenty-four, but I couldn't save him. I had been a poor son and a poor brother and

I followed a poor father. There was not much to be proud of, when I came out of the Tower."

She waited.

"There was nowhere for me to go but to her stepmother's house at Stanfield Hall, Norfolk," he said, the bitterness in his voice still sharp. "Everything we owned: the London house, the great estates, the house at Syon, were all gone. Poor Amy had even lost her own inheritance, her father's farm at Syderstone." He gave a short laugh. "Queen Mary had put the nuns back into Syon. Imagine it! My home was a nunnery once more and they were singing the *Te Deum* in our great hall."

"Did her family treat you kindly?" she asked, guessing the answer.

"As anyone would treat a son-in-law who had presented himself as the greatest man in the kingdom, and then came home as a penniless prisoner with a touch of jail fever," he said wryly. "Her stepmother never forgave me for the seduction of John Robsart's daughter and the collapse of his hopes. She swore that he had died of heartbreak because of what I had done to his daughter, and she never forgave me for that either. She never gave me more than a few pence to have in my pocket. And when they learned I had been in London to a meeting, they threatened to throw me out of the house in my boots."

"What meeting?" she asked, a conspirator from long habit.

He shrugged. "Oh, to put you on the throne," he said, his voice very low. "I never stopped plotting. My great terror was that your sister would have a son and we would be undone. But God was good to us."

"You risked your life in plotting for me?" she asked, her dark eyes wide. "Even then? When you had just been released?"

He smiled at her. "Of course," he said easily. "Who else for me, but England's Elizabeth?"

She took a little breath. "And after that you were forced to stay quiet at home?"

"Not I. When the war came my brother Henry and I volunteered to serve under Philip against the French in the Low Countries." He smiled. "I saw you before I sailed. D'you remember?"

Her look was warm. "Of course. I was there to bid farewell to Philip and to taunt poor Mary, and there were you, as handsome an adventurer who ever went away to war, smiling down at me from the royal ship."

"I had to find a way to raise myself up again," he said. "I had to get away from Amy's family." He paused. "And from Amy," he confessed.

"You had fallen out of love with her?" she asked, finally getting to the part of the story that she had wanted all along.

Robert smiled. "What pleases a young man who knows nothing at sixteen cannot hold a man who has been forced to look at his life, to study what he holds dear, and to start from the bottom once again. My marriage was over by the time I came out of the Tower. Her stepmother's humiliation of me as she stood by and watched only completed the end. Lady Robsart brought me as low as I could go. I could not forgive Amy for witnessing it. I could not forgive her for not taking my side. I would have loved her better if we had walked out of that house together into disaster. But she sat by the fireside on her little stool and reminded me from time to time, when she looked up from hemming shirts, that God orders us to honor our father and our mother, and that

we were utterly dependent on the Rob-
sarts."

He broke off, his face darkened with remembered anger. Elizabeth listened, hiding
her relish.

"So . . . I went to fight in the Low Countries, and thought I would make my name
and my fortune in that war." He gave a short
laugh. "That was my last moment of vanity,"
he said. "I lost my brother and I lost most of
my troop and I lost Calais. I came home a
very humbled man."

"And did she care for you?"

"That was when she thought I should be
a teamster," he said bitterly. "Lady Robsart
ordered me to labor in the fields."

"She never did!"

"She would have had me on my knees. I
walked out of the house that night and
stayed at court or with what friends would
have me. My marriage was over. In my
heart, I was a free man."

"A free man?" she asked in a very quiet
voice. "You would call yourself a free man?"

"Yes," he said firmly. "I am free to love
once more, and this time I will have nothing
but the best. I will not allow base coin to
drive out gold."

"Indeed," said Elizabeth, suddenly cool, withdrawing rapidly from dangerous intimacy. She turned and beckoned forward the lady-in-waiting. "I will have that shawl now," she said. "You may walk with us."

They walked in silence, Elizabeth taking in what he had told her, sifting the evidenced truth from the gloss. She was not such a fool as to believe the word of a married man. At her side Dudley reviewed what he had said, determinably ignoring an uncomfortable feeling of disloyalty to Amy whose love, he knew, had been more faithful, and continued more strongly than he chose to portray. Of course, his remaining love for her he had completely denied.

*   *   *

Cecil, Sir Francis Knollys, and the queen's young uncle, the twenty-three-year-old Thomas Howard, Duke of Norfolk, were head to head in the private window bay of the presence chamber; behind them, the queen's court stood around, chatting, plotting, flirting. The queen on her throne was talking with the Spanish ambassador in fluent Spanish. Cecil, one ear cocked for any danger from that quarter, was nonetheless very intent upon Sir Francis.

"We have to find a means to search everyone before they come to the queen, even the gentlemen of the court."

"We would give much offense," the duke demurred. "And surely the threat comes from the common people?"

"It comes from every convinced Papist," Cecil said bluntly. "The Pope's declaration, when it is published, will make her a lamb for the slaughter as she has never been before."

"She cannot dine in public anymore," Sir Francis said thoughtfully. "We will have to refuse permission for people to come in and see her at her dinner."

Cecil hesitated. Access to the monarch, or even to the great lords in their halls, was part of the natural order, the way things had always been done. If that were to be changed, then the court would have signaled very clearly to the people that they trusted them no more, and that they were retreating behind locked doors.

"It will look odd," he said begrudgingly.

"And she can hardly make any more public processions," Sir Francis said. "How can it be done?"

Before Cecil could stop him, Sir Francis

beckoned Robert Dudley, who excused himself from the group around him and started to come toward them.

"If you add him to our councils I'm away," the duke said abruptly, and turned aside.

"Why?" Sir Francis asked. "He knows how this can be done better than any of us."

"He knows nothing but his own ambition, and you will rue the day you ever include him in anything," Thomas Howard said rudely and turned his back as Dudley joined the others.

"Good day, Sir William, Sir Francis."

"What ails young Howard?" Sir Francis asked as the duke pushed past another man and strode away.

"I think he mourns the rising of my little star," Dudley said, amused.

"Why?"

"His father hated mine," Dudley said. "Actually, Thomas Howard arrested my father and my brothers and me and marched us into the Tower. I don't think he expected me to come marching out again."

Sir Francis nodded, taking it in. "You must be afraid that he will influence the queen against you?"

"He'd better fear that I will influence her

against him," Dudley replied. He smiled at Cecil. "She knows who her friends are. She knows who stood as her friends through the years of her troubles."

"And the troubles are not over now," Sir Francis said, turning to the matter in hand. "We are talking of the safety of the queen when she goes abroad. Sir William here has news that the Pope has sanctioned the use of force against her by ordinary men and women."

Dudley turned a stunned face to the older man. "It cannot be true? He would never do such a thing? It is ungodly!"

"It is under consideration," Cecil said flatly. "And we shall hear the confirmation soon enough. And then the people will learn of it."

"I've heard nothing of this," Robert exclaimed.

Oh, have you not? Cecil hid his smile. "Nonetheless, I am sure of it."

Dudley was silent for a moment, shocked by the news, but noting at the same time that Cecil had a spy in the very court of the Bishop of Rome. Cecil's network of intelligencers and informers was growing to impressive proportions. "It is to overthrow the natural order," he said. "She was anointed by one of his own bishops. He cannot do it. He cannot set the dogs on a sacred person."

"He will do it," Cecil said, irritated by the young man's slowness. "Indeed, by now, he probably has done it. What we are considering is how to prevent anyone obeying it."

"I was saying that she must be kept from the people," Sir Francis said.

A bright laugh from the throne made all three of them break off, turn, and smile at where the queen was flirting with her fan and laughing at Ambassador Feria, who was colored up—torn between frustration and laughter. They all three smiled at her, she was irresistible in her joy, in her playfulness, in the brightness of her energy.

"The people are her greatest safety," Dudley said slowly.

Cecil shook his head, but Sir Francis checked him with a hand on his sleeve. "What d'you mean?"

"The Pope makes this a matter of the common people, he invites them to attack her; but he does not know this queen. She should not hide from the few men or women who would do her harm; she should go out and draw the love of all the rest. Her greatest safety would be if every man, woman, or child in this country would lay down their lives for her."

"And how would we achieve that?"

"You know it already," Dudley said bluntly to Cecil. "You saw it. In the coronation procession she won every single heart in that crowd. We have to take the risk to take her out to the people and know that they will be the ones that protect her. Every Englishman should be one of the queen's guard."

Sir Francis slowly nodded. "And when it comes to an invasion they would fight for her."

"A single man with a single poignard is almost unstoppable," Cecil said bleakly. "She may win over a hundred, but if one is against her, and he is the one with the knife, then she is dead, and it is at our door." He paused. "And a Catholic queen inherits, and England is a cat's-paw of France, and we are ruined."

"As you say, unstoppable," Robert rejoined, not at all overwhelmed by the gloom of this picture. "But your way, you give her twenty guards, perhaps thirty. My way: I give her the whole of England."

Cecil grimaced at the younger man's romantic language.

"There will still be some places that we cannot admit the people," Sir Francis pursued. "When she is dining, when she goes through the halls to her chapel. There are too many and they press too close."

"That, we should restrict," Robert concurred. "And we can serve her dinner without her being there."

Cecil drew breath. "Without her being there? What is the purpose of that?"

"The people come to see the throne and the plate and the great ceremony," Robert said airily. "They will come anyway. Provided that there is a good show they don't need to see her in person. High days and holidays she must be there to show that she is well and in good spirits. But most of the time she can eat in private with her friends, in safety. As long as it is grand enough and the trumpets play and it is served in state, then the people will go away feeling that they have seen a good show. They will go away knowing that the country is wealthy and secure. That is what we need to do. We need to give them the show of the throne.

The queen need not always be there herself, as long as everyone can feel her presence."

"Serve her dinner to an empty throne?" Cecil demanded quizzically.

"Yes," Dudley replied. "And why not? It's been done before. When the young King Edward was sick they served his dinner on gold plates every night to an empty throne and the people came to watch and went away satisfied. My father ruled it so. We gave them a great show of grandeur, of wealth. And when they *do* see her, she has to be beloved, reachable, touchable. She has to be a queen for the people."

Cecil shook his head but Sir Francis was persuaded.

"I shall speak with her about it," he said, glancing back at the throne. The Spanish ambassador was taking his leave, he was handing over a letter sealed ostentatiously with the royal coat of arms of the Spanish emperor. With the eyes of the court upon her, Elizabeth took it and—apparently un- aware that everyone was watching her— held it against her heart.

"I think you will find that Elizabeth under- stands how to put on a show," Robert said drily. "She has never disappointed an audience in her life."

*   *   *

Robert Dudley's own steward came himself from London to escort Amy for the short journey to Bury St. Edmunds, and to bring her a purse of gold, a length of warm red velvet for a new dress, and her husband's affectionate compliments.

He also brought a lady companion with him: Mrs. Elizabeth Oddingsell, the widowed sister of one of Robert Dudley's old and faithful friends, who had been with Amy at Gravesend and then went with her to Chichester. Amy was glad to see the little dark-haired, brisk woman again.

"How your fortunes do rise," Mrs. Oddingsell said cheerfully. "When I heard from my brother that Sir Robert had been appointed Master of Horse I thought I would write to you, but I did not want to seem to be pushing myself forward. I thought you must have many friends seeking your acquaintanceship now."

"I expect my lord has many new friends," Amy said. "But I am still very secluded in the country here."

"Of course, you must be." Mrs. Oddingsell cast a quick glance around the small, chilly hall which formed the main body of the square stone-built house. "Well, I hear we are to make a round of visits. That will be pleasant. We shall be on progress like a queen."

"Yes," Amy said quietly.

"Oh! And I was forgetting!" Mrs. Oddingsell unwound a warm scarf from her throat. "He has sent you a lovely little black mare. You are to name her as you please. That will make our journey merry, won't it?"

Amy ran to the window and looked out into the yard. There was a small escort loading Amy's few trunks into a cart, and at the back of the troop was a sweet-faced black mare, standing quite still.

"Oh! She is so pretty!" Amy exclaimed. For the first time since Elizabeth's coming to the throne she felt her spirits lift.

"And he sent a purse of gold for you to settle his debts here, and to buy yourself anything you might like," Mrs. Oddingsell said, delving into the pocket of her cape and pulling out the money.

Amy took the heavy purse into her hand. "For me," she said. It was the most money she had held for years.

"Your hard times are over," Mrs. Odd-ingsell said gently. "Thank God. For all of us, the good times have come at last."

Amy and Mrs. Oddingsell started their journey a little after dawn on a cold winter morning. They broke their journey at New-borough, and rested two nights, then they went on. It was an uneventful journey marred only by the cold, the wintry dark-ness, and the state of the roads. But Amy enjoyed her new horse, and Mrs. Oddingsell kept her spirits up as they rode down the muddy lanes and splashed through icy pud-dles.

*   *   *

Mr. and Mrs. Woods at Bury St. Edmunds greeted Amy kindly, and with every appear-ance of pleasure. They assured her that she was welcome to stay as long as she liked; Sir Robert had mentioned in his letter that she would be with them until April.

"Did he send a letter for me?" Amy de-manded. The brightness drained from her face when they said "No." It was just a brief note to tell them when to expect her and the duration of her stay.

"Did he say that he was coming here?" she asked.

"No," Mrs. Woods said again, feeling uncomfortable at the shadow that passed over Amy's face. "I expect he's very busy at court," she continued, trying to gloss over the awkward moment. "I doubt he'll be able to get home for weeks."

She could have bitten off her tongue in irritation at her own clumsiness as she realized that there was no home for this young woman and her husband. She fell back on the good manners of hospitality. Would Amy like to rest after her journey? Would she like to wash? Would she like to take her supper at once?

Amy said abruptly that she was sorry, that she was very tired, and she would rest in her room. She went quickly from the hall, leaving Mrs. Woods and Mrs. Oddingsell alone.

"She is tired," Mrs. Oddingsell said. "I am afraid she is not strong."

"Shall I send for our physician at Cambridge?" Mr. Woods suggested. "He's very good, he would come at once. He's very much in favor of cupping the patient to adjust the humors. She is very pale; is she of a watery humor, d'you think?"

Elizabeth Oddingsell shook her head. "She is in much discomfort," she said.

Mr. Woods thought that she meant indigestion, and was about to offer arrowroot and milk, but Mrs. Woods, remembering the glimpse she had seen of Robert Dudley, dark-eyed on a black horse at the coronation procession, riding behind the queen as if he were prince consort himself, suddenly understood.

*   *   *

It was Cecil, not Dudley, who was at the queen's side after dinner. She had been served with all the grandeur of the Tudor tradition, great plates passed down the long dining hall of Whitehall Palace, checked by the taster for poison, and presented to her on bent knee. Three of the servers were new and clumsy. They were Cecil's men, spies put in place to watch and guard her, learning how to serve on bended knee at the same time.

Elizabeth took a very little from each plate and then sent them to her favorites, seated in the body of the hall. Sharp eyes watched where the best dishes went, and when a dish of stewed venison was sent to Dudley there were a few muttered complaints. The loud, joyful rumble of the court at dinner filled the great hall, the servants cleared the tables, and then Cecil was beckoned up to the dais and stood before the queen.

She gestured that the musicians should play; no one could hear their quiet conversation. "Any news of any hired killers?" she asked.

He saw the strain on her face. "You are safe," he said steadily, though he knew he could never truly say that to her again. "The ports are watched, your gates are guarded. A mouse cannot come in without us knowing."

She found a weak smile. "Good. Tell them to stay alert."

He nodded.

"And as to Scotland: I read your note this afternoon. We cannot do what you propose," she said. "We cannot support rebels against a queen, that is to subvert the rule of law. We have to wait and see what happens."

It was as Cecil had expected. She had a mortal terror of making a mistake. It was as if she had lived on the brink of disaster for so long that she could bear to step neither forward nor back. And she was right to be cautious. Every decision in England had a hundred opponents, every change had a thousand. Anything that threatened a man's individual prosperity made an enemy of him, anything that was to his benefit made him a grasping, unreliable ally. She was a queen new-come to her throne and the crown was dangerously unsteady on her head. She did not dare consider anything that might undermine the power of queens.

Cecil made sure that no sign of these thoughts showed on his face. It was his deep-rooted belief that the intelligence of a woman, even one as formidably educated as this, could not carry the burden of too much information, and the temperament of a woman, especially this one, was not strong enough to take decisions.

"I could never support a rebellion against a ruling queen," she specified.

Tactfully Cecil avoided mentioning the years when Elizabeth had been the focus and sometimes instigator of a dozen plots against her pure-blood, anointed half-sister.

"It is all very well you wanting us to support the Scots Protestants against the regent, Queen Mary of Guise, but I cannot support any rebels against a ruling king or queen. I cannot meddle in another's kingdom."

"Indeed, but the French princess will meddle in yours," he warned her. "Already she has the arms of England quartered on her shield, she considers herself the true heir to England, and half of England and most of Christendom would say she has the right. If her father-in-law, the French king, decides to support her claim to your throne, the French could invade England tomorrow, and what more useful stepping-stone than Scotland and the north? Her mother, a Frenchwoman, holds Scotland for them as regent, already the French soldiers are massing on your northern border; what are they doing there, if not waiting to invade? This is a battle that must come. Better that we fight the French army in Scotland, with the Protestant Scots on our side, than we wait for them to come marching down the Great North Road when we do not know who might rise up for us and who might rise up for them."

Elizabeth paused; the appearance of the English leopards on the shield of the daughter of Mary of Guise was an offense which went straight to her jealously possessive heart. "She dare not try to claim my throne. No one would rise up for her in preference to me," she said boldly. "No one would want another Catholic Mary on the throne."

"Hundreds would," Cecil said dampeningly. "Thousands."

That checked her, as he had known it would. He could see that she lost a little color.

"The people love me," she asserted.

"Not all of them."

She laughed but there was no real merriment in her voice. "Are you saying I have more friends in Scotland than in the north of England?"

"Yes," he said bluntly.

"Philip of Spain would stand my ally if there was an invasion," she declared.

"Yes, as long as he thinks that you will be his wife. But can you keep him thinking that for much longer? You cannot really mean to have him?"

Elizabeth giggled like a girl and, unaware of betraying herself, glanced across the room toward Robert Dudley, seated between two other handsome young men. Effortlessly, he outshone them. He tipped back his head to laugh and snapped his fingers for more wine. A servant, studiously ignoring other thirsty diners, leapt to do his bidding.

"I might marry Philip," she said. "Or I might keep him waiting."

"The important thing," Cecil said gently, "is to choose a husband and get us an heir. That is the way to make the country safe against the Princess Mary. If you have a strong husband at your side and a son in the cradle, no one would want another queen. People would even overlook religion for a safe succession."

"I have been offered no one I could be sure to like as a husband," she said, warming to her favorite, most irritating theme. "And I am happy in my single state."

"You are the queen," Cecil said flatly. "And queens cannot choose the single state."

Robert raised his goblet in a toast to the health of one of Elizabeth's ladies, his most recent mistress; her friend nudged her and she simpered across the room to him. Elizabeth apparently saw nothing, but Cecil knew that she had missed none of it.

"And Scotland?" he prompted.

"It is a very great risk. All very well to say that the Scottish Lords Protestant might rise up against Mary of Guise, but what if they do not? Or if they do, and are defeated? Where are we then, but defeated in a war of our own making? And meddling in the affairs of an anointed queen. What is that to do, but to go against God's will? And to invite a French invasion."

"Either in Scotland or in England we will have to face the French," Cecil predicted. "Either with the Spanish on our side or without them. What I am advising, Your Grace— nay, what I am begging you to understand— is that we will have to face the French and we should do it at a time and a place of our choosing, and with allies. If we fight now, we have the Spanish as our friends. If you leave it too long, you will have to fight alone. And then you will certainly lose."

"It will anger the Catholics in England if we are seen to join the Protestant cause against a rightful Catholic queen," she pointed out.

"You were known as the Protestant princess; it will come as little surprise to them, and it makes it no worse for us. And many of them, even stout Catholics, would be glad to see the French soundly beaten.

Many of them are Englishmen before they are Catholics."

Elizabeth shifted irritably on her throne. "I don't want to be known as the Protestant queen," she said crossly. "Have we not had enough inquiry into men's faiths that we have to chase after their souls once more? Can't people just worship in the way that they wish, and leave others to their devotions? Do I have to endure the constant inquiry from the bishops to the Commons as to what I think, as to what the people should think? Can't it be enough for them that we have restored the church to what it was in my father's time but without his punishments?"

"No," he said frankly. "Your Grace," he added when she shot him a hard look. "You will be forced again and again to take a side. The church needs leadership; you must command it or leave it to the Pope. Which is it to be?"

He saw her gaze wander; she was looking past him to Robert Dudley, who had risen from his place at table and was strolling across the room to where the ladies-in-waiting were seated on their table. As he approached they all turned toward him, without seeming to move; their heads all swiveled like flowers seeking the sun, his current favorite blushing in anticipation.

"I shall think about it," she said abruptly. She crooked her finger to Robert Dudley and smoothly, he altered his course and came to the dais and bowed. "Your Grace," he said pleasantly.

"I should like to dance."

"Would you do me the honor? I have been longing to ask you, but did not dare to interrupt your talk, you seemed so grave."

"Not only grave but urgent," Cecil reminded her grimly.

She nodded, but he saw he had lost her attention. She rose from her seat, her eyes only for Robert. Cecil stepped to one side and she went past him to the center of the floor. Robert bowed to her, as graceful as an Italian, and took her hand. A faint hint of color came into Elizabeth's cheek at his touch. She turned her head away from him.

Cecil watched the set of dancers form behind the couple, Catherine and Francis Knollys behind them, Robert's sister, Lady Mary Sidney, and her partner, other ladies and gentlemen of the court behind them, but no pair even half as handsome as the queen and her favorite. Cecil could not help but smile on the two of them, a radiant pair of well-matched beauties. Elizabeth caught his indulgent look and gave him a cheeky grin. Cecil bowed his head. After all, she was a young woman, as well as a queen, and it was good for England to have a merry court.

*   *   *

Later that night, in the silent palace, under an unbroken black sky, the court slept, but Cecil was wakeful. He had thrown a robe over his linen nightshirt and sat at his great desk, his bare feet drawn onto the furred edge of his gown against the wintry coldness of the stone floor. His pen scratched on the manuscript as he made out his list of candidates for the queen's hand, and the advantages and disadvantages of each match. Cecil was a great one for lists; their march down the page matched the orderly progression of his thinking.

Husbands for the Queen.
1. King Philip of Spain—he will need dispensation from the Pope/he would support us against France and save us from the danger of

the French in Scotland/ but he will use England in his wars/the people will never accept him a second time/can he even father a child?/she was attracted to him before but perhaps it was spite, and only because he was married to her sister.

2. *Archduke Charles—Hapsburg but free to live in England/Spanish alliance/said to be fanatically religious/said to be ugly and she cannot tolerate ugliness even in men.*

3. *Archduke Ferdinand—his brother so same advantages but said to be pleasant and better-looking/ younger so more malleable?/she will never brook a master, and neither will we.*

4. *Prince Erik of Sweden—a great match for him and would please the Baltic merchants, but of no help to us elsewhere/ would make the French and the Spanish our bitter enemies and for the scant benefit of a weak ally/Protestant of course/ rich too, which would be a great help.*

5. *Earl of Arran—heir to the Scottish throne after Princess Mary/could lead the Scottish campaign for us/handsome/ Protestant/poor (and thus grateful to me). If he were to defeat the French in Scotland our worst danger is gone/and a son to him and the queen would finally unite the kingdoms/a Scottish-- English monarchy would solve everything . . .*

6. *An English commoner—she is a young woman and sooner or later is bound to take a liking to someone who always hangs about her/this would be the worst choice: he would further his own friends and family/would anger other families/would seek greater power from his knowledge of the country/disaster for me . . .*

Cecil broke off and brushed the feather of the quill against his lips.

It cannot be, he wrote. We cannot have an overmighty subject to further his own family and turn her against me and mine. Thank God that Robt. Dudley is already married or he would be scheming to take this flirtation further. I know him and his . . .

He sat in the silence of the nighttime palace. Outside on the turret an owl hooted, calling for a mate. Cecil thought of the sleeping queen and his face softened in a smile that was as tender as a father's. Then he drew a fresh piece of paper toward him and started to write.

To the Earl of Arran:
My lord,
   At this urgent time in your affairs the bearer of this will convey to you my good wishes and my hopes that you will let him assist you to come to England, where my house and my servants will be honored to be at your disposal . . .

Elizabeth, in her private apartment at Whitehall Palace, was rereading a love-letter from Philip of Spain, the third of a series that had grown increasingly passionate as the correspondence had gone on. One of her ladies-in-waiting, Lady Betty, craned to see the words upside down but could not make out the Latin, and silently cursed her poor education.

"Oh, listen," Elizabeth breathed. "He says that he cannot eat or sleep for thinking of me."

"He'll have got dreadfully scrawny then," Catherine Knollys said robustly. "He was always too thin; he had legs like a pigeon."

Lady Mary Sidney, Robert Dudley's sister, giggled.

"Hush!" Elizabeth reprimanded them primly; she was always sensitive to the status of a fellow monarch. "He is very distinguished. And anyway, I daresay he is eating. It is just poetry, Catherine. He is just saying it to please me."

"Just nonsense," Catherine said under her breath. "And Papist nonsense, at that."

"He says he has struggled with his conscience, and struggled with his respect for my faith and my learning, and that he is sure that we can somehow find a way that allows us both to continue in our faith, and yet bring our hearts together."

"He will bring a dozen cardinals in his train," Catherine predicted. "And the Inquisition behind them. He has no affection for you at all, this is just politics."

Elizabeth looked up. "Catherine, he does have an affection for me. You were not here, or you would have seen it for yourself. Everybody remarked it at the time, it was an utter scandal. I swear that I would have been left in the Tower or under house arrest for the rest of my life if he had not intervened for me against the queen's ill wishes. He insisted that I be treated as a princess and as heir . . ." She broke off and smoothed down the golden brocade skirt of her gown . . . "And he was very tender to me." Her voice took on its typical, narcissistic lilt. Elizabeth was always ready to fall in love with herself. "He admired me, to tell the truth; he adored me. A real prince, a real king, and desperately in love with me. While my sister was confined we spent much time together, and he was . . ."

"A fine husband he will make," Catherine interrupted. "One who flirts with his sister-in-law while his wife is in confinement."

"She was not really confined," Elizabeth said with magnificent irrelevance. "She only thought she was with child because she was so swollen and sick . . ."

"All the kinder of him then," Catherine triumphed. "So he flirted with his sister-in-law when his wife was ill and breaking her heart over something she could not help. Your Grace, in all seriousness, you cannot have him. The people of England won't have the Spanish king back again. He was hated here the first time; they would go mad if he came back again. He emptied the treasury, he broke your sister's heart, he did not give her a son, he lost us Calais, and he has spent the last few months in the most disgraceful affairs with the ladies of Brussels."

"No!" Elizabeth said, instantly diverted from her love-letter. "So is that what he means when he says he neither eats nor sleeps?"

"Because he is always bedding the fat burghers' wives. He is as lecherous as a sparrow!" Catherine beamed at her cousin's irresistible giggle. "You must be able to do better than your sister's leftovers, surely! You are not such an old maid that you have to settle for cold meats, a secondhand husband. There are better choices."

"Oh! And who would you want me to have?" Elizabeth asked.

"The Earl of Arran," Catherine said

promptly. "He's young, he's Protestant, he's handsome, he's very very charming—I met him briefly and I lost my heart to him at once—and when he inherits the throne, you join England and Scotland into one kingdom."

"Only if Mary of Guise were to helpfully drop dead, followed by her daughter," Elizabeth pointed out. "And Mary of Guise is in good health and her daughter is younger than me."

"Stranger things happen to further God's will," Catherine said confidently. "And if the regent Mary lives, why should she not be pushed off her throne by a handsome Protestant heir?"

Elizabeth frowned and glanced around the room to see who was listening. "Enough, Catherine, matchmaking doesn't suit you."

"It is both matchmaking and the safety of our nation and our faith," Catherine said, unrepentant. "And you have the chance to secure Scotland for your son, and save it from the Antichrist of Popery by marrying a handsome young man. It sounds to me as if there is no decision to take. Who would not want the Earl of Arran, fighting on the side of the Scottish lords for God's kingdom on earth, and the kingdom of Scotland as his dowry?"

*   *   *

Catherine Knollys might be certain in her preference for the young Earl of Arran, but at the end of February another suitor appeared at Elizabeth's court: the Austrian ambassador, Count von Helfenstein, pressing the claims of the Hapsburg archdukes, Charles and Ferdinand.

"You are a flower pestered by butterflies." Robert Dudley smiled as they walked in the cold gardens of Whitehall Palace, two of Elizabeth's new guards following them at a discreet distance.

"Indeed, I must be, for I do nothing to attract."

"Nothing?" he asked her, one dark eyebrow raised.

She paused to peep up at him from under the brim of her hat. "I invite no attention," she claimed.

"Not the way that you walk?"

"For sure, I go from one place to another."

"The way you dance?"

"In the Italian manner, as most ladies do."

"Oh, Elizabeth!"

"You may not call me Elizabeth."

"Well, you may not lie to me."

"What rule is this?"

"One for your benefit. Now, to return to the subject. You attract suitors in the way that you speak."

"I am bound to be polite to visiting diplomats."

"You are more than polite, you are . . ."

"What?" she asked with a giggle of laughter in her voice.

"Promising."

"Ah, I promise nothing!" she said at once. "I never promise."

"Exactly," he said. "That is the very snare of you. You sound promising, but you promise nothing."

She laughed aloud in her happiness. "It's true," she confessed. "But to be honest, sweet Robin, I have to play this game, it is not just my own pleasure."

"You would never marry a Frenchman for the safety of England?"

"I would never turn one down," she said. "Any suitor of mine is an ally for England. It is more like playing chess than a courtship."

"And does no man make your heart beat a little faster?" he asked, in a sudden swoop to intimacy.

Elizabeth looked up at him, her gaze straight, her expression devoid of coquetry, absolutely honest. "Not a one," she said simply.

For a moment he was utterly taken aback.

She crowed with laughter. "Got you!" She pointed at him. "You vain dog! And you thought you had caught me!"

He caught the hand and carried it to his mouth. "I think I will never catch you," he said. "But I should be a happy man to spend my life in trying."

She tried to laugh, but at his drawing closer, the laugh was caught in her throat. "Ah, Robert . . ."

"Elizabeth?"

She would have pulled her hand away, but he held it close.

"I will have to marry a prince," she said unsteadily. "It is a game to see where the dice best falls, but I know that I cannot rule alone and I must have a son to come after me."

"You have to marry a man who can serve your interests, and serve the interests of the country," he said steadily. "And you would be wise to choose a man that you would like to bed."

She gave a little gasp of shock. "You're very free, Sir Robert."

His confidence was quite unshaken, he still held her hand in his warm grip. "I am very sure," he said softly. "You are a young woman as well as a queen. You have a heart as well as a crown. And you should choose a man for your desires as well as for your country. You're not a woman for a cold bed, Elizabeth. You're not a woman that can marry for policy alone. You want a man you can love and trust. I know this. I know you."

Spring 1559

The lent lilies were out in Cambridgeshire in a sprawl of cream and gold in the fields by the river, and the blackbirds were singing in the hedges. Amy Dudley went out riding with Mrs. Woods every morning and proved to be a charming house guest, admiring their fields of sheep and knowledgeable about the hay crop which was starting to green up through the dry blandness of the winter grass.

"You must long for an estate of your own," Mrs. Woods remarked as they rode through a spinney of young oaks.

"I hope that we will buy one," Amy said happily. "Flitcham Hall, near my old home. My stepmother writes to me that squire Symes is ready to sell and I have always liked it. My father said he would give his fortune for it. He hoped to buy it a few years ago for Robert and me but then . . ." She broke off. "Anyway, I hope that we can have it now. It has three good stands of woodland, and two fresh rivers. It has some good wet meadows where the rivers join, and on the higher land the earth can support a good crop, mostly barley. The higher fields are for sheep of course, and I know the flock, I have ridden there since childhood. My lord liked the look of the place and I think he would have bought it, but when our troubles came . . ." She broke off again. "Anyway," she said more happily, "I have asked Lizzie Oddingsell to write to tell him that it is for sale, and I am waiting for his reply."

"And have you not seen him since the queen inherited?" Mrs. Woods asked incredulously.

Amy laughed it off. "No! Is it not a scandal? I thought he would come home for Twelfth Night, indeed, he promised that he would; but since he is Master of Horse, he was in charge of all the festivities at court, and he had so much to do. The queen rides or hunts every day, you know. He has to manage her stables and all the entertainments of the court as well, masques and balls and parties and everything."

"Don't you want to join him?"

"Oh, no," Amy said decidedly. "I went to London with him when his father was alive and the whole family was at court and it was dreadful!"

Mrs. Woods laughed at her. "Why, what was so terrible about it?"

"Most of the day there is nothing to do but to stand about and talk of nothing," Amy said frankly. "For men of course there is the business of the Privy Council and parliament to discuss, and endless seeking of pensions and places and favors. But for women there is only service in the queen's rooms and nothing more, really. Very few ladies take an interest in the business of the realm, and no man would want my opinion anyway. I had to sit with my mother-in-law for days and days at a time, and she had no interest in anyone but the duke, her husband, and her sons. My husband's four brothers were all brilliant and very loyal to each other, and he has two sisters, Lady Catherine and Mary . . ."

"That is Lady Sidney now?"

"Yes, her. They all think that Sir Robert is a very god, and so no one would ever have been good enough for him. Least of all me. They all thought I was a fool and by the time I was allowed to leave, I absolutely agreed with them."

Mrs. Woods laughed with Amy. "What a nightmare! But you must have had opinions; you were in a family at the very heart of power."

Amy made a little face. "You learned very quickly in that family that if you had opinions that did not agree with the duke, then you had better not voice them," she said. "Although my husband rode out against her, I always knew that Queen Mary was the true queen, and I always knew that her faith would triumph. But it was better for me, and better for Robert, if I kept my thoughts and my faith to myself."

"But such a test of fortitude! Never to argue when they were so overbearing!"

Amy giggled. "I cannot begin to tell you," she said. "And the worst of it is that Sir Robert is not like that. When I first met him at my father's house he was such a boy, so sweet and loving. We were going to take a little manor house and keep sheep and he was going to breed horses. And here I am, still waiting for him to come home."

"I always longed to go to court," Mrs. Woods remarked into the wistful pause. "Mr. Woods took me once to see the old queen at her dinner and it was very grand."

"It takes forever," Amy said flatly. "And the food is always cold, and half the time it is so badly cooked that everyone goes back to their own rooms and has their own food cooked for them there, so they can have something good to eat. You aren't allowed to keep your own hunting dogs, and you cannot have more servants than the Lord Chamberlain allows, and you have to keep court hours . . . up late and to bed late till you are so tired you could die."

"But that life pleases Sir Robert?" Mrs. Woods observed acutely.

Amy nodded and turned her horse for home. "It does for now. He was born in the palaces with the royal family. He lived like a prince. But in his heart I know that he is still the young man that I fell in love with who wanted nothing more than some good pastureland to breed beautiful horses. I know I must be true to that—whatever it costs me."

"But what about you?" Mrs. Woods

asked gently, bringing her horse alongside the younger woman.

"I keep faith," Amy said staunchly. "I wait for him, and I trust that he will come home to me. I married him because I loved him just as he is. And he married me because he loved me, just as I am. And when the newness of this queen and the reign has worn off, when all the pensions and the places have been snapped up and the privileges all dispensed, then, when he has the time, he will come home to me, and there I will be, in our lovely house, with his beautiful foals at foot by the mares in the field, and everything just as it should be."

*   *   *

Elizabeth's flirtation by private letter with Philip of Spain went far enough to alarm William Cecil, went far enough to alarm Catherine Knollys. But Mary Sidney, in low-voiced consultation with her beloved brother Robert Dudley, was reassuring.

"I am certain she is only securing him as an ally," she said quietly. "And amusing herself, of course. She has to have constant admiration."

He nodded. They were riding together, ambling home from hunting on a long rein, both horses sweaty and blowing. Ahead, the queen was riding with Catherine Knollys on one side and a new, sweet-faced young man on the other. Robert Dudley had taken a good look at him and was not concerned. Elizabeth would never fall for a pretty face; she needed a man who would make her catch her breath.

"As an ally against France?" he suggested.

"It's the pattern," she said. "Philip stood with us against France when they took Calais; we stood with him when they threatened the Netherlands."

"Does she want him to stand her friend so that she can go against the Scottish regent?" he asked. "Does she like Cecil's plan to support the Scottish Protestants? Does she say anything when she is quiet and alone with you women? Is she planning for war, as Cecil says she must?"

Mary shook her head. "She is like a horse with flies. She cannot be at peace. Sometimes she seems to think that she should help them, she shares their faith, and of course the French are the greatest threat to our peace. But other times she is too afraid to make the first move against an anointed monarch. She worries what enemies she might unleash here. And she is in living terror of someone coming against her secretly, with a knife. She dare not do anything to increase the number of her enemies."

He frowned. "Cecil is very sure that France is our greatest danger and that we must fight them now, while the Scots themselves are turning against their masters. This is our moment while they are calling on us for help."

"Cecil would have her marry Arran," Mary guessed. "Not Philip. Cecil hates the Spanish and Popery more than anyone, though he always speaks so calmly and so measured."

"Have you ever seen Arran?"

"No, but Catherine Knollys speaks very highly of him. She says he is handsome and clever, and of course his claim to the throne of Scotland is second only to Mary, Queen of Scots. If the queen marries him and he defeats the regent and takes the throne, then their son would unite the kingdoms."

She saw Dudley's face darken. "He is our greatest danger," he said, and she knew he was not speaking of the danger to England but the danger to themselves.

"She likes you better than any other man at court," she said, smiling. "She is always saying how skilled you are and how handsome. She is always remarking on it, and even the youngest maids-in-waiting know that if they want to please her they only have to say how well you ride, or how well the horses are managed, or what wonderful taste you have in clothes. Laetitia Knollys is positively unmaidenly in the way she talks about you, and the queen laughs."

She had thought he would laugh, but his face was still sullen. "What good is that to me, since I have a wife?" he asked. "And besides, Elizabeth would not marry to disoblige the throne."

He shocked her into complete silence.

"What?" she asked.

He met her astounded gaze frankly. "Elizabeth would not marry against policy, whatever her desires," he said flatly. "And I am not free."

"But of course not!" she stumbled. "Robert, brother, I knew you were her favorite—all the world can see that! We all tease the queen that she has eyes only for you. Half the men at court hate you for it.

But I never dreamed that you thought of anything more."

He shrugged. "Of course I think of it," he said simply. "But I cannot imagine how it might come to me. I am a married man and my wife is not strong; but she is not likely to die within the next twenty years, and I would not wish it on her. Elizabeth is a Tudor through and through. She will want to marry both for power and for desire, just as her sister did, just as her father always did. Arran would be a brilliant match for her; he could unite the Scots against the French and defeat them in Scotland, then he could marry her and make England and Scotland into one unbeatable kingdom. Then he would dismiss me."

Mary Sidney shot an anxious sideways glance at her brother. "But if it is best for England?" she suggested shyly. "Then we should side with Arran? Even if it might be against our own personal desires? If it is best for England?"

"There is no England," he said brutally. "Not as you mean. There is no entity that knows itself as England. There is just a neighborhood of great families: us, the Howards, the Parrs, the Cecils, up-and-coming, the Percys, the Nevilles, the Seymours, and the greatest bandit-tribe of them all: the Tudors. What is good for England is good for the greatest family of them all, and the greatest family of them all is the one that manages its own business the best. That is what our father knew; that is the plan he had for us. Now, the greatest family in the land is the Tudors, not so long ago it was us. It will be us again. You watch for the good of our family as I do, sister, and England will benefit."

"But however you plan for our family, you cannot hope to marry the queen," she said, her voice very low. "You know you cannot. There is Amy . . . and the queen herself would not."

"There is no point in being the favorite unless you raise yourself to the first man in the land," Robert said. "Whatever title you take."

*   *   *

Just as suddenly as she had arrived at the Woods' house, in mid-March Amy told them that she must leave them.

"I am so sorry you are going," Mrs. Woods said warmly. "I had hoped you would be here in time to see the May in."

Amy was distracted by happiness. "I will come another year, if I can," she said rapidly. "But Sir Robert has just sent for me to go to meet him at Camberwell. My mother's cousins the Scotts have a house there. And of course, I have to go at once."

Mrs. Woods gasped. "To Camberwell? Does he mean you to go to the City? Will he take you to court? Shall you see the queen?"

"I don't know," Amy said, laughing with pleasure. "I think he may want to buy a London house for us, so that he can entertain his friends. His family had Syon House before; perhaps she will give him that again."

Mrs. Woods put her hands to her cheeks. "That enormous palace! Amy! How grand he is becoming. How grand you will be. You must not forget us. Write and tell me all about it when you go to court."

"I will! I will write and tell you all. Everything! What the queen is wearing, and who is with her, and everything."

"Perhaps she will take you as one of her ladies-in-waiting," Mrs. Woods said, visions of Amy's importance unfolding before her. "His sister is at court in her service, is she not?"

At once Amy shook her head. "Oh no! I couldn't do it. He would not ask it of me. He knows I cannot bear court life. But if we had Flitcham Hall for all the summer, I could live with him in London in the winter."

"I should think you could!" Mrs. Woods giggled. "But what about your gowns? Do you have everything you need? Can I lend you anything? I know I'm probably terribly out of fashion . . ."

"I shall order everything new in London," Amy declared with quiet joy. "My lord always liked me to spend a small fortune on clothes, when he was at the height of his glory. And if I see some stuff that would make you a riding cloak like mine, I shall be sure to send it to you."

"Oh, please do," Mrs. Woods said, visions of her friendship with Amy introducing her to the glamorous circle of court. "And I shall send you the strawberries, as soon as they come out. I promise."

Mrs. Oddingsell put her head around the door; already she was wearing her traveling cloak with her hood up against the cold morning air. "My lady?" she asked. "The horses are waiting."

Mrs. Woods gave a little cry. "Such a hurry!"

But Amy was halfway out of the door. "I cannot delay; my lord wants me. If I have forgotten anything I will send a man back to fetch it."

Mrs. Woods saw her out to the waiting horses. "And do come again," she said. "Perhaps I may call on you in London. Perhaps I shall call on you in your new London house."

The waiting groom lifted Amy into the saddle and she gathered up the reins. She beamed down at Mrs. Woods. "Thank you," she said. "I have had such a merry visit. And when my lord and I are settled in our new house you shall come and stay with me."

*   *   *

Cecil wrote Elizabeth one of his memoranda, in his own hand, for her eyes only.

Whitehall Palace
The twenty-fourth day of March.

Reference your constant correspondence with Philip of Spain.

1. Philip of Spain is a committed Catholic and will expect his wife to follow his religious practice. If he tells you any different he is lying.

2. He may protect us from France in this present peril with Scotland, but he will also lead us into war with France on his terms and for his cause. I remind you that they would not have attacked Calais but for him. And he will not help us win it back.

3. If you were to marry him we would lose the support of the Protestant English who hate him.

4. And not gain the support of the Catholic English who hate him too.

5. He cannot marry you since he was married to your half-sister, unless he has Papal dispensation.

If you acknowledge the power of Pope to rule then you have to accept his ruling that your father and Katherine of Aragon were truly married, in which case your own mother was no more than the king's mistress and you would be regarded as a bastard.

And so, not the rightful heir to the throne.

> *So why would he then marry you?*
> 6. *Any child born to King Philip of Spain would be brought up as a Catholic.*
> 7. *This would be your child. You would have put a Catholic prince on the throne of England.*
> 8. *Clearly you will not marry him, so at some point you will have to jilt King Philip.*
> 9. *If you leave it too long you will make the most powerful man in Europe look a great fool.*
> 10. *That would not be a wise move.*

"I am so sorry," Elizabeth said sweetly to Count Feria, the Spanish ambassador. "But it is impossible. I admire your master more than I can say."

Count Feria, after months of uneasy marriage negotiations with a woman he had always disliked and mistrusted, bowed low, and hoped to keep the conversation within the bounds of reason and in diplomatically acceptable language.

"As he admires you, Your Grace," he said. "He will be saddened by your decision, but he will always be your friend, and a friend to your country."

"I am a heretic, you see," Elizabeth said hastily. "I absolutely deny the authority of the Pope. Everybody knows that I do. The king cannot possibly marry me. I would embarrass him."

"He will be your brother, then," the count said. "Your loving brother, as he always has been."

"It would have been quite, quite impossible," Elizabeth repeated, even more earnestly than before. "Please convey to him my sorrow and my regret."

The count, bowing low, was getting himself out of the presence chamber as speedily as he could, before this volatile young queen embarrassed them both. Already he could see tears gathering in her eyes, and her mouth was trembling.

"I will write to him at once," he said soothingly. "He will understand. He will understand completely."

"I am so sorry!" Elizabeth cried as the ambassador backed away swiftly the double doors. "Pray tell him that I am so filled with regret!"

He raised his head from his bow. "Your

Grace, think no more of it," he said. "There was no offense given and no offense taken. It is a matter of regret for both parties, that is all. You remain the warmest friend and ally that Spain could desire."

"Allies always?" Elizabeth begged, her handkerchief to her eyes. "Can you promise me that, from your master? That we will be allies always?"

"Always," he said breathlessly.

"And if I need his help I can count on him?" She was near to breaking down, as at last the doors opened behind him. "Whatever happens in the future?"

"Always. I guarantee it for my master." He bowed his way through to the safety of the gallery outside.

As the doors closed on his hasty retreat, Elizabeth dropped the handkerchief and gave Cecil a triumphant wink.

*   *   *

Elizabeth's Privy Council was meeting in her presence chamber. The queen, who should have been sitting in state at the head of the table, was pacing between the windows like an imprisoned lioness. Cecil looked up from his neat pages of memoranda and hoped that it was not going to be an impossibly difficult meeting.

"The treaty of Cateau-Cambrésis puts us in a far stronger position than ever before," he began. "It ensures peace between Spain, France, and ourselves. We can count ourselves as safe from invasion for the time being."

There was a chorus of self-satisfied assent. The treaty which guaranteed peace between the three great countries had been a long time in negotiation but was a first triumph for Cecil's diplomacy. At last England could be sure of peace.

Cecil glanced nervously at his mistress, who was always irritable with the smug male style of the Privy Council. "This is almost entirely thanks to Her Grace's skill with the Spanish," he said quickly.

Elizabeth paused in her tracks to listen.

"She has kept them as our friends and allies for long enough to frighten France into agreement, and when she released Philip of Spain from his promises to her, she did it with such skill that Spain stays our friend."

Elizabeth, soothed by flattery, came to the head of the table and perched on the arm of her great wooden chair, head and shoulders above the rest of them. "That's true. You may go on."

"The treaty, and the security it brings us, gives us the safety to make the reforms that we need," he went on. "We can leave the question of Scotland for the moment, since the treaty assures us that the French will not invade. And so we are free to turn to the urgent business of the country."

Elizabeth nodded, waiting.

"The first should be to make Her Grace supreme governor of the church. As soon as we have got that passed, we will adjourn parliament."

Elizabeth sprang up and stalked to the window once more. "Is this our first business indeed?" she demanded.

"Good idea," said Norfolk, ignoring his niece, the queen. "Send them back to their fields before they start getting ideas in their thick heads. And get the church bolted down."

"All our troubles over," said one idiot.

It was the spark to the tinder of Elizabeth's temper. "Over?" she spat, erupting from the window like an enraged kitten. "Over? With Calais still in French hands and small chance of buying it back? With Mary still quartering English arms on her shield? How are our troubles over? Am I Queen of France or am I not?"

There was a stunned silence.

"You are," said Cecil quietly, when no one else dared to speak. In theory she was. The English monarchs had always called themselves King of France even when the English holdings in France had shrunk to the pale of Calais. Now it seemed that Elizabeth would continue the tradition even though Calais was gone.

"Then where are my French forts, and my French territories? I will tell you. In the hands of an illegal force. Where are my guns and my walls and my fortifications? I will tell you. Pulled down or turned on England. And when my ambassador goes to dine at the French court, what does he see on the plates of the French princess?"

They were all looking down at the table, willing the storm to pass them by.

"My coat of arms!" Elizabeth shouted. "On French plate. Has that been resolved in this treaty which you are all so thrilled with? No! Has anyone even addressed it? No! And you think that the most important business of the kingdom is the leadership of the church. Not so! My lords! Not so! The most important business is to get me back my Calais, and get that woman to stop using my coat of arms on her damned plates!"

"It will be resolved," Cecil said soothingly. He glanced around the table. They were all thinking as one man: that these council meetings would be so much easier if only she would marry a reasonable man and let him do the business of kingship.

To his horror, he saw that her dark eyes were filling with tears. "And Philip of Spain." Her voice was husky. "Now, I hear that he is to marry."

Cecil looked at her aghast. The last thing he had imagined was that she had actually felt anything for the man she had tormented during his wife's lifetime and then had strung along for months after.

"A marriage to seal the treaty," he said hesitantly. "I don't believe there is any courtship, any preference. There is no attraction, no rival attraction involved. He does not prefer her to . . . to . . ."

"You urged me to marry him," she said, her voice throbbing with emotion, looking along the bowed heads of her Privy Council. "Still you continually persuade me to one man or another, and see? The man of your choice, *your* preferred suitor, has no fidelity. He swore that he loved me; but see? He will marry another. You would have had me marry a faithless flirt."

"None could suit her better," Norfolk said, so low that nobody could hear but his neighbor, who snorted with suppressed laughter.

It was pointless even to attempt reason with her, Cecil knew. "Yes," he said simply. "We were most mistaken in his nature. Thank God that Your Grace is so young and so very beautiful that there will always be suitors for your hand. It is for you to choose, Your Grace. There will always be men who long to marry you. All we can do is advise your own wise preference."

A sigh like a passing breeze passed through the beleagured council. Once again, Cecil had hit exactly the right note. Sir Francis Knollys rose to his feet and guided his cousin to her chair at the head of the table. "Now," he said. "Although they are less important indeed, we *do* have to talk about the bishops, Your Grace. We cannot go on like this. We have to make a settlement with the church."

*

Amy's cousin and her husband, a prosperous merchant with an interest in the Antwerp trade, greeted her on the doorstep on their large square-built house in Camberwell.

"Amy! You'll never guess! We heard from Sir Robert this very morning!" Frances Scott said breathlessly. "He is coming to dine this very day, and staying at least one night!"

Amy flushed scarlet. "He is?" She turned to her maid. "Mrs. Pirto, unpack my best gown, and you'll need to press my ruff." She turned back to her cousin. "Is your hairdresser coming?"

"I told him to come an hour early for you!" her cousin laughed. "I knew you would want to look your best. I have had my cook at work ever since I heard the news. And they are making his favorite: marchpane."

Amy laughed aloud, catching her cousin's excitement.

"He has become a great man again," Ralph Scott said, coming forward to kiss his cousin-in-law. "We hear nothing but good reports of him. The queen honors him and seeks his company daily."

Amy nodded and slid from his embrace to

the open front door. "Am I to have my usual room?" she asked impatiently. "And can you ask them to hurry to bring my chest with my gowns up?"

*   *   *

But after all the rush of preparations, the pressing of the gowns, the sending the maid out in a panic to buy new stockings, Sir Robert sent his apologies and said that he would be delayed. Amy had to wait for two hours, sitting by the window in the Scotts' elegant modern parlor, watching the road for her husband's entourage.

It was nearly five in the afternoon when they came trotting down Camberwell High Street, six men abreast mounted on the most superb matched bay horses, wearing the Dudley livery, scattering chickens and pedestrians and shouting children ahead of them. In the middle of them rode Robert Dudley, one hand on the reins, one hand on his hip, his gaze abstracted, his smile charming: his normal response to public cheers.

They pulled up before the handsome new house and Dudley's groom came running to hold the horse while Dudley leapt lightly down.

Amy, in the bay window, had been on her feet at the first sound of the rattle of hoofs on cobblestones. Her cousin, running in to warn her that Sir Robert was at the door, found her, quite entranced, watching him through the window. Frances Scott dropped back, saying nothing, and stood in the hall beside her husband as their two best menservants flung open the door and Sir Robert strode in.

"Cousin Scott," he said pleasantly, gripping the man's hand. Ralph Scott blushed slightly with pleasure at the recognition.

"And my cousin Frances," Sir Robert said, recovering her name from his memory just in time to kiss her on both cheeks and see her color rise under his touch, which was always the case with women, and then her eyes darkened with desire, which was also a frequent occurrence.

"My dearest cousin Frances," Dudley said more warmly, watching her more closely.

"Oh, Sir Robert," she breathed and rested her hand on his arm.

Oho, thought Robert. *A plum ripe and ready for the picking, but hardly worth the uproar when we were discovered, which we undoubtedly would be.*

The door behind her opened, and Amy stood, framed in the doorway. "My lord," she said quietly. "I am so glad to see you."

Gently, Dudley released Frances Scott and stepped to his wife. He took her hand in his and bent his dark head to kiss her fingers, and then he drew her closer to him and kissed her cheek, first one and then the other, and then her warm ready lips.

At the sight of him, at his touch, at the scent of him, Amy felt herself melt with desire. "My lord," she whispered. "My lord, it has been so long. I have waited to see you for so long."

"I'm here now," he said, as quick as any man to deflect reproach. He slid his arm around her waist and turned back to their host. "But I am damnably late, cousins, I hope you will forgive me. I was playing bowls with the queen and I could not get away until Her Grace had won. I had to feint and cheat and dissemble until you would have thought I was half blind and half-witted in order to lose to her."

The nonchalance of this was almost too much for Frances Scott but Ralph rose to the occasion. "Of course, of course, the ladies must have their entertainments," he said. "But did you bring an appetite?"

"I am as hungry as a hunter," Dudley assured him.

"Then come to dinner!" Ralph said and gestured that Sir Robert should walk with him, down the hall to the dining room at the rear of the house.

"What a pretty place you have here," Sir Robert said.

"Very small compared with a country house, of course," Frances said, deferentially following them with Amy.

"But new-built," Dudley remarked with pleasure.

"I planned much of it myself," Ralph said smugly. "I knew I had to build a new house for us and I thought—why try to make a great palace on the river and employ an army to keep it warm and clean? Then you have to build a great hall to feed them all, then you have to house them and keep them. So I thought, why not a snugger, tighter house which can be more easily run and still have room for a dozen friends for dinner?"

"Oh, I agree with you," Dudley replied insincerely. "What reasonable man would want more?"

Mr. Scott threw open the double door to the dining hall which, though tiny by the standards of Whitehall or Westminster, could still seat a dozen guests and their followers, and led the way, through the other diners, half a dozen dependents and a dozen upper servants, to the top table. Amy and Frances followed. Mrs. Oddingsell and Frances's companion came in as well and the Scotts' oldest children, a girl and a boy of ten and eleven, very stiffly dressed in adult clothes, eyes down, awed into complete silence by the grandeur of the occasion. Dudley greeted them all with pleasure, and sat down at his host's right hand, with Amy on his other side. Concealed by the table and the great sweep of the banqueting cloth, Amy moved her stool so that she could be close to him. He felt her little slipper press against his riding boot and he leaned toward her so that she could feel the warmth and strength of his shoulder.

Only he heard her little sigh of desire and felt her shiver, and he reached down his hand and touched her waiting fingers.

"My sweetheart," he said.

*

Dudley and Amy could not be alone to-gether until bedtime, but when the house was quiet they sat either side of their bed-room fire and Robert heated two mugs of ale.

"I have some news," he said quietly. "Something I need to tell you. You should hear it first from me, and not from some cor-ner gossip."

"What is it?" Amy asked, looking up and smiling at him. "Good news?"

He thought for a moment what a young smile hers still was: the smile of a girl whose hopes are always ready to rise, the open gaze of a girl who has reason to think that the world is filled with promise for her.

"Yes, it is good news." He thought it would be a hard-hearted man who could bear to tell this childish woman that any-thing had gone wrong, especially when he had already brought her so much grief.

She clapped her hands together. "You have bought Flitcham Hall! I didn't dare hope you would! I knew it! I absolutely knew it!"

He was thrown from his course. "Flitcham? No. I sent Bowes to look at it and to tell the owner that we were not interested."

"Not interested? But I told Lady Robsart to tell the owner that we would take it."

"It's impossible, Amy. I thought I told you before I left Chichester, when you first mentioned it?"

"No, never. I thought you liked it? You always said you liked it. You said to Father . . ."

"No. Anyway, it's not about Flitcham. I want to tell you . . ."

"But what did Mr. Bowes tell Mr. Symes? I had promised him we would almost certainly take it."

He realized that he had to answer her before she could listen to him. "Bowes told Mr. Symes that we did not want Flitcham after all. He was not upset, he understood."

"But *I* don't understand!" she said plaintively. "I don't understand. I thought you wanted to make Flitcham our home. I thought you loved it like I do. And it is so near to Syderstone, and to all my family, and Father always liked it . . ."

"No." He took her hands in his and saw her wounded indignation dissolve at once under his touch. He caressed the palms of her hands with his gentle fingertips. "Now, Amy, you must see, Flitcham Hall is not close enough to London. I would never see you if you buried yourself in Norfolk. And we could never be able to make it a big enough place for the visitors we will have."

"I don't want to be near London," she insisted stubbornly. "Father always said that nothing came from London but trouble . . ."

"Your father loved Norfolk, and he was a great man in his own country," Robert said, controlling his own irritation with an effort. "But we are not your father. I am not your father, Amy, my love. Norfolk is too small for me. I do not love it as your father did. I want you to find us a bigger house, somewhere more central, near Oxford. Yes? There is more to England than Norfolk you know, my dearest."

He saw she was soothed by the endearments, and in her quietness he could broach the rest that he had to tell her. "But this is not what I wanted to tell you. I am to be honored by the queen."

"An honor? Oh! She will give you a seat on the Privy Council?"

"Well, there are other honors," he said,

concealing his frustration that he still had no political power.

"She would never make you an earl!" she exclaimed.

"No, not that!" he corrected. "That would be ridiculous."

"I don't see why," she said at once. "I don't see why being an earl would be ridiculous. Everyone says that you are her favorite."

He checked, wondering exactly what scandal might have come to her ears. "I'm not her favorite," he said. "Her favorite is Sir William Cecil for counsel and Catherine Knollys for company. I assure you, my sister and I are only two of very many among her court."

"But she made you Master of her Horse," Amy objected reasonably. "You cannot expect me to believe that she does not like you above all others. You always said that she liked you when you were children together."

"She likes her horses to be well managed," he said hastily. "And of course she likes me, we are old friends, but that's not what I meant . . . I . . . ."

"She must like you a great deal," she pursued. "Everyone says that she goes out with you every day." She took care not to let a jealous note into her voice. "Someone even told me that she neglects her royal business for riding."

"I take her riding, yes . . . but it is my work, not my preference. There is nothing between us, no especial warmth."

"I should hope not," she said sharply. "She had better remember that you are a married man. Not that such a fact has restrained her in the past. Everyone says that she . . ."

"Oh, for saints' sake, stop!"

She gave a little gasp. "You may not like it, Robert, but it is no more than everyone says about her."

He took a breath. "I beg your pardon, I did not mean to raise my voice."

"It is not very pleasant for me, knowing that you are her favorite and that she has no good reputation for being chaste." Amy finished her complaint in a breathless rush. "It is not very pleasant for me, knowing that your names are linked."

He had to take a long deep breath. "Amy, this is ridiculous. I have told you I am not a particular favorite. I ride with her because I am her Master of Horse. I am a favored man at court because of my abilities, thank God for them, and because of my family. We should both be glad that she favors me as she should. As to her reputation, I am surprised you would lower yourself to gossip, Amy. I am indeed. She is your anointed queen. It is not for you to pass comment."

She bit her lip. "Everyone knows what she's like," she said stubbornly. "And it is not very nice for me when your name is linked with hers."

"I do not wish my wife to gossip," he said flatly.

"I only repeated what everyone—"

"Everyone is wrong," he said. "It is almost certain that she will marry the Earl of Arran and secure his claim to the Scottish throne. I tell you this in the deepest secrecy, Amy. So that you know that there is nothing between her and me."

"Do you swear?"

Robert sighed as if he were weary, to make his lie more persuasive. "Of course, I swear there is nothing."

"I trust you," she said. "Of course I do. But I cannot trust her. Everyone knows that she—"

"Amy!" He raised his voice even louder, and she fell silent at last. Her sliding glance at the door told him that she was afraid her cousin would have heard his angry tone.

"Oh, for God's sake. It doesn't matter if anyone heard."

"What will people think . . ."

"It doesn't matter what they think," he said with the simple arrogance of a Dudley.

"It does."

"Not to me," he said grandly.

"To me, it does."

He bit his lip on his argument. "Well, it should not," he said, trying to keep his temper with her. "You are Lady Dudley, and the opinion of some London merchant and his wife should be nothing to you."

"My own mother's cousin . . ." He could just hear a few words of her whispered defiance. "Our hosts. And always very civil to you."

"Amy . . . please," he said.

"I have to live with them, after all," she said with a childish stubbornness. "It's not as if you will be here next week . . ."

He rose to his feet and saw her flinch.

"Wife, I am sorry," he said. "I have gone all wrong about this."

At the first hint of retraction she was quick to meet him. Her head came up, a little smile on her face. "Oh, are you unwell?"

"No! I . . ."

"Are you overtired?"

"No!"

"Shall I get you a hot possett?" Already she was on her feet and wanting to serve him. He caught her hand and had to make himself hold her gently, and not shake her in his anger.

"Amy, please be still and let me talk to you. I have been trying to tell you one small thing since we came up, and you don't let me speak."

"How ever could I stop you?"

He answered her with silence, until obediently, she sank to her stool and waited.

"The queen is to honor me by awarding me the Order of the Garter. I am to have it with three other noblemen and there is to be a great celebration. I am honored indeed."

She would have interrupted with congratulations but he pressed on to the more difficult topic. "And she is to give me land, and a house."

"A house?"

"The Dairy House at Kew," he said.

"A London house for us?" she asked.

He could imagine Elizabeth's response if he tried to install a wife in the pretty little bachelor's nest in the garden of the royal palace.

"No, no. It's just a little place for me. But my idea was that you could stay with the Hydes and find a house for us? A house that we could make our own? A bigger house than Flitcham Hall, a grander place altogether? Somewhere near them in Oxfordshire."

"Yes, but who will run your house at Kew?"

He dismissed it. "It is little more than a few rooms. Bowes will find me servants; it is nothing."

"Why does she not want you to live at the palace anymore?"

"It's just a gift," he said. "I may not even use it."

"So why give it to you?"

Robert tried to laugh it off. "It's just a sign of her favor," he said. "And my rooms in the palace are not of the best." Already, he knew, the gossips were speculating that the queen had given him a place where the two of them could go to be alone together, hidden from the eyes of the court. He had to ensure that Amy would dismiss such rumors if they ever came to her ears. "In truth, I think Cecil wanted it, and she is teasing him by giving it to me."

She looked disapproving. "And would Cecil have lived there with his wife?"

He was pleased to be on safe ground. "Cecil has not seen his wife since the queen's accession," he said. "She is overseeing the building of his new house, Burghley. He is in the same strait as I. He wants to get home but he is kept too busy. And I want you to be like his wife; I want you to build a house for us, that I can come to in summer. Will you do it for me? Will you find us a really lovely house or site, and make a home for us, a proper home at last?"

Her face lightened as he knew it would. "Oh, I would love to," she said. "And we would live there and be together all the time?"

Gently he took both her hands. "I would have to be at court for much of the time," he said. "As you know. But I would come home to you, as often as I could, and you would like to have a proper home of your own, wouldn't you?"

"You would come home to me often?" she stipulated.

"My work is at court," he pointed out. "But I never forget that I am married and that you are my wife. Of course I will come home to you."

"Then yes," Amy said. "Oh, my lord. I would like it so much."

He drew her toward him and felt her warmth through the thin linen gown.

"But you will take care, won't you?"

"Take care?" He was cautious. "Of what?"

"Of her trying . . ." She chose her words carefully so as not to irritate him. "Of her trying to draw you in."

"She is the queen," Robert said gently. "It flatters her vanity to be surrounded by men. I am a courtier; it is my work to be drawn in by her. It means nothing."

"But if she favors you so much, you will make enemies."

"What d'you mean?"

"I just know that anyone who is favored by the king or the queen makes enemies. I just want you to take care."

He nodded, relieved that she had nothing more to go on. "You're right, I have my enemies, but I know who they are and what they threaten. They envy me but they are powerless against me while I have her favor. But you are right to warn me, wife. And I thank you for your wise counsel."

*   *   *

That night Robert Dudley and his wife slept in the same bed in some accord. He bedded her as gently and as warmly as he could, and Amy, desperate for his touch, accepted the false coin of his kindness as love. She had waited so long for his kiss, for the gentle press of his body against hers, that she whimpered and cried with joy within the first few minutes, and he, falling easily into the well-known rhythm of their lovemaking, with her familiar body surprising him with pleasure, found her easy to please and was glad of that, if for nothing more. He was used to whores, and the ladies of the court, and it was a rare pleasure for him to bed a woman whom he cared for; it was strange for him to hold back out of consideration. As he felt the sweet rush of Amy's response, his mind wandered to what it would be like to have Elizabeth cling to him, as Amy was clinging now—and the fantasy was so powerful that his lust came like a storm and left him gasping with the thought of a white throat flung back, dark eyelashes fluttering with lust, and a mass of tumbled bronze hair.

Amy fell asleep at once, her head resting on his shoulder, and he leaned up on his elbow to look at her face in the moonlight which came, all pale and watery, through the glass of the leaded window pane. It gave her skin an odd, greenish pallor, like that of a drowned woman, and her hair spread out on the pillow was like that of a woman rocking on the deep water of a river and sinking down.

He looked at her with irritated compassion: this wife, whose happiness was so solely dependent upon him, whose desire revolved around him, who was lost without him and infuriating with him, the wife who could never now satisfy him. He knew too that, although she would deny it to her very death, in truth, he could never make her truly happy. They were two such different people, with such different lives, he could not see how they could ever now be joined as one.

He sighed and leaned back, his dark head resting on the crook of his arm. He thought of his father's warning against marrying a pretty face for love, and his mother saying sourly to him that little Amy Robsart was as much use to an ambitious man as a primrose in his buttonhole. He had wanted then to show his parents that he was not a son like Guilford, who would marry a girl who hated him, at his father's command. He had wanted to choose his own wife, and Amy had been so young and so sweet and so willing to agree to anything he proposed. He had thought then that she could learn to be a courtier's wife, he had thought she could be an ally to him, a source of power and information—as his mother was to his father. He had thought that she could be a loyal and effective partner in the rise of his family to greatness. He did not realize that she would always be the contented daughter of Sir John Robsart, a big man in a small country, rather than an ambitious wife to Robert Dudley, a man who was finding greatness so unreliable, and so hard to win.

*   *   *

Robert woke early and felt the old familiar rush of irritation that the woman beside him in bed was Amy, and not some London whore whom he could dismiss before she had the temerity to speak. Instead, his wife stirred as he stirred, as if even in sleep every sense had been on the watch for him. She opened her eyes almost as soon as he did, and as soon as she saw him she smiled that familiar, vacuous smile, and said, as she always said, "Good morning, my lord. God be with you. Are you well?"

He hated too that when he replied brusquely, a shadow passed across her face as if he had slapped her in her very first moments of waking, which forced him to smile in his turn and ask her if she had slept well, with extra concern in his voice in an attempt to make amends.

The repetitive dullness of it made him grit his teeth and spring out of bed as if he were urgently needed elsewhere, though in fact, he had told everyone at court that he would spend some days with his wife in Camberwell. The predictable interplay of his irritation and her hurt was unbearable.

"Oh, are you getting up?" she asked, as if she could not see him swing his cloak around his naked shoulders.

"Yes," he said shortly. "I have remembered something I should have done at court; I shall have to go back early."

"Early?" She could not keep the disappointment from her voice.

"Yes, early," he said abruptly, and went quickly from the room.

He had hoped to break his fast alone and be on his horse and away before the household was stirring, but Amy flung herself from their bed and wakened everyone. Mr. and Mrs. Scott came tumbling down the stairs, Mrs. Scott pinning her hair as she trotted in her husband's wake, Mrs. Oddingsell behind them; he could hear the heels of Amy's expensive shoes rattling along the wooden floorboards as she hurried down too. He forced a smile on his face and prepared himself to repeat his lies of urgent business overlooked.

A more sophisticated family would have guessed at once the simple truth: their noble guest could not endure another minute. But for the Scotts, and for their cousin Amy, it was a surprise and a disappointment, and Amy in particular was worried that he was overburdened by the business at court.

"Can they not get someone else to do it for you?" she asked, hovering over him with maternal concern and watching him drink ale and eat bread.

"No," he said, his mouth full.

"They ask you to do so much," she said proudly. She glanced at Mrs. Scott, at Mrs. Oddingsell. "Can they not manage without you? They should not put so much on your shoulders."

"I am Master of Horse," he said. "It is my duty to do the task she has given me."

"Can't William Cecil do it for you?" Amy asked at random. "You could send him a note."

Dudley would have laughed if he had not been so irritated. "No," he said. "Cecil has his own work, and the last thing I want is him interfering in mine."

"Or your brother then? Surely you could trust him? And then you could stay here another night."

Dudley shook his head. "I am sorry to leave you all," he said, including the Scotts in the charm of his apology. "And if I could stay, I would do so. But I woke myself in the night with the sudden realization that there is to be a great outing on barges after the ceremony of the Order of the Garter and I have not ordered the barges. I have to get back to court and put it all in hand."

"Oh, if it is just ordering some boats you

can do it by letter," Amy reassured him. "And one of the pages can take it at once."

"No," he repeated. "I have to be there. The boats have to be checked and the rowers allotted. I have to prepare a water pageant and get a boat for the musicians; there's a lot to do. It's not just a matter of ordering the boats. I cannot think how I could have overlooked it."

"If I came too, I could help you, perhaps."

Robert rose from the table. He could not bear the wistfulness in her face. "How I wish you could!" he said warmly. "But I have another job for you, a far more important task. Don't you remember? And you have promised to undertake it for me, for us."

The smile came back to her face. "Oh, yes!"

"I want that done as soon as possible. I will leave you now, and you can tell our friends all about it."

He was out of the door before she could again ask him to stay. His men in the stable yard were saddling up, ready to leave. He ran an expert eye over them. Dudley was famous for having his escort as smart as outbound soldiers. He nodded and took the reins of his big hunter and led him round to the front of the house.

"I must thank you for your hospitality to me," he said to Mr. Scott. "I know that you require no thanks for my wife's stay; I know how dear she is to you."

"It is always a pleasure to have my cousin here," the man said smoothly. "And a great honor to see you. But I was hoping to have time for a little word."

"Oh?"

Mr. Scott drew Robert Dudley to one side. "I have some difficulty in reclaiming a debt from a merchant in Antwerp; I have his bond but I cannot make him honor it. I would rather not present it to the magistrates; there are some clauses in it which are rather complicated for their simple minds, and my debtor knows this, and is taking advantage of it and will not pay."

Robert decoded this at his usual speed as meaning that Mr. Scott had lent some money to an Antwerp merchant at an illegally high rate of interest and that now the man was reneging on the debt, secure in the knowledge that no reputable London merchant would want it known that he was lending money to the vulnerable at twenty-five percent.

"What's the total sum?" Robert asked cautiously.

"Nothing, to such a great man as you. A mere three hundred pounds. But a worry for me."

Robert nodded. "You can write to Sir Thomas Gresham at Antwerp, and say you are my wife's cousin and I am asking him to act in this matter," he said easily. "He will oblige me by looking into it for you, and then you can tell me what he concludes."

"I am most grateful, cousin," Mr. Scott said warmly.

"It is my pleasure to be of service to you." Robert bowed gracefully, and turned to kiss Mrs. Scott and then to Amy.

At the moment of his leaving her, she could not hide her distress. Her face drained of color and her fingers trembled in the confident clasp of his warm hands. She tried to smile but her eyes filled with tears.

He bent his head and kissed her on the lips, and felt the sad downward curve under his mouth. Last night, underneath him, she had been smiling as he kissed her, she had wrapped her arms and legs around him and whispered his name, and the taste of her had been very sweet.

"Be happy, Amy," he urged her, whispering quietly in her ear. "I hate it when you are sad."

"I see you so seldom," she breathed urgently. "Can't you stay? Oh, please stay, just till dinner time . . ."

"I have to go," he said, holding her close.

"You're hurrying away to see another woman?" she accused, suddenly filled with rage, her voice a hiss in his ear like a serpent.

He pulled away from her grasp. "Of course not. It is as I have told you. Be happy! Our family is on the rise. Be happy for me, please, send me away with your smile."

"As long as you swear to me on your mother's honor that there is no one else."

He grimaced at the exaggerated language. "Of course, I promise," he said simply. "Now you be happy for me."

Amy tried to smile, though her lips trembled. "I am happy," she lied at once. "I am happy for you in your success and I am so happy that we are to have a house at last."

Her voice dropped. "If you swear you have kept faith with me."

"Of course. Why else would I want you to make a home for us? And I will meet you at the Hydes' at Denchworth, within a fortnight or so. I will let you know by a note to Mrs. Oddingsell."

"Write to me," she urged him. "I like it when they bring your letters to me."

Robert gave her a little hug. "Very well then," he said, thinking it was like pacifying a child. "I will write to you and seal it, and it can come to you and you can break the seal yourself."

"Oh, I never break them. I lift them off the page and I keep them. I have a whole collection of them in my jewel-box drawer, from all the letters you have ever sent me."

He turned away from the thought of her treasuring something as trivial as his sealing wax, and ran down the steps and vaulted into the high saddle of his horse.

Robert swept his hat from his head. "I'll say farewell for now," he said pleasantly. "And look to our next meeting." He could not bear to meet her eyes. He glanced at Mrs. Oddingsell and saw that she was nearby, ready to support Amy once he had gone. There was no point in prolonging the farewell. He nodded to his company of horse and they fell in behind him, his standard-bearer ahead, and they trotted off, the noise of the horses very loud as the street narrowed toward the end of the road.

Amy watched them go until they turned the corner and were out of sight. Still she waited on the steps until she could no longer hear the clatter of the hooves and the jingle of the bits. Even then she waited in case he miraculously changed his mind and came riding back, wanting a last kiss, or wanting her to go with him. For half an hour after he had gone, Amy lingered near the front door in case he would come back. But he never did.

Robert rode the long way back to court in a circuitous route at breakneck pace that tested the horsemanship of his escort, and the stamina of their mounts. When they finally rattled into the stable yard of Whitehall Palace the horses were blowing, their necks darkened with sweat, and the standard-bearer was gritting his teeth on the pain in his arms from riding one-handed at a half gallop for almost an hour.

"Good God, what is burning the man?"

he asked as he fell from the saddle into the arms of one of his companions.

"Lust," said the other crudely. "Lust or ambition or a guilty conscience. That's our lord in a nutshell. And today, seeing that he is riding hell for leather from his wife to the queen, it's guilty conscience, then ambition, then lust."

As Robert dismounted, one of his household, Thomas Blount, stood up from where he had been lounging in the shadows and came forward to hold the horse's reins.

"Some news," he said quietly.

Robert waited.

"At the Privy Council meeting, the queen tore into them over the treaty of Cateau-Cambrésis failing to return Calais to England, and not forcing the French princess to surrender the English coat of arms. They agreed to build two new warships, by subscription. You'll be asked for money, as well as everyone else."

"Anything else?" Dudley asked, his face a mask.

"About the church. Cecil to draw up a bill to go through parliament to decide what the services are to be. Agreed that they should base it on King Edward's prayer book with some small changes."

Dudley narrowed his eyes, thinking. "Did they not press her to go further?"

"Aye, but Cecil said that anything more would provoke a rebellion from the bishops and the lords. He couldn't promise to get it through as it is. And some of the councillors said they were opposed anyway. It's to go before parliament by Easter; Cecil hopes to work on the opposition by then."

"Anything else?"

"Nothing of matter. Some outburst of jealousy from the queen about Philip of Spain's marriage. And some discussion among themselves when she was gone that she would do best to marry Arran. Cecil in favor of Arran. Most of the council in agreement, especially if Arran can deliver Scotland. Some harsh words against you."

"Against me?"

"For distracting her from marriage plans, turning her head, flirtation, that sort of thing."

"Just hard words?"

"Norfolk said you should be sent back to the Tower or he'd run you through himself and think it a job well done."

"Norfolk is a puppy; but watch him for me," Robert said. "You've done very well. Come and see me later today; I have some other business for you."

The man bowed and faded into the background of the stable yard as if he had never been there. Robert turned for the palace and took the steps up to the hall two at a time.

*   *   *

"And how was your wife?" Elizabeth asked sweetly, the demure tone quite contradicted by the sharp glance she threw at him.

Robert was too experienced a philanderer to hesitate for a moment. "Well indeed," he said. "Blooming in health and beauty. Every time I see her she is prettier."

Elizabeth, who was ready to crow over any admission of Amy's imperfections, was caught unawares. "She is well?"

"In the best of health," he assured her. "And very happy. She is staying with her cousin, a very prosperous lady, married to Mr. Ralph Scott, a London merchant, a very successful man. I had to drag myself away from them; they were a merry party indeed."

Her dark eyes snapped. "You need not have put yourself to any trouble, Sir Robert.

You could have stayed as long as you wished in—where was it?—Kendal?"

"Camberwell, Your Grace," he replied. "Just down the road from London. A pretty little village. You would like it. I'm surprised you have never heard of it. Amy adores it there and she has wonderful taste."

"Well, you were not missed here. There has been nothing here but courtships and suitors and romancing."

"I don't doubt it," he said, smiling down at her. "For you missed me so little that you thought me in Kendal."

She pouted. "How am I to know where you are, or what you do? Aren't you supposed to be at court all the time? Is it not your duty to be here?"

"Not my duty," Sir Robert said. "For I would never neglect my duty."

"So you admit that you neglect me?"

"Neglect? No. Flee? Yes."

"You flee from me?" Her ladies saw her face alight with laughter as she leaned forward to hear him. "Why would you flee from me? Am I so fearsome?"

"You are not, but the threat you pose is dreadful, worse than any Medusa."

"I have never threatened you in my whole life."

"You threaten me with every breath that you take. Elizabeth, if I let myself love you, as I could do, what would become of me?"

She leaned back and shrugged. "Oh, you would pine and weep for a sennight and then you would visit your wife again in Camberwell and forget to come back to court."

Robert shook his head. "If I let myself love you, as I want to love you, then everything would change for me, forever. And for you . . ."

"For me what?"

"You would never be the same again," he promised her, his voice dropping to a whisper. "Your life would never be the same again. You would be a woman transformed; everything would be . . . revalued."

Elizabeth wanted to shrug and laugh but his dark gaze was utterly hypnotic, far too serious for the flirtatious tradition of courtly love. "Robert . . ." She put her hand to the base of her throat where her pulse was hammering, her face flushed pink with desire. But experienced philanderer as he was, he did not attend to the color in her cheeks but to the slow, revealing stain that spread from the base of her neck to the tips of her earlobes where two priceless pearls danced. It was the rose-red stain of lust and Robert Dudley had to bite his lip not to laugh aloud to see the virgin Queen of England as red as any slut with lust for him.

*　　*　　*

In the house at Camberwell Amy went into the parlor with the Scotts and Mrs. Oddingsell, swore them to the strictest of confidence, and announced that her husband was to be given the very highest order of chivalry, the Order of the Garter, a pretty little house at Kew, a grant of lands, a profitable office, and that best of all he had asked her to find them a suitable house in Oxfordshire.

"Well, what did Mrs. Woods tell you?" Mrs. Oddingsell demanded of her radiant charge. "And what did I say? You will have a beautiful house and he will come home every summer, and perhaps even the court will visit on progress, and you will entertain the queen in your own house and he will be so proud of you."

Amy's little face glowed at the thought of it.

"This is to rise high indeed," Ralph Scott

said delightedly. "It's no knowing how far he may go on the queen's favor like this."

"And then he will need a London house, he will not be satisfied with a little place at Kew, you will have Dudley House or Dudley Palace, and you will live in London every winter, and give such grand feasts and entertainments that everyone will want to be your friend, everyone will want to know the beautiful Lady Dudley."

"Oh, really," Amy said, blushing. "I don't seek it . . ."

"Yes, indeed. And think of the clothes you will order!"

"When did he say he would join you at Denchworth?" Ralph Scott asked, thinking that he might call on his cousin in Oxfordshire and promote his relationship with her husband.

"Within a fortnight, he said. But he is always late."

"Well, by the time he comes, you will have had time to ride all around the country and to find a house he might like," Mrs. Oddingsell said. "You know Denchworth already, but there are many old houses that you have never seen. I know it is my home, and so I am partial; but I think Oxfordshire is the most beautiful country in England. And my brother and sister-in-law will be so pleased to help us look. We can all go out together. And then, when Sir Robert finally comes, you will be able to ride out with him and show him the best land. Master of the Queen's Horse! Order of the Garter! I would think he could buy up half of the country."

"We must pack!" Amy cried, seized with urgency. "He says he wants me to go at once! We must leave at once."

She dragged her friend to her feet, Mrs. Oddingsell laughing at her. "Amy! It will take us only two or three days to get there. We don't have to rush!"

Amy danced to the door, her face as bright as a girl's. "He's going to meet me there!" she beamed. "He wants me there now. Of course we have to go at once."

*   *   *

William Cecil was in low-voiced conference with the queen in the window embrasure at Whitehall Palace, a March shower pelting the thick glass of the window behind them. In various states of alertness the queen's court waited for her to break from her advisor and turn, looking for entertainment. Robert Dudley was not among them;

he was in his great chambers organizing river barges with the head boatmen. Only Catherine Knollys stood within earshot, and Cecil trusted Catherine's loyalty to the queen.

"I cannot marry a man I have never seen." She repeated the answer she was using to everyone to delay the courtship of the Archduke Ferdinand.

"He is not some shepherd swain that can come piping and singing to court you," Cecil pointed out. "He cannot come halfway across Europe for you to look him over like a heifer. If the marriage is arranged then he could come for a visit and you could be married at the end of it. He could come this spring and you could be married in the autumn."

Elizabeth shook her head, instantly retreating from the threat of decisive action, at the very mention of a date on the calendar. "Oh, not so soon, Spirit. Don't press me."

He took her hand. "I don't mean to," he said earnestly. "But your safety lies this way. If you were betrothed to a Hapsburg archduke, then you have an alliance for life, unbreakable."

"They say Charles is very ugly, and madly Catholic," she reminded him.

"They do," he agreed patiently. "But it is his brother Ferdinand that we are considering. And they say he is handsome and moderate."

"And the emperor would support the match? And we would have a treaty of mutual support if I married him?"

"Count Feria indicated to me that Philip would see this as a guarantee of mutual goodwill."

She looked impressed.

"Last week, when I advised you in favor of the Arran match, you said you thought this match the better one," he reminded her. "Which is why I speak of it now."

"I did think so then," she concurred.

"It would rob the French of their friendship with Spain, and reassure our own Papists," he added.

She nodded. "I'll think about it."

Cecil sighed and caught Catherine Knollys's amused sidelong smile. She knew exactly how frustrating Elizabeth could be to her advisors. He smiled back. Suddenly there was a shout and a challenge from the doorway and a bang against the closed door of the presence chamber. Elizabeth blanched and started to turn, not knowing where she could go for safety. Cecil's two secret bodyguards stepped quickly toward her; everyone looked at the door. Cecil, his pulse hammering, took two steps forward. *Good God, it has happened. They have come for her,* he thought. *In her own palace.*

Slowly the door opened. "Beg pardon, Your Grace," the sentry said. "It's nothing. A drunk apprentice. Just stumbled and fell. Nothing to alarm you."

Elizabeth's color flowed back into her cheeks, and her eyes filled with tears. She turned into the window bay to hide her stricken face from the court. Catherine Knollys came forward and put her arm around her cousin's waist.

"Very well," Cecil said to the soldier. He nodded to his men to step back against the walls again. There was a buzz of concern and interest from the courtiers; only a few of them had seen the sudden leap of Elizabeth's fear. Cecil loudly asked Nicholas Bacon a question and tried to fill the silence with talk. He glanced back. Catherine was talking steadily and quietly to the queen, reassuring her that she was safe, that there was nothing to fear. Elizabeth managed to smile, Catherine patted her hand, and the two women turned back to the court.

Elizabeth glanced around. Count von Helfenstein, the Austrian ambassador representing the Archduke Ferdinand, was just coming into the long gallery. Elizabeth went toward him with her hands outstretched.

"Ah, Count," she said warmly. "I was just complaining that there was no one to divert me on this cold day, and praise be! here you are like a swallow in springtime!"

He bowed over her hands and kissed them.

"Now," she said, drawing him to walk beside her through the court. "You must tell me all about Vienna and the ladies' fashions. How do they wear their hoods, and what sort of ladies does the Archduke Ferdinand admire?"

*　　*　　*

Amy's energy and determination to meet her husband meant that she had packed her goods and clothes, organized her escort, and said farewell to her cousins within days. Her spirits did not flag on the long journey from Camberwell to Abingdon, though they spent three nights on the road and one of them in a very inferior inn where there was nothing to eat at dinner but a thin mutton broth and only gruel for breakfast. Sometimes she rode ahead of Mrs. Oddingsell, cantering her horse on the lush spring grass verges, and the rest of the time she kept the hunter to a brisk walk. In the warm, fertile countryside with the grass greening, the pasture and the crops starting to fill the fields, the escort felt safe to drop behind the two women; there was no threat from any beggars or other travelers as the empty road wound over an empty plain, unmarked by hedges or fields.

Now and again Robert's armed escort closed up as the way led the party through a wood of old oak trees, where some danger might be waiting, but the countryside was so open and empty, except for the solitary man plowing behind a pair of oxen, or a lad watching sheep, that it was not likely that anything could threaten Lady Dudley as she rode, merrily from one friendly house to another, secure of her welcome and hopeful of a happier future at last.

Mrs. Oddingsell, accustomed to Amy's mercurial changes of mood which depended so much on the absence or promise of Sir Robert, let the young woman ride ahead, and smiled indulgently when she heard the snatches of song that drifted back to her.

Clearly, Sir Robert, with his candidate on the throne, with a massive income flowing into his coffers, would look around for a great house, would look around for a handsome estate, and in very short order would want to see his wife at the foot of his table and a son and heir in the nursery.

What was the value of influence at court and a fortune in the making without a son to pass it on to? What was the use of an adoring wife if not to run the estate in the country and to organize the house in London?

Amy loved Robert very deeply and would do anything to please him. She wanted him to come home to her and she had all the knowledge and skills to run a successful country estate. Mrs. Oddingsell thought that the years of Amy's neglect and Robert's years under the shadow of treason were over at last, and the couple could start again. They would be partners in a venture typical of their time, furthering the fortunes of a family: the man wheeling and dealing at court, while his wife managed his land and fortune in the country.

Many a good marriage had started on nothing more tender than this, and forged itself into a strong good partnership. And—who could tell?—they might even fall in love again.

Mr. Hyde's house was a handsome place, set back a little from the village green, with a good sweep of a drive up to it and high walls built in the local stone. It had once been a farmhouse and successive additions had given it a charming higgledy-piggledy roof line, and extra wings branching from the old medieval hall. Amy had always enjoyed staying with the Hydes; Mrs. Oddingsell was sister to Mr. Hyde and there was always a warm sense of a family visit which hid the awkwardness that Amy sometimes felt when she arrived at one of Robert Dudley's dependents. Sometimes it seemed as if she were Robert's burden which had to be shared equally among his adherents; but with the Hydes she was among friends. The rambling farmhouse set in the wide open fields reminded her of her girlhood home in Norfolk, and the small worries of Mr. Hyde, the dampness of the hay, the yield of the barley crop, the failure of the river to flood the water meadows since a neighbor had put in an overly deep carp pond, were the trivial but fascinating business of running a country estate that Amy knew and loved.

The children were on the watch for their Aunt Lizzie and Lady Dudley; when the little cavalcade came up the drive the front door opened and they came tumbling out, waving and dancing around.

Lizzie Oddingsell tumbled off her horse and hugged them indiscriminately, and then straightened up to kiss her sister-in-law, Alice, and her brother, William.

They all three turned and hurried to help Amy down from her horse.

"My dear Lady Dudley, you are most welcome to Denchworth," William Hyde said warmly. "And are we to expect Sir Robert?"

Her blaze of a smile warmed them all. "Oh, yes," she said. "Within a fortnight, and I am to look for a house for us and we are going to have an estate here!"

*   *   *

Robert, walking around the Whitehall Palace stable yard on one of his weekly inspections, turned his head to hear a horse trotting rapidly on the cobbled road and then saw Thomas Blount jump from his hard-ridden mare, throw the reins at a stable lad, and march toward the pump as if urgently needing to sluice his head with water. Obligingly, Robert worked the pump handle.

"News from Westminster," Thomas said quickly. "And I think I am ahead of anyone else. Perhaps of interest to you."

"Always of interest. Information is the only true currency."

"I have just come from parliament. Cecil has done it. They are going to pass the bill to change the church."

"He's done it?"

"Two bishops imprisoned, two said to be ill, and one missing. Even so, he did it by only three votes. I came away as soon as I had counted the heads and I am sure of it."

"A new church," Dudley said thoughtfully.

"And a new head of the church. She's to be supreme governor."

"Supreme governor?" Dudley demanded, querying the curious name. "Not head?"

"That's what they said."

"That's an odd thing," Dudley said, more to himself than to Blount.

"Sir?"

"Makes you think."

"Does it?"

"Makes you wonder what she might do."

"Sir?"

"Nothing, Blount." Dudley nodded to the man. "My thanks." He walked on, shouted for a stable lad to move a halter rope, finished his inspection in a state of quiet elation, then turned and went slowly up the steps toward the palace.

On the threshold he met William Cecil, dressed for the journey to his home at Theobalds.

"Oh, Lord Secretary, good day. I was just thinking about you." Dudley greeted him jovially and patted him on the shoulder.

Cecil bowed. "I am honored to occupy your thoughts," he said with the ironic courtesy that he often used to keep Dudley at a safe distance, and to remind them both that the old relationship of master and servant no longer applied.

"I hear you have triumphed and remade the church?" Dudley inquired.

How the devil does he know that? Cecil demanded of himself. *And why can't he just dance with her and ride with her and keep*

*her happy till I can get her safely married to
the Earl of Arran?*

"Yes, a pity in many ways. But at last we
have agreement," Cecil said, gently detach-
ing his sleeve from the younger man's de-
taining hand.

"She is to be governor of the church?"

"No more and no less than her father, or
her brother."

"Surely they were called head of the
church?"

"St. Paul was thought to have ruled
against a woman's ministry," Cecil volunteered. "So she could not be called head.
Governor was deemed to be acceptable.
But if you are troubled in your conscience,
Sir Robert, there are spiritual leaders who
can guide you better than I."

Robert gave a quick laugh at Cecil's wonderful sarcasm. "Thank you, my lord. But
my soul can generally be trusted to look after itself in these matters. Will the clergy
thank you for such a thing?"

"They will not thank us," Cecil said carefully. "But they may be coerced and slid and
argued and threatened into agreement. I expect a struggle. It will not be easy."

"And how will you coerce and slide them and argue with them and threaten them?"

Cecil raised an eyebrow. "By administering an oath, the Oath of Supremacy. It's been done before."

"Not to a church that was wholly opposed," Dudley suggested.

"We have to hope that they will not be wholly opposed when it comes to a choice between swearing an oath or losing their livelihood and their freedom," Cecil said pleasantly.

"You don't propose to burn?" Dudley asked baldly.

"I trust it will not come to that, though her father would have done so."

Robert nodded. "Does all the power come to her, despite the different name? Does it give her all the powers of her father? Of her brother? Is she to be Pope in England?"

Cecil gave a little dignified bow, preparatory to making his leave. "Yes indeed, and if you will excuse me . . ."

To his surprise the younger man no longer detained him but swept him a graceful bow and came up smiling. "Of course! I should not have delayed you, Lord Secretary. Forgive me. Are you on your way home?"

"Yes," Cecil said. "Just for a couple of days. I shall be back in plenty of time for your investiture. I must congratulate you on the honor."

So how does he know about that? Dudley demanded of himself. *She swore to me that she would tell no one till nearer the time. Did he get it by his spies, or did she tell him herself? Does she indeed tell him everything?* Aloud he said, "I thank you. I am too much honored."

You are indeed, Cecil said to himself, returning the bow and making his way down the steps to where his short-backed horse was waiting for him, and his entourage was assembling. *But why should you be so delighted that she is head of the church? What is it to you, you sly, unreliable, handsome coxcomb?*

She is to be the English Pope, Robert whispered to himself, strolling like a prince at leisure in the opposite direction. The soldiers at the end of the gallery threw open the double doors for him and Robert passed through. The intense charm of his smile made them duck their heads and shuffle their feet, but his smile was not for them. He was smiling at the exquisite irony of Cecil serving Robert, all unknowing. Cecil, the great fox, had fetched home a game bird, and laid it at Robert's feet, as obedient as a Dudley spaniel.

He has made her Pope in everything but name. She can grant a dispensation for a marriage, she can grant an annulment of a marriage, she can rule in favor of a divorce, Robert whispered to himself. *He has no idea what he has done for me. By persuading those dull squires to make her supreme governor of the Church of England he has given her the power to grant a divorce. And who do we know who might benefit from that?*

*   *   *

Elizabeth was not thinking of her handsome Master of Horse. Elizabeth was in her presence chamber, admiring a portrait of Archduke Ferdinand, her ladies around her. From the ripple of approval as they noted the Hapsburg darkness of his eyes and the high fashion of his clothes Robert, entering the room at a leisurely stroll, understood that Elizabeth was continuing her public courtship of this latest suitor.

"A handsome man," he said, earning a smile from her. "And a good stance."

She took a step toward him, Robert, alert as a choreographer to every move of a dance, stood stock still and let her come to him.

"You admire the archduke, Sir Robert?"

"Certainly, I admire the portrait."

"It is a very good likeness," the ambassador Count von Helfenstein said defensively. "The archduke has no vanity, he would not want a portrait to flatter or deceive."

Robert shrugged, smiling. "Of course not," he said. He turned to Elizabeth. "But how could one choose a man from canvas and paint? You would never choose a horse like that."

"Yes; but an archduke is not a horse."

"Well, I would want to know how my horse would move, before I gave myself up to desire for him," he said. "I would want to put him through his paces. I would want to know how he felt when I gentled him under my hand, smoothed his neck, touched him everywhere, behind the ears, on the lips, behind the legs. I would want to know how responsive he was when I was on him, when I had him between my legs. You know,

I would even want to know the smell of him, the very scent of his sweat."

She gave a little gasp at the picture he was drawing for her, so much more vivid, so much more intimate, than the dull oil on canvas before them.

"If I were you, I would choose a husband I knew," he said quietly to her. "A man I had tested with my own eyes, with my own fingers, whose scent I liked. I would only marry a man I knew I could desire. A man I already desired."

"I am a maid," she said, her voice a breath. "I desire no man."

"Oh, Elizabeth, you lie," he whispered with a smile.

Her eyes widened at his impertinence, but she did not check him. He took silence for encouragement, as he always would. "You lie: you *do* desire a man."

"Not one who is free to marry," she shot back.

He hesitated. "Would you want me to be free?"

At once she half turned her head away from him and he saw that he had lost her to her habitual coquetry. "Oh, were we speaking of you?"

Immediately, he let her go. "No. We are speaking of the archduke. And he is a handsome young man indeed."

"And agreeable," the ambassador interposed, hearing only the tail of their low-voiced conversation. "A fine scholar. His English is all but perfect."

"I am sure," Sir Robert replied. "Mine is remarkably good too."

*   *   *

Amy was blooming in the April weather. Every day she rode out with Lizzie Oddingsell or with Alice or William Hyde to look at land that might be bought, woods that might be felled to clear a space for a house, or farmhouses that might be rebuilt.

"Will he not want something much grander than this?" William Hyde asked her one day as they were riding around an estate of two hundred acres with a pretty red-tiled farmhouse in the center.

"We would rebuild the house, of course," Amy said. "But we don't need a great palace. He was very taken with my cousin's house at Camberwell."

"Oh, a merchant's house in the town, yes," Mr. Hyde agreed. "But will he not want somewhere that he can entertain the queen when the court is on progress? A house where he can entertain the whole court? A big house, more like Hampton Court, or Richmond?"

She looked quite shocked for a moment. "Oh, no," she said. "He wants something that we would have as our home, that would feel like a proper home. Not a great big palace of a place. And surely the queen would stay at Oxford if she came to this part of the country?"

"If she wanted to hunt?" Alice suggested. "He is her Master of Horse. Would he not want enough land for a great deer park?"

Amy's confident laugh rang out. "Ah, you would have me buy the New Forest!" she exclaimed. "No. What we want is a place like my home in Norfolk, but just a little bigger. Somewhere like Flitcham Hall that we nearly bought, just a little grander and bigger than that. Somewhere that we can add a wing and a gateway, so that it is a handsome house, he would not want anything mean, and with pleasure gardens and an orchard and fish ponds of course, and some pretty woods and some good rides, and the rest would be farmland and he will breed horses for the court. He spends all his time in palaces; he will want to come home to a house which feels like a home and not a great cathedral filled by a band of mummers, which is what the royal palaces are like."

"If you are sure it is what he wants, then we can ask them the price for this place," William Hyde said cautiously, still unconvinced. "But perhaps we should write to him to make sure he does not want something more imposing, with more chambers, and more land."

"There is no need," Amy said confidently. "I know what my husband wants. We have been waiting to make a home like this for years."

*   *   *

Robert Dudley was deep in planning the greatest court feast since the high point of the queen's coronation. Ostensibly it was to honor St. George's Day, the great day of English celebration that the Tudors had introduced to the court calendar. It would be the day that he and three other great noblemen accepted the Order of the Garter, the highest award of chivalry, from the queen's hand. The order was given only to men who had excelled themselves in defense of the crown. The queen was awarding it to Robert Dudley; to her young kinsman Thomas Howard, the Duke of Norfolk; to Sir William Parr, her late stepmother's brother; and to the Earl of Rutland.

There were those who suggested that Robert Dudley was an odd addition to this array of family, or senior councillors, and perhaps, since he had been part of the expedition that had lost Calais for England, he had not made a particularly dazzling defense of the realm.

Also, said the gossips, planning a few processions could hardly qualify a man for the highest order of English chivalry, especially since his grandfather and father had been condemned traitors. How could a man like Robert Dudley have earned such exceptional honor? But no one said it very loud. And no one said it anywhere near the queen.

There would be jousting all the afternoon, the knights would come into the jousting ring in costume and in disguises, they would recite witty and beautiful verses to explain their role. The theme of the feast was to be Arthurian.

"Is it Camelot?" Sir Francis Knollys asked

Robert with gentle irony, in the tilt yard, where he was supervising the flying of the flags with medieval crests. "Are we enchanted?"

"I hope you will be enchanted," Robert said pleasantly.

"Why Camelot, exactly?" Sir Francis was determinedly uncomprehending.

Dudley dragged his eyes from the tilt yard which was being swatched in gold cloth, economically saved and reused from the coronation pageants. "Obvious."

"Not to me. Tell me," Sir Francis pleaded.

"Beautiful queen," Robert said shortly, ticking off the elements on his long, slim fingers. "Perfect England. Unified under one magical monarch. No religious issues, no marriage issues, no bloody Scots. Camelot. Harmony. And the adoration of the Lady."

"The Lady?" Sir Francis queried, thinking of the shrines all around England to the Lady Mary, mother of Jesus, now slowly falling into disuse, as the country people were persuaded that what had been the core of their honest faith was error, even heresy.

"The Lady. The queen. Elizabeth," Robert replied. "The Queen of Our Hearts, the

Queen of the Joust, in her summertime court, ruling forever. Hurrah."

"Hurrah," Sir Francis chorused obediently. "But hurrah to what exactly? Unless to celebrate your ascent to the Order of the Garter, for which greatest congratulations."

Robert flushed slightly. "I thank you," he said with simple dignity. "But it is not to celebrate my honor. It goes further, far beyond someone as humble as me, far beyond the noble lords, even."

"Goes?"

"Out to the country. To the people. Every time we have a pageant or a day of festivities, it is copied, in every town and every village up and down the country. Don't you think that giving them all the idea that the queen is a ruler as wonderful as Arthur reminds them that they should love and revere and defend her? Reminding them that she is young and beautiful and that her court is the most handsome of all of Europe doesn't just play well in England; the word goes everywhere: to Paris, to Madrid, to Brussels. They have to admire her, so they have to recognize her power. It makes her as safe as Cecil's treaty."

"I see you are a politician," Sir Francis

said. "And it is as we agreed. That she should be seen to be loveable so that she is beloved, so that they will keep her safe."

"Please God," Robert assented, and then made a little irritated tut as a clumsy page-boy dropped his end of a bolt of cloth and it trailed on the tilt yard's sandy floor. "Pick it up, lad! It's getting dirty!"

"And have you thought of her safety at this day?" Sir Francis confirmed. "Most of the people have heard now that the Pope has blessed an attack on her."

Dudley faced him. "I think of nothing but her safety," he said flatly. "Night and day. I think of nothing but her. You will find no more faithful man in her service. I think of her as if my life depended on it. Indeed, my life does depend on it."

Sir Francis nodded. "I don't doubt you," he said honestly. "But these are anxious times. I know that Cecil has a spy network across all of Europe to catch anyone who might come to England to threaten her. But what of Englishmen? Men and women that have passed as our friends? People who might even now be thinking that it is their duty, their sacred duty, to assassinate her?"

Robert squatted down and drew with his

finger on the sandy floor of the jousting arena. "Royal entrance here. Only members of the court allowed in. Merchants, citizens of London, general gentry here: kept from her by the gentlemen pensioners. Apprentices here, farther back: since they are always the worst troublemakers. Country people, anyone who has come here without invitation, farther back still. At each corner an armed man. Cecil's men to go among the crowds, watching. I have a few trusted men of my own who will pass around and keep their eyes open."

"But what about the threat from her friends? Gentry and nobility?" Sir Francis asked softly.

Robert rose up and brushed off his hands. "Pray God that they all now understand that their loyalty is first to her, however they like to celebrate Mass." He paused. "And, to tell you the truth, most of those that you would doubt are already being watched," he volunteered.

Sir Francis gave a sharp crack of laughter. "By your men?"

"Mostly Cecil's," Robert said. "He has hundreds in his secret employ."

"Now there is a man I would not want for my enemy," Sir Francis remarked cheerfully.

"Only if you were certain you could win," Robert replied smoothly. He glanced over his shoulder and saw a pageboy unrolling a pennant and hauling it up a pole. "You! Look at what you're doing! That's upside down!"

"Well, I'll leave you to it," Sir Francis said, retreating as if in fear that he would be sent up a ladder.

Robert grinned at him. "Aye. I'll call you when the work is over," he said cheekily, and strode to the center stage. "I imagine you will return in good time for the feast once all the hard work is done. Are you jousting?"

"Good God, yes! I shall be a very noble gentil parfit knight! I shall be the very flower of chivalry. I am off now to polish my shield and my couplets," Sir Francis called mockingly from the stand. "Sing hey nonny nonny, sweet Robin!"

"Hey nonny nonny!" Robert shouted back, laughing.

He returned to his work, smiling at the exchange, and then he had a sense of being watched. It was Elizabeth, standing alone on the platform that would be decked out as the royal box, looking down at the empty jousting rails and the sandy arena.

Robert scrutinized her for a moment, noted her stillness, and the slight droop of her head. Then he picked up a flagpole as if still at work, and strolled past the royal box.

"Oh!" he exclaimed, as if he suddenly saw her. "Your Grace!"

She smiled at him and came to the front of the box. "Hello, Robert."

"Thoughtful?"

"Yes."

He wondered if she had overheard their conversation about the danger she walked through every day, if she had heard them name the dangers from every sort of person, from the lowest apprentices to her closest friends. How could a young woman bear to know that she was hated by her own people? That the greatest spiritual power in Christendom had declared her fit to die?

He stuck the flagpole in its stand and came before the box and looked up. "Anything I can help you with, my princess?"

Elizabeth gave him a shy little smile. "I don't know what to do."

He did not understand her. "Do? Do about what?"

She leaned over the rail of the box so that she could speak softly. "I don't know what to do at a tournament."

"You must have been to hundreds of tournaments."

"No, very few. I was not that often at court during my father's reign, and Mary's court was not merry and I was imprisoned for most of the time."

Again Robert was reminded that she had been in exile for most of her girlhood. She had educated herself with the passion of a scholar, but she had not prepared herself for the trivial entertainments of court life. She could not do so; there was no way to be at ease in the palaces or at the great events except through familiarity. He might relish the wit of thinking of a new theme to flavor a traditional event, but he knew the traditional event as one who had attended every joust since first coming to court, and indeed, had won most of them.

Robert's desire was to outdo the tournaments and entertainments that he knew only too well; Elizabeth's desire was to get through them without betraying her lack of ease.

"But you like jousting?" he confirmed.

"Oh, yes," she said. "And I understand the rules but not how I should behave, and when to clap, and when to show favor, and all the rest of it."

He thought for a moment. "Shall I make you out a plan?" he asked gently. "Like I did for your coronation procession? So that it shows you where you should be and what you should do and say at each point?"

At once she looked happier. "Yes. That would be good. Then I could enjoy the day instead of worrying about it."

He smiled. "And shall I make you a plan for the ceremony of the Order of the Garter?"

"Yes," she said eagerly. "Thomas Howard told me what I should do but I couldn't remember it all."

"How would he know?" Dudley said dismissively. "He was hardly uppermost at court in the last three reigns."

She smiled at his habitual rivalry with the duke, her uncle, their contemporary in age, and Robert's lifelong rival.

"Well, I will write it out for you," Robert said. "May I come to your room before dinner and go through it with you?"

"Yes," she said. Impulsively she reached

down her hand to him. He stretched up and could reach only her fingertips with his own, he kissed his hand and reached up to touch hers.

"Thank you," she said sweetly, her fingertips lingering against his.

"I'll always tell you, I'll always help you," he promised her. "Now that I know, I will draw you a table to show you where to go and what to do for every event. So that you always know. And when you have been to a dozen jousts you can tell me that you want it done differently, and you shall be the one that draws it up for me and shows me how you want everything changed."

Elizabeth smiled at that and then she turned and went from the royal box, leaving him with an odd sensation of tenderness toward her. Sometimes she was not like a queen come by luck and cunning to greatness. Sometimes she was more like a young girl with a task too difficult to manage alone. He was accustomed to desiring women; he was accustomed to using them. But for a moment in the half-prepared tilt yard he felt a new sensation for him—tenderness, of wanting her happiness more than his own.

*

Lizzie Oddingsell wrote a letter to Amy's dictation, and then Amy copied it herself, laboriously making the letters march straight along the ruled lines.

Dear Husband,

I hope this finds you in good health. I am happy and well, staying with our dear friends the Hydes. I think I have found us a house and land, as you asked me to do. I think you will be very pleased with it. Mr. Hyde has spoken to the squire who is selling up owing to ill health and has no son to come after him, and he says that he is asking a fair price.

I will go no further until I have your instructions, but perhaps you will come and see the house and land very soon. Mr. and Mrs. Hyde send you their good wishes and this basket of early salad leaves. Lady Robsart tells me we have eighty lambs born this year at Stanfield, our best ever year. I hope you will come soon.

Your devoted wife
Amy Dudley

PS I do hope you will come soon,
husband

Amy walked to church across the park with Mrs. Oddingsell, over the village green through the lych-gate into the churchyard and then into the cool, changeless gloom of the parish church.

Yet, it was not changeless, it was strangely changed. Amy looked around and saw a new great brass lectern at the head of the aisle and the Bible spread out on it, wide open as if anyone could be allowed to read it. The altar, where it was usually kept, was conspicuously empty. Amy and Lizzie Oddingsell exchanged one silent look and shut themselves into the Hyde family pew. The service proceeded in English, not the more familiar Latin, following King Edward's prayer book rather than the beloved Mass. Amy bowed her head over the new words and tried to feel the presence of God, even though his church was changed, and the language was changed, and the Host was hidden.

It came to the moment for the priest to pray for the queen, and he did so, his voice shaking only a little, but when it came for him to pray for their beloved bishop, Thomas Goldwell, the tears in his voice stopped him from speaking altogether and he fell silent. The clerk finished the prayer for him and the service went on, ending with the usual bidding prayer and blessing.

"You go on," Amy whispered to her friend. "I want to pray for a moment."

She waited until the church was empty, and then she came from the Hyde pew. The priest was on his knees at the rood screen, Amy quietly went and knelt beside him.

"Father?"

He turned his head. "Daughter?"

"Is there something wrong?"

He nodded. His head bowed low as if he were ashamed. "They are saying that our Bishop Thomas is not our bishop at all."

"How is this?" she asked.

"They are saying that the queen has not appointed him to Oxford, and yet he is no longer Bishop of St. Asaph. They are saying that he is betwixt and between, that he belongs nowhere, is bishop of nothing."

"Why would they say such a thing?" she demanded. "They must know he is a good and holy man, and he left St. Asaph to come to Oxford. He is appointed by the Pope."

"You should know as well as I," he said wearily. "Your husband knows how this court works."

"He does not . . . confide in me," she said, picking the right word carefully. "Not about court matters."

"They know our bishop is a man faithful till death," the priest said sadly. "They know he was Cardinal Pole's dearest friend, was at his deathbed, he gave him the last sacraments. They know he will not turn his coat to please this queen. He would not dishonor the Host as he is ordered to do. I think they will first strip him of his Holy Office, by this sleight of hand, and then murder him."

Amy gasped. "Not again," she said. "Not more killing. Not another Thomas More!"

"He has been ordered to appear before the queen. I am afraid it is to go to his death."

Amy nodded, white-faced.

"Lady Robsart, your husband is spoken of as one of the greatest men at court. Can you ask him to intercede for our bishop? I swear Father Thomas has never spoken a word against the accession of the queen, never a word against her as queen. He has only spoken out, as God has commanded him to do, in defense of our Holy Church."

"I cannot," she said simply. "Father, forgive me, God forgive me, but I cannot. I have no influence. My husband does not take my advice on court matters, on policy. He does not even know I think on such matters! I cannot advise him, and he would not listen to me."

"Then I will pray for you, that he turns to you," the priest said gently. "And if God moves him to listen, then, daughter: you speak. This is the life of our bishop at stake."

Amy bowed her head. "I will do what I can," she promised without much hope.

"God bless you, child, and guide you."

*   *   *

Robert's clerk handed him Amy's letter on the afternoon after his investiture as a knight of the garter. Robert had just hung the blue silk of the garter over the back of a chair and stepped back to admire it. Then he pulled on a new doublet, scanned the letter swiftly, and handed it back.

"Write her that I am busy now, but I will come as soon as I can," he said as he opened the door. His hand on the latch, he realized that the ill-formed letters were Amy's own hand, and that she must have dedicated hours to writing to him.

"Tell her that I am very glad she wrote to me herself," he said. "And send her a small purse of money to buy gloves or something she wants."

He paused, with a nagging sense that he should do more; but then he heard the herald's trumpet sound get the jousting and there was no time. "Tell her I'll come at once," he said, and turned and ran lightly downstairs to the stable yard.

*   *   *

The joust had all the pageantry and color that Elizabeth loved, with knights in disguise singing her praises, and composing extempore verses. The ladies gave out favors and the knights wore their ladies' colors over their heart. The queen was wearing one glove of white silk and holding the other in her hand, when she leaned forward to wish Sir Robert the best of fortune as he came to the royal box to look up at her, high above him, and pay his respects.

Accidentally, as she leaned forward, the glove slipped through her fingers, and it fell. At once, almost quicker than anyone could see, he had spurred his horse on, the great warhorse wheeled, responsive at once, and he caught the glove in mid-air before it fell to the ground.

"Thank you!" Elizabeth called. She nodded to a page boy. "Fetch my glove from Sir Robert."

With one hand holding back the curvetting big horse, he raised his visor with his other hand and put the glove to his lips.

Elizabeth, her color rising, watched him kiss her glove, did not demand its return, did not laugh away the gesture as part of the jousting courtesies.

"May I not keep it?" he asked.

She recovered herself a little. "Since you so cleverly caught it," she said lightly.

Robert brought his horse a little closer. "I thank you, my queen, for dropping it for me."

"I dropped it by accident," she said.

"I caught it by intent," he replied, his dark eyes gleaming at her, and tucked it carefully inside his breastplate, wheeled his horse around, and rode down to the end of the lists.

They jousted all afternoon in the hot April sunshine and when the evening came the queen invited all her special guests onto the river for an evening sail in the barges. Londoners, who had expected this end to the day, had begged and borrowed and hired boats in their thousands, and the river was as crowded as a marketplace with boats and barges flying gaily colored pennants and streamers, and every third craft with a singer or a lute player on board so that haunting tunes drifted across the water from one boat to another.

Robert and Elizabeth were in the queen's barge with Catherine and Sir Francis Knollys, Lady Mary Sidney and her husband, Sir Henry Sidney, a couple of the queen's other ladies, Laetitia Knollys, and another maid of honor.

A musicians' barge rowed beside them and the lingering notes of love songs drifted across the water, as the rowers kept pace to the gentle beat of a drum. The sun, setting among clouds of rose and gold, laid a path across the darkening Thames as if it would lead them all the way inland to the very heart of England.

Elizabeth leaned on the gold-leafed railing of the barge and looked out at the lapping waters of the river, and the panorama of the pleasure boats keeping pace with her own, at the bobbing lanterns which illuminated their own reflections in the water. Robert joined her and they stood side by side for a long while, watching the river in silence.

"You know, this has been the most perfect day of my life," Elizabeth said quietly to Robert.

For a moment the constant erotic tension between them was eased. Robert smiled at her, the affectionate smile of an old friend. "I am glad," he said simply. "I would wish you many more such days, Elizabeth. You have been generous to me and I thank you."

She turned and smiled at him, their faces so close that his breath stirred a strand of hair that had escaped from her hood.

"You still have my glove," she whispered.

"You have my heart."

*   *   *

Generous indeed, William Cecil said drily to himself, as the court rode out on May Day morning to visit Robert Dudley in his new home of the Dairy House at Kew, an enchantingly pretty place built at the very edge of the park, just ten minute's walk from the palace. A flight of grand white stone steps led to a double-height arched double door, framed by two windows. Inside, a great hall gave way to small, intimate retiring rooms that overlooked the gardens on each side. A hedge bordered the front of the house with two perfectly pruned trees as round as plums, on sentinel each side.

Robert Dudley greeted the small party at the front door and led them straight through the house to the pretty walled garden at the back. It was planted partly with flowers and partly as an orchard, very much in the new fashion of making a garden appear as much as possible like a flowery mead. A table was spread with a white linen cloth and a breakfast was ready for the queen. In a typical Dudley conceit, all the servants were dressed as milkmaids or shepherds, and there was a little flock of lambs, absurdly dyed the Tudor colors of green and white, gamboling under the blossom in the apple orchard.

Elizabeth clapped her hands in delight at the sight of it all.

"Oh, Robert, this is exquisite!"

"I thought you would like to be a simple country girl for the day," he said quietly into her ear.

She turned to him. "Did you? Why?"

He shrugged. "A crown is a weight as well as an honor. The people who flock about you all the time always take from you; they never give. I wanted you to have a day that was filled with pleasure and laughter, a day for a pretty girl, not an overburdened queen."

She nodded. "You understand. They want so much of me," she said resentfully.

"And these new suitors the worst," he said. "The two Hapsburg dukes, who want your glory to hitch them up from poor dukes in Austria to King of England in one great leap! Or the Earl of Arran, who wants to drag you into war with Scotland! They offer you nothing, and expect everything in return."

Elizabeth frowned, and for a moment he was afraid he had gone too far. Then she said, "All they offer me is trouble, but what they want from me is everything that I am."

"They want nothing of *you*," he corrected her. "Not the real you. They want the crown or the throne or the heir that you might give them. But they are counterfeit suitors, false gold, they do not know you, or love you as I . . ." He broke off.

She leaned forward, she could feel his warm breath on her face and he saw her breathe in with him.

"You?" she prompted.

"As I do," he whispered very low.

"Are we going to eat?" Cecil demanded plaintively, from the group waiting behind them. "I am weak with hunger. Sir Robert, you are a very Tantalus to spread a feast before us but never to bid us to dine."

Robert laughed and turned away from the queen, who took a moment to recover her sense of the others, of the eyes upon them, of the tables laid with the snowy cloths in the sunshine-filled orchard. "Please . . ." he said, gesturing like a grand lord that they should take their places.

They sat down to a breakfast that was as sophisticated as an Italian banquet but served with the stylish insouciance that was Dudley's signature, and then, when the meal was ended and the sugared plums were on the table, the shepherds and the milkmaids performed a country dance, and sang a song in praise of the shepherdess queen. A small boy, blond and cherubic, stepped forward and recited a poem to Elizabeth, Queen of all the Shepherds and

Shepherdesses, and presented her with a crown of may, and a peeled wand of willow, and then a band of musicians, uncomfortably hidden in the branches of the apple trees, played an opening chord and Robert offered Elizabeth his hand and led her out in a country dance, a May Day dance on this very day for courtship, when tradition had it that even the birds were marrying.

Pretty enough, William Cecil said to himself, glancing at the sun which was now almost overhead. *Half the day wasted and a mountain of letters for me to read when I get back to court. Bad news from Scotland, no doubt, and still no money forthcoming from the queen to support our coreligionists, though they beg us for our help and demand, with reason, what we think we are doing: abandoning them when they are on the very brink of victory?*

He looked a little closer. Robert Dudley's hand was not where it should be, on the queen's back as he guided her forward in the steps of the dance, but around her waist. And she, far from standing upright as she always did, was most definitely leaning toward him. *One might almost say yearning,* he thought.

Cecil's first thought was for her reputation, and the marriage plans. He glanced around. Praise God, they were among friends: the Knollys, the Sidneys, the Percys. The queen's irritable young uncle, the Duke of Norfolk, would not like to see his kinswoman in the arms of a man as if she were some serving wench at a roadside inn, but he would hardly report her to the Hapsburg ambassador. There might be spying servants in the party, but their words would carry little weight. Everyone knew that Elizabeth and Dudley were intimate friends. There was no harm done by the evident affection between the young couple.

And yet, Cecil said quietly to himself. *And yet, we should get her married. If she lets him caress her, we're safe enough, he is married and can do no more but light a fire which will have to burn out. But what if a single man took her fancy? If Dudley arouses her desires, what if some clever young buck presents himself, and happens to be both handsome and free? What if she thought to marry for love and undo England's policy for a girl's whim? Better get her married and soon.*

*

Amy was waiting for Robert's arrival.

The whole household was waiting for Robert's arrival.

"Are you sure that he said he was coming at once?" David Hyde asked his sister, Elizabeth Oddingsell, the second week in May.

"You saw the letter as well as I," she said. "First his clerk wrote he was busy but that he would come as soon as he could, then in the second sentence he corrects the first and says that he will come at once."

"My cousin in London, who is kin to the Seymour family, says that he is all day every day with the queen," Alice Hyde observed. "She went to the St. George's Day joust and she heard someone say that he carried the queen's glove in his breastplate."

Lizzie shrugged. "He is her Master of Horse; of course she favors him."

"Mr. Hyde's cousin says that in the evening he sailed with her in the royal barge."

"As he should be, honored among others," Lizzie maintained stoutly.

"She visited him for a May Day breakfast at his new house at Kew and stayed all the day."

"Of course," Lizzie said patiently. "A court breakfast might well last for most of the day."

"Well, my cousin says that the word is that she never lets him out of her sight. He is at her side all day and they dance together every night. She says that the queen's own kinsman the Duke of Norfolk has sworn that if he dishonors her, he is a dead man, and he would not make such a threat lightly or for no reason."

Lizzie's look at her sister-in-law was neither sisterly nor warm. "Your cousin is obviously well informed," she said irritably. "But you can remind her that Sir Robert is a married man about to buy land and build his first house with his wife and that this will happen at any day now. Remind her that he married his wife for love, and that they are planning their life together. And you can tell her that there is a world of difference between courtly love, which is all show and fol-de-rol and poetry and singing, done by every man at court to please the queen, and real life. And your cousin should bite her tongue before she gossips about her betters."

*

The Spanish ambassador, Count Feria, deeply weary of the dance of Elizabeth's courtship which he had gone through once on account of his master, Philip of Spain, did not think he could bear to watch it played out all over again with a fellow ambassador and another suitor: the Hapsburg archduke. At last, King Philip responded to his pleas and agreed to replace him with another ambassador: the astute Bishop de Quadra. Count Feria, barely able to hide his relief, asked Cecil for permission to take his leave of Elizabeth.

The experienced ambassador and the young queen were old adversaries. He had been the most loyal advisor to Queen Mary Tudor and had recommended consistently and publicly that she execute her troublesome heir and half-sister, Elizabeth. They were his spies who over and over again brought evidence of Elizabeth plotting with English rebels, plotting with French spies, plotting with the magician Dr. Dee, plotting with anyone who would offer to overthrow her sister by treason, by foreign armies, or by magic.

He had been Mary's truest and steadiest friend and he had fallen in love and married her most constant lady-in-waiting, Jane Dormer. Queen Mary would have released her beloved friend to no one but the Spanish ambassador, and she gave them her blessing on her deathbed.

Obeying tradition, the count brought his wife to court to say her farewell to her queen, and Jane Dormer, holding her head very high, walked into Whitehall Palace once more, having walked out of it in disgust the day that Elizabeth became queen. Now a Spanish countess, her belly curved with pregnancy, Jane Dormer returned, pleased to be saying good-bye. As luck would have it, the first person she met was a face from the old court: the royal fool, Will Somers.

"How now, Jane Dormer," he said warmly. "Or do I call you my lady countess?"

"You can call me Jane," she said. "As ever. How are you, Will?"

"Amusing," he said. "This is a court ready to be amused, but I fear for my post."

"Oh?" she asked.

The lady-in-waiting who was escorting Jane to the queen paused for the jest.

"In a court in which every man is played

for a fool, why should anyone pay me?" he asked.

Jane laughed out loud. The lady-in-waiting giggled. "Give you good day, Will," Jane said fondly.

"Aye, you will miss me when you are in Spain," he said. "But not miss much else, I would guess?"

Jane shook her head. "The best of England left it in November."

"God rest her soul," Will said. "She was a most unlucky queen."

"And this one?" Jane asked him.

Will cracked a laugh. "She has all the luck of her sire," he said with wonderful ambiguity, since Jane's conviction would always be that Elizabeth was the child of Mark Smeaton, the lute player, and his luck was stretched to breaking point on the rack before he danced on air from the gallows.

Jane gleamed at the private, treasonous joke, and then followed the lady-in-waiting toward the queen's presence chamber.

"You're to wait here, Countess," the lady said abruptly, and showed Jane into an anteroom. Jane rested one hand in the small of her back and leaned against the windowsill.

There was no chair in the room, no stool, no window seat, not even a table that she might lean on.

Minutes passed. A wasp, stumbling out of its winter sleep, struggled against the leaded window pane and fell silent on the sill. Jane shifted her weight from one foot to another, feeling the ache in her back.

It was stuffy in the room, the ache in the small of her back traveled down to the calves of her legs. Jane flexed her feet, going up and down on her toes, trying to relieve the pain. In her belly, the child shifted and kicked. She put her hand on her stomacher and stepped to the window embrasure. She looked out of the window to the inner garden. Whitehall Palace was a warren of buildings and inner courts; this one had a small walnut tree growing in the center with a circular bench around it. As Jane watched, a pageboy and a serving maid loitered for five precious minutes whispering secrets and then scampered off in opposite directions.

Jane smiled. This palace had been her home as the favorite lady-in-waiting of the queen, and she thought that she and the Spanish ambassador had met by that very seat themselves. There had been a brief, joyful time, one summer, between the queen's wedding and her triumphant announcement that she was with child, when this had been a happy court, the center of world power, united with Spain, confident of an heir, and ruled by a woman who had come to her own at last.

Jane shrugged. Queen Mary's disappointment and death had been the end of it all, and now her bright, deceitful little half-sister was sitting in her place, and using that place to insult Jane by this discourteous delay. *It was,* Jane thought, *a petty revenge on a dead woman, not worthy of a queen.*

Jane heard a clock strike from somewhere in the palace. She had planned to visit the queen before her dinner and already she had been kept waiting for half an hour. She felt a little light-headed from lack of food and hoped she would not be such a fool as to faint when she was finally admitted to the presence chamber.

She waited. More long minutes passed. Jane wondered if she could just slip away; but that would be such an insult to the queen from the wife of the Spanish ambassador that it would be enough to cause an international incident. But this long waiting was, in itself, an insult to Spain. Jane sighed. Elizabeth must still be a filled with spite, if she would take such a risk for the small benefit of insulting such a very unimportant person as herself.

At last the door opened. The lady-in-waiting looked miserably embarrassed. "Do forgive me. Will you come this way, Countess?" she asked politely.

Jane stepped forward and felt her head swim. She clenched her fists and her nails dug into the palms of her hands so the pain of it distracted her from her dizziness and from the ache in her back. *Not long now,* she said to herself. *She can't keep me on my feet for much longer.*

Elizabeth's presence chamber was hot and crowded, the lady-in-waiting threaded through the many people and a few of them smiled and acknowledged Jane, who had been well liked when she had served Queen Mary. Elizabeth, standing in blazing sunlight in the center of a window bay, deep in conversation with one of her Privy Councillors, seemed not to see her. The lady-in-waiting led Jane right up to her mistress. Still there was no acknowledgment. Jane stood and waited.

At last Elizabeth concluded the animated conversation and looked around. "Ah, Countess Feria!" she exclaimed. "I hope you have not been kept waiting?"

Jane's smile was queenly. "Not at all," she said smoothly. Her head was thudding now and her mouth was dry. She was very afraid of fainting at Elizabeth's feet; there was little more than determination holding her up.

She could not see Elizabeth's face, the window was a blaze of white light behind her, but she knew the taunting smile and the dancing black eyes.

"And you are expecting a child," Elizabeth said sweetly. "Within a few months?"

There was a suppressed gasp from the court. A birth within a few months would mean that the child had been conceived before the wedding.

Jane's calm expression never wavered. "In the autumn, Your Grace," she said steadily.

Elizabeth fell silent.

"I have come to bid you farewell, Queen Elizabeth," Jane said with glacial courtesy.

"My husband is returning to Spain and I am going with him."

"Ah yes, you are a Spaniard now," Elizabeth said, as if it were a disease that Jane had caught.

"A Spanish countess," Jane replied smoothly. "Yes, we have both changed our places in the world since we last met, Your Grace."

It was a shrewd reminder. Jane had seen Elizabeth on her knees and weeping with pretended penitence before her sister, had seen Elizabeth bloated with illness, under house arrest, under charge of treason, sick with terror, begging for a hearing.

"Well, I wish you a good journey anyway," Elizabeth said carelessly.

Jane sank to the ground in a perfect courtly curtsy; no one could have known that she was on the very edge of losing consciousness. She rose up and saw the room swim before her eyes, and then she walked backward from the throne, one smooth step after another, her rich gown held out of the way of her scarlet high heels, her head up, her lips smiling. She did not turn until she reached the door. Then she flicked her skirt around and left, without a backward glance.

*

"She did what?" Cecil demanded incredulously of an excitable Laetitia Knollys, reporting, as she was paid to do, on the doings of the queen's private rooms.

"Kept her waiting for a full half hour, and then suggested that she had the baby in her belly before marriage," Laetitia whispered breathlessly.

They were in Cecil's dark paneled study, the shutters closed although it was full day, a trusted man on the door and Cecil's other rooms barred to visitors.

He frowned slightly. "And Jane Dormer?"

"She was like a queen," Laetitia said. "She spoke graciously, she curtsyed—you should have seen her curtsy—she went out as if she despised us all, but gave said not one word of protest. She made Elizabeth look like a fool."

Cecil frowned slightly. "Watch your speech, little madam," he said firmly. "I would have been whipped if I had called my king a fool."

Laetitia bowed her bronze head.

"Did Elizabeth say anything when she had gone?"

"She said that Jane reminded her of her

sour-faced old sister and thank God those days were past."

He nodded. "Anyone reply?"

"No!" Laetitia was bubbling with gossip. "Everyone was so shocked that Elizabeth should be so . . . so . . . ." She had no words for it.

"So what?"

"So nasty! So rude! She was so unkind! And to such a nice woman! And her with child! And the wife of the Spanish ambassador! Such an insult to Spain!"

Cecil nodded. *It was a surprising indiscretion for such a controlled young woman,* he thought. *Probably the relic of some foolish women's quarrel that had rumbled on for years. But it was unlike Elizabeth to show her hand with quite such vulgarity.* "I think you will find that she can be very nasty," was all he said to the girl. "You had better make sure you never give her cause."

Her head came up at that, her dark eyes, Boleyn eyes, looked at him frankly. She smoothed her bronze hair under her cap. She smiled, that bewitching, sexually aware Boleyn smile. "How can I help it?" she asked him limpidly. "She only has to look at me to hate me."

*

Later that night Cecil called for fresh candles and another log for the fire. He was writing to Sir James Croft, an old fellow-plotter. Sir James was at Berwick but Cecil had decided that the time had come for him to visit Perth.

Scotland is a tinderbox, he wrote in the code that he and Sir James had used to each other since Mary Tudor's spy service had intercepted their letters, *and John Knox is the spark that will set it alight.*

My commission for you is to go to Perth and do nothing more than observe. You should get there before the forces of the queen regent arrive. My guess is that you will see John Knox preaching the freedom of Scotland to an enthusiastic crowd. I should like to know how enthusiastic and how effective. You will have to make haste because the queen regent's men may arrest him. He and the Scottish Protestant lords have asked for our help but I would know what sort of men they are before I commit the queen. Talk to them, take their measure. If they would celebrate their victory by turning the country against the French, and in alliance with us, they can be encouraged. And let me know at once. Information is a better coin than gold here.

Summer 1559

Robert finally arrived at Denchworth in the early days of June, all smiles and apologies for his absence. He told Amy that he could be excused from court for a few days since the queen, having formally refused the Archduke Ferdinand, was now inseparable from his ambassador, talking all the time about his master, and showing every sign of wishing to change her mind and marry him.

"She is driving Cecil mad," he said, smiling. "No one knows what she intends or wants at all. She has refused him but now she talks about him all the time. She has no time for hunting, and no interest for riding. All she wants to do is to walk with the ambassador or practice her Spanish."

Amy, with no interest in the flirtations of the queen or of her court, merely nodded at the news and tried to turn Robert's attention to the property that she had found. She ordered horses from the stables for Robert, the Hydes, Lizzie Oddingsell, and for herself, and led the way on the pretty cross-country drover's track to the house.

William Hyde found his way to Robert's side. "What news of the realm?" he asked. "I hear that the bishops won't support her."

"They say they won't take the oath confirming her as supreme governor," Robert said briefly. "It is treason, as I tell her. But she is merciful."

"What will she . . . er . . . mercifully do?" Mr. Hyde asked nervously, the burning days of Mary Tudor still very fresh in his memory.

"She'll imprison them," Robert said bluntly. "And replace them with Protestant clergy if she cannot find any Catholics to see reason. They have missed their chance. If they had called in the French before she was crowned they might have turned the country against her, but they have left it too late." He grinned. "Cecil's advice," he said. "He had their measure. One after another of them will cave in or be replaced. They did not have the courage to rise against her with arms; they only stand against her on theological grounds, and Cecil will pick them off."

"But she will destroy the church," William Hyde said, shocked.

"She will break it down and make it new," Dudley, the Protestant, said with pleasure. "She has been forced into a place where it is either the Catholic bishops or her own authority. She will have to destroy them."

"Does she have the strength?"

Dudley raised a dark eyebrow. "It does not take much strength to imprison a bishop, as it turns out. She has half of them under house arrest already."

"I mean strength of mind," William Hyde said. "She is only a woman, even though a queen. Does she have the courage to go against them?"

Dudley hesitated. It was always everyone's fear, since everyone knew that a woman could neither think nor do anything with any consistency. "She is well advised," he said. "And her advisors are good men. We know what has to be done, and we keep her to it."

Amy reined back her horse and joined them.

"Did you tell Her Grace that you were coming to look at a house?" she asked.

"Indeed yes," he said cheerfully as they crested one of the rolling hills. "It's been too long since the Dudleys had a family seat. I tried to buy Dudley Castle from my cousin, but he cannot bear to let it go. Ambrose, my brother, is looking for somewhere too. But perhaps he and his family could have a wing of this place. Is it big enough?"

"There are buildings that could be extended," she said. "I don't see why not."

"And was it a monastic house, or an abbey or something?" he asked. "A good-sized place? You've told me nothing about it. I have been imagining a castle with a dozen pinnacles!"

"It's not a castle," she said, smiling. "But I think it is a very good size for us. The land is in good heart. They have farmed it in the old way, in strips, changing every Michaelmas, so it has not been exhausted. And the higher fields yield good grass for sheep, and there is a very pretty wood that I thought we might thin and cut some rides through. The water meadows are some of the richest I have ever seen, the milk from the cows must be almost solid cream. The house itself is a little too small, of course, but if we added a wing we could house any guests that we had . . ."

She broke off as their party rounded the corner in the narrow lane and Robert saw the farmhouse before him. It was long and low, an animal barn at the west end built of worn red brick and thatched in straw like the house, only a thin wall separating the beasts from the inhabitants. A small tumbling-down stone wall divided the house from the lane and inside it, a flock of hens scratched at what had once been a herb garden but was now mostly weeds and dust. To the side of the ramshackle building, behind the steaming midden, was a thickly planted orchard, boughs leaning down to the ground and a few pigs rooting around. Ducks paddled in the weedy pond beyond the orchard; swallows swooped from pond to barn, building their nests with beakfuls of mud.

The front door stood open, propped with a lump of rock. Robert could glimpse a low, stained ceiling and an uneven floor of stone slabs scattered with stale herbs but the rest of the interior was hidden in the gloom since there were almost no windows, and choked with smoke since there was no chimney but only a hole in the roof.

He turned to Amy and stared at her as if she were a fool, brought to beg for his mercy. "You thought that I would want to live here?" he asked incredulously.

"Just as I predicted," William Hyde muttered quietly and pulled his horse gently away from the group, nodding to his wife for her to come with him, out of earshot.

"Why, yes," Amy said, still smiling confidently. "I know the house is not big enough, but that barn could become another wing, it is high enough to build a floor in the eaves, just as they did at Hever, and then you have bedrooms above and a hall below."

"And what plans did you have for the midden?" he demanded. "And the duck pond?"

"We would clear the midden, of course," she said, laughing at him. "That would never do! It would be the first thing, of course. But we could spread it on the garden and plant some flowers."

"And the duck pond? Is that to become an ornamental lake?"

At last she heard the biting sarcasm in his tone. She turned in genuine surprise. "Don't you like it?"

He closed his eyes and saw at once the doll's-house prettiness of the Dairy House at Kew, and the breakfast served by shepherdesses in the orchard with the tame lambs dyed green and white, skipping around the table. He thought of the great houses of his boyhood, of the serene majesty of Syon House, of Hampton Court, one of his favorite homes and one of the great palaces of Europe, of the Nonsuch at Sheen, or the Palace at Greenwich, of the walled solidity of Windsor, of Dudley Castle, his family seat. Then he opened his eyes and saw, once again, this place that his wife had chosen: a house built of mud on a plain of mud.

"Of course I don't like it. It is a hovel," he said flatly. "My father used to keep his sows in better sties than this."

For once, she did not crumple beneath his disapproval. He had touched her pride, her judgment in land and property.

"It is not a hovel," she replied. "I have been all over it. It is soundly built from brick and lathe and plaster. The thatch is only twenty years old. It needs more windows, for sure, but they are easily made. We would rebuild the barn, we would enclose a pleasure garden, the orchard could be lovely, the pond could be a boating lake, and the land is very good, two hundred acres of prime land. I thought it was just what we wanted, and we could make anything we want here."

"Two hundred acres?" he demanded. "Where are the deer to run? Where is the court to ride?"

She blinked.

"And where will the queen stay?" he demanded acerbically. "In the henhouse, out the back? And the court? Shall we knock up some hovels on the other side of the orchard? Where will the royal cooks prepare her dinner? On that open fire? And where will we stable her horses? Shall they come into the house with us, as clearly they do at present? We can expect about three hundred guests; where do you think they will sleep?"

"Why should the queen come here?" Amy asked, her mouth trembling. "Surely she will stay at Oxford. Why should she want to come here? Why would we ask her here?"

"Because I am one of the greatest men at

her court!" he exclaimed, slamming his fist down on the saddle and making his horse jump and then sidle nervously. He held it on a hard rein, pulling on its mouth. "The queen herself will come and stay at my house to honor me! To honor you, Amy! I asked you to find us a house to buy. I wanted a place like Hatfield, like Theobalds, like Kenning-hall. Cecil goes home to Theobalds Palace, a place as large as a village under one roof; he has a wife who rules it like a queen herself. He is building Burghley to show his wealth and his grandeur; he is shipping in stonemasons from all over Christendom. I am a better man than Cecil, God knows. I come from stock that makes him look like a sheepshearer. I want a house to match his, stone for stone! I want the outward show that matches my achievements.

"For God's sake, Amy, you've stayed with my sister at Penshurst! You know what I expect! I didn't want some dirty farmhouse that we could clean up so that at its best, it was fit for a peasant to breed dogs in!"

She was trembling, hard put to keep her grip on the reins. From a distance, Lizzie Oddingsell watched and wondered if she should intervene.

Amy found her voice. She raised her drooping head. "Well, all very well, husband, but what you don't know is that this farm has a yield of—"

"Damn the yield!" he shouted at her. His horse shied and he jabbed at it with a hard hand. It jibbed and pulled back, frightening Amy's horse who stepped back, nearly unseating her. "I care nothing for the yield! My tenants can worry about the yield. Amy, I am going to be the richest man in England; the queen will pour the treasury of England upon me. I don't care how many haystacks we can make from a field. I ask you to be my wife, to be my hostess at a house which is of a scale and of a grandeur—"

"Grandeur!" she flared up at him. "Are you still running after grandeur? Will you never learn your lesson? There was nothing very grand about you when you came out of the Tower, homeless and hungry; there was nothing very grand about your brother when he died of jail fever like a common criminal. When will you learn that your place is at home, where we might be happy? Why will you insist on running after disaster? You and your father lost the battle for Jane Grey, and it cost him his son and his own life. You lost Calais and came home without your brother and disgraced again! How low do you need to go before you learn your lesson? How base do you have to sink before you Dudleys learn your limits?"

He wheeled his horse and dug his spurs into its sides, wrenching it back with the reins. The horse stood up on its hind legs in a high rear, pawing the air. Robert sat in the saddle like a statue, reining back his rage and his horse with one hard hand. Amy's horse shield away, frightened by the flailing hooves, and she had to cling to the saddle not to fall.

His horse dropped down. "Fling it in my face every day if you please," he hissed at her, leaning forward, his voice filled with hatred. "But I am no longer Sir John Robsart's stupid young son-in-law, out of the Tower and still attainted. I am Sir Robert Dudley once more; I wear the Order of the Garter, the highest order of chivalry there is. I am the queen's Master of Horse, and if you cannot take a pride in being Lady Dudley then you can go back to being Amy Robsart, Sir John Robsart's stupid daughter, once more. But for me: those days are gone."

Fearful of falling from her frightened horse, Amy kicked her feet free and jumped from the saddle. On the safety of the ground she turned and glared up at him as he towered over her, his big horse curvetting to be away. Her temper rose up, flared into her cheeks, burned in her mouth.

"Don't you dare to insult my father," she swore at him. "Don't you dare! He was a better man than you will ever be, and he won his lands by honest work and not by dancing at some heretic bastard's bidding. And don't say yields don't matter! Who are you to say that yields don't matter? You would have starved if my father had not kept his land in good heart, to put food on your plate when you had no way of earning it. You were glad enough of the wool crop then! And don't call me stupid. The only stupid thing I ever did was to believe you and your braggart father when you came riding into Stanfield Hall, and not long after, you were riding into the Tower on a cart as traitors." She was almost gibbering in her rage. "And don't you dare threaten me. I shall be Lady Dudley to the day of my death! I have been through the worst with you when my name was a shame to me. But now neither you nor your heretic pretender can take it away from me."

"She can take it away," he said bitingly. "Fool that you are. She can take it away to-morrow, if she wants it. She's supreme governor of the church of England. She can take away your marriage if she wants it and better women than you have been divorced for less than this . . . this . . . shite-house pipe dream."

His big horse reared, Amy ducked away, and Sir Robert let the horse go, tearing up the earth with its big hooves, thundering away along the lane, leaving them in a sudden silence.

*   *   *

When they got home there was a man in the stable yard waiting for Robert Dudley. "Urgent message," he said to William Hyde. "Can you send a groom to guide me to where I might find him?"

William Hyde's square face creased with concern. "I don't know where he might be," he said. "He went for a ride. Will you come into the house and take a cup of ale while you're waiting?"

"I'll follow him," the man said. "His lordship likes his messages delivered at once."

"I don't know which direction he took," William said tactfully. "You'd better come inside to wait."

The man shook his head. "I'd be obliged to you for a drink out here, but I'll wait here for him."

He sat on the mounting block and did not shift until the sun dropped lower in the sky, until finally he heard the clip-clop of hooves and Robert rode up the lane and into the stable yard and tossed the reins of his weary horse to a waiting groom.

"Blount?"

"Sir Robert."

Robert drew him to one side, his rage with Amy all forgotten. "Must be important?"

"Sir William Pickering is back in England."

"Pickering? The queen's old flirt?"

"He was not sure if he would be welcomed, not sure how long her memory would be. There were rumors that he had served her sister. He did not know what she might have heard."

"She would have heard everything," Dudley said dourly. "You can trust to me and Cecil for that. Anyway, did she welcome him?"

"She saw him alone."

"What? A private audience? She saw him in private? Dear God, he's honored."

"No, I mean alone. Completely alone. For all the afternoon, five hours he was locked up with her."

"With her women in attendance," Robert stated.

The spy shook his head. "Completely alone, sir. Just the two of them. Five hours behind a closed door, before they came out."

Robert was staggered at a privilege that he had never had. "Cecil allowed this?" he demanded incredulously.

Thomas Blount shrugged. "I don't know, sir. He must have done, for the next day she saw Sir William again."

"Alone?"

"All the afternoon. From noon till dinner time. They are taking bets on him being her husband. He's the favorite; he's overtaken the archduke. They are saying that they've wedded and bedded in private, all that is lacking is an announcement."

Robert exclaimed and whirled away, and then turned back. "And what does he do now? Is he to stay at court?"

"He is the favorite. She has given him a suite of rooms near to hers in Greenwich Palace."

"How near?"

"They say there is a passageway that he can go to her at any time of the night or day. She has only to unlock the door and he can walk into her bedchamber."

Robert suddenly became very still and calm. He glanced at his horse as the groom walked it up and down the yard, noting the sweat on its neck and the foam at its mouth, as if he were contemplating starting his journey at once.

"No," he said softly to himself. "Better tomorrow, rested with a clear head. With a rested horse. Any other news?"

"That the Protestants are rioting against the French regent in Scotland, and she is massing her soldiers, calling for more men from France."

"I knew that before I left court," Robert said. "Does Cecil work on the queen to send support?"

"Still," the man said. "But she says nothing either one way or the other."

"Too busy with Pickering, I suppose," Robert said sourly, and turned to go into the house. "You can wait here and ride back with me tomorrow," he said shortly. "I obviously cannot risk being away for even a moment. We leave for Greenwich at first light. Tell my people that we leave at dawn and that we will ride hard."

*   *   *

Amy, sick with tears, was waiting, as humble as any petitioner, outside the door of Robert's privy chamber. She had seen him ride in on his lathered horse, and had hovered on the stairs hoping to speak to him. He had gone past her with a brief, courteous word of apology. He had washed and changed his clothes; she had heard the clink of jug against bowl. Then he had gone into his privy chamber, closed the door, and was clearly packing his books and his papers. Amy guessed that he was leaving, and she did not dare to knock on his door and beg him to stay.

Instead she waited outside, perched on the plain wooden window seat, like an apologetic child waiting to see an angry father.

When he opened the door she leapt to her feet and he saw her in the shadows. For a moment he had quite forgotten the quarrel, then his dark, thick eyebrows snapped together in a scowl. "Amy."

"My lord!" she said; the tears flooded into her eyes and she could not speak. She could only stand dumbly before him.

"Oh, for God's sake," he said impatiently and kicked open the door of his room with his booted foot. "You had better come in before the whole world thinks that I beat you."

She went before him into his room. As she had feared, it was stripped of all the papers and books that he had brought. Clearly, he was packed and ready to leave.

"You're not going?" she said, her voice tremulous.

"I have to," he said. "I had a message from court; there is some business which demands my attention, at once."

"You are going because you are angry with me," she whispered.

"No, I am going because I had a message from court. Ask William Hyde, he saw the messenger and told him to wait for me."

"But you *are* angry with me," she persisted.

"I was," he said honestly. "But now I am sorry for my temper. I am not leaving because of the house, nor what I said. There are things at court that I have to attend to."

"My lord . . ."

"You shall stay here for another month, perhaps two, and when I write to you, you can move to the Hayes' at Chislehurst. I will come and see you there."

"Am I not to find us a house here?"

"No," he said shortly. "Clearly, we have very different ideas as to what a house should be like. We will have to have a long conversation about how you wish to live and what I need. But I cannot discuss this now. Right now I have to go to the stables. I will see you at dinner. I shall leave at dawn tomorrow; there is no need for you to rise to see me off. I am in a hurry."

"I should not have said what I said. I am most sorry, Robert."

His face tightened. "It is forgotten."

"I can't forget it," she said earnestly, pressing him with her contrition. "I am sorry, Robert. I should not have mentioned your disgrace and your father's shame."

He took a breath, trying to hold back his sense of outrage. "It would be better if we forgot that quarrel, and did not repeat it," he cautioned her, but she would not be cautioned.

"Please, Robert, I should not have said what I did about you chasing after grandeur and not knowing your place—"

"Amy, I *do* remember what you said!" he broke in. "There is no need for you to remind me. There is no need to repeat the insult. I do remember every word and that you spoke loud enough for William Hyde, his wife, and your companion to hear it too. I don't doubt that they all heard you abuse me, and my father. I don't forget you named him as a failed traitor and blamed me for the loss of Calais. You blamed him for the death of my brother Guilford and me for the death of my brother Henry. If you were one of my servants I would have you whipped and turned away for saying half of that. I'd have your tongue slit for scandal. You would do better not to remind me, Amy. I have spent most of this day trying to forget your opinion of me. I have been trying to forget that I live with a wife who despises me as an unsuccessful traitor."

"It's not my opinion," she gasped. She was on the floor kneeling at his feet in one smooth movement, hammered down by his anger. "I do not despise you. It is not my opinion; I love you, Robert, and I trust you—"

"You taunted me with the death of my brother," he said coldly. "Amy, I do not want to quarrel with you. Indeed, I will not. You must excuse me now; I have to see about something in the stables before I go to dinner."

He swept her a shallow bow and went from the room. Amy scrambled up from her subservient crouch on the floor and ran to the door. She would have torn it open and gone after him but when she heard the brisk stride of his boots on the wooden floor she did not dare. Instead she pressed her hot forehead to the cool paneling of the door and wrapped her hands around the handle, where his hand had been.

* * *

Dinner was a meal where good manners overlaid discomfort. Amy sat in stunned silence, eating nothing; William Hyde and Robert maintained a pleasant flow of conversation about horses and hunting and the prospect of war with the French. Alice Hyde kept her head down, and Lizzie watched Amy as if she feared she would faint at the table. The ladies withdrew as soon as they could after dinner and Robert, pleading an early start, left soon after. William Hyde took himself into his privy chamber, poured himself a generous tumbler of wine, turned his big wooden chair to the fire, put his feet up on the chimney breast, and fell to considering the day.

His wife, Alice, put her head round the door and came quietly into the room, followed by her sister-in-law. "Has he gone?" she asked, determined not to meet with Sir Robert again, if she could avoid him.

"Aye. You can take a chair, Alice, Sister, and pour yourselves your wine if you please."

They served themselves and drew up their chairs beside his, in a conspiratorial semicircle around the fire.

"Is that the end of his plans to build here?" William asked Lizzie Oddingsell.

"I don't know," she said quietly. "All she told me was that he is very angry with her, and that we're to stay here another month."

A quick glance between William and Alice showed that this had been a matter of some discussion. "I think he won't build," he said. "I think all she showed him today was how far apart they have become. Poor, silly woman. I think she has dug her own grave."

Lizzie quickly crossed herself. "God's sake, brother! What do you mean? They had a quarrel. You show me a man and wife who have not had cross words."

"This is not an ordinary man," he said emphatically. "You heard him, just as she heard him, but neither of you have the wit to learn. He told her to her face: he is the greatest man in the kingdom. He stands to be the wealthiest man in the kingdom. He has the full attention of the queen; she is always in his company. He is indispensable to the first spinster queen this country has ever known. What d'you think that might mean? Think it out for yourself."

"It means he will want a country estate," Lizzie Oddingsell pursued. "As he rises at court. He will want a great estate for his wife and for his children, when they come, please God."

"Not for this wife," Alice said shrewdly. "What has she ever done but be a burden to him? She does not want what he wants: not the house, not the life. She accuses him of ambition when that is his very nature, his blood and his bone."

Lizzie would have argued to defend Amy, but William hawked and spat into the fire. "It does not matter if she pleases him or fails him," he said flatly. "He has other plans now."

"Do you think he means to put her aside?" Alice asked her husband.

Lizzie looked from the one grave face to the other. "What?"

"You heard him," William said to her patiently. "Like her, you hear him; but you don't attend. He is a man rising far from her."

"But they are married," she insisted uncomprehendingly. "Married in the sight of God. He cannot put her aside. He has no reason."

"The king put two wives aside for no reason," William Hyde said grimly. "And half the nobility have divorced their wives. Every Roman Catholic priest in England who married during the Protestant years had to put his wife aside when Queen Mary came to the throne, and now perhaps the Protestant clergy will have to do the same. The old laws do not stand. Everything can be remade. Marriage does not mean marriage now."

"The church . . ."

"The head of the church is the queen. Act of parliament. No denying it. What if the head of the church wants Sir Robert to be a single man once more?"

Lizzie Oddingsell's face was bleached with shock. "Why ever would she?" She dared him to name the reason.

"To marry him herself." Mr. Hyde's voice dropped to a low whisper.

Lizzie put down her wineglass, very slowly, and clasped her hands in her lap to stop them shaking. When she looked up she saw that her brother's face was not drawn like hers, but bright with suppressed excitement.

"What if our lord were to be the King of England?" he whispered. "Forget Amy for a moment, she has signed the warrant for her own exile, he will give up on her now, she is no use to him. But think about Sir Robert! Think about us! What if he were to be King of England! What would that mean for us? What of that, Sister?"

*   *   *

Amy waited in the porch of the church in the early hours of the morning for Father Wilson to come and unlock the great wooden doors. When he came up the churchyard path and saw her, pale in her white dress against the silvery wood door, he said nothing but gave her a slow, sweet smile and opened the door to her in silence.

"Father?" she said softly.

"Tell it to God and then to me," he said gently, and let her go in before him.

He waited at the back of the church, busying himself quietly until she rose from her knees and sat in the pew seat, and only then did he go to her. "Trouble?" he asked.

"I have angered my husband on another matter," she said simply. "And so I failed to plead for our bishop."

He nodded. "Don't reproach yourself for that," he said. "I think there is nothing any of us can do. The queen is to be called supreme governor of the church. All the bishops have to bow down to her."

"Supreme governor?" Amy repeated. "But how can she?"

"They say that she does no more than claim the title of her brother and her father," he said. "They don't say that she is a woman and filled with a woman's frailties. They don't say how a woman, bound by God to be the handmaiden to her husband, cursed by God for the first sin, can be supreme governor."

"What will happen?" Amy asked in a little thread of sound.

"I am afraid she will burn the bishops," he said steadily. "Already Bishop Bonner is arrested, and one by one, as they refuse to kneel to her, the others will be taken."

"And our bishop? Bishop Thomas?"

"He will go like the others, like a lamb to the slaughter," the priest said. "A great darkness is going to come over this country and you and I, daughter, can do nothing more than pray."

"If I can speak to Robert, I will," she promised. She hesitated, remembering his rapid departure, and the rage in his voice. "He is a great man now, but he knows what it is to be a prisoner, in fear of your life. He is merciful. He will not advise the queen to destroy these holy men."

"God bless you," the priest said. "There will be few who dare to speak."

"And what about you?" she asked. "Will you have to take an oath as well?"

"Once they have finished with the bishops they will come for men like me," he said certainly. "And I shall have to be ready. If I can stay, I will. I am sworn to serve these people, this is my parish, this is my flock. The good shepherd does not leave his sheep. But if they want me to take an oath which says that she is Pope then I don't see how I can do it. The words would choke me. I will have to take my punishment as better men than me are doing now."

"They will murder you for your faith?"

He spread out his hands. "If they must."

"Father, what will become of us all?" Amy asked.

He shook his head. "I wish I knew."

*   *   *

Robert Dudley, storming into court in no very sweet temper, found the place strangely quiet. The presence chamber held only a sprinkling of ladies and gentlemen of the court, and a handful of lesser gentry.

"Where is everyone?" he demanded of Laetitia Knollys, who was seated in a window bay ostentatiously reading a book of sermons.

"I am here," she said helpfully.

He scowled at her. "I meant anyone of any importance."

"Still me," she said, not at all dashed. "Still here."

Reluctantly, he laughed. "Mistress Knollys, do not try my patience, I have had a long hard ride from one damnably stubborn and stupid woman to another. Do not you make a third."

"Oh?" she said, opening her dark eyes very wide. "Who has been so unfortunate as to offend you, Sir Robert? Not your wife?"

"No one that need concern you. Where is the queen?"

"Out with Sir William Pickering. He has returned to England, did you know?"

"Of course I knew. We are old friends."

"Don't you adore him? I think he is the most handsome man I have ever seen in my life."

"Absolutely," Dudley said. "Are they riding?"

"No, walking. It's more intimate, don't you think?"

"Why aren't you with them?"

"Nobody is with them."

"Her other ladies?"

"No. Really, nobody. She and Sir William are quite alone today as they have been for the last three days. We all think it's a certainty."

"It?"

"Their betrothal. She cannot keep her eyes off him. He cannot keep his hands off her. It's such a love story. Like a ballad. It is Guinevere and Arthur, it truly is!"

"She will never marry him," Dudley said, with more certainty than he was feeling.

"Why should she not? He's the best-looking man in Europe, he's as rich as an emperor, he has no interest in politics or power so she can rule as she wants, and he has neither enemies in England nor a wife. I would have thought he was perfect."

Robert turned from her, unable to speak for rage, and almost collided with Sir William Cecil. "Your pardon, Lord Secretary. I was just leaving."

"I thought you had just arrived."

"Leaving to go to my rooms," Robert said, biting the inside of his mouth to contain his temper.

"I am glad you are back," Cecil said, walking beside him. "We have needed your counsel."

"I thought no work had been done at all."

"Your counsel with the queen," Cecil said flatly. "This whirlwind courtship may suit Her Grace, but I am not sure if it is beneficial for the country."

"Have you told her that?"

"Not I!" Cecil said with a little chuckle. "She is a young woman in love. I rather thought you might tell her."

"Why me?"

"Well, not tell her. I thought you might distract her. Divert her. Remind her that there are many handsome men in the world. She does not have to marry the first one that comes free."

"I'm a married man," Robert said bleakly. "In case you forgot. I can hardly compete with a bachelor dripping in gold."

"You are right to remind me," Cecil said blandly, charging tack. "Because if he marries her both of us will be able to go home to our wives. He won't want us advising her. He will put in his own favorites. Our work at court will be over. I can go home to Burghley at last, and you can go home to . . ." He broke off, if surprised to remember that Robert had no great family estate. "Wherever you choose, I suppose."

"I will hardly build a Burghley with my present savings," Dudley said furiously.

"No. Perhaps it would be better for both of us if Pickering were to have a rival. If he were to be troubled. If he were not to have everything quite his own way. Easy for him to be smiling and pleasant when he rides a straight road without competition."

Dudley sighed, as a man weary of nonsense. "I am going to my rooms."

"Shall I see you at dinner?"

"Of course I shall come to dinner."

Cecil smiled. "I am very glad to see you back at court," he said sweetly.

*   *   *

The queen sent a dish of venison down the hall to Sir William Pickering's table, and, even-handed, sent a very good game pie to Robert Dudley's table. When the boards had been cleared and the musicians struck up she danced with one man and then the other. Sir William sulked after a little of this treatment; but Robert Dudley was at his most debonair, and the queen was radiant. Robert Dudley stood up for a dance with Laetitia Knollys and had the pleasure of hearing the Spanish ambassador remark to the queen what a handsome couple they were together. He watched the queen pale with anger. Shortly after, she called for a pack of cards and Dudley bet her the pearl in his hat that he would have won on points by midnight. The two went head to head as if there were no one else in the room, no one else in the world; and Sir William Pickering retired early to bed.

July 1st 1559

Dear William,

Sir Nicholas Throckmorton, ambassador to Paris, addressed Cecil in a coded letter, freshly delivered by a hard-pressed messenger.

Incredible news. The king has, this very day, been wounded in a jousting tournament and the surgeons are with him now. The word I hear is that they are not hopeful; the blow may be fatal. If he dies, there is no doubt that the kingdom of France will be ruled in everything but name by the Guise family, and no doubt but that they will immediately send forces to strengthen their kinswoman Mary of Guise in Scotland, and move on to conquer England for her daughter, Mary, Queen of Scots. Given their wealth, power, and determination (and the justice of their claim in the eyes of all Roman Catholics), given the weakness, division, and uncertainty of our poor country, ruled by a young woman not long on the throne, with a debatable legitimacy, and without an heir, I think there can be no doubt of the outcome.

For God's sake, for all of our sakes, beg the queen to muster our troops and prepare to defend the borders or we are lost. If she does not fight this battle she will lose her kingdom without a struggle. As it is, I doubt that she can win. I shall send to you the moment that the king dies. Pray God that he rallies, for without him we are lost. I warn you that I do not expect it.

Nicholas.

William Cecil read the letter through twice and then pushed it gently into the hottest part of the fire in his privy chamber. Then he sat with his head in his hands for a long time. It seemed to him that England's future lay in the hands of the surgeons who were, at this very moment, struggling to keep King Henry II of France's breath in his failing body. The safety of England had been guaranteed at the peace of Cateau-Cambrésis by this king. Without him, there was no guarantor, there was no guarantee, there was no safety. If he died then the avaricious ruling family of France would ride their merciless cavalry through Scotland and then through all of England.

There was a knock at the door. "Yes?" Cecil said calmly, no trace of his fear in his voice.

It was his steward. "A messenger," he said shortly.

"Send him in."

The man came in, travel-stained, and walking with the stiff bow-legged stride of a rider who has spent days in the saddle. Cecil recognized Sir James Croft's most trusted servant and spy.

"William! I am glad to see you. Take a seat."

The man nodded at the courtesy and lowered himself gingerly into the chair. "Blisters," he said by way of an explanation. "Burst and bleeding. My lord said it was important."

Cecil nodded, waited.

"He said to tell you that all hell broke lose at Perth, that the French queen regent could not overcome the spirit of the Protestant lords. He said his bet is that she will never be able to get her troops to stand against them. They don't have the heart for it and the Protestant Scots are wild for a fight."

Cecil nodded.

"The Protestants are tearing the abbeys down all the way on the road to Edinburgh. Word is that the captain of Edinburgh Castle won't take sides; he'll bar the castle gates against them both until law is returned. My lord's own belief is that the queen regent will have to fall back on Leith Castle. He said if you are minded to take a gamble, he would put his fortune on Knox's men; that they are unbeatable while their blood is up."

Cecil waited in case there was any more.

"That's all."

"I thank you," Cecil said. "And what did you think of them yourself? Did you see much fighting?"

"I thought they were savage beasts," the man said bluntly. "And I would want them neither as allies nor as enemies."

Cecil smiled at him. "These are our noble allies," he said firmly. "And we shall pray every day for their success in their noble battle."

"They are wanton destroyers; they are a plague of locusts," the man said stoutly.

"They will defeat the French for us," Cecil prompted him, with more confidence than any sensible man would own. "If anyone asks you, they are on the side of the angels. Don't forget it."

*   *   *

That night, with Cecil's grave news beating a rhythm of fear into her very temples, Elizabeth refused to dance with either Sir William Pickering or Sir Robert Dudley, who eyed each other like two cats on a stable roof. What use was William Pickering or Robert Dudley when the French king was dying and his heirs were mustering an expedition to England, with the excuse of a war with the Scots to hand? What use was any Englishman, however charming, however desirable?

Robert Dudley smiled at her; she could hardly see him through the haze of pain behind her eyes. Simply, she shook her head at him and turned away. She beckoned the Austrian ambassador to take a chair beside her throne and to talk to her of Archduke Ferdinand, who would come with all the power of Spain at his back and who was the only man who might bring with him a big enough army to keep England safe for her.

"You know, I have no liking for the single state," Elizabeth said softly to the ambassador, ignoring Sir William's goggle-eyed glare at her. "I have only waited, as any sensible maid would do, for the right man."

*   *   *

Robert was planning a great tournament for when they returned to Greenwich, the last celebration before the court went on its summer progress. On his long refectory table in his pretty house at Kew, he had a scroll of paper unrolled, and his clerk was pairing the knights who would joust against each other. It was to be a tournament of roses, Robert had decided. There would be a bower of roses for the queen to sit in, with the red rose of Lancaster and the white rose of York and the Galicia rose which combined both colors and resolved the ancient enmity between England's greatest counties, as the Tudors themselves had done. There would be rose petals, scattered by children dressed in rose pink before the queen when she walked from the palace door at Greenwich down to the tilt yard. The yard itself was to be blazoned with roses and all the contenders had been told that they were to incorporate roses into their poetry, or into their arms, or armor.

There would be a tableau greeting Elizabeth as the Queen of the Roses and she would be crowned with a chaplet of rosebuds. They would eat sugared rose comfits and there would be a water fight with rose water; the very air would be scented with the amorous perfume; the tilt yard would be carpeted with petals.

The joust was to be the central event of the day. Dudley was painfully aware that Sir William Pickering was a powerful rival for the queen's affections, a blond, well-made, rich bachelor, widely read, well traveled, and well educated. He had intense charm; a smile from his dark blue eyes sent most women into a flutter, and the queen was always vulnerable to a commanding man. He had all the confidence of a man wealthy from boyhood, who came from wealthy and powerful parents. He had never been as low as Robert; he did not even know that a man could sink so low, and his whole bearing, his easy charm, his sunny disposition all showed a man to whom life had been

kind and who believed that the future would
be as blessed as the past.

Worst of all, from Dudley's point of view,
there was nothing to stop the queen marrying him tomorrow. She could drink a glass
of wine too many, she could be teased a little too hard, she could be aroused and engaged and provoked—and Pickering was a
master of subtle seduction—then he could
offer her a priceless diamond ring, and his
fortune, and the job would be done. The
gambling men were putting odds on Sir
William marrying the queen by autumn and
her constant ripple of laughter in his presence, and her amused tolerance of his rising
pride, gave everyone reason to believe that
his big blond style was more to her taste
than Dudley's dark good looks.

Robert had suffered many rivals for her
attention since she had come to the throne.
Elizabeth was a flirt and anyone with a valuable gift or a handsome smile could have
her evanescent attention. But Sir William
was a greater risk than these passing fan-
cies. He was phenomenally rich and Elizabeth, with a purse full of lightweight coins
and an empty treasury, found his wealth
very attractive. He had been a friend of hers

from the earliest days and she treasured fidelity, especially in men who had plotted to put her on the throne, however incompetent they had been. But more than anything else, he was handsome and new-come to court, and an English Protestant bachelor, so when she danced with him and they were the center of gossip and speculation, it was good-natured. The court smiled on the two of them. There was no one reminding her that he was a married man or a convicted traitor, or muttering that she must be mad to favor him. And although Dudley's rapid return to court had disturbed Sir William's smooth rise to favor and power, it had not prevented it. The queen was shamelessly delighted to have the two most desirable men in England competing for her attention.

Dudley was hoping to use the joust to unseat Sir William with one hard blow, preferably to his handsome face or thick head, and was drawing up the jousting list to ensure that Pickering and he would meet in the final round. He was absorbed in the work when suddenly his door banged open without a knock. Robert leapt up, his hand reaching for his dagger, heart thudding, knowing that at last the worst thing had happened: an uprising, an assassin.

It was the queen, quite alone, without a single attendant, white as a rose herself, who flung herself into the room toward him and said three words: "Robert! Save me!"

At once he snatched her to him and held her close. He could feel her gasping for breath; she had run all the way from the palace to the Dairy House, and run up the steps to his front door.

"What is it, my love?" he asked urgently. "What is it?"

"A man," she gasped. "Following me."

With his arm still around her waist he took his sword from where it hung on the hook, and threw open the door. Two of his men were outside, aghast at the queen's dashing past them.

"Seen anyone?" Robert asked tersely.

"No one, sir."

"Go and search." He turned to the fainting woman. "What did he look like?"

"Well dressed, brown suit, like a London merchant, but he dogged my feet while I was walking in my garden down to the river and when I went faster he came on, and when I ran he ran behind me, and I thought that he was a Papist, come to kill me . . ." She lost her breath for fear.

Robert turned to his stunned clerk. "Go with them, call out the guard and the Queen's Pensioners. Tell them to look for a man in a brown suit. Check the river first. If he is away in a boat, take a boat and follow him. I want him alive. I want him now." Robert sent the men off, and then drew Elizabeth back into the house, into his drawing room, and slammed the door and bolted it.

Gently, he put her into a chair and closed the shutters and bolted them. He unsheathed his sword and laid it to hand, on the table.

"Robert, I thought he had come for me. I thought he would murder me, where I walked in my own garden."

"You're safe now, my love," he said gently. He knelt beside her chair and took her hand. She was icy cold. "You are safe with me."

"I didn't know what to do, I didn't know where to run. I could only think of you."

"Quite right. You did quite right, and you were very brave to run."

"I wasn't!" she wailed suddenly, like a child.

Robert lifted her from the chair and drew her onto his knees. She buried her face in his neck and he felt her sweaty face and the wetness of her tears. "Robert, I wasn't brave at all. I wasn't like a queen at all; I was like a nothing. I was as full of fear as a market girl. I couldn't call for my guards, I couldn't scream. I didn't even think to turn and challenge him. I just went faster, and when he went faster, I went faster.

"I could hear his footsteps coming behind me faster and faster and all I could do . . ." She burst into another wail. "I feel such a child! I feel like I am such a fool! Anyone would think that I was the daughter of a lute player . . ."

The enormity of that shocked her into silence, and she raised her tearstained face from his shoulder. "Oh, God," she said brokenly.

Steadily, lovingly, he met her eyes, smiled at her. "No one will think anything of you, for no one will know," he said softly. "This is between us two and no one else will ever know."

She caught her breath on a sob and nodded.

"And no one, even if they knew, could

blame you for being afraid, if a man comes after you. You know the danger that you are in, every day. Any woman would be afraid, and you are a woman, and a beautiful woman as well as a queen."

Instinctively, she twisted a tendril of hair and tucked it back behind her ear. "I should have turned on him and challenged him."

Robert shook his head. "You did exactly the right thing. He could have been a madman; he could have been anyone. The wisest thing to do was to come and find me, and here you are, safe. Safe with me."

She nestled a little closer to him and he tightened his arms around her. "And no one could ever doubt your fathering," he said into her red hair. "You are a Tudor from your clever copper head down to your swift little feet. You are my Tudor princess and you always will be. I knew your father, remember, I remember how he used to look at you and call you his best girl Bessie. I was there. I can hear his voice now. He loved you as his true-born daughter and heir, and he knew you were his, and now you are mine."

Elizabeth tipped her head back at him, her dark eyes trusting, her mouth starting to curve upward in a smile. "Yours?"

"Mine," he said certainly and his mouth came down on hers and he kissed her deeply.

She did not resist for one moment. Her terror and then the feel of safety with him were as potent as a love potion. He could smell the sweat of her fear and the new scent of her arousal, and he went from her lips to her neck and down to the top of her gown, where her breasts pressed tight against the laced bodice as she panted lightly. He rubbed his face against her neck, and she felt the roughness of his chin and the eager licking of his tongue and she laughed and caught her breath all at once.

Then his hands were in her hair, slipping out the pins, and taking a handful of the great tumbling locks and pulling her head back so that he could have her mouth once more and this time he tasted of her own sweat, salty on his mouth. He bit her, licked her, filled her with the heat of his desire and with the very taste of him as he salivated as if she were a dish he would devour.

He rose up from the chair with her in his arms and she clung to his neck as he swept the scroll from the table and laid her on it, and then climbed up, like a stallion covering a mare, onto her. His thigh was pushing between her legs, his hands pulling up her gown so that he could touch her, and Elizabeth melted under his touch, pulled him closer to her, opened his mouth for his kisses, ravenous for the feel of him everywhere.

"My gown!" she cried in frustration.

"Sit up," he commanded. She did as he obeyed and twisted around, offering the laces on the back of the tight stomacher. He struggled with the threaded laces and then pulled it off her and threw it aside. With a groan of utter desire he buried his hands, and then his face, in her linen shift to feel the heat of her belly through the thin fabric, and the rounded firm curves of her breasts.

He threw off his own doublet and tore off his shirt and pressed down on her once more, his chest against her face as if he would smother her with his body, and he felt her sharp little teeth graze his nipple as her tongue lapped at the hairs on his chest and she rubbed her face against him, like a wanton cat.

His fingers fumbled at the ties of her skirt, and then, losing patience, he took the laces and with one swift tug, broke them and pushed her skirt down from her waist so that he could get his hand on her.

At his first touch she moaned and arched her back, pushing herself against his palm. Robert pulled back, unlaced his breeches, pulled them down, and heard her gasp as she saw the strength and power of him, and then her sigh of longing as he came toward her.

There was a loud hammering on the front door. "Your Grace!" came an urgent shout. "Are you safe?"

"Knock down the door!" someone commanded.

With a whimper, Elizabeth rolled away from him and flew across the room, snatching up her stomacher. "Lace me!" she whispered urgently, pressing the tight garment against her throbbing breasts, and turning her back to him.

Robert was pulling up his breeches and tying the ties. "The queen is here, and safe with me, Robert Dudley," he called, his voice unnaturally loud. "Who is there?"

"Thank God. I'm the commander of the watch, Sir Robert. I will take the queen back to her rooms."

"She is . . ." Dudley fumbled with the lacing of Elizabeth's gown and then thrust the laces into any holes he could manage and tied it up. From the front she looked quite presentable. "She is coming. Wait there. How many men have you?"

"Ten, sir."

"Leave eight to guard the door and go and fetch ten more," Robert said, buying time. "I will take no risks with Her Grace."

"Yes, sir."

They ran off. Elizabeth bent her head and tied what was left of the strings at the waistband of her skirt. Robert snatched up his doublet and pulled it on.

"Your hair," he whispered.

"Can you find my pins?"

She was twisting it into bronze ringlets and tucking it under the ebony combs that had survived his embrace. Robert dropped to his knees on the floor and hunted for pins under the bench and under the table and came up with four or five. Swiftly, she speared them into her hair, and pinned her hood on top.

"How do I look?"

He moved toward her. "Irresistible."

She clapped her hand over her mouth so that the men waiting outside should not hear her laugh. "Would you know what I had been doing?"

"At once."

"For shame! Would anyone else know?"

"No. They will expect you to look as though you have been running."

She put out her hand to him. "Don't come any closer," she said unsteadily when he stepped forward. "Just hold my hand."

"My love, I must have you."

"And I you," she breathed as they heard the tramp of the guard coming to the door.

"Sir Robert?"

"Aye?"

"I am here with twenty men."

"Stand back from the door," Robert said. He took up his sword and opened the drawing-room door, and then unbolted the front door. Carefully, he opened it a crack. The queen's men were outside, he recognized them, he threw open the door. "She is safe," he said, letting them see her. "I have her safe."

To a man they dropped to their knees.

"Thank God," said the commander. "Shall I escort you to your chambers, Your Grace?"

"Yes," she said quietly. "Sir Robert, you

will dine with me in my privy chamber tonight."

He bowed politely. "As you command, Your Grace."

*   *   *

"He was upset, because he was disappointed," Amy said suddenly at dinner to her hosts, as if she were continuing a conversation, though they had been eating in silence. William Hyde glanced at his wife; this was not the first time that Amy had tried to convince them that what they had seen was a small tiff between a comfortably married couple. As if she were trying to convince herself.

"I had been so foolish as to make him think that the place was finished, ready for us to move into this summer. Now he will have to stay at court, and go on progress with the queen. Of course he was disappointed."

"Oh yes," said Lizzie Oddingsell in loyal support.

"I misunderstood him," Amy continued. She gave an awkward little laugh. "You will think me a fool but I was still thinking of the plans we made when we were first married, when we were little more than children. I was thinking of a little manor house, and some rich meadows around it. And of course, now he needs more than that."

"Will you look for a bigger estate?" Alice Hyde asked curiously.

Lizzie glanced up from her place and gave her sister-in-law a sharp look.

"Of course," Amy said with simple dignity. "Our plans are unchanged. It was my mistake that I did not understand quite what my lord had in mind. But now that I know, I shall set about finding it for us. He needs a grand house set in beautiful parkland with good tenant farms. I shall find it for him, and I shall commission builders, and I shall see it built for him."

"You'll be busy," William Hyde said pleasantly.

"I shall do my duty as his wife," she said seriously, "as God has called me to do, and I shall not fail him."

*   *   *

Elizabeth and Dudley sat opposite each other at a table laid for two and ate breakfast in her privy chamber at Greenwich Palace, as they had done every morning since their return from Kew. Something had changed between them that everyone could see but no one could understand. Elizabeth did not even understand it herself. It had not been the sudden leaping up of her passion for Dudley; she had wanted him before, she wanted other men before, she was used to curbing her desires with a heavy hand. It was that she had run to him for safety. Instinctively, with a court of men bound to serve her, with Cecil's spies somewhere in her chamber, she had taken to her heels at the first sign of threat and run to Dudley as the only man she could trust.

Then she had wept in her terror like a child, and he had comforted her like a childhood friend. She would not speak of it to him, nor to anyone. She would not even think of it herself. But she knew that something had changed. She had showed herself and she had showed him that he was her only friend.

They were far from alone. Three servers waited on them, the server of the ewery stood behind the queen's chair, a page stood at each end of the table, four ladies-in-waiting sat in a little cluster in the window embrasure, a trio of musicians played, and a chorister from the queen's chapel sang love songs. Robert had to quell his desire, his frustration, and his anger as he saw that his royal mistress had walled herself in against him once more.

He chatted to her politely over the meal, with the easy intimacy that he could always summon, and with all the warmth that he genuinely felt for her. Elizabeth, returning to her confidence after her fright, delighting in the thrill of Robert's touch, laughed, smiled on him, flirted with him, patted his hand, pulled at his sleeve, let her little slippered foot slide to his under the shield of the table, but never once suggested that they should send the people away and be alone.

Robert, apparently unperturbed by desire, made a hearty breakfast, touched his lips with his napkin, held out his fingers to be washed and patted dry by the server, and then rose from the table.

"I must take my leave of you, Your Grace."

She was amazed, and she could not hide it. "You're going so early?"

"I am to meet a few men in the tilt yard, we are practicing for the joust of the roses. You would not want me unhorsed in the first tilt."

"No, but I thought you would sit with me for the rest of the morning."

He hesitated. "Whatever you command."

She frowned. "I would not keep you from your horse, Sir Robert."

He took her hand and bowed over it.

"You were not so quick to let me go when we were together in your rooms at Kew," she whispered to him as she had him close.

"You wanted me then as a woman wants a man, and that is how I want to come to you," he said, as fast as a striking snake. "But since then you have summoned me as a courtier and a queen. If that is what you want, I am at your service too, Your Grace. Always. Of course."

It was like a game of chess; he saw her turn her head and puzzle how she could outwit him.

"But I will always be queen," she said. "You will always be my courtier."

"I would want nothing less," he said, and then he whispered, so she had to lean forward to hear him, "but I long for so much more, Elizabeth."

She could smell the clean male scent of him and he felt her hand tremble in his. It took an effort for her to make herself move away, sit back in her chair, and let him go. He knew what it cost her; he had known women before who could not bear to lose a moment of his touch. He smiled at her, his dark, saturnine, knowing smile, and then bowed low, and went toward the door.

"Whatever you command, you know you will always be queen of my heart." He bowed again, his cloak swirled from his shoulders as he turned and he was gone.

*   *   *

Elizabeth let him go, but she could not settle without him. She called for her lute and she tried to play but she had no patience for it, and when a string broke she could not even be troubled to retune it. She stood at her writing table and read the memoranda that Cecil had sent her but his grave words of warning about Scotland made no sense. She knew that there was much that she should do, that the situation with the currency was desperate, and that the threat to Scotland and to England was a real and pressing one, the French king was on his deathbed and once he died then the safety of England died too; but she could not think. She put her hand to her head and cried: "I have a fever! A fever!"

At once they were all over her, the ladies fluttered around her, Kat Ashley was called and Blanche Parry. She was put to bed, she turned from their attentions, she could bear no one to touch her. "Close the shutters, the light burns my eyes!" she exclaimed.

They would send for physicians. "I will see no one," she said.

They would prepare a cooling draught, a soothing draught, a sleeping draught. "I want nothing!" she almost screamed with her irritation. "Just go! I want no one to watch me. I don't even want anyone outside my door. Wait in my presence chamber; I don't even want anyone in my privy chamber. I shall sleep. I must not be disturbed."

Like a troubled dovecote they fluttered out as they were bid, and went to the presence chamber to discuss her. In her bedchamber, through two closed doors, Elizabeth could still hear their concerned murmur and she turned her hot face to the pillow, wrapped her arms around her own slim body, and held herself tight.

* * *

Sir Robert, riding slowly up and down the line of the tilt yard, made his horse wheel at the bottom, and then took the line again.

They had been doing the exercise for more than an hour. Everything depended on the horse's willingness to ride a straight line, even though another horse, a warhorse, with a knight in full armor on its back, his lance down, was thundering from the other end, only a flimsy barrier between the two creatures. Sir Robert's horse must not swerve, not even drift aside, it must hold its line even when Sir Robert, lowering his own lance, was one-handed on the reins, it must hold to the line even if he rocked in the saddle from a blow, and all but let it go.

Robert wheeled, turned, did the line at a trot, wheeled, did the line again at full gallop. His horse was blowing when he pulled it up, a dark patina of sweat marking its neck. He wheeled it round and raced down the line once more.

A ripple of clapping came from the entrance to the yard. A serving girl was standing at the entrance where the riders came in and out, a shawl around her shoulders, a mobcap becomingly perched on her head, a lock of red hair showing, her face pale, her eyes black.

"Elizabeth," he said in quiet triumph, as he recognized her, and rode toward her. He pulled up the horse and dropped down from the saddle.

He waited.

She nipped her lip, she looked down, looked up again. He saw her gaze dart from his linen shirt where his sweat was darkening the cloth at his chest and on his back, to his tight riding breeches and his polished leather riding boots. He saw her nostrils flare as she took in the scent of him, her eyes narrow as she looked up at him again, at his dark head silhouetted against the bright morning sky.

"Robert," she breathed.

"Yes, my love?"

"I have come to you. I can be away from my rooms for no more than an hour."

"Then let us not waste one moment," he said simply and tossed the reins of his warhorse to his squire. "Put your shawl over your head," he said softly, and slid his arm around her waist, leading her, not to the palace, but to his private rooms over the stables. There was a small gated entrance from the garden; he opened the door and led her up the stairs.

In Robert's apartments, Elizabeth dropped the shawl and looked around. His chamber was a big room with two tall windows, the walls of dark linenfold paneling. The plans for the next day's tournament were spread out on the table; his desk was littered with business papers from the stables. She looked toward the door that was behind the desk, the door to his bedchamber.

"Yes, come," he said, following her gaze, and led her through the door into his chamber.

A handsome four-poster bed took up most of the room, a prie-dieu in the corner, a shelf with a small collection of books, a lute. His plumed hat was on the bed, his cloak on the back of the door.

"No one will come in?" she asked him breathlessly.

"No one," he assured her, and then shut the door and slid the heavy iron bolt.

He turned to her. She was trembling with anticipation, fear, and mounting desire.

"I cannot have a child," she specified.

He nodded. "I know. I will take care of that."

Still she looked anxious. "How can you be sure?"

He reached into the inner pocket of his

doublet and drew out a prophylactic, made of sheep's bladder sewn with tiny stitches and trimmed with ribbons. "This will keep you safe."

Torn between nerves and curiosity, she giggled. "What is it? How does it work?"

"Like armor. You must be my squire and put it on me."

"I cannot be bruised where my women might see."

He smiled. "I will not leave so much as a print of my lips on you. But inside, Elizabeth, you will burn up, I promise."

"I am a little afraid."

"My Elizabeth," he said softly, and stepped toward her, and took off the mob-cap. "Come to me, my love."

Her mass of red hair tumbled about her shoulders. Robert took a handful of the locks and kissed them, then, as she turned her entranced face toward him, kissed her full on the mouth. "My Elizabeth, at last," he said again.

Within moments she was in a dream of sensuality. He had always imagined that she would be responsive but under his skilled hands she stretched like a cat, reveling in pleasure. She was wanton: no hint of shame as she stripped to her skin and laid on his bed and reached out her arms for him. As his chest pressed against her face he smiled to find her feverish with desire, but then lost his own awareness in the rise of his feelings. He wanted to touch every inch of her skin, to kiss every fingertip, every dimple, every crevice of her body. He moved her one way and then another, touching, tasting, licking, probing, until she cried out loud that she must, she must have him, and then at last he allowed himself to enter her and watched her eyelids flicker closed and her rosy lips smile.

*   *   *

It was Sunday. The Hyde family, Lizzie Oddingsell, Lady Dudley, and all the Hyde servants were seated in a block in the parish church, the Hyde family and their guests in their high-walled pew, the servants arranged in strict order of precedence behind them, the women first, the men behind.

Amy was on her knees, her eyes fixed on Father Wilson as he held the Host toward them, preparing the communion in full sight of the congregation, in obedience to the new directive, though no bishop in the country had agreed, and most of them were either in the Tower or the Fleet prison. Oxford's own Bishop Thomas had escaped to Rome before they could arrest him, and the see was vacant. No one would come forward to fill it. Not one man of God would serve in Elizabeth's heretical church.

Amy's gaze was entranced, her lips silently moved as she watched him bless the Host, and then bid them come to take communion.

Like a sleeper in a dream she walked forward with the others and bent her head. The wafer was cloying on her tongue as she closed her eyes and knew that she was sharing in the very body of the living Christ, a miracle that no one could deny or explain. She returned to her pew and bent her head again. She whispered her prayer: "Lord God, send him back to me. Save him from the sin of ambition and from the sin that is that woman, and send him back to me."

After the service was over Father Wilson bade farewell to his parishioners at the lych-gate. Amy took his hand and spoke quietly to him, for his ears only.

"Father, I would confess, and celebrate Mass in the proper way."

He recoiled and glanced around at the

Hydes. No one but him had heard Amy's whispered request.

"You know it is forbidden now," he said quietly. "I can hear your confession but I have to pray in English."

"I cannot feel free from my sin without attending Mass in the old way," Amy said.

He patted her hand. "Daughter, is this true to your heart?"

"Father, truly, I am most in need of grace."

"Come to the church on Wednesday evening, at five o'clock," he told her. "But tell no one else. Just say you are coming to pray on your own. Take care not to betray us by accident. This is a life-and-death matter now, Lady Dudley; not even your husband must know."

"It is his sin that I must atone for," she said dully. "As well as my own in failing him."

He checked at the pain in the young woman's face. "Ah, Lady Dudley, you cannot have failed him," he exclaimed, speaking more as a man than a priest, prompted by pity.

"I must have done," she said sadly. "And many times. For he has gone from me, Father, and I don't know how to live without him. Only God can restore him, only God can restore me, only God can restore us to each other, if he can forgive me for my failures as a wife."

The priest bowed and kissed her hand, wishing that he could do more. He looked around. Mrs. Oddingsell was nearby; she came up and took Amy's arm.

"Let's walk home now," she said cheerfully. "It will be too hot to go out later."

*   *   *

It was the fifteenth of July, the day of the tournament, and all Elizabeth's court could think of was the clothes they would wear, the arrangements for the jousting, the roses they would carry, the songs they would sing, the dances they would dance, the hearts they would break. All Cecil could think of was his latest letter from Throckmorton in Paris.

July 9th

He is failing fast, I expect to hear of his death any day. I will send to you the moment I hear. Francis II will be King of France, and it is certain that Mary will style herself Queen of France, Scotland, and England; my intelligencer has seen the announcement that the clerks are drawing up. With the wealth of France and the generalship of the Guise family, with Scotland as their Trojan horse, they will be unstoppable. God help England and God help you, old friend. I think you will be England's last Secretary of State and all our hopes will lie in ruins.

Cecil translated the letter out of code, and sat with it for a few thoughtful minutes. Then he took the whole transcript to the queen in her privy chamber. She was laughing with her ladies as they prepared their costumes; Laetitia Knollys, in virginal white trimmed with the darkest rose red, was plaiting roses into a circlet for the queen to wear as a crown. Cecil thought that the news he had in the letter in his hand was like a summer storm which can blow up out of nowhere, and strip the petals from roses and destroy a garden in an afternoon.

Elizabeth was wearing a rose-pink gown with white silk slashings on the sleeves, trimmed with silver lace, and a white head-dress trimmed with pink and white seed pearls in gorgeous contrast to her copper hair.

She beamed at Cecil's surprised face and twirled before him. "How do I look?"

Like a bride, Cecil thought in horror. "Like a beauty," he said quickly. "A summertime queen."

She spread her skirts and bobbed him a curtsy. "And who do you favor for the champion?"

"I don't know," Cecil said distractedly. "Your Grace, I know this is a day for pleasure but I have to speak with you, forgive me, but I have to speak with you urgently."

For a moment she pouted and when she saw his face remained grave, she said: "Oh, very well, but not for long, Spirit, for they cannot start without me; and Sir Ro . . . and the riders will not want to wait in their heavy armor."

"Why, who is Sir Ro . . . ?" Laetitia asked playfully, and the queen giggled and blushed.

Cecil ignored the young woman, and instead drew the queen into the window bay and gave her the letter. "It is from Throckmorton," he said simply. "He warns of the French king's death. Your Grace, the moment that he dies we are in mortal danger. We should be arming now. We should be ready now. We should have sent funds to the Scottish Protestants already. Give me leave to send money to them now and to start the muster for an English army."

"You always say we have no funds," she said willfully.

Carefully, Cecil did not look at the pearls in her ears and the thick rope of pearls at her throat. "Princess, we are in the gravest of danger," he said.

Elizabeth twitched the letter from his hand and took it to the window to read. "When did you have this?" she asked, her interest sharpening.

"This very day. It came in code; I have just translated it."

"She cannot call herself Queen of England; she agreed to give up her claim in the treaty of Cateau-Cambrésis."

"No, you see, she did not. *She* agreed nothing. It was the king who made that agreement and the king that signed that treaty is dying. Nothing will stop her ambition now, the new king and his family will only egg her on."

Elizabeth swore under her breath and

turned from the merry court so that no one could see the darkening of her face. "Am I never to be safe?" she demanded in a savage undertone. "Having fought all my life for this throne, do I have to go on fighting for it? Do I have to fear the knife in the shadows and the invasion of my enemies forever? Do I have to fear my own cousin? My own kin?"

"I am sorry," Cecil said steadily. "But you will lose your throne and perhaps your life if you do not fight for it. You are in as much danger now as you have ever been."

She gave a harsh little cry. "Cecil, I have been all but charged with treason, I have faced the block, I have faced my own death from assassins. How can I be in more danger now?"

"Because now you face your death, and you face the loss of your inheritance, and you face the end of England," he said. "Your sister lost us Calais through her folly. Will you lose us England?"

She drew a breath. "I see," she said. "I see what must be done. Perhaps it will have to be war. I shall talk with you later, Spirit. As soon as the king dies and they show their hand we must be ready for them."

"We must," he said, delighted at her decision. "That is spoken like a prince."

"But Sir Robert says that we should prevail upon the Scottish Protestant lords to settle with their regent, Queen Mary. He says that if there is peace in Scotland there can be no excuse for the French to send in men and no reason for them to invade England."

Oh, does he? Cecil thought with scant gratitude for the unsolicited council. "He may be right, Your Grace; but if he is wrong then we are unprepared for a disaster. And older and wiser heads than Sir Robert's think we should strike at them now, before they reinforce."

"But he cannot go," she said.

I wish I could send him to hell itself, flashed through Cecil's irritated mind. "No, we should send a seasoned commander," he said. "But first we must send the Scots lords money to maintain the fight against the regent, Mary of Guise. And we must do that at once."

"Spain will stand our friend," Elizabeth reminded him.

"So can I send the Protestant lords some

funds?" He pressed her with the main point, the only point.

"As long as no one knows it is from me," Elizabeth said, her habitual caution uppermost as always. "Send them what they need, but I can't have the French accuse me of arming a rebellion against a queen. I can't be seen as a traitor."

Cecil bowed. "It shall be done discreetly," he promised her, hiding his immense sense of relief.

"And we may get help from Spain," Elizabeth repeated.

"Only if they believe that you are seriously considering the Archduke Charles."

"I am considering him," she said emphatically. She handed the letter back into his hand. "And after this news, I am considering him with much affection. Trust me for that, Spirit. I am not joking. I know I will have to marry him if it comes to war."

*   *   *

He doubted her word when she was in the royal box overlooking the tilt yard and he saw how her eyes searched the mounted riders for Dudley, how quickly she picked out his standard of the bear and ragged staff, how Dudley had a rose-pink scarf, the exact match of the queen's gown, unquestionably hers, worn boldly on his shoulder where anyone could see. He saw that she was on her feet with her hand to her mouth in terror when Dudley charged down the list, how she applauded his victories, even when he unseated William Pickering, and how, when he came to the royal box and she leaned over and crowned him with her own circlet of roses for being the champion of the day, she all but kissed him on the mouth, she leaned so low and so smilingly whispered to him.

But despite all that, she had the Hapsburg ambassador, Caspar von Breuner, in the royal box beside her, fed him with delicacies of her own choosing, laid her hand on his sleeve, and smiled up into his face, and—whenever anyone but Dudley was jousting—plied him with questions about the Archduke Ferdinand and gave him very clearly to understand that her refusal of his proposal of marriage, earlier in the month, was one that she was beginning to regret, deeply regret.

Caspar von Breuner, charmed, baffled, and with his head quite turned, could only think that Elizabeth was seeing sense at last and the archduke could come to England to meet her and be married by the end of the summer.

*　　　*　　　*

The next night Cecil was alone when there was a tap on the door. His manservant opened the door. "A messenger."

"I'll see him," Cecil said.

The man almost fell into the room, his legs weak with weariness. He put back his hood and Cecil recognized Sir Nicholas Throckmorton's most trusted man. "Sir Nicholas sent me to tell you that the king is dead, and to give you this." He proffered a crumpled letter.

"Sit down." Cecil waved him to a stool by the fire and broke the seal on the letter. It was short and scrawled in haste.

The king has died, this day, the tenth. God rest his soul. Young Francis says he is King of France and England. I hope to God you are ready and the queen resolute. This is a disaster for us all.

*　　　*　　　*

Amy, walking in the garden at Denchworth, picked some roses for their sweet smell and entered the house by the kitchen door to find some twine to tie them into a posy. As she heard her name she hesitated, and then realized that the cook, the kitchenmaid, and the spit boy were talking of Sir Robert.

"He was the queen's own knight, wearing her favor," the cook recounted with relish. "And she kissed him on the mouth before the whole court, before the whole of London."

"God save us," the kitchenmaid said piously. "But these great ladies can do as they please."

"He has had her," the spit lad opined. "Swived the queen herself! Now that's a man!"

"Hush," the cook said instantly. "No call for you to gossip about your betters."

"My pa said so," the boy defended himself. "The blacksmith told him. Said that the queen was nothing more than a whore with Robert Dudley. Dressed herself up as a serving wench to seek him out and that he had her in the hay store, and that Sir Robert's groom caught them at it, and told the blacksmith himself, when he came down here last week to deliver my lady's purse to her."

"No!" said the kitchenmaid, deliciously scandalized. "Not on the hay!"

Slowly, holding her gown to one side so that it would not rustle, barely breathing, Amy stepped back from the kitchen door, walked back down the stone passageway, opened the outside door so that it did not creak, and went back out into the heat of the garden. The roses, unnoticed, fell from her fingers; she walked quickly down the path and then started to run, without direction, her cheeks burning with shame, as if it were she who was disgraced by the gossip. Running away from the house, out of the garden and into the shrubbery, through the little wood, the brambles tearing at her skirt, the stones shredding her silk shoes. Running, without pausing to catch her breath, ignoring the pain in her side and the bruising of her feet, running as if she could get away from the picture in her head: of Elizabeth like a bitch in heat, bent over in the hay, her red hair tumbled under a mobcap, her white face triumphant, with Robert, smiling his sexy smile, thrusting at her like a randy dog from behind.

*

The Privy Council, traveling on summer progress with the court, delayed the start of their emergency meeting at Eltham Palace for Elizabeth; but she was out hunting with Sir Robert and half a dozen others and no one knew when she would return. The councillors, looking grim, seated themselves at the table and prepared to do business with an empty chair at the head.

"If just one man will join with me, and the rest of you will give nothing more than your assent, I will have him murdered," the Duke of Norfolk said quietly to this circle of friends. "This is intolerable. She is with him night and day."

"You can do it with my blessing," said Arundel, and two other men nodded.

"I thought she was mad for Pickering," one man complained. "What's become of him?"

"He couldn't stand another moment of it," Norfolk said. "No man could."

"He couldn't afford another moment of it," someone corrected him. "He's spent all his money on bribing friends at court and he's gone to the country to recoup."

"He knew he'd have no chance against

Dudley," Norfolk insisted. "That's why he has to be got out of the way."

"Hush, here is Cecil," said another and the men parted.

"I have news from Scotland. The Protestant lords have entered Edinburgh," Cecil said, coming into the room!

Sir Francis Knollys looked up. "Have they, by God! And the French regent?"

"She has withdrawn to Leith Castle. She is on the run."

"Not necessarily so," Thomas Howard, the Duke of Norfolk, said dourly. "The greater her danger, the more likely the French are to reinforce her. If it is to be finished, she must be defeated at once, without any hope of rallying, and it must be done quickly. She has raised a siege in the certain hope of reinforcements. All this means is that the French are coming to defend her. It is a certainty."

"Who would finish it for us?" Cecil asked, knowing the most likely answer. "What commander would the Scots follow that would be our friend?"

One of the Privy Councillors looked up. "Where is the Earl of Arran?" he asked.

"On his way to England," Cecil replied,

hiding his sense of smugness. "When he gets here, if we can come to an agreement with him, we could send him north with an army. But he is only young . . ."

"He is only young, but he has the best claim to the throne after the French queen," someone said farther down the table. "We can back him with a clear conscience. He is our legitimate claimant to the throne."

"There is only one agreement that he would accept and that we could offer," Norfolk said dourly. "The queen."

A few men glanced at the closed door as if to ensure that it did not burst open and Elizabeth storm in, flushed with temper. Then, one by one, they all nodded.

"What of the Spanish alliance with the archduke?" Francis Bacon, brother to Sir Nicholas, asked Cecil.

Cecil shrugged. "They are still willing and she says she is willing to have him. But I'd rather we had Arran. He is of our faith, and he brings us Scotland and the chance to unite England, Wales, Ireland, and Scotland. That would make us a power to reckon with. The archduke keeps the Spanish on our side, but what will they want of us? Whereas Arran's interests are the same as ours, and if they were to marry," he took a breath, his hopes were so precious he could hardly bear to say them, "if they were to marry we would unite Scotland and England."

"Yes: *if,*" Norfolk said irritably. "If we could make her seriously look twice at any man who wasn't a damned adulterous rascal."

Most of the men nodded.

"Certainly we need either Spanish help or Arran to lead the campaign," Knollys said. "We cannot do it on our own. The French have four times our wealth and manpower."

"And they are determined," another man said uneasily. "I heard from my cousin in Paris. He said that the Guise family will rule everything, and they are sworn enemies of England. Look at what they did in Calais; they just marched in. They will take one step in Scotland and then they will march on us."

"If she married Arran . . ." someone started.

"Arran! What chance of her marrying Arran!" Norfolk burst out. "All very well to consider which suitor would be the best for the country, but how is she to marry while she sees no one and thinks of no one but Dudley? He has to be put out of the way. She is like a milkmaid with a swain. Where the devil is she now?"

*   *   *

Elizabeth was lying under an oak tree on Dudley's hunting cape, their horses were hitched to a nearby tree, Dudley was leaning against the tree behind her, her head in his lap, twisting her ringlets around his fingers.

"How long have we been gone?" she asked him.

"An hour perhaps, no more."

"And do you always pull your mistresses off their horses and bed them on the ground?"

"D'you know," he said confidingly, "I have never done such a thing in my life before. I have never felt such desire before, I have always been a man who could wait for the right time, plan his time. But with you . . ." He broke off.

She twisted round so she could see his face and he kissed her on the mouth: a long, warm kiss.

"I am full of desire again," she said wonderingly. "I am becoming a glutton for you."

"I too," he said softly and pulled her up so that she was lying like a sinuous snake along him. "It's a satisfaction that brings with it only more appetite."

A long, low whistle alerted them. "That's Tamworth's signal," Robert said. "Someone must be coming near."

At once Elizabeth was up and on her feet, brushing the leaves off her hunting gown, looking around for her hat. Robert snatched up his cloak and shook it out. She turned to him. "How do I look?"

"Uncannily virtuous," he said, and was rewarded by the flash of her smile.

She went to her horse and was standing at its head when Catherine Knollys and her groom rode into the little glade followed by Tamworth, Dudley's valet.

"There you are! I thought I had lost you!"

"Where did you get to?" Elizabeth demanded. "I thought you were behind me."

"I pulled him up for a moment and then you were all gone. Where is Sir Peter?"

"His horse went lame," Robert said. "He is walking home in the sourest of moods. His boots are pinching. Are you hungry? Shall we dine?"

"I am starving," Catherine said. "Where are your ladies?"

"Gone ahead to the picnic," Elizabeth

said easily. "I wanted to wait for you, and Sir Robert stayed to keep me safe. Sir Robert, your hand if you please."

He threw her up into the saddle without meeting her eyes and then he mounted his own hunter. "This way," he said, and rode ahead of the two women to where the ride crossed a small river. On the far side, a pavilion hung with green and white had been erected and they could smell venison roasting on the fire and see the servants unpacking pastries and sweetmeats.

"I am so hungry," Elizabeth exclaimed with pleasure. "I have never had such an appetite before."

"You are becoming a glutton," Robert remarked to Catherine's surprise. She caught the quick, complicit look that passed between her friend and Sir Robert.

"A glutton?" she exclaimed. "The queen eats like a bird."

"A gluttonous peacock then," he said, quite unreproved. "Greed and vanity in one," and Elizabeth giggled.

*   *   *

On Wednesday evening Denchworth church seemed to be deserted, the door unlocked but shut. Tentatively, Amy turned the big iron handle and felt the door yield under her touch. An old lady in the pew at the back looked up and pointed silently toward the lady chapel at the side of the church. Amy nodded and went toward it.

The curtains were drawn across the stone tracery separating the chapel from the main body of the church. Amy drew them aside and slipped in. Two or three people were praying at the altar rail. Amy paused for a moment and then slipped into the rear pew near to the priest, who was in close-headed conference with a young man. After a few moments the youth, head bowed, took his place at the altar rail. Amy went beside Father Wilson and knelt on the worn cushion.

"Heavenly Father, I have sinned," she said quietly.

"What is your sin, my daughter?"

"I have failed in my love of my husband. I have set my judgment above his." She hesitated. "I thought I knew better than him how we should live. I see now that it was the sin of pride, my pride. Also, I thought I could win him from the court and bring him back to me and that we could live in a small way, a mean way. But he is a great man, born to be a great man. I am afraid that I have been envious of his greatness, and I think even my beloved father . . ." She strained her voice to speak the disloyal criticism. "Even my father was envious." She paused. "They were so far above our station . . . And I fear that in our hearts we both reveled in his fall. I think that secretly we were glad to see him humbled, and I have not been generous about his rise to power ever since. I have not been truly glad for him, as a wife and helpmeet should be."

She paused. The priest was silent.

"I have been envious of his greatness and the excitement of his life and his importance at court," she said softly. "And worse. I have been jealous of the love that he bears the queen and suspicious of that. I have poisoned my love for him with envy and jealousy. I have poisoned myself. I have made myself sick with sin and I have to be cured of this sickness and forgiven this sin."

The priest hesitated. In every alehouse in the land there were men who swore that Robert Dudley was the queen's lover and they were giving odds on that he would put his wife aside on some excuse, or poison her, or drown her in the river. There was little doubt in the priest's mind that Amy's worst fears were near to the truth. "He is your husband, set above you by God," he said slowly.

She lowered her head. "I know it. I shall be obedient to him, not just in my acts but in my thoughts too. I shall be obedient to him in my heart and not set myself up to judge him or to try to turn him from his great destiny. I shall try to teach myself to be glad for him in his fame, and not to hold him back."

The priest thought for a moment, wondering how to advise this woman.

"I am cursed by a picture in my head," Amy said, her voice very low. "I overheard someone say something about my husband, and now I see it all the time, in my head, in my dreams. I have to free myself from this . . . torment."

He wondered what she might have heard. Certainly, some of the talk that had come to his ears had been vile.

"God will free you," he said with more certainty than he felt. "Take this picture to God and lay it at his feet and he will free you."

"It's very . . . lewd," Amy said.

"You have lewd thoughts, daughter?"

"Not that give me any pleasure! They give me nothing but pain."

"You must take them to God and free your mind of them," he said firmly. "You must seek your own path to God. However your husband chooses to live his life, whatever his choices are, it is your duty to God and to him to bear it gladly and to draw nearer to God."

She nodded. "And what am I to do?" she asked humbly.

The priest considered for a moment. There were many stories in the Bible that described the sacred slavery that was the state of marriage, and he had exhorted many an independent-minded woman to obedience with them. But he did not have the heart to coerce Amy, whose face was so white and whose eyes were so pleading.

"You are to read the story of Mary Magdalene," he said. "And you are to consider the text "He that is without sin among you, let him first cast a stone." We are not ordered by God to judge each other. We are not even ordered by him to consider another person's sin. We are ordered by God to let Him consider it, to let Him be judge. Wait until God's will is clear to you and obey it, my child."

"And a penance?" she prompted.

"Five decades of the rosary," he said. "But pray on your own and in secret, my child; these are troubled times and devotion to the church is not justly respected."

Amy bowed her head for his whispered blessing and then joined the other five people at the altar rail. They heard the priest moving about behind them, followed by silence. Then, in his vestments, and carrying the bread and wine, he walked slowly up the aisle and went through the rood screen.

Amy watched through the network of her fingers, through the fretwork of the rood screen, as he turned his back to them and said the prayers in the timeless Latin, facing the altar. She felt an ache in her breast which she thought was heartbreak. The priest had not told her that her sorrows were imaginary, and that she should put them out of her mind. He had not recoiled from the suggestion and denied the gossip of the kitchenmaid, of the spitboy. He had not reproached her with the vanity of wicked suspicions against an honest husband. Instead, he had counseled her in her duty and in courage as if he thought she might have something to endure.

So he knows too, she thought to herself. *The whole country knows, from the Denchworth cook to the Denchworth priest. I must have been the last person in England to learn of it. Oh God, how deeply, how very deeply I am shamed.*

She watched him raise the bread and drew her breath at the miraculous moment of change, when the bread became the body of Christ and the wine became his blood. Every bishop in the land had defied Elizabeth to insist that this was the truth; every priest in the land still believed it, and hundreds continued secretly to celebrate Mass like this, in the old way, in hiding.

Amy, dazzled by the candles and comforted by the presence of the Living God, too sacred a being to be shown to the congregation, too sacred to be taken every Sunday, so sacred that He could only be watched through the lacing of her fingers, through the tracery of stone, prayed again that Robert might choose to come home to her, and that when he came, she should find some way to hold up her head, rinse those pictures from her mind, be free of sin and glad to see him.

* * *

Cecil managed to catch Elizabeth before the great banquet at the Duke of Arundel's magnificent palace, the Nonsuch, and delay her a moment in her privy chamber.

"Your Grace, I have to speak with you."

"Spirit, I cannot. The duke has prepared a banquet for an emperor. He has done every-thing but roll the meat in gold leaf. I cannot insult him by being late."

"Your Grace, I am duty-bound to warn you. The Pope has increased his threat against you, and there is much gossip against you in the country."

She hesitated and frowned. "What gos-sip?"

"They say that you are favoring Sir Robert over and above any other man." *Mealy-mouthed*, Cecil scolded himself. *But how can I tell her to her face that they are calling her Dudley's whore?*

"And so I should," she replied, smiling. "He is the finest man at my court."

Cecil found the courage to be clearer. "Your Grace, it is worse than that. There are rumors that you and he have a dishonorable relationship."

Elizabeth flushed red. "Who says this?"

Every alehouse in England. "It is widely said, Your Grace."

"Do we not have laws to prevent me being slandered? Do we not have blacksmiths to cut their tongues?"

Cecil blinked at her fierceness. "Your Grace, we can make arrests, but if something is widely spoken and widely believed we are at a loss. The people love you but . . ."

"Enough," she said flatly. "I have done nothing dishonorable, and neither has Sir Robert. I will not be traduced in my own hearing. You must punish the gossips that you catch and it will die down. If it does not I shall blame you, Cecil. No one else."

She turned but he detained her. "Your Grace!"

"What?"

"It is not just a matter of the common people gossiping about their betters. There are men in the court who say that Dudley should be dead before he brings you down."

Now he had her full attention. "He is threatened?"

"You are both endangered by this folly. Your reputation has suffered and there are many who say that it is their patriotic duty to kill him before you are dishonored."

She blanched white. "No one must touch him, Cecil."

"The remedy is easy. His safety is easy. Marry. Marry either the archduke or Arran and the gossip is silenced and the threat is gone."

Elizabeth nodded, her hunted, fearful look on her face again. "I will marry one of them, you can count on it. Tell people that I will marry one or the other, this autumn. It is a certainty. I know that I have to."

"Caspar von Breuner will be at dinner. Shall he be seated beside you? We have to recruit his support for our struggle with Scotland."

"Of course!" she said impatiently. "Who did you think would sit next to me? Sir Robert? I have given everyone to understand that I am reconsidering marriage with the archduke; I have shown his ambassador every attention."

"It would be better for us all if anyone

could believe you this time," Cecil said frankly. "The ambassador has hopes, you have seen to that; but I do not see you drawing up a marriage treaty."

"Cecil, it is August, I am on progress, this is not a time to draw up treaties."

"Princess, you are in danger. Danger does not stop because someone has cooked you a banquet and the hunting is good and the weather is perfect. The Earl of Arran should be in England any day now; tell me that I can bring him to you the moment that he arrives."

"Yes," she said. "You can do that."

"And tell me that I can draw funds for him and start to muster an army to go north with him."

"Not an army," she said at once. "Not till we know that he has the stomach to command one. Not till we know from him what his plans are. For all you know, Cecil, he could have a wife tucked away somewhere already."

That would hardly prevent you, judging from your present behavior with a married man, Cecil thought, ill tempered. Aloud, he merely said: "Your Grace, he cannot be victorious without our support, and he has the greatest claim to the Scottish throne. If he will lead our army to victory, and you will take him as your husband, then we have made England safe against the French not just for now, but forever. If you will do that for England, you will be the greatest prince that the country has ever had on the throne, greater than your father. Make England safe from France and you will be remembered forever. Everything else will be forgotten; you will be England's savior."

"I will see him," Elizabeth said. "Trust me, Cecil, I put my country before anything. I will see him and I will decide what I should do."

*   *   *

The candles and crucifix were brought out of storage, polished, and displayed on the altar of the Royal Chapel at Hampton Court. The court had returned from its summer progress in spiritual mood. Elizabeth, going to Mass, had taken to curtsying to the altar and crossing herself on arrival and departure. There was holy water in the stoop and Catherine Knollys ostentatiously walked out of the court every morning to ride to London to pray with a reformed congregation.

"What is all this now?" Sir Francis Bacon asked the queen as they paused at the open doorway of the chapel and saw the choristers polishing the altar rail.

"This is a sop," she said disdainfully. "For those who wish to see a conversion."

"And who are they?" he asked curiously.

"For the Pope who would see me dead," she said irritably. "For the Spanish whom I must keep as my friends, for the archduke to give him hope, for the English Papists to give them pause. For you, and all your fellow Lutherans, to give you doubt."

"And what is the truth of it?" he asked, smiling.

She shrugged her shoulder pettishly and walked on past the door. "The truth is the last thing that matters," she said. "And you can believe one thing of the truth and me: I keep it well hidden, inside my heart."

*   *   *

William Hyde had a letter from Robert's steward, Thomas Blount, requesting him to be ready for Robert's men who would come within three days to escort Amy and Mrs. Oddingsell to the Forsters at Cumnor Place for a brief visit, and then on to Chislehurst. A scrawled note inside from his lordship told William the latest news from court, of the gifts that Robert had received from the queen, now returned to Hampton Court, and indicated that William would shortly be appointed to a profitable post in one of the Oxford colleges, by way of thanks for his kindness to Lady Dudley, and to maintain his friendship for the future.

He went to Amy with the letter in his hand. "It seems that you are to leave us."

"So soon?" she said. "Did he say nothing about a house here?"

"The queen has given him a great place in Kent," he said. "He writes to tell me. Knole Place, do you know it?"

She shook her head. "So does he not want me to look for a house for him now? Are we not to live in Oxfordshire? Shall we live in Kent?"

"He does not say," he said gently, thinking that it was a shame that she should have to ask a friend where her home would be. Her very public quarrel with her husband had obviously wounded her deeply; he had watched her shrink inside herself as if shamed. In recent weeks she had become very devout and it was William Hyde's view that churchgoing was a comfort to women, especially when they were in the grip of unhappy circumstances over which they had no control. A good priest like Father Wilson could be counted on to preach resignation; and William Hyde believed, as did other men of his age, that resignation was a great virtue in a wife. He saw her hand go to her breast.

"Are you in pain, Lady Dudley?" he asked. "I often see you put your hand to your heart. Should you see a physician before you go?"

"No," she said with a swift, sad smile. "It is nothing. When does my lord say I am to leave?"

"Within three days," he said. "You are to go first to Cumnor Place to visit the Forsters, and then to your friend Mr. Hyde at Chislehurst. We shall be sorry to lose you. But I hope you will come back to us soon. You are like one of the family now, Lady Dudley. It is always such a pleasure to have you here."

To his discomfort, her eyes filled with tears and he went quickly to the door, fearing a scene.

But she only smiled at him and said, "You are so kind. I always like coming here; your house feels like a home to me now."

"I am sure you will come back to us soon," he said cheerfully.

"Perhaps you will come and see me. Perhaps I am to live at Knole," she said. "Perhaps Robert intends that to be my new home."

"Perhaps," he said.

*   *   *

Laetitia Knollys stood before William Cecil's great desk in his handsome rooms at Hampton Court, her hands clasped behind her, her face composed.

"Blanche Parry told the queen that she was playing with fire and she would burn down the whole house and us inside it," she reported.

Cecil looked up. "And the queen said?"

"She said she had done nothing wrong, and no one could prove anything of her."

"And Mistress Parry said?"

"She said that one only had to look at the two of them to know they were lovers." A quaver of laughter colored her solemn tone. "She said they were hot as chestnuts on a shovel."

Cecil scowled at her.

"And the queen?"

"Threw Blanche out of her rooms and told

her not to come back until she had rinsed her mouth of gossip or she would find her tongue slit for slander."

"Anything else?"

She shook her head. "No, sir. Blanche cried and said her heart was breaking; but I suppose that's not important."

"The queen sleeps always with a companion, a guard on the door?"

"Yes, sir."

"So there could be no truth in this vile gossip."

"No, sir," Laetitia repeated like a schoolgirl. "Unless . . ."

"Unless?"

"Unless there is a doorway behind the paneling, so that the queen could slip out of her bed when her companion is asleep and go through a secret door to Sir Robert, as they say her father the king used to do when he wanted to visit a woman."

"But no such passage exists," Cecil said flatly.

"Unless it is possible that a man can lie with a woman in the hours of daylight, and if they do not need a bed. If they can do it under a tree, or in a secret corner, or up against a wall in a hurry." Her dark eyes were brimful of mischief.

"All this may be true, but I doubt that your father would be pleased to know of your thoughts," Cecil said severely. "And I must remind you to keep such speculation to yourself."

Her dark eyes gleamed at him. "Yes, sir, of course, sir," she said demurely.

"You can go," Cecil said. *Good God, if that little minx can say that to my face, what can they be saying behind my back?*

* * *

Sir Robert was leaning down to whisper to the seated queen, when Cecil walked into the presence chamber, and saw the queen laugh up at him. The desire between the two of them was so powerful that for a moment Cecil thought he could almost see it, then he shook his head against such nonsense and went forward to make his bow.

"Oh, no bad news, Cecil, please!" Elizabeth exclaimed.

He tried to smile. "Not one word. But can I walk with you for a moment?"

She rose from her seat. "Don't go," she said quietly to Robert.

"I might go to the stables," he said.

Her hand flew out and touched his sleeve. "Wait for me, I'll only be a moment."

"I might," he said teasingly.

"You wait, or I'll behead you," she whispered.

"I'd certainly lie down for you and tell you when I was ready."

At her ripple of shocked laughter, the court looked around and saw Cecil, once her greatest friend and only advisor, waiting patiently, while she tore herself away from Sir Robert, her cheeks flushed.

Cecil offered his arm.

"What is it?" she asked, not very agreeably.

He waited until they had walked from the presence chamber into the long room of the gallery. Members of the court lingered here too, and some came strolling out of the presence chamber to watch Cecil and the queen, to wait their turn to catch her attention now that someone, at last, had separated her from Dudley.

"I hear from Paris that the French are to send reinforcements to Scotland to assist the queen regent."

"Well, we knew that they would," she said indifferently. "But some people think that the Scots will not man the siege for very long anyway. They never carry more than a fortnight's supplies; they will just give up and go home."

So says Sir Robert, does he? Cecil said quietly to himself. "We had better pray that they do not," he said with some asperity. "For those Scots lords are our first line of defense against the French. And the news I have is that the French are sending men to Scotland."

"How many?" she asked, determined not to be frightened.

"One thousand pikemen and one thousand arquebusiers. Two thousand men in all."

He had wanted to shock her but he thought he had gone too far. She went quite white and he put his hand on the small of her back to steady her.

"Cecil, that is more than they need to defeat the Scots."

"I know," he said. "That is the first wave of an invading force."

"They mean to come." She spoke in little more than a frightened whisper. "They really mean to invade England."

"I am certain that they do," he said.

"What can we do?" She looked up at him, sure that he would have a plan.

"We must send Sir Ralph Sadler to Berwick at once to make an agreement with the Scots lords."

"Sir Ralph?"

"Of course. He served your father faithfully in Scotland and he knows half the Scots lords by name. We must send him with a war chest. And he must inspect the border defenses and strengthen them to keep the French out of England."

"Yes," she agreed quickly. "Yes."

"I can put that in hand?"

"Yes," she said. "Where is Arran?"

He looked grim. "He's on his way; my man is bringing him in."

"Unless he has gone back to Geneva," she said bleakly. "Thinking the odds too great against him."

"He's on his way," said Cecil, knowing that his best man had been sent to Geneva with orders to bring Arran to London, whether he liked it or not.

"We have to make the Spanish pledge their support to us. The French are afraid of Spain. If we had them as our allies we would be safer."

"If you can do it," he warned her.

"I will," she promised him. "I'll promise them anything they want."

*   *   *

William Hyde took a moment to see his sister Lizzie while she was in the throes of packing to leave his house. "Does she really have no idea what people are saying about Sir Robert and the queen?"

"She speaks to so few people that she might hear nothing of it, and anyway, who would have the heart to say such a thing to her?"

"A friend might tell her," he prompted her. "A true friend. To prepare her."

"How could anyone prepare her?" She rounded on him. "Nobody knows what is going to happen. Nothing like this has ever happened before. I am not prepared, you are not prepared, how can his wife be? How can anyone prepare when nothing like this has ever happened before? What country has ever had a queen who acts like a whore with a married man? Who can tell what is going to happen next?"

*   *   *

"For God's sake, Princess, I must speak with you," Kat Ashley said in desperation in

Elizabeth's private room at Hampton Court Palace.

"What is it?" Elizabeth was seated before her looking glass, smiling at her reflection as they brushed her hair with soft ivory-backed brushes and then rubbed it with red silk.

"Your Grace, everyone is talking about you and Sir Robert, and the things they are saying are shameful. Things that should not be said of any young woman if she is to make a good marriage, things that should never be dreamed of in connection with the Queen of England."

To her surprise, Elizabeth, who as a princess had been so fearful of her reputation, turned her head away from her old governess and said dismissively, "People always talk."

"Not like this," Kat said, pressing on. "This is scandalous. It is dreadful to hear."

"And what do they say? That I am unchaste? That Sir Robert and I are lovers?" Elizabeth dared her to say the worst.

Kat drew a breath. "Yes. And more. They say that you bore his child and that is why the court went on progress this summer. They say the baby was born and hidden away with his wet nurse until you two can marry and bring him out. They say that Sir Robert is plotting to kill his wife, to murder her, to marry you. They say you are under an enchantment from him and you have lost your wits and all you can do is bed him, that you can think of nothing but lust. They say you are monstrous in your appetites, perverse in your pleasure in him. They say you neglect the business of the realm to go riding with him every day. They say he is king in all but name. They say he is your master."

Elizabeth flushed scarlet with rage. Kat dropped to her knees. "They say very detailed things about your bedding him, things anyone would blush to hear. Your Grace, I have loved you like a mother and you know what I have suffered for you in your service, and suffered it gladly. But I have never endured such anxiety as I feel now. You will throw yourself from your throne if you do not put Sir Robert aside."

"Put him aside!" Elizabeth sprang to her feet, scattering hair brushes and combs. "Why the devil should I put him aside?"

The other ladies in the chamber leapt to their feet and cleared out of her way, spreading themselves against the wall, eyes down, hoping to be invisible, desperate to avoid Elizabeth's fiery gaze.

"Because he will be the death of you!" Kat rose too, facing her young mistress, desperately earnest. "You cannot keep your throne and allow people to speak of you as they are doing. They say you are no better than a whore, Your Grace, God forgive me that I should say such a word to you. This is worse than it has ever been. Even with Lord Seymour . . ."

"Enough!" Elizabeth snapped. "And let me tell you something. I have never had a moment's safety in my life, you know that, Kat. I have never had a moment's joy. I have never had a man who loves me, nor a man that I could admire. In Sir Robert I have a great friend, the finest man I have ever known. I am honored by his love; I will never be shamed by it.

"And there is no shame in it. I know that he is a married man, I danced at his wedding, for God's sake. I sleep in my bedchamber every night with guards on the door and a companion in my bed. You know that as well as I. If I was a fool and I wanted to take a lover—and I do not—then it would be impossible for me to do so. But if I wanted to, then who should deny me? Not you, Kat, not the Privy Council, and not the Commons of England. If I wanted a lover then why should I, as Queen of England, be denied what any goose-girl can have for the asking?"

Elizabeth was shouting her justification, quite beyond herself with rage. Kat Ashley, backed against the wood-paneled wall, was sick with shock. "Elizabeth, my princess, Your Grace," she whispered. "I just want you to have a care."

Elizabeth whirled around and plumped down on her stool again, thrust her hairbrush at a white-faced Laetitia Knollys. "Well, I won't," Elizabeth replied flatly.

*   *   *

That night she slipped through the secret doorway into Robert's adjoining chamber. He was waiting for her, a warm fire in the grate, two chairs drawn up before it. His valet, Tamworth, had put out wine and little pastries for them, before leaving the room to stand guard outside the door.

Elizabeth, in her nightgown, slid into Robert's arms and felt his warm kisses on her hair.

"I had to wait forever," she whispered. "I

was sleeping with Laetitia and she chattered and chattered and would not sleep."

Resolutely he turned his mind from the picture of the exquisite young woman and his mistress in bed together, combing each other's copper hair, their white nightgowns open at the neck. "I was afraid you could not come."

"I will always come to you. Whatever anyone says."

"What has anyone said?"

"More scandal." She dismissed it with a shake of her head. "I can't repeat it. It's so vile."

He seated her in the chair and gave her a glass of wine. "Don't you long for us to be together openly?" he asked softly. "I want to be able to tell everyone how much I adore you. I want to be able to defend you. I want you to be mine."

"How could it ever be?"

"If we were to marry," he suggested quietly.

"You are a married man," she said, so low that not even the little greyhound sitting at her feet could hear. But Robert heard, he saw the shape her lips made, he never took his eyes from her mouth.

"Your father was a married man when he met your mother," he said gently. "And yet when he met her, the woman that he had to have, the woman that he knew was the great love of his life, he put his first wife aside."

"His first marriage was not valid," she responded instantly.

"And nor is mine. I told you, Elizabeth, my love for Amy Robsart is dead, as is hers for me, and she means nothing to me. She lives apart from me now, and has done for years, of her own choice. I am free to love you. You can set me free, and then you shall see what we shall be for each other."

"I can set you free?" she whispered.

"You have the power. You are head of the church. You can grant me a divorce."

She gasped. "I?"

Robert smiled at her. "Who else?"

He could see her brain working furiously. "You have been planning this?"

"How could I plan such a thing? How could I dream that this would happen to us? Parliament made you supreme governor and gave you the powers of the Pope without a word from me. Now you have the power to annul my marriage; the Commons of England gave you that power, Elizabeth. You can free me, Elizabeth, as your father freed himself. You can free me to be your husband. We can be married."

She closed her eyes so that he could not see the whirl of thoughts in her head, her immediate frightened rejection. "Kiss me," she said dreamily. "Oh, kiss me, my love."

*   *   *

Thomas Blount was in Robert's private chambers over the stables the very next morning, leaning against the door, cleaning his fingernails with a sharp knife, when the opposite door opened and Dudley came in from riding, a sheaf of farriers' bills in his hand.

"Thomas?"

"My lord."

"News?"

"The Earl of Arran, James Hamilton, has arrived and is in hiding."

"Arran?" Dudley was genuinely astonished. "Here?"

"Came into London three nights ago. Housed in some private rooms at Deptford."

"Good God! That was silently done. Who brought him in? Who pays his bills?"

"Cecil, for the queen herself."

"She knows he is here?"

"She commanded him. He is here at her invitation and request."

Dudley swore briefly, and turned to the window overlooking the vegetable gardens where they stretched down to the river. "If it's not one damned opportunity seeker, it is another. To what end? Do you know that?"

"My intelligencer, who knows the maid where the noble gentleman is staying, says that he is to meet the queen privately, to see if they can agree, and then when they have terms, she will publicly announce his arrival, they will be betrothed, and he will march to Scotland to claim his throne. When he is King of Scotland he will return in triumph and marry her, uniting the two kingdoms."

For a moment Dudley was so shocked that he could not speak. "And you are certain that this is the plan? You could be mistaken? This could be Cecil's plan and the queen might know nothing of it."

"Perhaps. But my man is sure of it, and the maid seemed to think she had it right. She's a whore as well as a maid and he was bragging to her when he was drunk. She is sure that the queen had consented."

Dudley tossed him a purse of coins from

a drawer in the desk. "Watch him, as you would watch your own baby," he said shortly. "Tell me when he sees the queen. I want to know every detail, I want to know every word, every whisper, every creak of the floorboard."

"He has seen her already," Blount said with a grimace. "He came here under cover of darkness last night and she saw him last night, after dinner, after she withdrew for bed."

Dudley had a very vivid memory of the previous night. He had knelt at her bare feet and her hair had tumbled over his face as she leaned toward him, enfolding him in her arms. He had rubbed his face against her breasts and belly, warm and sweet-smelling through her linen.

"Last night?"

"So they say." Thomas Blount thought that he had never seen his master look so grim.

"And we know nothing of what was said?"

"I didn't pick up the trail until this morning. I am sorry, my lord. Cecil's men had him well hidden."

"Aye," Dudley said shortly. "He is the

master of shadows. Well, watch Arran from now on, and keep me informed."

He knew he should mind his temper and bite his tongue but his quick pride and quicker anger got the better of him. He flung open the door, leaving the papers blowing off his desk, and stormed out of his room and down the twisting private stairs to the garden where the court was watching a tennis match. The queen was in her chair at the side of the court, a golden awning over her head, her ladies around her, watching two players jostle for the prize: a purse of gold coins.

Robert bowed and she smiled on him and gestured to him to come to sit at her side.

"I must see you alone," he said abruptly.

At once she turned her head, took in the white line around his compressed lips. "Love, what is wrong?"

"I have heard some news which has troubled me." He could hardly speak, he was so angry. "Just now. I must ask you if it is true."

Elizabeth was too passionate to tell him to wait until the end of the tournament, even though there were only a few games left to be played. She rose to her feet and all the court rose too, the men on the court let the ball bounce off the roof and roll out of play. Everything was suspended, waiting for the queen.

"Sir Robert would speak with me privately," she said. "We will walk alone in my privy garden. The rest of you can stay here and watch the tournament to the finish and . . ." She glanced around. "Catherine can award the prize in my place."

Catherine Knollys smiled at the honor, and curtsyed. Elizabeth led the way from the court and turned into her privy garden. The guards on the wooden door set into the gray stone wall leapt to attention, swung it open. "Let no one else in," Elizabeth commanded them. "Sir Robert and I would be alone."

The two men saluted and closed the door behind them. In the sunlit empty garden, Elizabeth turned to Robert. "Well, I think I have done enough to earn me another lecture from Kat on indiscretion. What is it?"

As she saw his dark expression the smile drained from her face. "Ah, love, don't look like that, you are frightening me. What is it? What is wrong?"

"The Earl of Arran," he said, his tone biting. "Is he in London?"

She turned her head this way and that, as if his glare was a beam of light shining on her. He knew her so well he could almost see the quick denials flying through her head. Then she realized she could not lie directly to him. "Yes," she said unwillingly. "He is in London."

"And you met with him last night?"

"Yes."

"He came to you in secret, you met him alone?"

She nodded.

"In your bedchamber?"

"Only in my privy chamber. But, Robert—"

"You spent the first part of the night with him and then came to me. All that you told me about having to wait for Lettice Knollys to fall asleep: all that was a lie. You had been with him."

"Robert, if you are thinking—"

"I am thinking nothing," he said flatly. "I cannot bear what I might think. First Pickering, when my back is turned, and now Arran while we are lovers, declared lovers . . ."

She sank down on a circular seat built around a wide-trunked oak tree. Robert rested one boot on the seat beside her so that he towered over her. Pleadingly, she looked up at him.

"Must I tell you the truth?"

"Yes. But tell me everything, Elizabeth. I cannot be played with as a fool."

She drew a breath. "It is a secret."

He gritted his teeth. "Before God, Elizabeth, if you have promised yourself in marriage to him you will never see me again."

"I have not! I have not!" she protested. "How could I? You know what you are to me! What we are to each other!"

"I know what I feel when I hold you in my arms and I kiss your mouth and bite your neck," he said bitterly. "I don't know what you feel when you meet another man just moments before you come to me, with a pack of lies in your mouth."

"I feel as if I am going mad!" she cried out at him. "That is what I feel! I feel as if I am being torn apart! I feel as if you are driving me mad. I feel that I cannot stand another moment of it."

Robert recoiled. "What?"

She was on her feet, squaring up to him like a fighter. "I have to play myself like a piece in a chess game," she panted. "I am my own pawn. I have to keep the Spanish on our side, I have to frighten the French, I have to persuade Arran to get himself up to Scotland and claim his own, and I have nothing to bring to bear on any of these but my own weight. All I can promise any of them is myself. And . . . and . . . and . . ."

"And what?"

"I am not my own!"

He was silenced. "You are not?"

Elizabeth gave a sobbing breath. "I am yours, heart and soul. God knows, as God is my witness, I am yours, Robert . . ."

He reached out for her, took her hands, started to draw her close.

"But . . ."

He hesitated. "But what?"

"I have to play them, Robert," she said. "I have to make them think that I will marry. I have to look as if I will take Archduke Ferdinand; I have to give Arran hope."

"And what d'you think happens to me?" he asked her.

"You?"

"Yes. When you are known to be spending hours of time with Pickering, when the court is abuzz with the word that you will marry the archduke."

"What happens to you?" She was genuinely puzzled.

"Then my enemies mass against me. Your kinsman Norfolk, your advisor Cecil, Francis Bacon, his brother Nicholas, Catherine Knollys, Pickering, Arundel, they hunt in a pack like hounds waiting to bring down a stag. When you turn from me they know that their time has come. They will bring charges against me, pull me down, accuse me. You have raised me so high, Elizabeth, that I am envied now. The hour that you announce your betrothal to another man is the hour that I am ruined."

She was aghast. "I did not know. You did not tell me."

"How should I tell you?" he demanded. "I am not a child to run crying to my nurse because the other children threaten me. But it is true. The moment they know that you have turned from me to another man I am ruined or worse."

"Worse?"

"Dead," he said shortly. "Every day I half expect to be dragged into some dark alley and knifed."

She looked up at him, still clinging to his

hands. "My love, you know I would do any-thing to make you safe and keep you safe."

"You cannot make me safe, unless you declare your love for me. Elizabeth, you know that I would do anything to love you and protect you. Marry me, for God's sake, and let us have a child. Marriage and a son and heir will make us safer than any other way, and you will have me at your side for-ever. You need not play yourself like a pawn. You can be yourself, your dear, lovely self, and belong to no one but me."

Elizabeth twisted her hands from him and turned away. "Robert, I am so afraid. If the French come into England from Scotland they will march through the northern king-doms as welcome friends. Where can I stop them? Who can stop the French army? Mary lost us Calais and they still curse her name. What will they say of me if I lose Berwick? Or Newcastle? Or York? What if I lose London itself?"

"You won't lose," he urged her. "Marry me and I shall take an army north for you. I have fought the French before. I don't fear them. I shall be the man to fight for you, my love. You need not beg for help from others; I am yours, heart and soul. All you have to do is trust yourself to me."

Her hood had fallen back; she took the thick tresses of hair at her temples in her fists and pulled them, as if she hoped that pain would steady her thoughts. She gave a shuddering sob. "Robert, I am so afraid, and I don't know what to do. Cecil says one thing, and Norfolk another, and the Earl of Arran is nothing but a pretty boy! I had hopes of him until I met him last night; but he is a child dressing up as a soldier. He is not going to save me! The French are coming, there is no doubt that they are coming, and I have to find an army, and find a fortune, and find a man to fight for England and I don't know how to do it, or who to trust."

"Me," Robert said instantly. Roughly he pulled her into his arms, overwhelming her protests with his weight and his strength. "Trust me. Declare your love for me, marry me, and we will fight this together. I am your champion, Elizabeth. I am your lover. I am your husband. You can trust no one but me, and I swear I will keep you safe."

She struggled in his grip, pulled her face

free; he could hear only the word: "England?"

"I will keep England safe for you, for me, and for our son," he swore. "I can do it for him, and I will do it for you."

*   *   *

Amy, on the road again to Chislehurst, after a brief visit with Robert's friends the Forsters at Cumnor Place, kept her rosary in her pocket and every time she had a jealous thought she put her hand to the beads and said a silent "Hail Mary." Lizzie Oddingsell, watching her companion ride quietly through the dry August countryside at the end of a hard summer, wondered at the change in her. It was as if, under the burden of terrible uncertainty, she had grown from being a petulant child into a woman.

"Are you well, Amy?" she asked. "Not too tired? Not finding it too hot?"

Instinctively Amy's hand went to her heart. "I am well," she said.

"Do you have a pain in your breast?" Elizabeth asked.

"No. There is nothing wrong with me."

"If you feel at all ill, we could call in at London on the way and see his lordship's physician."

"No!" Amy said hastily. "I don't want to go to London without my lord's invitation. He said we were to go to Chislehurst; there is no need for us to go through London."

"I didn't mean we should go to court."

Amy flushed slightly. "I know you did not, Lizzie," she said. "I am sorry. It is just that . . ." She broke off. "I believe that there is much talk in the country about Robert and the queen. I would not want him to think I was coming to London to spy on him. I would not want to look like a jealous wife."

"No one could ever think you were that," Lizzie said warmly. "You are the most tender-hearted and forgiving wife a man could wish for."

Amy turned her head away. "Certainly, I love him," she said in a very small voice. They rode on for a few more minutes. "And have you heard much gossip, Lizzie?" she asked very quietly.

"There is always gossip about a man like Sir Robert," Lizzie said stoutly. "I wish I could have a shilling for every unfounded rumor I have heard about him; I would be a rich woman now. D'you remember what they said about him when he was with King Philip in the Netherlands? And how distressed you were when he came home with that French widow from Calais? But it all meant nothing, and nothing came of it."

Amy's hand went to the cool round beads of the rosary in her pocket. "But have you heard a rumor of him and the queen?" Amy pressed her friend.

"My sister-in-law told me that her cousin in London had said that the queen favors Sir Robert above any other, but there is nothing there that we did not know already," Lizzie said. "They were friends in childhood, he is her Master of Horse. Of course they are friendly together."

"She must be amusing herself," Amy said bitterly. "She knows he is a married man, she knows that she has to marry the archduke, she is just enjoying the summer in his company."

"Flighty," Lizzie said, watching Amy's face. "She is a flighty young woman. There was gossip enough about *her* in her girlhood. If you want to think of scandal—Elizabeth was it!"

Hidden by the flap of her pocket, Amy wrapped her rosary around her fingers. "It is not for us to judge," she reminded herself.

"It is my duty to stay loyal to my lord and wait for his return home."

"She would do better to mind the affairs of state," Lizzie Oddingsell volunteered. "They say there must be a war with the French and we are quite unprepared. She would do better to marry a good man who could run the kingdom safely for us all. Her sister married as soon as she came to the throne and chose a man who brought his own army."

"It is not for me to judge," Amy said, holding her beads. "But God guide her back to the path of right."

Autumn 1559

The court, newly arrived in September at one of Elizabeth's favorite houses, Windsor Castle, started the preparations for her birthday celebrations. Robert planned a day of festivities with the queen awakened by choristers, a choreographed hunt in which huntsmen would pause to sing her praises, woodland nymphs would dance, and a tamed deer with a garland round its neck would lead the queen to a dinner laid out in the greenwood. That night there would be a great banquet, with dancing, singing, and a tableau depicting the Graces, with goddesses in attendance and Diana, symbolizing Elizabeth the huntress, taking the crown.

The ladies-in-waiting were to dance as

goddesses and the maids-in-waiting were to be the Graces. "Which Grace am I?" Laetitia Knollys asked Robert as he allocated parts in a quiet corner of the queen's presence chamber.

"If there was a Grace called Unpunctuality, you could be her," he recommended. "Or if there was a Grace called Flirtation, you could be her."

She shot him a look that was pure Boleyn: promising, provocative, irresistible. "I?" she said. "Do *you* call me flirtatious? Now that is praise indeed."

"I meant it to be abuse," he said, pinching her chin.

"From such a master at his trade it is a great compliment."

He tapped her on the nose, as he would have reproved a kitten. "You are to be Chastity," he said. "I could not resist it."

She widened her slanting, dark eyes at him. "Sir Robert!" she pouted. "I do not know what I can have done to so offend you. First you call me unpunctual, then you call me flirtatious, and then you say that you could not resist giving me the part of Chastity. Have I annoyed your lordship?"

"Not at all. You delight my eye."

"Have I troubled you?"

Robert winked at her. He was very certain he was not going to tell this young woman that he sometimes found it hard to look away from her when she was dancing, that once when he had danced with her and the movement of the dance had put her into his arms he had felt an instantaneous, irresistible thud of desire, stronger than he had ever felt for so slight a touch in his life before.

"How could a little ninny such as you trouble a man such as me?" he asked.

She raised her eyebrows. "I can think of a dozen ways. Can't you? But the question is not how I would; but whether I do?"

"Not at all, Miss Shameless."

"Chastity, if you please. And what do I wear?" she asked.

"Something fearfully immodest," he promised her. "You will be delighted. But you must show it to your mother, to make sure that she approves. The queen's wardrobe has it for you. It is quite indecent."

"Should I not come and show it to you?" she asked him provocatively. "I could come to your rooms before dinner."

Robert glanced around. The queen had

come in from the garden and was standing in a window bay, withdrawn from the rest, in close conversation with Sir William Cecil. The young man picked out to be Laetitia's husband was leaning against the wall, his arms crossed, looking thoroughly surly. Robert judged he should bring this tantalizing conversation to a close.

"Most certainly, you will not come to my rooms," he said. "You will attempt to behave like a lady. You could be polite to poor young Devereux, your unhappy betrothed, while I go and talk with your mistress."

"Your mistress," she said impertinently.

Robert hesitated and looked gravely at her. "Do not overreach yourself, Mistress Knollys," he said quietly. "You are enchanting, of course, and your father is a powerful man, and your mother beloved of the queen, but not even they can save you if you are found to be spreading scandal."

She hesitated, a pert reply ready on her tongue; but then at the steadiness of his gaze, and the firmness of his expression, her dark eyes fell to the toes of his boots. "I am sorry, Sir Robert, I was only speaking in jest."

"Well and good," he said, and turned

away from her, feeling absurdly that although she had been in the wrong, and had
apologized, he had been a pompous bore.

Elizabeth, in the window bay, talking low-
voiced with Cecil, was so absorbed that she
was not scanning the room for Robert.

"And he has gone safely?"

"Gone, and your agreement with him."

"But nothing in writing."

"Your Grace, you cannot think of denying
your word. You said if he attempted the
Scottish throne and was successful then
you would marry him."

"I know I did," she said coolly. "But if he
were to die in his attempt I would not want
such a letter found on him."

Well, thought Cecil, *my dream that she
would be so taken with him, pretty boy that
he is, can be forgotten, if she can imagine
him dying in her cause, and all she cares is
if he is carrying incriminating papers.*

"There was nothing in writing, but you
have given your word, he has given his, and
I have given mine," Cecil reminded her. "You
are promised to marry if he wins Scotland
from the French."

"Oh, yes," she said, opening her dark
eyes very wide. "Yes, indeed."

She was about to turn away from him but he stood his ground. "There is something else, Your Grace."

She hesitated. "Yes?"

"I have intelligence of a possible attempt on your life."

At once she was alert. He saw her face quiver with fear. "A new plot? Another one?"

"I am afraid so."

"The Pope's men?"

"Not this time."

She drew a shaky breath. "How many more men will come against me? This is worse than it was for Mary and she was hated by everyone."

There was nothing he could say; it was true. Mary had been hated; but no monarch had ever been more threatened than this one. Elizabeth's power was all in her person, and too many men thought that if she were dead then the country would be restored.

She turned back to him. "At any rate, you have captured the men who planned it?"

"I have only an informant. I hope he will lead me onward. But I draw it to your attention at this stage because it was not only you who was threatened by this plot."

She turned, curious. "Who else?"

"Sir Robert Dudley."

Her face drained pale. "Spirit, no!"

Good God, does she love him so much? Cecil exclaimed to himself. *She takes a threat to herself as a matter of concern; but when I name him as a victim you would think she was in mortal terror.*

"Indeed, yes. I am sorry."

Elizabeth's eyes were dilated. "Spirit, who would hurt him?"

Cecil could almost feel his thoughts clicking into place as a strategy formed in his mind. "A word with you?"

"Walk with me," she said quickly, and put her hand on his arm. "Walk me away from them all."

Through the velvet of his slashed sleeve he could feel the heat of her palm. *She is sweating with fear for him,* he thought. *This has gone further than I had thought; this has gone to the very madness of forbidden love.*

He patted her hand, trying to steady himself and hide the thoughts that whirled in his head. The courtiers parted before Cecil and the queen; he saw a glimpse of Francis Knollys with his wife, his daughter demurely talking to young Walter Devereux, Mary Sidney, the Bacon brothers in conversation with the queen's uncle, the Duke of Norfolk, a few men from the Spanish ambassador's train, half a dozen hangers-on, a couple of City merchants with their sponsors, nothing out of the ordinary, no strange face, no danger here.

They reached the relative privacy of the gallery and walked away from the others, so that no one could see the bleak agony on her face.

"Cecil, who could dream of hurting him?"

"Your Grace, there are so many," he said gently to her. "Has he never told you that he has enemies?"

"Once," she said. "Once, he said to me that he was surrounded with enemies. I thought . . . I thought he meant rivals."

"He does not know the half of them," Cecil said grimly. "The Catholics blame him for the changes in the church. The Spanish think that you love him, and if he was dead you would take their candidate in marriage. The French hate him since he fought for Philip at St. Quentin, the Commons of England blame him for taking you from your duties of queenship, and every lord of the land, from Arundel to Norfolk, would pay to see him dead because they envy him for your love, or they blame him for the terrible scandal that he has generated about you."

"It cannot be that bad."

"He is the most hated man in England, and the more that you are seen under his influence the greater the danger to you. I spend days and nights on tracking down plots against you; but he . . ." Cecil broke off and shook his head regretfully. "I don't know how to keep him safe."

Elizabeth was white as her ruff; her fingers plucked at his sleeve. "We must have him guarded, Spirit. We must put guards about him, you must find out who would hurt him and arrest them, rack them, find out who they are leagued with. You must stop at nothing; you must take these plotters to the Tower and torture them till they tell us . . ."

"Your own uncle!" he exclaimed. "Half the lords of England! Dudley is widely despised, Your Grace. Only you and half a dozen people tolerate him."

"He is beloved," she whispered.

"Only by his kinsmen, and those he pays," he said loftily.

"Not you?" she said, turning her dark

gaze on him. "You don't hate him, Spirit? You must stand his friend, if only for my sake. You know what he is to me, what joy he brings to my life. He must have your friendship. If you love me, you must love him."

"Oh, I stand his friend," he said carefully. *For I am not such a fool as to let you or him think otherwise.*

She took a shuddering sigh. "Oh, God, we must keep him safe. I could not live if . . . Spirit, you must guard him. How can we make him safe?"

"Only by letting him decline in your favor," Cecil replied. *Careful,* he warned himself. *Care and steadiness here.* "You cannot marry him, Princess; he is a married man and his wife is a virtuous, pleasant woman, pretty and sweet-tempered. He can never be more than a friend to you. If you want to save his life you have to let him go. He has to be your dear courtier, and your Master of Horse; but no more."

She looked quite haggard. "Let him go?"

"Send him home to his wife; it will still the gossips. Set your mind on Scotland and the work we have to do for the country. Dance with other men, set yourself free of him."

"Free of him?" she repeated like a child.

Despite himself, Cecil was moved by the pain in her face. "Princess, this can go nowhere," he said quietly to her. "He is a married man; he cannot put his wife aside for no reason. You cannot sanction a divorce to serve your own lust. He can never marry you. You may love him, but it will always be a dishonorable love. You cannot be husband and wife, you cannot be lovers, you cannot even be seen to desire him. If there is any more scandal spoken against you, it could cost you your throne; it could even cost you your life."

"My life has been on a thread since I was born!" She reared up.

"It could cost *his* life," Cecil switched quickly. "Your favoring of him, as openly as generously as you do, will be his death warrant."

"You will protect him," she said stubbornly.

"I cannot protect him from your friends and family," Cecil replied steadily. "Only you can do that. Now I have told you how. You know what you have to do."

Elizabeth gripped his arm. "I cannot let him go," she said to him in a low moan. "He is the only one . . . he is my only love . . . I cannot send him home to his wife. You must have a heart of stone to suggest it. I cannot let him go."

"Then you will sign his death warrant," he said harshly.

He felt a deep shudder run through her.

"I am unwell," she said quietly. "Get Kat."

He walked her to the end of the gallery and sent a page flying to the queen's rooms for Kat Ashley. She came and took one look at Elizabeth's pallor, and one look at Cecil's grave face. "What's the matter?"

"Oh, Kat," Elizabeth whispered. "The worst thing, the worst thing."

Kat Ashley stepped forward to shield her from the eyes of the court and took her quickly away to her rooms. The court, fascinated, looked at Cecil, who blandly smiled back at them all.

*   *   *

It was raining, the gray drops pouring like a stream down the leaded window panes of Windsor Castle, pattering like tears. Elizabeth had sent for Robert and told her ladies to seat themselves round the fire while he and she talked in the window seat. When Robert came into the room in a swirl of dark red velvet the queen was alone in the window seat, like a solitary girl without friends.

He came up at once and bowed and whispered: "My love?"

Her face was white and her eyelids red and sore from crying. "Oh, Robert."

He took a rapid step toward her and then checked himself, remembering that he must not snatch her to him in public. "What is the matter?" he demanded. "The court thinks you have been taken ill; I have been desperate to see you. What is the matter? What did Cecil say to you this morning?"

She turned her head to the window and put a fingertip to the cold green glass. "He warned me," she said quietly.

"Of what?"

"A new plot, against my life."

Robert's hand instinctively went to where his sword should be, but no man carried arms in the queen's apartments. "My love, don't be afraid. However wicked the plot I should always protect you."

"It was not just against me," she broke in. "I would not be sick with fear like this, just for a plot against me."

"So?" His dark eyebrows were drawn together.

"They want to kill you too," she said quietly. "Cecil says that I have to let you go, for our safety."

That damned cunning sly old fox, Robert cursed inwardly. *What a brilliant move: to use her love against me.*

"We are in danger," he acknowledged quietly to her. "Elizabeth, I beg of you, let me put my wife aside and let me marry you. Once you are my wife and you have my child then all these dangers are gone."

She shook her head. "They will destroy you, as you warned me. Robert, I am going to give you up."

"No!" He spoke too loud in his shock, and the conversation at the fireplace was silenced and all the women looked toward him. He drew closer to the queen. "No, Elizabeth. This cannot be. You cannot just give me up, not when you love me, and I love you. Not when we are happy now. Not after so many years of waiting and waiting for happiness!"

She had herself under the tightest control, he saw her bite her lip to stop the tears coming to her eyes. "I have to. Don't make it harder for me, my love, I think my heart is breaking."

"But to tell me here! In the full glare of the court!"

"Oh, d'you think I could have told you anywhere else? I am not very strong with you, Robert. I have to tell you here, where you cannot touch me, and I have to have your word that you will not try to change my mind. You have to give me up, and give up your dream of our marriage. And I have to let you go, and I have to marry Arran if he is victorious, and the archduke if he is not."

Robert raised his head and would have argued.

"It is the only way to stop the French," she said simply. "Arran or the archduke. We have to have an ally against the French in Scotland."

"You would give me up for a kingdom," he said bitterly.

"For nothing less," she replied steadily. "And I ask something more of you."

"Oh, Elizabeth, you have my heart. What can I give you more?"

Her dark eyes were filled with tears; she put out a shaking hand to him. "Will you still be my friend, Robert? Though we can never be lovers again, even though I will have to marry another man?"

Slowly, oblivious now of the ladies' stares, he took her cold hand in his own, and bent his head and kissed it. Then he knelt to her and held up his hands in the age-old gesture of fealty. She leaned forward and took his praying hands in her own.

"I am yours," he said. "Heart and soul. I always have been since you are my queen, but more than that: you are the only woman I have ever loved and you are the only woman I ever will love. If you want me to dance at your wedding, I will do it as well as I can. If you will recall me from this misery, I will return to joy with you in a second. I am your friend for life, I am your lover forever, I am your husband in the sight of God. You have only to command me, Elizabeth, now and ever, I am yours till death."

They were both trembling, gazing into each other's eyes as if they could never tear themselves away. It was Kat Ashley who had the courage to interrupt them, after long minutes when they had been hand-clasped and silent.

"Your Grace," she said gently. "People will talk."

Elizabeth stirred and released Robert, and he rose to his feet.

"You should rest, my lady," Kat said quietly. She glanced at Robert's white, shocked face. "She's not well," she said. "This is too much for her. Let her go now, Sir Robert."

"May God bring you to good health and happiness," he said passionately, and at her nod he bowed and took himself out of the room before she could see the despair in his own face.

*   *   *

Mr. Hayes's father had been born a tenant of the Dudleys but had risen through the wool trade to the position of mayor at Chislehurst. He had sent his son to school and then to train as a lawyer and when he died, he left the young man a small fortune. John Hayes continued the family connection with the Dudleys, advising Robert's mother on her appeal to reclaim the title and estates, and as Robert rose in power and wealth, running the various wings of Robert's steadily increasing businesses in the City and countrywide.

Amy had often stayed with him at Hayes Court, Chislehurst, and sometimes Robert joined her there to talk business with John

Hayes, to gamble with him, to hunt his land, and to plan their investments.

The Dudley train reached the house at about midday, and Amy was glad to be out of the September sun, which was still hot and bright.

"Lady Dudley." John Hayes kissed her hand. "How good to see you again. Mrs. Minchin will show you to your usual room; we thought you preferred the garden room?"

"I do," Amy said. "Have you heard from my lord?"

"Only that he promises himself the pleasure of seeing you within the week," John Hayes said. "He did not say which day—but we don't expect that, do we?" He smiled at her.

Amy smiled back. *No, for he will not know which day the queen will release him,* said the jealous voice in her head. Amy touched the rosary in her pocket with her finger. "Whenever he is free to come to me, I shall be glad to see him," she said, and turned and went up the stairs behind the house-keeper.

Mrs. Oddingsell came into the house, pushing back her hood and shaking the dust from her skirt. She shook hands with John Hayes; they were old friends.

"She looks well," he said, surprised, nodding his head in the direction of Amy's bedroom. "I heard she was very sick."

"Oh, did you?" said Lizzie levelly. "And where did you hear that from?"

He thought for a moment. "Two places, I think. Someone told me in church the other day, and my clerk mentioned it to me in the City."

"Did they say what ailed her?"

"A malady of the breast, my clerk said. A stone, or a growth, too great for cutting, they said. They said that Dudley might put her aside, that she would agree to go to a convent and annul the marriage because she could never have his child."

Lizzie folded her mouth in a hard line. "It is a lie," she said softly. "Now who do you think would have an interest in spreading such a lie? That Dudley's wife is sick and cannot be cured?"

For a moment he looked at her quite aghast.

"These are deep waters, Mrs. Oddingsell. I had heard that it had gone very far . . ."

"You had heard that they are lovers?"

He glanced around his own empty hall as if nowhere was safe to speak of the queen and Dudley, even if their names were not mentioned.

"I heard that he plans to put his wife aside, and marry the lady of whom we speak, and that she has the power and desire that he should do so."

She nodded. "It seems everyone thinks so. But there are no grounds, and never could be."

He thought for a moment. "If she were known to be too sick to bear children she might step aside," he whispered.

"Or if everyone thought she was ill, then no one would be surprised if she died," Lizzie said, even lower.

John Hayes exclaimed in shock and crossed himself. "Jesu! Mrs. Oddingsell, you must be mad to suggest such a thing. You don't really think that? He would never do such a thing, not Sir Robert!"

"I don't know what to think. But I do know that everywhere we rode from Abingdon to here, there was gossip about his lordship and the queen, and a belief that my lady is sick to death. At one inn the landlady asked me if we needed a doctor before we had even dismounted. Everyone is talking of my lady's illness, and my lord's love affair. So I don't know what to think except that someone is being very busy."

"Not his lordship," he said staunchly. "He would never hurt her."

"I don't know anymore," she repeated.

"Then, if it is not him, who would spread such a rumor, and to what end?"

She looked blankly at him. "Who would prepare the country for his divorce and remarriage? Only the woman who wanted to marry him, I suppose."

*   *   *

Mary Sidney was seated before the fireplace in her brother's apartments at Windsor, one of his new hound puppies on the floor at her feet, gnawing at the toe of her riding boot. Idly, she prodded his fat little belly with the other foot.

"Leave him alone, you will spoil him," Robert commanded.

"He will not leave me alone," she returned. "Get off me, you monster!" She gave him another prod and the puppy squirmed with delight at the attention.

"You would hardly think he was true bred," Robert remarked, as he signed his name on a letter and put it to one side, and then came to the fireplace and drew up a stool on the other side. "He has such low tastes."

"I have had highly bred puppies slavering at my feet before now," his sister said with a smile. "It is no mark of bad breeding to adore me."

"And rightly so," he replied. "But would you call Sir Henry your husband a low-bred puppy?"

"Never to his face." She smiled.

"How is the queen today?" he asked more seriously.

"Still very shaken. She could not eat last night and she only drank warmed ale this morning and ate nothing. She walked in the garden on her own for an hour and came in looking quite distracted. Kat is in and out of her bedroom with possets, and when Elizabeth dressed and came out she would not talk or smile. She is doing no business; she will see nobody. Cecil is striding about with a sheaf of letters and nothing can be decided. And some people say we will lose the war in Scotland because she has despaired already."

He nodded.

She hesitated. "Brother, you must tell me. What did she say to you yesterday? She looked as if her heart was breaking, and now she looks halfway to death."

"She has given me up," he said shortly.

Mary Sidney gasped and put her hand to her mouth. "Never!"

"Indeed, yes. She has asked me to stand her friend but she knows she has to marry. Cecil warned her off me, and she has taken his advice."

"But why now?"

"Firstly the rumors, and then the threats against me."

She nodded. "The rumors are every-where. My own waiting woman came to me with a story of Amy and poison and a whole string of slanderous lies that made my hair stand on end."

"Beat her."

"If she had made up the stories I would do so. But she was only repeating what is being said at every street corner. It is shameful what people are saying about you, and about the queen. Your pageboy was set on at the stables the other day, did you know?"

He shook his head.

"Not for the first time. The lads are saying they won't wear our livery if they go into the City. They are ashamed of our coat of arms, Robert."

He frowned. "I didn't know it was that bad."

"My maid told me that there are men who swear they will see you dead before you marry the queen."

Robert nodded. "Ah, Mary, it could never happen. How could it? I am a married man."

Her head came up in surprise. "I thought you . . . and she . . . had some plan? I thought perhaps . . ."

"You are as bad as these people who dream of divorce and death and dethroning!" he said, smiling. "It is all nonsense. The queen and I had a summertime love affair which has been all dancing and jousting and flowery meadows and now the summer is ended and the winter is coming I have to visit John Hayes with Amy. The country has to go to war with Scotland—Cecil predicted it; and Cecil is right. The queen has to be a queen indeed; she has been Queen of Camelot, now she has to be queen in deadly reality. She has had her summer at leisure, now she has to marry to secure the safety of the kingdom. Her choice has fallen on Arran if he can win her Scotland, or else Archduke Charles, as the best choice for the safety of the country. Whatever she may have felt for me in July, she knows she has to marry either one of them by Christmas."

"She does?" Mary was amazed.

He nodded.

"Oh, Robert, no wonder she sits and stares and says nothing. Her heart must be breaking."

"Aye," he said tenderly. "Her heart may break. But she knows it has to be done. She won't fail her country now. She has never lacked courage. She would sacrifice anything for her country. She will certainly sacrifice me and her love for me."

"And can you bear this?"

Her brother's face was so dark that she thought she had never seen him so grim since he came out of the Tower to face ruin. "I have to face it like a man. I have to find the courage that she has to find. In a way, we are still together. Her heart and mine will break together. We will have that scant comfort."

"You will go back to Amy?"

He shrugged. "I have never left her. We

had a few cross words when we last met, and she may have been distressed by the gossip. In my temper, and in my pride, I swore I should leave her, but she did not believe me for a moment. She stood her ground and said to my face that we were married and could never be divorced. And I knew she was right. In my heart I knew that I could never divorce Amy. What has she ever done to offend? And I knew that I was not going to poison the poor woman or push her down the well! So what else could happen but that the queen and I would have a summer of flirtation and kissing . . . yes! I admit to the kissing . . . and more. Very delicious, very sweet, but always, always, going nowhere. She is Queen of England, I am her Master of Horse. I am a married man and she must marry to save the kingdom."

He glanced over. There were tears in his sister's eyes. "Robert, I am so afraid that you will never love anyone but Elizabeth. You will have to live the rest of your life loving her."

He gave her a wry smile. "That's true. I have loved her from childhood and in these last months I have fallen in love, more deeply and more truly than I every thought possible. I thought myself hard of heart, and yet I find she is everything to me. Indeed, I love her so much that I am going to let her go. I am going to help her to marry Arran or the archduke. Her only safety lies that way."

"You will give her up for her own safety?"

"Whatever it costs me."

"My God, Robert, I never thought you could be so . . ."

"So what?"

"So selfless!"

He laughed. "I thank you!"

"I mean it. To help the woman you love to marry another is a truly selfless thing to do." She was silent for a moment. "And how will you bear it?" she asked tenderly.

"I shall treasure a memory of loving a beautiful young queen in the very first year of her reign," he said. "In the golden summer when she came to her throne in her youth and her beauty and she thought she could do anything—even marry a man like me. And I shall go home to my wife and make a nursery full of heirs and I shall name all the girls Elizabeth."

She put her sleeve to her eyes. "Oh, my dearest brother."

He covered her hand with his own. "Will you help me do this, Mary?"

"Of course," she whispered. "Of course, anything."

"Go to the Spanish ambassador, de Quadra, and tell him that the queen needs his help in concluding the match with the archduke."

"I? But I hardly know him."

"It doesn't matter. He knows us Dudleys well enough. Go to him as if you were coming directly from the queen, not at my request. Tell him that she felt she could not approach him directly, not after this summer when she has blown hot and cold on the plan. But if he will come to her with a renewed proposal, she will say 'yes' at once."

"This is the queen's own wish?" Mary asked.

He nodded. "She wants to signal to everyone that I have not been rejected, that she stands my friend, that she loves me and you too. She wants the Dudley family to broker this marriage."

"It's a great honor to take such a message," she said solemnly. "And a great responsibility too."

"The queen thought we should keep it in

the family." He smiled. "Mine is the sacrifice, you are the messenger, and together, the deed is done."

"And what of you, when she is married?"

"She will not forget me," he said. "We have loved each other too well and too long for her to turn from me. And you and I will be rewarded both by her and by the Spanish for faithful dealing now. This is the right thing to do, Mary; I have no doubts. It ensures her safety and it takes me out of the reach of lying tongues . . . and worse. I don't doubt that there are men who would see me dead. This is my safety as well as hers."

"I will go tomorrow," she promised him.

"And tell him you come from her, at her bidding."

"I will," she said.

*   *   *

Cecil, sitting at his fireside in the silence of the palace at midnight, rose from his chair to answer a discreet tap at the door. The man who entered the room put back his black hood and went to the fire to warm his hands.

"Do you have a glass of wine?" he asked in a light Spanish accent. "This mist on the river will give me an ague. If it is this damp in September, what will it be like in midwinter?"

Cecil poured the wine and gestured the man to a chair by the fire. He threw on another log. "Better?"

"Yes, I thank you."

"It must be interesting news to bring you out on such a cold night as this," Cecil remarked to no one in particular.

"Only the queen herself, proposing marriage to Archduke Charles!"

Cecil's response was wholly satisfying. His head came up; he looked astounded. "The queen has proposed marriage?"

"Through an intermediary. Did you not know of this?"

Cecil shook his head, refusing to answer. Information was currency to Cecil and, unlike Gresham, he believed that there was neither good nor bad coinage in the currency of information. It was all valuable.

"Do you know the intermediary?" he asked.

"Lady Mary Sidney," the man said. "One of the queen's own ladies."

Cecil nodded; perhaps this was the ripple from the stone he had thrown. "And Lady Mary had a proposal?"

"That the archduke should come at once to pay the queen a visit, as if in politeness. That she will accept a proposal of marriage at that visit. The terms will be drawn up at once, and that the wedding will take place by Christmas."

Cecil's face was a frozen mask. "And what did His Excellency think of this proposal?"

"He thought it could be done now or never," the man said bluntly. "He thinks she hopes to save her reputation before any worse is said of her. He thinks she has seen reason at last."

"He said this aloud?"

"He dictated it to me to translate into code to send to King Philip."

"You do not bring me a copy of the letter?"

"I dare not," the man said briefly. "He is no fool. I risk my life even telling you this much."

Cecil waved the danger aside. "Lady Mary would no doubt have told me in the morning, had I not known of it already from the queen herself."

The man looked a little dashed. "But would she tell you that my master has written to the archduke this very night to recommend that he comes at once on this visit? That Caspar von Breuner has sent for Austrian lawyers to draw up the marriage contract? That this time we believe the queen is in earnest and we are going ahead? And the archduke should be here by November?"

"No, that is good news," Cecil said. "Anything else?"

The man looked thoughtful. "That is all. Shall I come again when I have more?"

Cecil reached into the drawer of his desk and drew out a small leather purse. "Yes. This is for now. And as for your papers, they will be drawn up for you . . ." He paused.

"When?" the man asked eagerly.

"When the marriage is solemnized," Cecil said. "We can all rest safe in our beds when that takes place. Did you say Christmas?"

"The queen herself named Christmas as her wedding day."

"Then I shall give you your papers to allow you to stay in England when your master, the archduke, is named Elizabeth's consort."

The man bowed in assent and then hesitated before leaving. "You always have a purse for me in that drawer," he said curiously. "Do you expect me to come, or do so many men report to you that you have their fee ready?"

Cecil, whose informants now numbered more than a thousand, smiled. "Only you," he said sweetly.

*　　*　　*

Robert arrived at Hayes Court in September, in quiet and somber mood, his face grim.

Amy, watching him from an upper window, thought that she had not seen that desolate look on his face since he had come home from the siege of Calais when England had lost its last foothold in France. Slowly, she went downstairs, wondering what he had lost now.

He was dismounting from his horse; he greeted her with a cursory kiss on the cheek.

"My lord," Amy said in greeting. "Are you unwell?"

"No," he said shortly. Amy wanted to cling to him, to treasure his touch but gently he put her aside. "Let me go, Amy, I am dirty."

"I don't mind!"

"But I do." He turned; his friend John Hayes was coming down the front steps of the house.

"Sir Robert! I thought I heard horses!"

Robert clapped John on the back. "No need to ask how you are," he said cheerfully. "You're putting on weight, John. Obviously not hunting enough."

"But you look dreadful." His friend was concerned. "Are you sick, sir?"

Robert shrugged. "I'll tell you later."

"Court life?" John said, guessing quickly.

"It would be easier to dance the volta in hell than survive in London," Robert said precisely. "Between Her Grace, and Sir William Cecil, and the women of the queen's chamber, and the Privy Council, my head is spinning from dawn when I get up to check the stables, till midnight when I can finally leave the court and go to bed."

"Come and have a glass of ale," John offered. "Tell me all about it."

"I stink of horse," Robert said.

"Oh, who cares for that?"

The two men turned and went toward the house. Amy was about to follow them and then she dropped back and let them go on. She thought that perhaps her husband would be relieved if he could talk alone with his friend, and would perhaps be easier, not constrained by her presence. But she crept after them and sat on the wooden chair in the hall, outside the closed door, so that she should be there for him when he came out.

*   *   *

The ale helped Robert's bad temper, and then a wash in hot, scented water and a change of clothes. A good dinner completed the change; Mrs. Minchin was a famously lavish housekeeper. By six in the evening when the four of them, Sir Robert, Amy, Lizzie Oddingsell, and John Hayes, sat down to a game of cards, his lordship was restored to his usual sweet temper and his face was less drawn. By nightfall he was tipsy and Amy realized that she would get no sense from him that evening. They went to bed together, and she hoped that they would make love, but he merely turned away, heaved the covers high over his shoulders, and fell into a deep sleep. Amy, lying awake in the darkness, did not think that she should wake him since he was tired, and in any case, she never initiated their lovemaking. She wanted him; but she did not know where to begin—his smooth unyielding back did not respond to her tentative touch. She turned away herself, and watched the moonlight coming through the slats of the shutters, listened to his heavy breathing, and remembered her duty before God to love her husband whatever the circumstances. She resolved to be a better wife to him in the morning.

* * *

"Would you like to ride with me, Amy?" Robert asked politely at breakfast. "I have to keep my hunter fit, but I shan't go too far or too fast today."

"I should like to come," she said at once. "But don't you think it will rain?"

He was not listening; he had turned his head and ordered his manservant to get the horses ready.

"I beg your pardon?"

"I only said I was afraid it will rain," she repeated.

"Then we will come home again."

Amy flushed, thinking that she had sounded like a fool.

On the ride it was not much better. She could think of nothing to say but the most obvious banalities about the weather and the fields on either side of them, while he rode, his face dark, his eyes abstracted, his gaze fixed on the track ahead of them but seeing nothing.

"Are you well, my lord?" Amy asked quietly when they turned for home. "You do not seem yourself at all."

He looked at her as if he had forgotten that she was there. "Oh, Amy. Yes, I am well enough. A little troubled by events at court."

"What events?"

He smiled as if he were being interrogated by a child. "Nothing for you to worry about."

"You can tell me," she assured him. "I am your wife. I want to know if something troubles you. Is it the queen?"

"She is in great danger," he said. "Every day there is news of another plot against her. There never was a queen who was more loved by half the people and yet more hated by the others."

"So many people think she has no right to the throne," Amy remarked. "They say that since she was a bastard, it should have gone to Mary, Queen of Scots, and then the kingdoms would be united now, without a war, without the change to the church, without the trouble that Elizabeth brings."

Robert choked on his surprise. "Amy, whatever are you thinking? This is treason that you are speaking to me. Pray God you never say such a thing to anyone else. And you should never repeat it, even to me."

"It's only the truth," Amy observed calmly.

"She is the anointed Queen of England."

"Her own father declared her to be a bastard, and that was never revoked," Amy said reasonably enough. "She has not even revoked it herself."

"There is no doubt that she is his legitimate daughter," Robert said flatly.

"Excuse me, husband, but there is every doubt," Amy said politely. "I don't blame you for not wanting to see it, but facts are facts."

Robert was astounded by her confidence. "Good God, Amy, what has come over you? Who have you been talking to? Who has filled your head with this nonsense?"

"No one, of course. Who do I ever see but your friends?" she asked.

For a moment, he thought she was being sarcastic and he looked sharply at her, but her face was serene, her smile as sweet as ever.

"Amy, I am serious. There are men all round England with their tongues slit for less than you have said."

She nodded. "How cruel of her to torture innocent men for speaking nothing but the truth."

They rode for a moment in silence, Robert utterly baffled by the sudden uprising in his own household.

"Have you always thought like this?" he asked quietly. "Even though you have always known that I supported her? That I was proud to be her friend?"

Amy nodded. "Always. I never thought her claim was the best."

"You have never said anything to me."

She shot him a little smile. "You never asked me."

"I would have been glad to know that I had a traitor in my household."

She gave a little laugh. "There was a time when you were the traitor and I was right-thinking. It is the times that have changed, not us."

"Yes, but a man likes to know if his wife is plotting treason."

"I have always thought that she was not

the true heir; but I thought she was the best choice for the country, until now."

"Why, what has happened now?" he demanded.

"She is turning against the true religion, and supporting the Protestant rebels in Scotland," she said levelly. "She has imprisoned all the bishops, except those that have been forced into exile. There is no church anymore, just frightened priests not knowing what they should do. It is an open attack on the religion of our country. What does she hope for? To make England and Scotland and Wales and Ireland all Protestant? To rival the Holy Father himself? To make a Holy Empire of her own? Does she want to be a Pope in petticoats? No wonder she does not marry. Who could bear such a wife as she would be?"

"True religion?" Robert exclaimed. "Amy, you have been a Protestant all your life. We were married by King Edward's service in his presence. Who have you been talking with to get such ideas in your head?"

She looked at him with her usual mildness. "I have been talking with no one, Robert. And our household was Papist for all of Queen Mary's years. I do think, you know. In the long hours that I spend alone, I have nothing to do but to think. And I travel around the country, and I see what Elizabeth and her servants are doing. I see the destruction of the monasteries and the poverty of the church lands. She is throwing hundreds into beggary; she is leaving the poor and sick without hospitals. Her coins are worth next to nothing, and her churches cannot even celebrate Mass. No one who looked at England under Elizabeth could think of her as a good queen. All she has brought is trouble."

She paused, seeing his appalled expression. "I don't talk like this to anyone else," she reassured him. "I thought it would be all right to share my thoughts with you. And I have wanted to speak to you about the Bishop of Oxford."

"The Bishop of Oxford can rot in hell!" he burst out. "You cannot talk to me of these matters. It's not fitting. You are a Protestant, Amy, like me. Born and bred. Like me."

"I was born a Catholic; then I was a Protestant when King Edward was on the throne," she said calmly. "And then I was Roman Catholic when Queen Mary was on the throne. Changed and changed about.

Just as you have been. And your father re-canted his Protestantism and called it a great error, didn't he? He blamed all the sor-rows of the country on his heresy, those were his very words. We were all Catholics then. And now you want to be Protestant, and you want me to be Protestant, just be-cause she is. Well, I am not."

At last he heard a note that gave him the key to her. "Ah, you are jealous of her."

Amy's hand went to her pocket to touch the cool beads of her rosary. "No," she said steadily. "I have sworn I will not feel jeal-ousy, not of any woman in the world, least of all her."

"You have always been a jealous woman," he said frankly. "It is your curse, Amy—and mine."

She shook her head. "I have broken my curse then. I will never be jealous again."

"It is your jealousy that leads you into these dangerous speculations. And all this theology is just a mask for your jealous ha-tred of her."

"Not so, my lord. I have sworn I will re-nounce jealousy."

"Oh, admit it," he said, smiling. "It is noth-ing but a woman's spite."

She reined in her horse and looked at him so steadily that he had to meet her eyes. "Why, what cause have I for jealousy?" she demanded.

For a moment Robert blustered, shifting in the saddle, his horse nervous under a tightened rein.

"What cause have I?" she demanded again.

"You will have heard talk about her and me?"

"Of course. I assume that all the country has heard it."

"That would make you jealous. It would make any woman jealous."

"Not if you can assure me that there is no foundation to it."

"You cannot think that she and I are lovers!" He made it into a joke.

Amy did not laugh; she did not even smile. "I will not think it, if you can assure me it is not true." In her pocket she was gripping tight on her rosary. It felt like a rope that might save her from drowning in the deeps of this dangerous conversation.

"Amy, you cannot think that I am her lover and plotting to divorce you, or to murder you as the gossipmongers say!"

Still she did not smile. "If you assure me that the rumors are false then I will not attend to them," she said steadily. "Of course I have heard them, and very vivid and unpleasant they are."

"They are most scurrilous and untrue," he said boldly. "And I would take it very badly in you, Amy, if you were to listen to them."

"I don't listen to them, I listen to you. I am listening very carefully now. Can you swear on your honor that you are not in love with the queen and that you have never thought of a divorce?"

"Why do you even ask me?"

"Because I want to know. Do you want a divorce, Robert?"

"Surely, you would never consent to a divorce if such a thing were ever proposed?" he asked curiously.

Amy's eyes flew to his face and he saw her blench as if she were sickened. For a moment she was frozen on her horse before him, her mouth a little open as she gasped, and then, very slowly, she touched her horse with her little heel and preceded him down the track toward home.

Robert followed her. "Amy . . ."

She did not stop, nor turn her head. He

realized that he had never before called her name without her immediate response. Amy always came when he called her; generally she was at his side long before he called her. It felt very strange and unnatural that little Amy Robsart should ride away from him with her face as white as death.

"Amy . . ."

Steadily she rode on, looking neither to right nor left, certainly not looking back to see if he was following. In silence, she rode all the way home, and when she got to the stable yard she handed her reins to the groom and went into the house in silence.

Robert hesitated, and then followed her up the stairs to their bedroom. He did not know how to manage this strange new Amy. She went into their room and closed the door; he waited in case he could hear the sound of her turning the key in the lock. If she barred the door against him he could be angry, if she locked him out he was within his legal rights to break down the door, he had a legal right to beat her—but she did not. She closed the door; she did not lock it. He went forward and opened the door, as was his right, and went in.

She was seated at the window in her

usual seat, looking out, as she so often looked out for him.

"Amy," he said gently.

She turned her head. "Robert, enough of this. I need to know the truth. I am sickened to my heart by lies and rumor. Do you want a divorce or not?"

She was so calm that he felt, incredulously, a glimmer of hope. "Amy, what is in your mind?"

"I want to know if you want to be released from our marriage," she said steadily. "I am perhaps not the wife you need, now that you are become such a great man. That has become clear to me over recent months.

"And God has not blessed us with children yet," she added. "These alone might be reasons enough. But if half the gossip is true then it is possible that the queen would take you as her husband if you were free. No Dudley could resist such a temptation. Your father would have boiled his wife in oil for such a chance, and he adored her. So I ask you, please tell me honestly, my lord: do you want a divorce?"

Slowly Robert realized what she was saying; slowly it dawned on him that she had been preparing herself for this, but instead of a sense of opportunity he felt rage and distress growing in him like a storm.

"It's too late now!" he exploded. "My God! That you should say this to me now! It's no good you coming to your senses now, after all these years, it's too late. It's too late for me!"

Startled, Amy looked up at him, her face shocked at the suppressed violence in his voice. "What d'you mean?"

"She has given me up," he cried, the truth bursting out of him in his agony. "She loved me and she knew it; she wanted to marry me and I her, but she has to have an ally for a war against France and she has given me up for the archduke or that puppy Arran."

There was an appalled silence. "Is that why you are here?" she asked. "And why you are so grave and quiet?"

He sank into the window seat and bowed his head. Almost he felt he might weep like a woman. "Yes," he said shortly. "Because it is all over for me. She has told me she has to be released and I have let her go. There is nothing left for me but you; whether you are the right woman or not, whether we have children or not, whether we will waste the rest of our lives together, and die hating each other, or not."

He had his hand to his mouth; he closed his teeth on his knuckles, forcing any more words back into silence.

"You are unhappy," she remarked.

"I have never been in a worse case in all my life," he said shortly.

She said nothing, and in a few moments Robert mastered himself, swallowing his grief, and raised his head to look at her.

"Were you lovers?" she asked very quietly.

"What does it matter, now?"

"But were you? You can tell me the truth now, I think."

"Yes," he said dully. "We were lovers."

Amy rose, and he looked up at her as she stood before him. Her face, against the brightness of the window, was in shadow. He could not see her expression. He could not tell what she was thinking. But her voice was as calm as ever.

"Then I must tell you: you have made a very grave mistake, my lord. A mistake in my nature, and in what insults I will tolerate, a mistake in yourself and how you should live. You must be mad indeed if you make such a confession to me, hoping that I might sympathize. Me, of all women: who am most hurt by this, I, who know what it is to love without return. I, who know what it is to waste a life in loving.

"You are a fool, Robert, and she is a whore indeed, as half the country thinks. She will have to invent another new religion entirely to justify the hurt that she has done to me, and the peril she has led you to. She has brought you to sin and danger; she has brought this country to the brink of ruin, to heartbreak and poverty; and she is only in the first year of her reign. What wickedness will she undertake before she is done?"

Then she drew her skirts back from him as if she would not have him touch even the hem of her gown, and walked out of the room they had shared.

*   *   *

The November mist was cold on the river. The queen, looking down on the shrouded Thames from the high windows of White-hall, shivered and drew her furred gown a little closer around her.

"Still a lot better than Woodstock." Kat Ashley smiled at her.

Elizabeth made a face. "Better than arrest

in the Tower," she said. "Better than a lot of places. But not better than midsummer. It's freezing cold and deadly dull. Where is Sir Robert?"

Kat did not smile. "Visiting his wife still, Princess."

Elizabeth hunched her shoulder. "There's no need to look like that, Kat. I have a right to know where my Master of Horse is. And I have a right to expect him to attend court."

"And he has a right to see his wife," Kat said stoutly. "Letting him go was the best day's work you ever did, Princess. I know it is painful for you, but . . ."

Elizabeth's face was peaked with the loss of him. "It's not a good day's work done; your congratulations are too early," she said sulkily. "It is a sacrifice I have to make fresh, every day. It was not the work of one day, Kat, every single day of my life I have to live without him and to know that he is living without me. Every morning I wake and know that I may not smile at him and see him look at me with love. Every night I lie down to sleep aching for him. I don't see how to bear it. It has been forty-one days since I sent him from me, and still I am sick with love for him. It does not ease at all."

Kat Ashley looked at the young woman whom she had known from girlhood. "He can be your friend," she said consolingly. "You don't have to lose him altogether."

"It's not his friendship I miss," Elizabeth said bluntly. "It's him. The very person of him. His presence. I want his shadow on my wall, I want the smell of him. I can't eat without him, I can't do the business of the realm. I can't read a book without wanting his opinion, I can't hear a tune without wanting to sing it to him. It's like all the life and color and warmth has bled out of the world when he is not with me. I am not missing my friend, Kat. I am missing my eyes. I can't see without him. Without him I am a blind woman."

The doors opened and Cecil came in, his face grave. "Sir William," Elizabeth said without much warmth. "And bringing bad news, if I judge you rightly."

"Just news," he said neutrally, until Kat Ashley stepped away from the two of them.

"It's Ralph Sadler," he said shortly, naming their agent in Berwick. "He sent our money, a thousand crowns of it, to the Lords Protestant; and Lord Bothwell, a turncoat Protestant serving the regent Mary of

Guise, intercepted him and stole it. We can't get it back."

"A thousand crowns!" She was appalled. "That's nearly half of all the money we raised for them."

"And we were right to do so. The Lords Protestant are selling their very knives and plates to arm their forces. And who would have thought that Bothwell would dare betray his fellow lords? But we have lost the money, and, worse than the loss, the queen regent will know now that we are arming her enemies."

"It was French crowns, not English coins," she said rapidly, rushing to a lie. "We can deny everything."

"It came from our man, Sadler at Berwick. They can hardly doubt it was our money."

Elizabeth was appalled. "Cecil, what are we going to do?"

"It is sufficient reason for the French to declare war against us. With this, we have given them just cause."

She turned and walked away from him, her fingers rubbing at the cuticles on her nails. "They won't declare war on me," she said. "Not while they think I will marry a Hapsburg. They wouldn't dare."

"Then you will have to marry him," he pressed her. "They will have to know that it is going ahead. You will have to announce your betrothal and name the date of your marriage: Christmas."

Her look was bleak. "I have no choice?"

"You know you have not. He is making ready to come to England right now."

She tried to smile. "I shall have to marry him."

"You will."

*   *   *

Robert Dudley came back to find the court in feverish mood. Duke John of Finland had arrived to represent his master, Prince Erik of Sweden, and was scattering money and promising favors to anyone who would support his proposal of marriage to the queen.

Elizabeth, sparkling with counterfeit gaiety, danced with him, walked and talked with the archduke's ambassador, and mystified them both as to her real intentions. When Cecil drew her to one side the smiles fell from her face like a dropped mask. The news from Scotland was grim. The Lords Protestant were encamped before Leith Castle, hoping to starve out the regent before reinforcements arrived from France; but

the castle was impregnable, the queen regent inside was well supplied, and the
French would be coming soon. No one
trusted the Scots to hold the siege. They
were an army for a speedy attack and victory; they had no discipline for a long war.
And now everyone knew that it was a war,
not some petty rebellion. It was a full-blown,
perilous war and none of the court's brittle
gaiety could conceal its anxiety.

Elizabeth greeted Robert pleasantly but
coolly, and never invited him to be alone
with her. In return, he gave her a slow, sweet
smile and kept his distance.

"Is it all over between you forever?" Mary
Sidney asked him, glancing from the queen
seated very straight on her chair, watching
the dancing, to her brother's dark gaze,
watching Elizabeth.

"Doesn't it look like that?" he asked.

"It's obvious that you no longer seek each
other out. You are never alone with her anymore," she said. "I wondered what you were
feeling."

"Like death," he said simply. "Every day I
wake and know that I will see her and yet
I cannot whisper in her ear, or touch her

hand. I cannot tempt her away from her meetings, I cannot steal her away from others. Every day I greet her like a stranger and I see the pain in her eyes. Every day I hurt her with my coldness and she destroys me with hers. It is as bad being away from court as it is being near her. The coldness between us is killing us both and I cannot even tell her that I pity her."

He glanced briefly at his sister's aghast face and then he looked back at the queen. "She is so alone," he said. "I see her holding herself together by a thread. She is so afraid. And I know that, and I cannot help her."

"Afraid?" Mary repeated.

"She is afraid for her own life, she is afraid for her country, and I imagine she is utterly terrified that she is going to have to take us into war with the French. The old Queen Mary fought the French and they defeated her and destroyed her reputation. And they are stronger now than they were then. And this time the war will be on English soil in England."

"What will she do?"

"Delay as long as she can," Robert predicted. "But the siege has to break one way or another, and then what?"

"And what will you do?"

"Watch her from a distance, pray for her, miss her like a mortal ache."

*   *   *

In the middle of November Robert's question was answered. The worst news came: the French queen regent's forces had stormed out of the trap of Leith Castle and thrown their Protestant tormentors back to Stirling. The regent, for her daughter Mary, Queen of Scots, held Edinburgh once more, and the Protestant cause in Scotland was utterly defeated.

Winter 1559-60

Amy traveled on the cold, wet roads back to Stanfield Hall, her girlhood home in Norfolk, for the winter season. The skies arching above the flat landscape were gray with rain clouds, the land beneath was brown speckled with gray flints, as drab as homespun and as poor. Amy rode through the cold with her hood up and her head down.

She did not expect to see Robert again before Christmas; she did not expect to see him at any time during the twelve days of the Christmas feast. She knew that he would be engaged at court, planning the festivities, organizing the masques, the players, the parties, and the hunting, for the court was determined to celebrate the winter feast, thinking, but not saying aloud, that it might be their last with Elizabeth as queen. She knew that her husband would be constantly at the side of the young queen: her lover, her friend, her intimate companion. She knew that whether they were lovers or whether they were estranged there was no one in the world for Robert but Elizabeth.

"I don't blame him," she whispered on her knees in Syderstone parish church, looking toward the blank space on the altar where the crucifix had once stood, looking to the plinth where a statue of the Virgin Mary had once raised her kindly stone hand to bless the faithful. "I won't blame him," she whispered to the empty spaces that were all that Elizabeth's new priest had left for the faithful to turn to in prayer. "And I won't blame her. I don't want to blame either of them, anyone. I have to be free from my own rage and my own grief. I have to say that he can walk away from me, he can go to another woman, he can love her more than he ever loved me, and I have to release my jealousy and my pain and my grief from my heart. I have to let it all go, or it will destroy me."

She dropped her head to her hands. "This

pain in my breast which throbs all the time is my wound of grief," she said. "It is like a spear thrust into my heart. I have to forgive him to make it heal. Every time I pluck at it with my jealousy the pain breaks out afresh. I will make myself forgive him. I will even make myself forgive her."

She lifted her head from her hands and looked toward the altar. Faintly against the stone she could see the outline where the crucifix had hung. She closed her eyes and prayed to it as if it were still there. "I will not agree to the heresy of divorce. Even if he was to come back to me and say that she had changed her mind and she wanted them to marry, even then I would not consent to it. God joined Robert and me together; no one can put us apart. I know that. He knows that. Probably even she, in her poor sinful heart, knows that."

*   *   *

In his grand rooms in Whitehall Cecil was laboring over the writing of a letter. It was addressed to the queen, but it was not in his usual brisk style of numbered points. It was a far more formal letter, composed by him for the Scottish Protestants to send to her. The circuitous route of the letter, from

Cecil to Scotland, copied by the Scots lords in their own hands and sent back south urgently to the queen, was justified in Cecil's mind because something had to shake Elizabeth into sending an English army into Scotland.

The French garrison at Leith had burst out of the siege and defeated the Scottish Protestants encamped before the castle. In the horror of his defeat the Earl of Arran, Cecil's great hope in Scotland, was behaving most oddly: alternately raving with rage and lapsing into silence and tears. No feats of heroic leadership could be expected from poor James Hamilton, and no triumphant marriage with Elizabeth; the poor sweet-faced young man was clearly half mad and his defeat was pushing him over the brink. The Scottish lords were leaderless, on their own. Without Elizabeth's support they were friendless too. What was a retreat now would be a rout when the French reinforcements landed, and Sir Nicholas Throckmorton, newly arrived from Paris, frantic with fear, warned that the French fleet was massing in all the Normandy ports, the troops were armed and would set sail as soon as there was a favorable wind. The ambassador swore that the French had no doubt that they would first conquer Scotland, and then march on England. They had no doubt at all that they would win.

Your Grace, Cecil wrote for the Scots.

As a fellow religionist, as an ally who fears the power of the French, as a neighbor and a friend, we beg you to come to our aid. If you do not support us, we stand alone against the usurping French, and there can be no doubt that after Scotland falls, the French will invade England. On that day, you will wish that you had helped us now, for there will be none of us alive to help you.

We are not disloyal to Queen Mary of Scotland; we are defying her wicked advisors, the French, not her. We are defying the regent Mary of Guise who is ruling in the place of our true Queen Mary. The regent's countrymen, French troops, are already engaged, any treaty you have with the French is already broken since they have taken up arms against us, on our soil. The regent's family are our sworn enemies, and yours.

If we had appealed like this to your father, he would have defended us and so united the kingdom; it was his great plan. Please, be your father's true daughter and come to our aid.

You can add what you like, Cecil wrote in a postscript to the Scots lords, but take care that you do not sound like rebels against a legitimate ruler; she will not support an outright rebellion. If the French have murdered any women and children by the time you come to write, you should tell her of it, and do not stint in the telling. Do not mention money; give her good reason to think that it will be a swift and cheap campaign. I leave you to tell her the current situation when this letter comes to you and you copy it and send it on. God speed, and God help you.

And God help us all, he said fearfully to himself as he folded it up and sealed it in three places with a blank seal. He had left it unsigned. Cecil only rarely put his name to anything.

*

A new masque, planned by Robert, was to have the ever-popular theme of Camelot; but not even he, with his determined charm, could put much joy in it.

The queen played the spirit of England, and sat on the throne while the young ladies of her chamber danced before her and the players came later with a specially written play to celebrate the greatness of Arthur's England. There was an anti-masque of characters who threatened the golden glory of the round table, let no one doubt that one of the signs of a great kingdom was the existence of its enemies, but they were thrown down without much difficulty; in Robert's fictional England there was no sign of Elizabeth's constant terror of war.

Elizabeth, looking around the court through the dancers, saw Robert and made herself look past him. Robert, standing near enough to the throne to be summoned, should she want to speak to him, saw her dark eyes go by him and knew that he had been caught gazing at her.

Like a greensick boy, he said angrily to himself.

She looked once directly at him and gave

him a faint smile, as if they were ghosts already, as if the shade of Elizabeth had dimly seen, through mist, the young man she had loved as a boy; and then she turned her head to Caspar von Breuner, the archduke's ambassador, the ally that she must have, the husband she must marry, to ask him when he thought the archduke would arrive in England.

The ambassador was not to be diverted. Not even Elizabeth, with all her charm deployed, could bring a smile to his face. Finally he rose from his seat, pleading ill health.

"See the trouble you have caused?" Norfolk said sharply to Dudley.

"I?"

"Baron von Breuner thinks my cousin the queen unlikely to marry while she is openly in love with another man, and has advised the archduke not to come to England yet."

"I am the queen's loyal friend, as you know," Dudley said disdainfully. "And I want nothing but what is best for her."

"You are a damned aspiring dog," Norfolk swore at him. "And you have stood in her light so that no prince in Europe will have her. D'you think they don't hear the gossip?

D'you think that they don't know that you are all over her like the Sweat? D'you think they believe that you and she have called it off now? Everyone thinks that you have just stepped back for her to pick her cuckold, and no man of honor will have her."

"You insult her; I will see you for it," Dudley said, white with anger.

"I may insult her, but you have ruined her," Norfolk threw back at him.

"Because some archduke won't come to pay court?" Dudley demanded. "You are neither a true friend nor a true Englishman if you think she should marry a foreigner. Why should we have another foreign prince on the English throne? What good did Philip of Spain do us?"

"Because she must be married," Norfolk said in a heat of rage. "And to royal blood, at any rate to a better man than a dog like you."

"Gentlemen." The cool tones of Sir Francis made them turn. "Noblemen indeed. The queen is looking your way; you are breaking up the pleasant harmony of the feast."

"Tell him," Norfolk said, pushing past Dudley. "I am beyond listening to this nonsense while my kinswoman is ruined and the country sinks without allies."

Robert let him go. Despite himself he glanced at the throne. Elizabeth was looking toward him. The ambassador had left and in her concern for what her uncle was saying to the man she loved, she had not noticed even his farewell bow.

*   *   *

The Scots Protestants' letter, duly travel-stained and authentically rewritten, came to the queen's hand at the end of November. Cecil brought it to her and laid it on her desk as she was prowling around the room, unable to concentrate on anything.

"Are you ill?" he asked, looking at the pallor of her skin and her restlessness.

"Unhappy," Elizabeth said shortly.

That damned Dudley, he thought to himself, and moved the letter a little closer so that she would open it.

She read it slowly.

"This gives you cause to send an army to Scotland," Cecil said to her. "This is an appeal by the united lords of Scotland for your help in resisting a usurping power: the French. No one can say you are invading for your own ends. No one can say that you are overthrowing a legitimate queen. This is your invitation from the legitimate lords, citing their justifiable grievances. You can say 'yes.'"

"No," she said nervously. "Not yet."

"We have sent funds," Cecil enumerated. "We have sent observers. We know that the Scots lords will fight well. We even know that they can defeat Mary of Guise; they threw her back right to the very shore of the sea at Leith. We know that the French will come, but they have not yet set sail. They are waiting for the weather to change. Only the wind stands between us and invasion. Only the very air stands between us and disaster. We know this is our moment. We have to take it."

She rose from her desk. "Cecil, half the Privy Council warn me that we are certain to lose. Lord Clinton, the High Admiral, says he cannot guarantee that our navy could hold off a French fleet; they have better ships and better guns. The Earl of Pembroke, the Marquess of Winchester advise me against going into Scotland; your own brother-in-law, Nicholas Bacon, says the risk is too great. Caspar von Breuner warns me in secret that although he and the emperor are my friends, they are certain that we will lose. The French court laughs out loud at the thought of us trying to make war against them. They find it laughable that we should even dream of it. Everyone I ask tells me that we are certain to lose."

"We are certain to lose if we leave it too late," Cecil said. "But I think we can possibly win if we send our army now."

"Perhaps in the spring," she temporized.

"In the spring the French fleet will be moored in Leith dock and the French will have garrisoned every castle in Scotland against us. You might as well send them the keys now and be done with it."

"It is a risk, it is such a risk," Elizabeth said miserably, turning to the window, rubbing at her fingernails in her nervousness.

"I know it. But you have to take it. You have to take the risk because the chance of winning now is greater than you will ever have later."

"We can send more money," she said miserably. "Gresham can borrow more money for us. But I dare not do more."

"Take advice," he urged her. "Let us see what the Privy Council has to say."

"I have no advisors," she said desolately.

Dudley again, Cecil thought. *She can barely live without him.* Aloud he said bracingly: "Your Grace, you have a whole council of advisors. We shall consult them tomorrow."

*   *   *

But the next day, before the meeting of the Privy Council, there came a visitor from Scotland. Lord Maitland of Lethington came in disguise, authorized by the other Scots lords secretly to offer the queen the crown of Scotland if she would only support them against the French.

"So, they have despaired of Arran," Cecil said, his joy so great that he could almost taste it on his tongue. "They want you."

For a moment Elizabeth's ready ambition leapt up. "Queen of France, Scotland, Wales, Ireland, and England," she breathed. "Lands from Aberdeen to Calais. I would be one of the greatest princes in Europe, one of the richest."

"This makes the future of the kingdom a certainty," Cecil promised her. "Think of what England could do if joined with Scotland! We would be safe at last, and safe forever from the danger of invasion from the north. We would break the risk of invasion from the French. We could use the strength and wealth of Scotland to go onward and forward. We would become a mighty power in Christendom. Who can tell what we might achieve? The Crown of England and Scotland together would be a power in the world that would be recognized by everyone! We would be the first great Protestant kingdom that the world has ever known."

For a moment he thought he had managed to give her his own vision of the destiny she could claim.

Then she turned her head away. "This is to entrap me," she complained. "When the French invade Scotland I would have to fight them. They would be on my land; I could not ignore it. This would force us to fight them."

"We will have to fight them anyway!" Cecil exclaimed at the circularity of her thinking. "But this way, if we win, you are Queen of England and Scotland!"

"But if we lose then I am beheaded as Queen of England and Scotland."

He had to control his impatience. "Your Grace, this is an extraordinary offer from the Scots lords. This is the end of years . . . no . . . of *centuries* of enmity. If we win, you have united the kingdom, as your father wanted, as your grandfather dreamed. You have the chance to be the greatest monarch England has ever known. You have the chance to make a united kingdom of these islands."

"Yes," Elizabeth said unhappily. "But what if we lose?"

*   *   *

It was Christmas Eve, but the court was far from merry. Elizabeth sat very still in her chair at the head of the table, her Privy Councillors around her, her only movement the constant rubbing at the cuticles of her fingernails, buffing her nails with her fingertips.

Cecil concluded his arguments in favor of war, certain that no one of any sense could disagree with the relentless plod of his logic. There was a silence as his peers took in his long list.

"But what if we lose?" the queen said bleakly.

"Exactly." Sir Nicholas Bacon agreed with her.

Cecil saw she was in an agony of fear.

"Spirit," she said, her voice very low. "God help me, but I cannot order a war on

France. Not on our own doorstep. Not without certainty of winning. Not without—" She
broke off.

She means not without Dudley's support,
he thought. *Oh, merciful God, why did you
give us a princess when we so desperately
need a king? She cannot take a decision
without the support of a man, and that man
is a fool and a traitor.*

The door opened and Sir Nicholas
Throckmorton came in, bowed to the
queen, and laid a paper before Cecil. He
glanced at it and then looked up at the
queen and his fellow councillors. "The wind
has changed," he said.

For a moment Elizabeth did not understand what he meant.

"The French fleet has sailed."

There was a sharply indrawn breath from
every councillor. Elizabeth blanched a paler
white. "They are coming?" she whispered.

"Forty ships," Cecil said.

"We only have fourteen," Elizabeth said,
and he could hardly make out the words,
her lips were so stiff and cold she could
hardly speak.

"Let them set sail," Cecil whispered to
her, as persuasive as a lover. "Let our ships

get out of harbor where they can at least intercept the stragglers of the French fleet, perhaps engage them. For God's sake, don't keep them in port where the French can sail in and burn them as they go by!"

The fear of losing her ships was greater than her fear of war. "Yes," she said uncertainly. "Yes, they should set sail. They must not be caught in port."

Cecil bowed swiftly, dashed off a note, and took it to the doorway for a waiting messenger. "I am obliged to you," he said. "And now we must declare war on the French."

*   *   *

Elizabeth, her lips nipped raw and her cuticles picked away, walked through the court on her way to take communion on Christmas Day like a haunted woman, a smile pinned on her face like a red frayed ribbon.

In her chapel she looked across and found that Robert Dudley was looking at her. He gave her a little smile. "Courage!" he whispered.

She looked at him as if he was the only friend she had in the world. He half rose from his seat, as if he would go to her, crossing the aisle of the church before the whole of the court. She shook her head and turned away so that she should not see the longing in his eyes, so that he should not see the hunger in hers.

*   *   *

The Christmas Day feast was carried out with joyless competence. The choristers sang, the ranks of serving men presented course after course of elaborate and glorious dishes, Elizabeth pushed aside one plate after another. She was beyond eating; she was beyond even pretending to eat.

After dinner, when the ladies were dancing in a masque specially prepared for the occasion, Cecil came and stood behind her chair. "What?" she said ungraciously.

"The Hapsburg ambassador tells me that he is planning to return to Vienna," Cecil said quietly. "He has given up hopes of the marriage between you and the archduke. He does not want to wait anymore."

She was too exhausted to protest. "Oh. Shall we let him go?" she asked dully.

"You will not marry the archduke?" Cecil said. It was hardly a question.

"I would have married him if he had come," she said. "But I could not marry a man I had never seen, and Cecil, as God is my witness, I am pulled so low I cannot think of courtship now. It is too late to save me from war whether he stays or goes, and I never cared a groat for him anyway. I need a friend I can trust, not a suitor who has to have everything signed and sealed before he will come to me. He promised me nothing and he wanted every guarantee a husband could have."

Cecil did not correct her. He had seen her under house arrest, and in fear of her own death, and yet he thought he had never seen her so drained of joy as she was at this feast, only her second Christmas on the throne.

"It's too late," Elizabeth said sadly, as if she were already defeated. "The French have sailed. They must be off our coasts now. They were not enough afraid of the archduke; they knew they would defeat him as they defeated Arran. What good is he to me now the French are at sea?"

"Be of good cheer, Princess," Cecil said. "We still have an alliance with Spain. Be merry. We can beat the French without the archduke."

"We can lose without him too," was all she said.

*

Three days later Elizabeth called another meeting of the Privy Council. "I have prayed for guidance," she said. "I have spent all night on my knees. I cannot do this. I dare not take us to war. The ships must stay in port; we cannot take on the French."

There was a stunned silence, then every man waited for Cecil to tell her. He looked around for an ally; they all avoided his eyes.

"But the ships have gone, Your Grace," he said flatly.

"Gone?" She was aghast.

"The fleet set sail the moment you gave the command," he said.

Elizabeth gave a little moan and clung to the high back of a chair as her knees gave way. "How could you do this, Cecil? You are a very traitor to send them out."

There was a sharp indrawn breath from the council at her use of that potent, dangerous word, but Cecil never wavered.

"It was your own order," he said steadily. "And the right thing to do."

*   *   *

The court waited for news from Scotland and it came in contradictory, nerve-racking snippets that sent people into nervous, whispering huddles in corners. Many men were buying gold and sending it out of the country to Geneva, to Germany, so that when the French came, as they were almost certain to do, an escape might be easily made. The value of English coin, already rock bottom, plummeted to nothing.

There was no faith in the English fleet, hopelessly outnumbered and outgunned, no faith in the queen, who was clearly ill with fear. Then came disastrous news: the entire English fleet, Elizabeth's precious fourteen ships, had been caught in a storm and were all missing.

"There!" the queen cried out in wild grief to Cecil before the whole Privy Council. "If you had let me delay them, they would have avoided the gales, and I would have a fleet ready to go, instead of all my ships missing at sea!"

Cecil said nothing; there was nothing he could say.

"My fleet! My ships!" she mourned. "Lost by your impatience, by your folly, Cecil. And now the kingdom open to invasion, and no sea defense, and our poor boys, lost at sea."

It was long days before the news came

that the ships had been recovered, and a fleet of eleven of the fourteen had anchored in the Firth of Forth and were supplying the Scots lords as they laid siege once more to Leith Castle.

"Three ships lost already!" Elizabeth said miserably, huddled over a fire in her privy chamber, picking at the skin around her fingers, more like a sulky girl than a queen. "Three ships lost, and not a shot fired!"

"Eleven ships safe," Cecil said stubbornly. "Think of that. Eleven ships safe and in the Firth of Forth, supporting the siege against Mary of Guise. Think how she must feel, looking from her window and seeing the Scots beneath her walls and the English fleet in her harbor."

"She only sees eleven ships," she said stubbornly. "Three lost already. God save that they are not the first losses of many. We must call them back while we still have the eleven. Cecil, I dare not do this without certainty of winning."

"There is never a certainty of winning," he declared. "It will always be a risk but you have to take it now, Your Grace."

"Spirit, please, don't ask it of me."

She was panting, working herself into one

of her tantrums, but he continued to press her. "You may not rescind the order."

"I am too afraid."

"You cannot play the woman now; you have to have the heart and stomach of a man. Find your courage, Elizabeth. You are your father's daughter; play the king. I have seen you be as brave as any man."

For a moment he thought that the flattering lie had persuaded her. Her chin came up, her color rose, but then he saw the spark suddenly drain from her eyes and she drooped again.

"I cannot," she said. "You have never seen me be a king. I have always been nothing more than a clever and duplicitous woman. I can't fight openly. I never have. There will be no war."

"You will have to learn to be a king," Cecil warned her. "One day you will have to say that you are just a weak woman but you have the heart and stomach of a king. You cannot rule this kingdom without being its king."

She shook her head, stubborn as a frightened red-headed mule. "I dare not."

"You cannot recall the ships; you have to declare war."

"No."

He took a breath and tested his own resolve. Then he drew his letter of resignation
from inside his doublet. "Then I have to beg
you to release me."

Elizabeth whirled around. "What? What is
this?"

"Release me. I cannot serve you. If you
will not take my advice on this matter which
so nearly concerns the safety of the kingdom then I cannot serve you. In failing to
convince you, I have failed you, and I have
failed my office. Anything in the world I can
do for you, I will. You know how dear you
are to me, as dear as a wife or a daughter.
But if I cannot prevail upon you to send our
army to Scotland then I have to leave your
service."

For a moment she went so white that he
thought she might faint. "You are jesting
with me," she said breathlessly. "To force
me to agree."

"No."

"You would never leave me."

"I have to. Someone else who can convince you of your right interest should serve
you. I am become the base that drives

out the good. I am disregarded. I am light-weight. I am counterfeit like a coin."

"Not disregarded, Spirit. You know . . ."

He bowed very low. "I will do anything else Your Grace commands, any other service though it were in Your Majesty's kitchen or garden; I am ready without respect of estimation, wealth, or ease to do Your Majesty's commandment to my life's end."

"Spirit, you cannot leave me."

Cecil started to walk backward to the door. She stood like a bereft child, her hands outstretched to him. "William! Please! Am I to be left with no one?" she demanded. "This Scotland has already cost me the only man I love; is it going to cost me my greatest advisor and friend? You, who have been my constant friend and advisor since I was a girl?"

He paused at the door. "Please take steps to defend yourself," he said quietly. "As soon as the Scots have been defeated, the French will come through England faster than we have ever seen an army move. They will come here and throw you from your throne. Please, for your own sake, prepare a refuge for yourself and a way to escape to it."

"Cecil!" It was a little wail of misery.

He bowed again and went to the door. He went out. He waited outside. He had been certain that she would run after him, but there was silence. Then he heard, from inside the room, a muffled sob as Elizabeth broke down.

*   *   *

"You are so devout, people are starting to say that you pray like a Papist," Lady Robsart of Stanfield Hall remarked critically to her stepdaughter Amy. "It doesn't reflect very well on us; your brother-in-law said only the other day that you looked very odd in church, you were still on your knees as people were going out."

"I am very much in need of grace," Amy said, not in the least embarrassed.

"You're not like yourself at all," her stepmother went on. "You used to be so . . . lighthearted. Well, not lighthearted, but not pious. Not one for constant prayer, at any rate."

"I was once secure in my father's love, and then secure in my husband's love, and now I have neither," Amy said flatly. Her voice did not quaver; there were no tears in her eyes.

Lady Robsart was stunned into momentary silence. "Amy, my dear, I know there has been much gossip about him but . . ."

"It is true," she said shortly. "He told me the truth himself. But he has given her up so that she can marry the archduke to get Spain to join with us in a war against the French."

Lady Robsart was stunned. "He told you this? He confessed it all?"

"Yes." For a moment Amy looked almost rueful. "I think he thought I would be sorry for him. He was so sorry for himself he thought I must sympathize. I have always sympathized with him before. He is in the habit of bringing his sorrows to me."

"Sorrows?"

"This has cost him very dear," Amy said. "There must have been a moment when he thought she might love him, and I might let him go, and he might fulfill his father's dream and put a Dudley on the throne of England. His brother married the heir to the throne, Jane Grey; his sister is married to Henry Hastings, next in line after Mary, Queen of Scots; he must feel it is his family's destiny." She paused. "And of course, he is deeply in love with her," she said, matter-of-fact.

"In love," Lady Robsart repeated, as if she had never heard such words before. "In love with the Queen of England."

"I can see it in everything he says," Amy said quietly. "He loved me once, but everyone thought he condescended to the marriage, and it was always true that he thought very highly of himself. But with her it is different. He is a man transformed. She is his lover but still his queen; he admires her as well as desires her. He . . ." She paused to find the words. "He aspires to love her, whereas I was always an easy love."

"Amy, are you not heartbroken?" her stepmother asked, feeling her way with this new, composed woman. "I thought he was everything to you?"

"I am sick to my very soul," Amy said quietly. "I never knew that anyone could feel such a grief. It is like an illness, like a canker which eats at me every day. That is why I seem devout. The only relief for me is to pray that God will take me to his own and then Robert and she can do as they please, and I will be free from pain at last."

"Oh, my dear!" Lady Robsart stretched

out her hand to Amy. "Don't say that. He's not worth it. No man in the world is worth shedding a tear for. Least of all him who has cost you so much already."

"I think my heart is really broken," Amy said quietly. "I think it must be. The pain in my breast is so sharp and constant that I think it will be the death of me. It is truly heartbreak. I don't think it will mend. It doesn't matter whether he is worth it or not. It is done. Even if she were to marry the archduke and Robert were to come riding home to me and say that it was all a mistake, how could we be happy again? My heart is broken and it will always be broken from now on."

*　　　*　　　*

The queen's ladies could do nothing to please her; she stalked about her rooms at Whitehall Palace like a vexed lioness. She sent for, and then dismissed, her musicians. She would not read. She could not rest. She was in a frenzy of worry and distress. She wanted to send for Cecil; she could not imagine how she would manage without him. She wanted to send for her uncle, but no one knew where he was, and then she changed her mind and did not want to see him anyway. There were petitioners waiting to see her in her chamber but she would not go out to them; the dressmaker came with some furs from Russia but she would not even look at them. Prince Erik of Sweden had written her a twelve-page letter, pinned with a diamond, but she could not be troubled to read it.

Nothing could free Elizabeth from the terror that rode her like a hag. She was a young woman in only the second year of her reign, and yet she had to decide whether or not to commit her kingdom to war against an unbeatable enemy, and the two men she trusted above all others had both left her.

Sometimes she was certain that she was making a mistake from her own cowardice; at other moments she was certain she was protecting her country from disaster; all the time she was terrified that she was making a deep and grave mistake.

"I'm going for Sir Robert," Laetitia Knollys whispered to her mother after watching Elizabeth's frantic turning all morning from one unfinished activity to another.

"Not without her order," Catherine replied.

"Yes," Laetitia insisted. "He's the only man

who can comfort her, and if she goes on like this she will make herself ill and drive us all mad."

"Lettice!" her mother said sharply but already the girl had slipped from the room and gone to Robert's chambers.

He was paying bills, a great money chest open before him, his steward presenting accounts and counting out coins for the huge costs of the stables.

Laetitia tapped on the door and peeped into the room.

"Mistress Knollys," Robert said levelly. "This is an improper honor indeed."

"It's about the queen," she said.

At once he leapt up, his quizzical look quite gone. "Is she safe?"

Laetitia noted that his first thought was that Elizabeth might have been attacked. So her father was right; they were all in the greatest of danger, all the time.

"She is safe, but much distressed."

"She sent for me?"

"No. I came without being told. I thought you should come to her."

He gave her a slow smile. "You are a most extraordinary girl," he said. "Why did you take such a task on yourself?"

"She's beside herself," Laetitia confided. "It's the war with Scotland. She can't decide, and she has to decide. And now she has lost Cecil, and she seems to have lost you. She has no one. Sometimes she thinks 'yes', sometimes she thinks 'no', but she's not happy with either decision. She is as jumpy as a rabbit with a ferret on its scut."

Robert frowned at the impertinence of her language. "I'll come," he said. "And I thank you for telling me."

She slid him a flirtatious smile under her dark eyelashes. "If I was the queen, I would want you at my side all the time," she said. "War or no war."

"And how are your wedding plans?" he asked urbanely. "Dress made? Everything ready? Groom impatient?"

"Thank you, yes," she said, quite composed. "And how is Lady Dudley? Not ill, I hope? Coming to court soon?"

*   *   *

In the queen's chambers, Elizabeth was at her seat by the fire, her ladies scattered around the room, tensely waiting for what she might next demand. Other courtiers stood about, hoping to be invited to speak with her, but Elizabeth would hear no petitions, would be distracted by no one.

Dudley came in, and at the sound of his step she turned at once. The leap of joy into her face could not be hidden. She rose to her feet: "Oh, Robert!"

Without further invitation he went up to her and drew her with him into a window bay, away from the curious stares of her ladies. "I knew you were unhappy," he said. "I had to come. I could not stay away a moment longer."

"How did you know?" she demanded. She could not stop herself leaning toward him. The very scent of his clothes, of his hair, was a deep comfort to her. "How did you ever know that I need you so badly?"

"Because I cannot rest without being near you," he said. "Because I need you too. Has something upset you?"

"Cecil has left me," she said brokenly. "I cannot manage without him."

"I knew he had gone, of course; but why?" Robert asked, though he had received a full report from Thomas Blount on the day that Cecil left.

"He said he would not stay with me unless we made war on the French and I don't dare, Robert, I really don't dare, and yet how can I rule without Cecil at my side?"

"Good God, I thought he would never leave you. I thought you and he had sworn an oath."

Elizabeth's mouth was working. "I thought he never would," she said. "I would have trusted him with my life. But he says he cannot serve me if I will not listen to him, and Robert . . . I am too afraid."

The last words were a little thread of sound; she glanced around the room as if her fear were a most shameful secret that she could only trust to him.

Ah, it's not just the war, he thought. *Cecil is like a father to her. He's the advisor she has trusted for years. And Cecil has a view of this country unlike any other. He really does think of it as a nation in its own right, not a motley crew of warring families which was my father's view . . . mine too. Cecil's love of England, his very belief in England, is a greater vision than mine or hers. He keeps her steady, he keeps her faithful, even if it's nothing but a dream.*

"I'm here now," he said, as if his presence would be enough to comfort her. "We'll talk together after dinner, and we will decide what should be done. You're not alone, my love. I am here to help you."

She leaned closer. "I can't do it on my own," she whispered to him, "It's too much. I can't decide, I am too afraid. I don't know how to decide. And I never see you now. I gave you up for Scotland, and now it has cost me Cecil too."

"I know," Robert said. "But I will be at your side again, I'll stand your friend. No one can blame us. The archduke has cooled of his own accord, and Arran is defeated, good for nothing. No one can say that I'm standing between you and a good marriage. And I'll get Cecil back for you. He shall advise us and we shall decide. You don't have to be the judge of it on your own, my love, my dearest love. I shall be with you now. I shall stay with you."

"It can make no difference to us." She hesitated. "I can't be your lover ever again. I shall have to marry someone. If not this year, then next."

"Just let me be at your side until then," he said simply. "Neither of us can bear our lives when we are apart."

*

That night at dinner the queen laughed at her fool for the first time in many weeks, and Sir Robert sat at her side once more and poured her wine.

"This wet weather has got into the very timbers of the roof," he remarked as the servants took the meats and the puddings off the table and brought the sweetmeats and the sugared fruits. "My room is so damp, you can see the steam coming off my linen when Tamworth holds it before the fire in the morning."

"Tell them to change your rooms," she said lightly. "Tell the groom of the household to put you back in your old rooms beside mine."

*   *   *

He waited. He knew the way forward with Elizabeth was not to press her. He decided that he would do nothing more than wait for her.

At midnight, the door between the two rooms slid open and she came quietly in. She was wearing a dark blue robe over her white shift, her red hair was brushed and shining over her shoulders.

"My Robert?"

The table before the fire was laid with

supper for two, the fire was lit, the bed was turned down, the door was locked, and Tamworth, Sir Robert's valet, was on guard outside.

"My love," he said and took her in his arms.

She nestled close. "I cannot live without you," she said. "We have to keep this secret, a most deep secret. But I cannot be queen without you, Robert."

"I know," he said. "I cannot live without you."

She looked up at him. "What will we do?"

He shrugged his shoulders, his smile was almost rueful. "I think we have gone beyond choice. We will have to marry, Elizabeth."

She glanced toward the window where one of the shutters stood open. "Close the shutters," the queen said in sudden superstitious fear. "I don't want even the moon to see us."

*   *   *

In her old bedroom at Stanfield Hall Amy woke with a start and found that the covers had slid from her bed and that she was freezing cold. She reached down to her feet and grabbed the linen sheets, the woolen rugs, and pulled them up to her shivering shoulders. She had left one of the shutters open, and the moon, a big, bold, creamy moon, was laying a path of light on her pillow. She lay down and looked out of the window to the moon.

"The same moon that is shining on me is shining on my lord," she whispered. "Perhaps it will wake him too, and make him think of me. Perhaps God will waken his love for me in his heart once more. Even now, perhaps he is thinking of me."

*   *   *

"You played me as a fool!" Mary Sidney raged at her brother, striding up to him in the Whitehall Palace stable yard. He and half a dozen other men were practicing for a joust, his horse was already armed, his squire standing by with his beautifully polished breastplate, his helmet, his lance.

Robert was distracted. He snapped his fingers for his pageboy with his gauntlets. "What is it, Mary? What have I done?"

"You sent me on a fool's errand to tell the ambassador that the queen would marry the archduke. You sent me knowing that since I believed you, since I was deeply, deeply grieved for you, that I would tell a convincing tale. I was the best person in court to send to him. D'you know I wept as I told him that you had given her up? And so of course, he believed me, and yet all along it was just a plot to throw dust in the eyes of the court."

"What dust?" Robert was all innocence.

"You and the queen are lovers," she spat at him. "You probably have been from the first day. You probably were lovers when I thought you were grieving for the loss of her. And you made me play pander to you."

"The queen and I agreed to part for her safety," he said steadily. "That was true. As I told you. But she needs friends, Mary, you know that. I have come back to her side to be her friend. And we are friends, as I said we would be."

She pulled away from his outstretched hand. "Oh, no, not another pack of lies, Robert; I won't hear them. You are faithless to Amy, and you are dishonest with me. I told the ambassador that I knew for a fact that the queen and you were true friends and that she was a virgin, free to marry and a chaste princess. I swore on my immortal soul that there was nothing between you but friendship and a few kisses."

"And there is not!"

"Don't speak to me!" she cried passion-ately. "Don't lie to me. I won't hear another word."

"Come with me to the tilt yard. . . ."

"I shan't watch you, I shan't talk with you. I don't even want to see you, Robert. There is nothing to you but ambition. God help your wife, and God help the queen."

"Amen," he said, smiling. "Amen to both, for they are both good women and innocent of any wrongdoing, and indeed God bless me and all Dudleys as we rise in the world."

"And what has Amy done that she should be shamed before the world?" she de-manded of him. "What sin has she ever done, for everyone in England to know that you have no liking for her? That you prefer another woman instead of her, your own true wife?"

"She has done nothing," he said. "And I have done nothing. Really, Mary, you shouldn't throw such accusations around."

"Don't you dare speak to me!" she swore again, quite beyond herself with rage. "I have nothing to say to you, and I will never have another word to say to you on this. You have played me as a fool and played the Spanish as fools and played your poor wife as a fool, and all along you have been lovers with the queen and you stay as lovers with the queen."

In one swift stride Robert was at her side with her wrist in a hard grip. "Now that is enough," he said. "You have said quite enough, and I have heard more than enough. The queen's reputation is beyond comment. She is going to marry the right suitor as soon as he comes along. We all know that. Amy is my wife and I will hear nothing against her. I visited her in October, and I shall visit her again shortly. Cecil himself gets home no more frequently than that."

"Cecil loves his wife and no one doubts his honor!" she flared up.

"And no one questions mine," he said sharply. "You can keep your poisonous little tongue off my affairs or you will spoil more than you understand. Be warned, Mary."

She was unafraid. "Are you mad, Robert?" she demanded. "Do you think you can fool the best spies in Europe as you fool your sister and your wife? In Madrid, in Paris, in Vienna, they know that you and the queen have adjoining rooms once more. What do you think they make of it? The Hapsburg archduke won't come to England while you and the queen sleep behind locked doors, one panel of wood between you. Everyone but your poor wife believes that you are lovers; the whole country knows it. You have ruined the queen's prospects with your lusts; you have ruined Amy's love for you. Pray God you do not ruin the kingdom too."

*   *   *

Mary's warning came too late, and could not prevent the scandalous intimacy between the queen and her Master of Horse. With Robert at her side once more, Elizabeth's color came back into her cheeks, her fingernails were buffed and shining and the cuticles smooth. She glowed in his company, her constant nervousness was quieted when he was near. It did not matter what anyone might say, they were clearly born for each other, and they could not conceal it. They rode together every day, they danced together every night, and Elizabeth had the courage to open her letters and listen to petitions once more.

In the absence of Cecil, Robert was her only trusted advisor. No one was seen by the queen except by Dudley's introduction;

she never spoke to anyone without him standing, discreetly, in the background. He was her only friend and her ally. She took no decision without him; they were inseparable. Duke John of Sweden danced around the court but hardly pressed his suit, William Pickering retired quietly to the country to try to economize on his massive debts, Caspar von Breuner came only rarely to court and everyone had forgotten the Earl of Arran.

Cecil, staying firmly on the outskirts of the young couple and their courtiers, remarked to Throckmorton that this was no way to rule a country on the brink of war and learned that she had just appointed Dudley as Lord Lieutenant and Constable of Windsor Castle, with fees to match.

"He will be the richest man in England if this goes on," Cecil observed.

"Rich: nothing. He means to be king," Sir Nicholas replied, saying the unsayable. "And then how d'you think the country will be run?"

Cecil said nothing. Only the evening before a man whose face was hidden by his hat pulled down low on his brow had tapped at Cecil's door and in a gruff voice asked him if he would join with three others in an attack on Dudley.

"Why come to me?" Cecil asked. "I take it you can bludgeon him to death on your own account without my permission."

"Because the queen's guards protect him and they follow your rule," the stranger said. Cecil moved a branch of candles on his desk and caught a glimpse of the angry face of Thomas Howard half hidden under the concealing cap. "And when he is dead, she will ask you to discover his murderers. We don't want your spies on us. We don't want to hang for him any more than we would hang for killing vermin."

"You must do as you think best," Cecil said, choosing his words with care. "But I will not protect you after the murder."

"Would you prevent us from doing it?"

"I am responsible for the safety of the queen. I daresay, sadly, I cannot prevent you."

The man laughed. "In short you wouldn't mind him dead but you won't take a risk," he taunted.

Cecil had nodded equably. "I think no one in England but the queen and his wife would mind at all," he said frankly. "But I will not be party to a plot against him."

"What's amusing you?" Throckmorton asked, glancing round the court for the reason for Cecil's smile.

"Thomas Howard," Cecil answered. "He's not exactly a master of subtlety, is he?"

Throckmorton glanced over. Thomas Howard had managed to enter the double open doors to the presence chamber just as Dudley was coming out. Everyone gave way to Dudley now, with the exception perhaps of Cecil, and Cecil would never have timed his entrance so that he was head to head with the royal favorite. Howard was standing his ground like an angry heifer.

In a moment, Cecil thought, *he will paw the floor and bellow.*

Dudley eyed him with the coolest of contempt, and then went to pass him.

At once Howard sidestepped and jostled him. "I beg your pardon but I am coming in," he said loudly enough for everyone to hear. "I! A Howard! And the Queen's uncle."

"Oh, please, do not beg my pardon for I am leaving," Dudley said, the laughter warm in his voice. "It is those hapless men that you are about to join who deserve your apology."

Howard choked on his words. "You are offensive!" he spluttered.

Dudley went quietly by him, serene in his power.

"You are a damned upstart, from nowhere!" Thomas Howard shouted at his back.

"Will he let that go, d'you think?" Throckmorton asked Cecil, quite fascinated at the little drama before them. "Is he as cool as he seems? Will he ignore Thomas Howard?"

"Not him," Cecil said. "And he probably knows that he is in real danger."

"A plot?"

"One of dozens. I think we can expect to see young Thomas Howard as the next ambassador to the Turkish court. I think it will be the Ottoman empire for the Howards, and a long posting."

Cecil was wrong only in the destination.

"I think Thomas Howard should strengthen our defenses in the north," Dudley remarked to the queen that night when they were alone, a slight smile warming his glance. "He is so fierce and warlike."

At once Elizabeth was alert, fearful for him. "Is he threatening you?"

"That puppy? Hardly," Robert said proudly. "But you do need someone you can trust in the north, and since he is spoiling for a fight, let him fight the French rather than me."

The queen laughed, as though Robert's words were meant as a joke, but the next day she awarded her uncle a new title: he was to be Lieutenant General of the Scottish border.

He bowed as he accepted the commission. "I know why I am sent away, Your Grace," he said with the prickly dignity of a young man. "But I will serve you faithfully. And I think you may find I am a better servant to you in Newcastle than some who hide behind your petticoats in London, far from danger."

Elizabeth had the grace to look abashed. "I need someone I can trust," she said. "We must hold the French north of Berwick. They cannot come into the heart of England."

"I am honored with your trust," he said sarcastically, and took his leave, ignoring the rumors that swirled around his departure, the gossip that said that Elizabeth had put her own family in the very front of the line, rather than embarrass her lover.

"Why not just behead him and get it over with?" Catherine Knollys asked.

Elizabeth giggled to her cousin, but faced a reprimand from her old governess as soon as they were alone together.

"Princess!" Kat Ashley exclaimed despairingly. "This is as bad as it ever was. What will everyone think? Everyone believes that you are as much in love with Sir Robert as ever. The archduke will never come to England now. No man would risk being so insulted."

"If he had come for me when he had promised, I would have married him. I gave my word," Elizabeth said lightly, secure in the knowledge that he would not come now, and that if he did, Robert would think of some way out of it.

But Kat Ashley, Mary Sidney, and all the court were right: he would not come now. The ambassador, deeply offended, asked to be recalled, and wrote to his master that he thought the whole episode of Lady Sidney coming to him and begging him to propose once more to the queen had been nothing more than a plot to take the attention from the clandestine love affair which was notorious once more throughout England and throughout Europe. He wrote that the queen had become a young woman inured to shame, corrupted without hope, and that he could recommend no honorable man to marry her, let alone a prince. She was living as a whore to a married man and their only way out was a semi-legal divorce, or the death of his wife: which was hardly likely.

Cecil, reading the first draft of this letter, retrieved by Cecil's agent from the ambassador's kindling paper basket, thought that his foreign policy lay in ruins, that England's safety could not be guaranteed, and that the Queen of England had run mad for lust and would lose the war in Scotland and then her head, and all for a smile from a dark-eyed man.

*   *   *

But when Elizabeth summoned Cecil by name he came to her at once.

"You were right, I am sure of it now," she said quietly. "I have found the courage you wanted me to find. I am quite decided on war."

Cecil glanced past her to where Sir

Robert leaned against the shutters of the window, apparently absorbed in a game of bowls taking place in the cold garden below.

So we have the benefit of your advice, do we? And you, in your wisdom, have decided to adopt a policy I have been begging her to deploy for months. Aloud, Cecil asked: "What has Your Grace decided?"

"We shall invade Scotland and defeat the French," she said calmly.

Cecil bowed, hiding his sense of intense relief. "I shall see that the moneys are raised and the army mustered," he said. "You will want to meet with the Privy Council and issue a proclamation of war."

Elizabeth glanced toward Robert. Minutely, he nodded his head. "Yes," she said.

Cecil, too wise to object to advice that agreed with his own, merely bowed again.

"And Cecil, you will be my Lord Secretary again, won't you? Now that I have taken your advice?"

"What of the archduke?" he asked.

Robert, at the window, recognized at once that the question was not as irrelevant as it seemed, striking as it did at the very heart of what he was doing there, within earshot of the queen and her most trusted advisor, nodding through her decisions as if he were her husband and king-consort. But this time, the queen did not even look at Robert.

"I shall be betrothed to the archduke as soon as he comes to England," she said. "I know that the alliance with Spain is more vital than ever."

"You know very well that he will not come," Cecil said flatly. "You know that his ambassador is leaving London."

Robert levered himself up from the shutter. "Doesn't matter," he said briefly to Cecil. "King Philip of Spain will stand her ally against France, marriage or no marriage. He cannot risk the French creating a kingdom in England. Their borders would run from Perth to the Mediterranean; they would destroy Spain after they had enslaved us."

You think so, do you? Cecil demanded silently. *And I am to save this kingdom for your bastards to inherit, am I?*

"What matters now," Dudley ruled, "is that we call up the men and arm them. The survival of the kingdom and the queen herself depends on swift action. We are looking to you, Cecil."

*

That night Cecil worked furiously, sending out the hundreds of instructions that were needed to recruit, arm, and supply the army that must march north at once. He wrote to Lord Clinton, the High Admiral, to say that the navy must intercept the French fleet in the North Sea, they must prevent at all costs the French reinforcements landing in Scotland, but they must destroy his letter and seemingly attack on their own initiative. He wrote to his spies with the Scots, and to his men positioned at Berwick and to his most secret correspondents at the court of the queen regent, Mary of Guise, to say that at last the Queen of England had found a warlike resolution, and that England was to defend the Lords Protestant of Scotland, and her own borders, and that he needed the fullest information and at once.

Cecil worked so speedily and so efficiently that when the Privy Council met, a few days later, in the last days of February, and the queen announced that, on reflection, she had changed her mind, and that since the risk was too great, there would be no venture in Scotland, he apologized but said it was too late.

"You will recall the fleet," she commanded, white to her ruff.

Cecil spread his hands. "They have sailed," he said. "With orders to attack."

"Bring back my army!"

He shook his head. "They are marching north, recruiting as they go. We are on a war footing; we cannot reverse the decision."

"We cannot go to war with the French!" she almost screamed at him.

The Privy Councillors bowed their heads to the table. Cecil alone faced her. "The die is already cast," he said. "Your Grace, we are at war. England is at war with France. God help us."

Spring 1560

Robert Dudley came to Stanfield Hall in March, a bad month for traveling on ill-maintained roads, and arrived chilled and bad-tempered.

No one was waiting for him; he had sent no warning that he would be coming, and Amy, a reluctant listener to the constant rumors that said that he and the queen were once more inseparable, hardly expected ever to see him again.

As soon as the horses clattered into the yard Lady Robsart came to find her.

"He's here!" she said coldly.

Amy leapt to her feet. "He" could only ever mean one man at Stanfield Hall. "My lord Robert?"

"His men are unsaddling in the yard."

Amy trembled as she stood. If he had come back to her, after their last parting when she had insisted that she would always be his wife, it could mean only one thing: that he had finished with Elizabeth and wanted to reconcile with his wife. "He is here?" she said again, as if she could not believe it.

Lady Robsart smiled wryly at her stepdaughter in the shared triumph of women over men. "It looks as if you have won," she said. "He is here and looking very cold and sorry for himself."

"Then he must come in!" Amy exclaimed and dashed toward the stairs. "Tell Cook he's here, and send word to the village that he will need a couple of hens and someone must slaughter a cow."

"A fatted calf, why not?" Lady Robsart said under her breath; but she went to do her stepdaughter's bidding.

Amy dashed down the stairs and flung open the front door. Robert, travel-stained and weary, walked up the short flight of steps, and Amy stepped into his arms.

From old habit he held her close to him, and Amy, feeling his arms come around her, and that familiar touch of his hand on her waist and the other on her shoulder blade, leaned her head against his warm, sweat-smelling neck and knew that he had come home to her at last, and that despite it all, all of it, she would forgive him as easily as accepting his kiss.

"Come in, you must be half frozen," she said, drawing him into the hall. She threw logs on the fire and pressed him into her father's heavy carved chair. Lady Robsart came in with hot ale and cakes from the kitchen and dipped a curtsy.

"Good day to you," she said neutrally. "I have sent your men to find beds in the village. We cannot accommodate such a large company here."

To Amy she remarked, "Hughes says he has some well-hung venison that he can let us have."

"I don't wish to put you out," Robert said politely, as if he had not once cursed her to her face.

"How could you put us out?" Amy demanded. "This is my home; you are always welcome here. There is always a place for you here."

Robert said nothing at the thought of Lady Robsart's cold house being their home, and her ladyship took herself out of the room to see about beds, and a pudding.

"My lord, it is so good to see you." Amy put another log on the fire. "I shall get my maid Mrs. Pirto to lay out your linen; the shirt you left here last time is all mended, you can't see the darn, I did it so carefully."

"Thank you," he said awkwardly. "Surely Mrs. Pirto does the mending for you?"

"I like to do your linen myself," Amy said. "Shall you want to wash?"

"Later," he said.

"Only I will have to warn Cook, to heat the water."

"Yes, I know. I lived here long enough."

"You were hardly here at all! And anyway, things are much better now."

"Well, in any case I remember that you cannot have a jug of hot water without mentioning it first thing in the morning on the third Sunday in the month."

"It's just that we have a small fireplace and . . ."

"I know," he said wearily. "I remember all about the small fireplace."

Amy fell silent. She did not dare ask him the one thing that she wanted to know: how long he would stay with her. When he broodingly watched the fire in silence she put on another log and they both watched the sparks fly up the dark chimney.

"How was your journey?"

"All right."

"Which horse did you bring?"

"Blithe, my hunter," he said, surprised.

"Did you not bring a spare horse?"

"No," he said, hardly hearing the question.

"Shall I unpack your bags?" She rose to her feet. "Did you bring many bags?"

"Just the one."

Robert did not see her face fall. She understood at once that one horse and one bag meant a short visit.

"And Tamworth will have done it already."

"You are not planning on a long stay, then?"

He looked up at her. "No, no, I am sorry, I should have said. Matters are very grave; I have to get back to court. I just wanted to see you, Amy, about something important."

"Yes?"

"We'll talk tomorrow," he decided. "But I need your help, Amy. I'll tell you all about it later."

She blushed at the thought of him coming

to her for help. "You know that anything I can do for you, I will do."

"I know it," he said. "I am glad of it." He rose to his feet and put his hands to the blaze.

"I like it when you ask things of me," she said shyly. "It always used to be like that."

"Yes," he said.

"You are cold; shall I light a fire in our bed-chamber?"

"No, no," he said. "I'll change my shirt and come down at once."

Her smile lit up her face like a girl's. "And we shall have such a good dinner; the family here has been living on mutton and I am heartily sick of it!"

*   *   *

It was a good dinner, with venison steaks, a mutton pasty, a chicken broth, and some puddings. There were hardly any vegetables in season, but Amy's father had been an enthusiast for wines and his cellar was still good. Robert, thinking he would need some help in getting through dinner with the two women, and Lady Robsart's daughter and son-in-law John Appleyard, fetched up four bottles and prevailed upon them all to help him drink them.

When they went to bed at a little after nine o'clock the women were tipsy and giggling, and Robert stayed downstairs to finish his glass in good-humored solitude. He left plenty of time for Amy to get into bed and did not go up until he thought she would be asleep.

He shed his clothes as quietly as he could, and put them on the chest at the foot of the bed. She had left a candle burning for him and in the flickering golden light he thought she looked like a sleeping child. He felt filled with tenderness for her as he blew out her candle and slipped into bed beside her, careful not to touch her.

Half asleep, she turned toward him and slid her naked leg between his thighs. At once he was aroused, but he shifted a little away from her, firmly taking her waist in his hands and holding her from him, but she gave a little sleepy sigh and put her hand on his chest, and then slid it inexorably down his belly to caress him.

"Amy," he whispered.

He could not see her in the darkness, but the even pace of her breathing told him that although she was still asleep, she was moving toward him in sleep, she was stroking him, sliding toward him, and finally rolling on her back so that he could take her in a state of aroused sleepiness that he, knowing that he was a fool, could not resist. Even as he took his pleasure, even as he heard her cry, her familiar, breathy little cry of delight as she woke to find him inside her, Robert knew that he was doing the wrong thing, the worst thing that he could do: for himself, for Amy, and for Elizabeth.

*   *   *

In the morning Amy was glowing, confident, a woman restored to love, a wife restored to her place in the world. He did not have to wake to her timid smile; she was up and in the kitchen as he was getting dressed, stirring the cook to bake breakfast bread just as he liked it. She had fetched the honey from their own hive; she brought fresh butter from the dairy with the Stanfield Hall seal on the pat. From the meat larder she had brought a good cut of ham borrowed from someone in the village, and there were some cold venison cutlets left over from last night.

Amy, presiding over a good table, poured small ale for her husband and tucked back a curl behind her ear.

"Shall you ride today?" she asked. "I can send Jeb to the stable to tell them to saddle your horse. We can ride together if you wish."

He could not believe that she had forgotten their last ride together, but her pleasure in the night had restored her to the Amy that he had once loved, the confident little mistress of her kingdom, Sir John Robsart's favorite child.

"Yes," he said, delaying the moment when he would have to speak honestly with her. "I should have brought my hawk; I shall soon eat you out of house and home."

"Oh no," she said. "For the Carters have already sent over a newly weaned calf as a compliment to you, and now that everyone knows you are here we shall be half buried in gifts. I thought we might ask them to come over for the day; you always find them good company."

"Tomorrow, perhaps," he said cravenly. "Not today."

"All right," she said agreeably. "But you will be hard put to eat the calf on your own."

"Tell them I will ride in an hour," he said, abruptly rising from the table. "And I should be glad of your company."

"Could we ride toward Flitcham Hall?" she asked. "Just to remind you what a fine house it is? I know you said it is too far from London, but they still have not found a buyer."

He winced. "Wherever you wish," he said, avoiding the issue of the house. "In an hour."

And so I avoid speaking to her until dinner, Robert berated himself, taking the stairs two at a time. *Because I shall never again try and talk sense to a woman while riding with her. But tonight, after dinner, I have to talk to her. I cannot lie with her again. I make a cheat of myself, and a fool of her.* He kicked open the door to Sir John's private room, and threw himself into the old man's chair. *Damn you,* he addressed his dead father-in-law. *Damn you for saying I would break her heart and damn you for being right.*

*   *   *

Robert waited until after dinner when Lady Robsart left them alone, and Amy was seated opposite him on the other side of the small fireplace.

"I am sorry we have no company," Amy remarked. "It must be so dull for you, after court. We could have had the Rushleys to visit, you remember them? They would come tomorrow, if you would like to invite them."

"Amy," he said hesitantly. "I have something to ask you."

Her head came up at once, her smile sweet. She thought he was going to ask for her forgiveness.

"We spoke once of a divorce," he said quietly.

A shadow crossed her face. "Yes," she said. "I have not had a happy moment since that day. Not until last night."

Robert grimaced. "I am sorry for that," he said.

She interrupted him. "I know," she said. "I knew you would be. And I thought that I would never be able to forgive you; but I can, Robert, and I do. It is forgiven and forgotten between us and we need never speak of it again."

This is something like ten thousand times harder because I was a lustful fool, Robert swore to himself. Aloud he said, "Amy, you will think me wicked, but my mind has not changed."

Her honest, open eyes met his. "What do you mean?" she asked simply.

"I have to ask you something," he said. "When we last spoke, you saw Elizabeth as your rival, and I understand your feelings. But she is the Queen of England, and she has done me the honor of loving me."

Amy frowned; she could not think what he wanted to ask her. "Yes, but you said you had given her up. And then you came to me . . ." She broke off. "It is like a miracle to me that you came to me, as if we were boy and girl again."

"We are at war with Scotland," Robert plowed on. "We could not be in more peril. I want to help her, I want to save my country. Amy, the French are very likely to invade."

Amy nodded. "Of course. But . . ."

"Invade," he repeated. "Destroy us all."

She nodded, but she could not care for the French when her own happiness was unfolding before her.

"And so I want to ask you to release me from my marriage with you, so that I can offer myself to the queen as a free man. The archduke will not propose to her; she needs a husband. I want to marry her."

Amy's eyes widened as if she could not believe what she had just heard. He saw her hand go to her pocket and he saw her fingers clench on something there.

"What?" she asked disbelievingly.

"I want you to release me from my marriage with you. I have to marry her."

"Are you saying that you want me to divorce you?"

He nodded. "I do."

"But last night . . ."

"Last night was a mistake," he said brutally and saw the color flush to her cheeks and the tears fill her eyes as rapidly as if he had slapped her till her head rang.

"A mistake?" she repeated.

"I could not resist you," he said, trying to soften the blow. "I should have done so. I love you, Amy, I always will. But my destiny has come for me. John Dee once said—"

She shook her head. "A mistake? To lie with your own wife? Did you not whisper: "I love you"? Was that a mistake too?"

"I didn't say that," he said quickly.

"I heard you say that."

"You may think you heard me, but I didn't say it."

She got up from her little chair and turned away from him to the table that she had prepared for dinner with such joy. It was all spoiled now; the broken meats gone to the servants, the waste gone to the pigs.

"You told me of Sir Thomas Gresham once," she said irrelevantly. "That he thought the worst thing about bad coinage is that it brings everything, even good coins, down to its own worthless value."

"Yes," he said, not understanding.

"That is what she has done," she said simply. "I am not surprised that a pound is not worth a pound, that we are at war with France, that the archduke will not marry her. She has made everything bad; she is the false coin of the kingdom and she has brought everything, even honorable love, even a good marriage begun in love, down to the value of a counterfeit coin."

"Amy . . ."

"So that in the night you say 'I love you' and everything you do tells me that you love me, and then in the day, the very next day, you ask me to release you."

"Amy, please!"

She stopped at once. "Yes, my lord?"

"Whatever you think of her, she is the anointed Queen of England; the realm is in danger. The Queen of England needs me and I am asking you to release me."

"You can command her armies," she observed.

Robert nodded. "Yes, but there are other, more skilled soldiers."

"You can advise her as to what she should do; she could appoint you to her Privy Council."

"I advise her already."

"Then what more can you do? And what more can you honorably ask for?" she burst out.

He gritted his teeth. "I want to be at her side, day and night. I want to be her husband and be with her all the time. I want to be her companion on the throne of England."

He braced himself for tears and rage, but to his surprise she looked at him dry-eyed, and spoke very quietly. "Robert, do you know, if it was in my gift, I would give it to you. I have loved you so much and for so long that I would even give you this. But it is not in my gift. Our marriage is an act of God; we stood together in a church and swore we would not be parted. We cannot be parted now, just because the queen wants you, and you want her."

"Other people in the world divorce!" he exclaimed.

"I don't know how they will answer for it."

"The Pope himself allows it, he says that they will not answer for it, there is no sin."

"Oh, shall you go to the Pope?" she inquired with a sudden rush of malice. "Is the Pope to rule that our marriage, our Protestant marriage, is invalid? Is Elizabeth the Protestant princess going to bow her knee to the Pope again?"

He leapt up from his chair and faced her. "Of course not!"

"Then who?" she persisted. "The Archbishop of Canterbury? Her creature? Appointed despite his own misgivings, the single turncoat in the church while all her other bishops are thrown into prison or exile because they know she is a false claimant to be head of the church?"

"I don't know the details," he said sulkily. "But with goodwill it could be done."

"It would have to be her, wouldn't it?" Amy challenged him. "A woman of twenty-six years old, blinded by her own lust, wanting another woman's husband and ruling that her desire is God's will. That she knows that God wants him to be free." She drew a breath and let out a wild, ringing laugh. "It is a nonsense, husband. You will make yourselves a laughingstock. It is a sin against God, it is a sin against man, and it is an insult to me."

"It is no insult. If your father were alive . . ."

It was the worst thing he could have said. Amy's family pride sprang up. "You dare say his name to me! My father would have horsewhipped you for even thinking of such a thing. He would have killed you for saying such a thing to me."

"He would never have laid a finger on me!" Robert swore. "He would not have dared."

"He said you were a braggart and I was worth ten of you," she spat at him. "And he was right. You are a braggart and I am worth ten of you. And you did say you loved me last night; you are a liar."

He could hardly see her for the mist that rose before his eyes with his blinding anger. His tight voice came out short, as if it were wrested from him. "Amy, no man in the world would abuse me as you have done and live."

"Husband, I can promise you that thousands will call you worse. They will call you her boy, her plaything, a common little colt that she rides for lust."

"They will call me King of England," he shouted.

She whirled around and caught him by the collar of the linen shirt that she had darned so carefully for him, and shook him in her rage. "Never! You will have to murder me before she can have you."

He snatched her hands from his neck and thrust her away from him, down into the chair. "Amy, I will never forgive you for this; you will turn me from your husband and lover to your enemy."

She looked up at him and she collected spittle in her mouth and spat at him. At once, blind with rage, he rushed toward her and, quick as thought, she put her little feet up and kicked out, driving him back.

"I know *that*," she shouted at him. "Fool that you are! But what difference does your hatred make, when you lie like a swine with her and then lie with me and say 'I love you' to us both?"

"I never said it!" he yelled, quite beyond himself.

Behind him, Lady Robsart opened the

door wide and stood in silence, looking at the two of them.

"Go away!" Amy shouted.

"No, come in," Robert said quickly, turning from Amy and dabbing at the spittle on his shirt and pulling at his collar that she had wrenched. "For God's sake, come in. Amy is distressed, Lady Robsart, help her to her room. I shall sleep in the guest room and leave tomorrow at first light."

"No!" Amy screamed. "You will come to me, Robert. You know you will. Your lust, your filthy lust, will wake you and you will want me again, and you will say, 'I love you. I love you.' You liar. You wicked, wicked liar."

"Take her away, for God's sake, before I murder her," he said to Lady Robsart, and brushed past her out of the room, avoiding Amy's clutching hands.

"You will come to me or I will kill you," she screamed.

Robert broke into a run up the narrow wooden stairs, and got away from his wife before she could shame them both anymore.

*   *   *

In the morning Amy was too sick to see him. Lady Robsart, her voice like ice, spoke of a night of hysterical weeping and told him that Amy had risen in the early hours of the morning and fallen to her knees and prayed for God to release her from this agony that was her life.

Robert's escort was waiting outside. "You'll know what it's all about, I suppose," he said shortly.

"Yes," Lady Robsart replied. "I suppose so."

"I rely on your discretion," he said. "The queen would be much offended by any gossip."

Her eyes flew to his face. "Then she should not give the gossips such rich pickings," she said bluntly.

"Amy has to see reason," he said. "She has to agree to a divorce. I don't want to force her. I don't want to send her out of the country to a convent against her will. I want a fair agreement and a good settlement for her. But she has to agree."

He saw the shock in her face at his frankness. "It would be worth your while," he said silkily. "I would stand your friend if you would advise her of her best interests. I have spoken to her brother-in-law, John Appleyard, and he agrees with me."

"John agrees? My son-in-law thinks that she should give you a divorce?"

"And your son Arthur."

Lady Robsart was silenced at this evidence of the unanimity of men. "I can't say what her best interests would be in such a case," she said with weak defiance.

"Just as I have said," Robert said bluntly. "Just as we say: us men. She either consents to a divorce with a good settlement, or she is divorced anyway and sent out of the country to a convent with no fortune. She has no other choice."

"I don't know what her father would have made of this. She is crying and wishing for death."

"I am sorry for it; but they will not be the first tears shed nor, I suppose, the last," he said grimly, and went out of the door without another word.

*   *   *

Robert Dudley arrived at the queen's apartments at Westminster during an impromptu recital of a new composition of some man's song, and had to stand by, smiling politely, until the madrigal—with much fa-la-la-ing—was over. Sir William Cecil, observing him quietly from a corner, was amused by the scowl on the younger man's face, and then surprised that even when he bowed to the queen his expression did not become any more pleasing.

Now what are they doing, that he should look so sour and she so concerned for him? Cecil felt his heart plunge with apprehension. *What are they planning now?*

As soon as the song was ended Elizabeth nodded Robert to a window bay and the two of them stepped to one side, out of earshot of the attentive courtiers.

"What did she say?" Elizabeth demanded, without a word of greeting. "Did she agree?"

"She went quite mad," he said simply. "She said she would die rather than agree to a divorce. I left her after a night of weeping herself sick, praying for death."

Her hand flew out to his cheek, she stopped herself before she embraced him before the whole court.

"Oh, my poor Robin."

"She spat in my face," he said, darkening at the memory. "She kicked out at me. We were all but brawling."

"No!" Despite the seriousness of their situation Elizabeth could not help but be diverted at the thought of Lady Dudley fighting like a fishwife. "Has she run mad?"

"Worse than that," he said shortly. He glanced around to make sure that no one could hear them. "She is full of treasonous thoughts and heretical opinions. Her jealousy of you has driven her to the most extreme ideas. God knows what she will say or do."

"So we will have to send her away," Elizabeth said simply.

Robert bowed his head. "My love, it will make such a scandal, I doubt we can do it at once. You can't risk it. She will fight me, she will raise a storm against me, and I have many enemies who would support her."

She looked at him directly, all the passion of a new love affair apparent in her flushed face.

"Robert, I cannot live without you. I cannot rule England without you at my side. Even now Lord Grey is marching my army into Scotland, and the English fleet, God help them, are trying to prevent three times their number of French ships getting to Leith Castle where that wicked woman has raised a siege again. I am on a knife edge, Robert. Amy is a traitor to make things worse for me. We should just arrest her for treason, put her in the Tower, and forget about her."

"Forget her now," he said swiftly, his first desire to soothe the anxious young woman he loved. "Forget her. I'll stay at court with you, I'll be at your side night and day. We will be husband and wife in everything but name, and when we have won in Scotland and the country is safe and at peace, we will deal with Amy and we will be married."

She nodded. "You won't see her again?."

He had a sudden unbidden memory of Amy's hand caressing him, and her sleepy unfolding of herself beneath him, of the way her hand had stroked his back and of his own whispered words in the darkness which might have been "Oh, I love you," speaking from desire, not calculation.

"I won't see her," he assured her. "I am yours, Elizabeth, heart and soul."

Elizabeth smiled, and Dudley tried to smile reassuringly back at her, but for a moment it was Amy's dreamy, desirous face that he saw.

"She is a fool," Elizabeth said harshly. "She should have seen my stepmother Anne of Cleves when my father asked for a divorce. Her first thought was to oblige him and her second to obtain a reasonable settlement for herself. Amy is a fool, and a wicked fool to try to stand in our way. And she is doubly a fool not to ask you for a good settlement."

"Yes," he assented, thinking that Anne of Cleves had not married for love, and longed for her husband every night for eleven years, nor had she been in his arms making passionate love the very night before he asked her to release him.

*   *   *

The court waited for news of the queen's uncle, Thomas Howard, who had been sent away to suit the convenience of the lovers, but was now a key player on the sensitive border. He was to negotiate and to sign an alliance with the Scots lords in his headquarters in Newcastle, but they waited and waited and heard nothing from him.

"What is keeping him so long?" Elizabeth demanded of Cecil. "Surely he would not play me false? Not because of Sir Robert?"

"Never," Cecil averred steadily. "These things take time."

"We have no time," she snapped.

"Thanks to you we have rushed into war and we are not prepared."

The English army, led by Lord Grey, was supposed to have assembled in Newcastle by January, and to have advanced on Scotland by the end of the month. But January had come and gone and the army had not stirred from their barracks.

"Why does it take so long?" Elizabeth demanded of Cecil. "Did you not tell him he was to march on Edinburgh at once?"

"Yes," Cecil said. "He knows what he is to do."

"Then why does he not do it?" she cried out in her frustration. "Why does no one press forward; or if they cannot, why do they not retreat? Why do we have to wait and wait and all I hear is excuses?"

She was rubbing at her fingernails, pushing the cuticles back from the nails in a nervous parody of her daily manicure. Cecil stopped himself from taking her hands.

"News will come," he maintained. "We have to be patient. And they were ordered not to retreat."

"We must proclaim our friendship with the French," she decided.

Cecil glanced at Dudley. "We are at war with the French," he reminded her.

"We should write a declaration that if their soldiers go home, we have no quarrel with France," Elizabeth said, her fingers working furiously. "Then they know that we are ready for peace, even at this late stage."

Dudley stepped forward. "Now that is an excellent idea," he said soothingly. "You write it. Nobody can marshal an argument like you."

An argument that is pure self-contradiction, Cecil thought to himself, and saw from the flash of Robert's smile toward him that Dudley knew it too.

"When do I have time to write?" Elizabeth demanded. "I can't even think; I am so anxious."

"In the afternoon," Dudley said soothingly to her. "And nobody can write like you can."

He gentles her like one of his Barbary mares, Cecil thought wonderingly. *He manages her in a way that no one else can do.*

"You shall compose it and I shall take your dictation," Robert said. "I shall be your clerk. And we shall publish it, so that everyone knows that you are not the war maker. If it comes to war they will know that your intentions were always peaceful. You will show that it is all the fault of the French."

"Yes," she said, encouraged. "And perhaps it will avert war."

"Perhaps," the men reassured her.

*   *   *

The only piece of good news that came in March was that the French preparations for war had been thrown into disarray by an uprising of French Protestants against the French royal family.

"This doesn't help us at all," Elizabeth miserably predicted. "Now Philip of Spain will turn against all Protestants; he will be in terror of it spreading, and refuse to be my friend."

But Philip was too clever to do anything that would help the French in Europe. Instead he offered to mediate between the French and the English, and the Seigneur de Glajon arrived with great pomp to meet with Elizabeth in April.

"Tell him I am ill," she whispered to Cecil, eyeing the powerful Spanish diplomat through a crack in the door from her private apartments to the audience chamber. "Keep him off me for a while. I can't stand to see him, I really can't, and my hands are bleeding."

Cecil stalled the Spanish don for several days until the news came from Scotland that Lord Grey had finally crossed the border with the English army. The soldiers of England were marching on Scottish soil. There was no denying it any longer: the two nations were finally at war.

Elizabeth's fingernails were immaculately buffed, but her lips bitten into sore strips when she finally met the Spanish ambassador.

"They will force us into peace," she whispered to Cecil after the meeting. "He all but threatened me. He warned me that if we cannot make peace with the French then Philip of Spain will send his own armies and force a peace on us."

Cecil looked aghast. "How should he do such a thing? This is not a quarrel of his."

"He has the power," she said angrily. "And it is your fault for inviting his support. Now he thinks it is his business, he thinks he has a right to come into Scotland. And if both France and Spain have armies in Scotland, what will become of us? Whoever wins will occupy Scotland forever, and will soon look to the border and want to come south. We are now at the mercy of both France and Spain; how could you do this?"

"Well, it was not my intention," he said wryly. "Does Philip think he can impose peace on France as well as us?"

"If he can force them to agree then it might be our way out," Elizabeth said, a little more hopefully. "If we make a truce with him, he has promised me that we will get Calais back."

"He lies," Cecil said simply. "If you want Calais, you will have to fight for it. If you want to keep the French out of Scotland, you will have to fight them. We have to prevent the Spanish from coming in. We have to face the two greatest countries in Christendom and defend our sovereignty. You have to be brave, Elizabeth."

He always called her by her title. It was a mark of her distress that she did not reprove him. "Spirit, I am not brave. I am so very afraid," she said in a whisper of a voice.

"Everyone is afraid," he assured her. "You, me, probably even the Sieur de Glajon. Don't you think Mary of Guise, ill in Edinburgh Castle, is afraid too? Don't you think that the French are afraid, with the

Protestants rising up against them in the heart of France itself? Don't you think that Mary, Queen of Scots, is afraid with them hanging hundreds of French rebels before her very eyes?"

"No one is alone as I am!" Elizabeth rounded on him. "No one faces two enemies on the doorstep but me! No one has to face Philip and face the French with no husband and no father and no help, but me!"

"Yes," he agreed sympathetically. "Indeed you have a lonely and a difficult part to play. But you must play it. You have to pretend to confidence even when you are afraid, even when you feel most alone."

"You would turn me into one of Sir Robert's new troop of players," she said.

"I would see you as one of England's players," he returned. "I would see you play the part of a great queen." *And I would rather die than trust Dudley with the script,* he added to himself.

*   *   *

Spring came to Stanfield Hall, and Lizzie Oddingsell arrived to be Amy's traveling companion, but no word came from Sir Robert as to where his wife was to go this season.

"Shall I write to him?" Lizzie Oddingsell asked Amy.

Amy was lying on a day bed, her skin like paper, her eyes dull, as thin as a wasted child. She shook her head, as if it were too much effort to speak. "It does not matter to him where I am anymore."

"It's just that this time last year we went to Bury St. Edmunds, and then Camberwell," Lizzie remarked.

Amy shrugged her thin shoulders. "Not this year, it seems."

"You cannot stay here all the year round."

"Why not? I lived here all the years of my girlhood."

"It's not fitting," Lizzie said. "You are his wife, and this is a little house with no gay company, and no good food or music or dancing or society. You cannot live like a farmer's wife when you are the wife of one of the greatest men in the country. People will talk."

Amy raised herself up on her elbow. "Good God, you know as well as I that people say far worse things than that I do not keep a good table."

"They speak of nothing but the war against the French in Scotland," Lizzie lied.

Amy shook her head and leaned back

and closed her eyes. "I am not deaf," she observed. "They say that my husband and the queen will be married within a year."

"And what will you do?" Lizzie prompted gently. "If he insists? If he puts you aside? I am sorry, Amy, but you should consider what you would need. You are a young woman, and—"

"He cannot put me aside," Amy said quietly. "I am his wife. I will be his wife till the day of my death. I cannot help it. God bound us together; only God can part us. He can send me away, he can even marry her, but then he is a bigamist and she is a whore in the eyes of everyone. I cannot do anything but be his wife until my death."

"Amy," Lizzie breathed. "Surely . . ."

"Please God my death comes soon and releases us all from this agony," Amy said in her thin thread of a voice. "Because this is worse than death for me. To know that he has loved me and turned from me, to know that he wants me far away, never to see him again. To know, every morning that I wake, every night that I sleep, that he is with her, that he chooses to be with her rather than to be with me. It eats into me like a canker,

Lizzie. I could think myself dying of it. This is grief like death. I would rather have death."

"You have to reconcile yourself," Lizzie Oddingsell said, without much faith in the panacea.

"I have reconciled myself to heartbreak," Amy said. "I have reconciled myself to a life of desolation. No one can ask more of me."

Lizzie stood up and turned a log on the fire. The chimney smoked and the room was always filled with a light haze that stung the eyes. Lizzie sighed at the discomfort of the farmhouse and of the late Sir John's determination that what he had established was good enough for anyone else.

"I shall write to my brother-in-law," she said firmly. "They are always glad to see you. At least we can go to Denchworth."

*   *   *

Westminster Palace
March 14th 1560
William Cecil to the Commander of the
Queen's Pensioners.

Sir,

    1. It has come to my attention that the French have hatched a conspiracy against the life of the queen and of the noble gentleman

Sir Robert Dudley. I am informed that they are determined that one or the other shall be killed, believing that this will give them an advantage in the war in Scotland.

2. I hereby advise you of this new threat and commend you to redouble your guard on the queen and to command them to remain alert at all times.

Be alert also for anyone approaching or following the noble gentleman, and for anyone hanging round his apartments or the stables.

God Save the Queen.

Sir Francis Knollys with Sir Nicholas Bacon sought out William Cecil.

"For God's sake, is there no end to these threats?"

"Apparently not," Cecil said quietly.

Sir Robert Dudley joined them. "What's this?"

"More death threats against the queen," Sir Francis told him. "And against you."

"Me?"

"From the French, now."

"Why would the French want to kill me?" Dudley asked, shocked.

"They think the queen would be distressed by your death," Nicholas Bacon said tactfully, when no one else answered.

Sir Robert took a swift, irritated turn on his heel. "Are we to do nothing while Her Majesty is threatened on all sides? When Frenchmen threaten her, when the Pope himself threatens her? When Englishmen plot against her? Can't we confront this terror and destroy it?"

"The nature of terror is that you don't know quite what it is or what it can do," Cecil observed. "We can protect her, but only up to a point. Short of locking her up in a gated room we cannot preserve her from danger. I have a man tasting everything she eats. I have sentries at every door, under every window. No one comes into court without being vouched for and yet still, every other day, I hear of a new plot, a new murder plan against her."

"How would the French like it if we murdered the young Queen Mary?" Sir Robert demanded.

William Cecil exchanged a glance with the other more experienced man, Sir Fran-

cis. "We can't reach her," he admitted. "I
had Throckmorton look at the French court
when he was in Paris. It can't be done without them knowing it was us."

"And is that your only objection?" Robert
bristled.

"Yes," Cecil said silkily. "I have no objection in theory to assassination as an act of
state. It could be a great saver of life and a
guarantee of safety for others."

"I am utterly and completely opposed to
it," Dudley said indignantly. "It is forbidden
by God, and it is against the justice of man."

"Yes, but it's you they want to kill, so
you would think that," Sir Nicholas said
with scant sympathy. "The bullock seldom
shares the beliefs of the butcher, and you,
you are dead meat, my friend."

*   *   *

Amy and Lizzie Oddingsell, escorted by
Thomas Blount, with men in the Dudley livery riding before and behind them, came in
silence to the Hyde house. The children,
watching for them as usual, came running
down the drive toward them and then hesitated when their aunt had nothing more for
them than a wistful smile, and their favorite

guest, the pretty Lady Dudley, did not seem to see them at all.

Alice Hyde, hurrying out to greet her sister-in-law and her noble friend, felt for a moment as if a shadow had fallen on their house and gave a little involuntary shiver as if the April sunshine had suddenly turned icy. "Sister! Lady Dudley, you are most welcome."

Both women turned to her faces that were pale with strain. "Oh, Lizzie!" Alice said, in shock at the weariness on her face, and then went to help her sister-in-law down from the saddle as her husband came out and helped Lady Dudley to dismount.

"May I go to my room?" Amy whispered to William Hyde.

"Of course," he said kindly. "I will take you myself, and have a fire lit for you. Will you take a glass of brandy to keep out the cold and put some roses in those pretty cheeks again?"

He thought she looked at him as if he addressed her in a foreign language.

"I am not ill," she said flatly. "Whoever told you that I was ill, is lying."

"No? I'm glad to hear of it. You look a little wearied by your journey, that's all," he said soothingly, leading her into the hall and then up the stairs to the best guest bedroom. "And are we to expect Sir Robert here, this spring?"

Amy paused at the door of her room. "No," she said very quietly. "I do not expect to see my husband this season. I have no expectations of him at all."

"Oh," William Hyde said, quite at sea.

Then she turned and put both her hands out to him. "But he is my husband," she said, almost pleading. "That will never change."

At a loss, he chafed her cold hands. "Of course he is," he soothed her, thinking that she was talking at random, like a madwoman. "And a very good husband too, I am sure."

Somehow, he had said the right thing. The sweet smile of Amy the beloved girl suddenly illuminated the bleak face of Amy the deserted wife.

"Yes, he is," she said. "I am so glad that you see that too, dear William. He is a good husband to me and so he must come home to me soon."

*   *   *

"Good God, what have they done to her?" William Hyde demanded of his sister, Lizzie

Oddingsell, when the three of them were seated around the dinner table, the covers cleared and the door safely closed against prying servants. "She looks near to death."

"It is as you predicted," Lizzie said shortly. "Just as you said when you were so merry about what would happen if your master were to marry the queen. He has done what you thought he might do. He has thrown her off and is going to marry the queen. He told her to her face."

A long, low whistle from William Hyde greeted this news. Alice was quite dumbstruck.

"And the queen has proposed this? She thinks she can get such a thing past the Lords and Commons of England?"

Lizzie shrugged. "He speaks as if all that stands in their way is Amy's consent. He speaks as if he and the queen are quite agreed and are picking out names for their firstborn."

"He will be consort. She might even call him king," William Hyde speculated. "And he will not forget the services we have done him and the kindness we have shown him."

"And what of her?" Lizzie asked fiercely, nodding her head to the chamber above them. "When he is crowned and we are in Westminster Abbey shouting hurrah? Where do you think she is then?"

William Hyde shook his head. "Living quietly in the country? At her father's old house? At the house she fancied here—old Simpson's place?"

"It will kill her," Alice predicted. "She will never survive the loss of him."

"I think so," Lizzie said. "And the worst of it is, that I think in his heart, he knows that. And I am sure that the she-devil queen knows that too."

"Hush!" William said urgently. "Even behind closed doors, Lizzie!"

"All her life Amy has been on a rack of his ambition," Lizzie hissed. "All her life she has loved and waited for him and prayed long, sleepless nights for his safety. And now, at the moment of his prosperity, he tells her that he will cast her aside, that he loves another woman, and that this other woman has such power that she can throw a true-wedded wife to the dogs.

"What do you think this will do to her? You saw her. Doesn't she look like a woman walking toward her grave?"

"Is she sick?" asked William Hyde, a

practical man. "Does she have this canker in her breast that they all say is killing her?"

"She is sick to death from heartache," Lizzie said. "That is all the pain in her breast. And he may not understand this, but I warrant the queen does. She knows that if she plays cat and mouse with Amy Dudley for long enough then her health will simply break down and she will take to her bed and die. If she does not kill herself first."

"Never! A mortal sin!" Alice exclaimed.

"It has become a sinful country," Lizzie said bleakly. "What is worse? A woman throwing herself headfirst downstairs or a queen taking a married man to her bed and the two of them hounding the true wife to her death?"

*   *   *

Thomas,

Cecil wrote in code to his old friend Thomas Gresham at Antwerp.

> *1. I have your note about the Spanish troopships, presumably, they are arming to invade Scotland. The great numbers that you have seen*

must indicate that they plan to in-vade England as well.

2. *They have a plan to invade Scot-land on the pretext of imposing peace. I assume that they are now putting this into practice.*

3. *On receipt of this, please inform your clients, customers, and friends that the Spanish are on the brink of invading Scotland, that this will take them into war with the French, with the Scots and with ourselves, and warn them most emphatically that all the English trade will leave Antwerp for France. The cloth mar-ket will leave the Spanish Nether-lands forever, and the loss will be incalculable.*

4. *If you can create utter panic in the commercial and trading quarters with this news I would be much obliged. If the poor people were to take it into their heads that they will starve for lack of English trade, and riot against their Spanish masters, it would be even better. If the Spanish could be brought to think*

*they are facing a national revolt it
would be very helpful.*

Cecil did not sign the letter nor seal it with his crest. He rarely put his name to anything.

*   *   *

Ten days later Cecil stalked into the queen's privy chamber like a long-legged, triumphant raven and laid a letter before her on her desk. There were no other papers, her anxiety about Scotland was so great that she did no other work. Only Robert Dudley could distract her from her terrified interrogation of the progress of the war; only he could comfort her.

"What is this?" she asked.

"A report from a friend of mine in Antwerp that there has been a panic in the city," Cecil said with quiet pleasure. "The respectable merchants and tradesmen are leaving in their hundreds; the poor people are barricading the streets and firing the slums. The Spanish authorities have been forced to issue a proclamation to the citizens and traders that there will be no expedition to Scotland or against England. There was a run on the currency, there were people leaving the town. There was absolute panic. They feared a rebellion would start that would flare into a civil war. They had to give their word that the ships in port are not headed for our shores. The Spanish have been forced to reassure the traders of the Spanish Netherlands that they will not intervene in Scotland against us, that they will stay our friend and ally, whatever takes place in Scotland. The risk to their commercial interest was too great. They have publicly declared their alliance to us, and that they will not invade."

The color flooded into her cheeks. "Oh, Spirit! We are safe!"

"We still have to face the French," he cautioned her. "But we need not fear the Spanish coming against us at the same time."

"And I need not marry the archduke!" Elizabeth laughed merrily.

Cecil checked.

"Although I still expect to do so," she corrected herself hastily. "I have given my word, Cecil."

He nodded, knowing she was lying. "And so shall I write to Lord Grey to take Leith Castle at once?"

He caught her for once in a confident

mood. "Yes!" she cried. "At last something is going well for us. Tell him to set the siege and win it at once!"

*   *   *

Elizabeth's bright, confident mood did not last long. The attack on Leith Castle in May failed miserably. The scaling ladders were too short and more than two thousand men died scrabbling against the castle walls, unable to get up or down, or fell wounded into the blood and mire below.

The horror of the injury, illness, and death of her troops haunted Elizabeth as much as the humiliation of failing before the very windows of Mary of Guise. Some said that the stone-hearted Frenchwoman had looked out and laughed to see Englishmen spitted on lances at the top of their scaling ladders and falling down like shot doves.

"They must come home!" Elizabeth swore. "They are dying as they drown in the mud before her door. She is a witch; she has called down rain on them."

"They cannot come home," Cecil told her.

Her nails shone with the frantic polishing of her fingers, her cuticles were pushed back till they were red and raw. "They must come home; we are fated to lose Scotland," she said. "How could the ladders be too short? Grey should be court-martialed. Norfolk should be recalled. My own uncle and a treacherous fool! A thousand men dead on the walls of Leith! They will call me a murderess, to send good men to their deaths for such folly."

"War always means death," Cecil said flatly. "We knew that before we started."

He checked himself. This passionate, fearful girl had never seen a battlefield, had never walked past wounded men groaning for water. A woman could not know what men endured; she could not rule as a king would rule. A woman could never learn the determination of a man made in the image of God.

"You have to adopt the courage of a king," he said to her firmly. "Now more than ever. I know you fear that we are failing, but the side that wins in a war is often the one which has the most confidence. When you are at your most fearful, that is when you have to appear your bravest. Say whatever comes into your head, put up your chin and swear that you have the stomach of a man. Your sister could do it. I saw her turn the

City of London around in a moment. You can do it too."

Elizabeth flared up. "Don't name her to me! She had a husband to rule for her."

"Not then," he contradicted her. "Not when she faced the Wyatt rebels as they came right up to the City and camped at Lambeth. She was a woman alone then; she called herself the Virgin Queen and the London militia swore they would lay down their lives for her."

"Well, *I* cannot do it." She was wringing her hands. "I cannot find the courage. I cannot say such things and make men believe me."

Cecil took her hands and held them tight. "You have to," he said. "We have to go forward now because we cannot go back."

She looked pitifully at him. "What must we do? What can we do now? Surely it is over?"

"Muster more troops, reinstate the siege," he said.

"Are you sure?"

"I would put my own life on it."

Reluctantly, she nodded.

"I have your permission to send out the

orders?" he pressed. "For more men, to put the siege back on Leith?"

"Very well." She breathed the words like a coerced girl.

*   *   *

Only Robert Dudley could comfort Elizabeth. They rode out less and less, she was too exhausted by sleepless nights of worry. Day flowed into night in the queen's private rooms when she paced the floor till four in the morning and then fell into an exhausted dream-filled doze in the early afternoon. They closed the door of her privy chamber, defiant of the gossips, and he sat with her beside the fire in the cold gray afternoons. She took off her heavy jewel-encrusted hood and let down her hair and laid her head in his lap, and he stroked her long bronze locks until the strained, anxious look melted from her face and she sometimes closed her eyes and slept.

Kat Ashley sat in the window seat for form's sake but she kept her eyes fixed on her needlework or read a book; she never so much as glanced at the lovers as Robert nursed Elizabeth as tenderly as a mother. Kat knew that soon Elizabeth would collapse under the strain. She had watched Elizabeth through a dozen nervous illnesses. She was accustomed to examining Elizabeth's slim fingers and wrists for any telltale signs of swelling which would show that her recurring disease of dropsy was about to exile her to bed. And Kat knew, as only Elizabeth's closest friends knew, that nothing brought on her illness faster than fear.

Outside the door, seated in the presence chamber trying to look as if nothing was wrong, Catherine Knollys, sewing a shirt for her husband, was acutely aware of the empty throne and the waiting court, of the whispers that the queen and Sir Robert had been locked up for half the day and would not come out till dinner time. Catherine kept her head up and her face blank, refusing to reply to people asking what her cousin the queen was doing alone with Sir Robert, refusing to hear the muttered comments.

Mary Sidney, aghast at where her brother's ambition was taking him, but unswerving in her family loyalty, dined with Catherine Knollys and walked with Kat Ashley, avoiding anyone who might question her as to what Robert Dudley thought he was doing.

The Privy Council, the Lords, any man

who was not on Dudley's payroll, swore that someone would soon run the man through for dishonoring the queen and bringing her name into the gossip of every alehouse in the land. Some said that Thomas Howard, desperately fortifying castles along the northern border and trying to persuade men to enlist, had still found time to send an assassin south to court to kill Dudley and have done with him once and for all. No one could deny that the world would be a better place if Dudley were to be gone. He endangered the realm more than the French. Locked up with the queen in her own rooms, whoever was in with them, whoever was on the door, was to bring the queen into fatal disrepute.

But no one could stop Dudley. When reproached by someone he trusted, like Sir Francis Knollys, he pointed out that the queen's health would break under her anxiety if he did not comfort her. He reminded any loyal friends that the queen was a young woman all alone in the world. She had no father, no mother, no guardian. She had no one to love her and care for her but himself, her old and trusted friend.

To everyone else he merely gave his impertinent, dark-eyed smile and thanked them sarcastically for their concern for his well-being.

Laetitia Knollys strolled into Cecil's apartments and took a seat at his desk with all the dignity of a betrothed woman.

"Yes?" Cecil asked.

"She wants him to negotiate a peace with the French," Laetitia remarked.

Cecil hid his shock. "Are you sure?"

"I am sure that she asked him." The young woman shrugged her slim shoulders. "I am sure that he said he would see what he could do. Whether she is of the same mind now, I couldn't say. That was this morning and now it is past noon. When does she ever stay in the same mind for more than two hours?"

"On what terms?" Cecil asked, ignoring Laetitia's impertinence.

"That they can have Scotland if they will return Calais, and take her coat of arms from the Queen of Scots."

Cecil compressed his lips on any comment.

"I thought you wouldn't like it." Laetitia smiled. "A whole country in exchange for a city. Sometimes she acts as if she is going quite mad. She was crying and clinging to him and asking him to save England for her."

Oh God, and in front of a girl like you who would tell anyone. "And he said?"

"What he always says: that she is not to fear, that he will care for her, that he will arrange everything."

"He promised nothing specific? Nothing at once?"

She smiled again. "He's too clever for that. He knows she'll change her mind in a moment."

"You were right to come and tell me," Cecil said. He reached into the drawer of the desk and, judging by touch, drew out one of the heavier purses. "For a gown."

"I thank you. It's extraordinarily expensive, being the best-dressed woman at court."

"Does the queen not give you her old gowns?" he asked, momentarily curious.

Laetitia gleamed at him. "D'you think she'd risk a comparison?" she asked mischieviously. "When she can't live without Robert Dudley? When she can't bear him even to glance at another woman? I wouldn't put me in one of her old gowns if I was her. I wouldn't beg the comparison."

*   *   *

Cecil, at the head of his spy ring, gathering gossip about the queen, hearing rumors that half the country thought her married to Dudley already and the other half thought her dishonored, gathered threatening whispers against the pair as a spider collects the threads of its web and lays its long legs along them, alert for any tremor. He knew that there were tens of men who threatened to drag Dudley to his death, and swore to knife him, hundreds who said they would help, and thousands who would see it happen and not lift a finger to defend him.

Please God someone does it, and soon, and brings an end to this, Cecil whispered to himself, watching Elizabeth and Dudley dining in her rooms before half the court, but whispering together as if they were quite alone, his hand on her leg underneath the table, her eyes fixed on his.

But even Cecil knew that Elizabeth could not rule without Dudley at her side. At this stage in her life—so young and surrounded by so many dangers—she had to have a friend. And although Cecil was willing to be at her side night and day, Elizabeth wanted a confidant: heart and soul. Only a man besottedly in love with her could satisfy Elizabeth's hunger for reassurance; only a man publicly betraying his wife every moment of every day could satisfy Elizabeth's ravenous vanity.

"Sir Robert." Cecil bowed to Dudley as the younger man stepped down from the dais at the end of dinner.

"I am just going to command the musicians, the queen wants to hear a tune I have composed for her," Sir Robert said negligently, unwilling to pause.

"Then I won't detain you," Cecil said. "Has the queen spoken to you about a peace with France at all?"

Dudley smiled. "Not to any effect," he said. "We both know, sir, that it cannot be. I let her talk, it eases her fears, and then later I explain it to her."

"I am relieved," Cecil said politely. *You explain, do you? When you and yours know nothing but double-dealing and treason!* "Now, Sir Robert, I was drawing up a list of ambassadors to the courts of Europe. I thought we should have some fresh faces, once this war is won. I wondered if you would like to visit France? We could do with a trustworthy man in Paris and Sir Nicholas would like to come home." He paused. "We would need a man to reconcile them to defeat. And if any man could turn the head of the Queen of France, and seduce her from her duty, it would be you."

Robert ignored the ambiguous compliment. "Have you spoken to the queen?"

No, Cecil thought, *For I know what the answer would be. She cannot let you out of her sight. But if I can persuade you, then you would persuade her. And I could do with a handsome rogue like you to flirt with Mary, Queen of Scots, and spy for us.* Aloud, he said: "Not yet. I thought I would ask if it pleased you first."

Sir Robert gave his most seductive smile. "I think it may not," he said. "Between the two of us, Sir William, I think that by this time next year I will have another task in the kingdom."

"Oh?" Cecil said. *What does he mean?* he thought rapidly. *He cannot mean my post? Does she mean to give him Ireland? Or, dear God, she would never put this puppy in charge of the north?*

Sir Robert laughed delightedly at Cecil's

puzzled face. "I think you will find me in a very great position," he said quietly. "Perhaps the greatest in the land, Master Secretary; do you understand me? And if you stand my friend now, I will be your friend then. Do you understand me now?"

And Cecil felt that he lost his balance, as if the floor had opened like a chasm beneath his feet. Finally, he did understand Sir Robert. "You think she will marry you?" he whispered.

Robert smiled, a young man in the confidence of his love. "For certain. If someone doesn't kill me first."

Cecil delayed him with a touch to his sleeve. "You mean this? You have asked her and she has agreed?" *Stay calm, she never agrees to marriage and means it. She never gives her word and keeps it.*

"She asked me herself. It is agreed between us. She cannot bear the burden of the kingdom alone, and I love her and she loves me." For a moment the blaze of the Dudley ambition was softened in Robert's face. "I do love her, you know, Cecil. More than you can imagine. I will make her happy. I will devote my life to making her happy."

Aye, but it is not a matter of love, Cecil

thought miserably. *She is not a milkmaid; you are not a shepherd boy. You are neither of you free to marry for love. She is Queen of England and you are a married man. If she goes on this way she will be queen in exile and you will be beheaded.* Aloud he said: "Is it firmly agreed between you?"

"Only death can stop us." Dudley smiled.

*   *   *

"Will you come for a ride?" Lizzie Oddingsell invited Amy. "The daffodils are out by the river and they are a beautiful sight. I thought we could ride down and pick some."

"I'm tired," Amy said faintly.

"You've not been out for days," Lizzie said.

Amy found a thin smile. "I know, I am a very dull guest."

"It's not that! My brother is concerned for your health. Would you like to see our family physician?"

Amy put out her hand to her friend. "You know what is wrong with me. You know that there is no cure. Have you heard anything from the court?"

The guilty evasive slide of Lizzie Oddingsell's gaze told Amy everything.

"She is not going to marry the archduke? They are together?"

"Amy, people are speaking of their marriage as a certainty. Alice's cousin, who goes to court, is sure of it. Perhaps you should consider what you will do when he forces a divorce on you."

Amy was silent. Mrs. Oddingsell did not dare to say anything more.

"I will talk to Father Wilson," Amy decided.

"Do so!" Mrs. Oddingsell said, relieved of some of the burden of caring for Amy. "Shall I send for him?"

"I'll walk down to the church," Amy decided. "I'll walk down and see him tomorrow morning."

*   *   *

The garden of the Hyde's house backed on to the churchyard; it was a pleasant walk down the winding path through the daffodils to the lych-gate, set into the garden wall. Amy opened the gate and went up the path to the church.

Father Wilson was kneeling before the altar, but at the sound of the opening door, he rose to his feet and came down the aisle. When he saw Amy, he checked.

"Lady Dudley."

"Father, I need to confess my sins and ask your advice."

"I am not supposed to hear you," he said. "You are ordered to pray directly to God."

Blindly, she looked around the church. The beautiful stained-glass windows that had cost the parish so dear were gone, the rood screen pulled down. "What has happened?" she whispered.

"They have taken the stained glass from the window, and the candles, and the cup, and the rood screen."

"Why?"

He shrugged. "They called them Popish entrapments for the soul."

"Can we talk here then?" Amy gestured to the pew.

"God will hear us here, as anywhere else," the priest assured her. "Let us kneel down and ask him for his help."

He rested his head in his hands and prayed for a moment very earnestly that he might find something to say which would comfort this young woman. Having heard some of the gossip from court he knew that the task was beyond his doing; she had been deserted. But God was merciful, perhaps something would come.

Amy knelt with her face buried in her hands and then spoke quietly through the shield of her fingers. "My husband, Sir Robert, proposes to marry the queen," she said softly. "He tells me that it is her wish. He tells me that she can force a divorce upon me, that she is Pope in England today."

The priest nodded. "And what did you say, my child?"

Amy sighed. "I am guilty of the sin of anger, and jealousy," she said. "I was vile and vicious, and I am ashamed of what I said and did."

"May God forgive you," the priest said gently. "I am sure you were in great pain."

She opened her eyes and shot him one dark look. "I am in such pain that I think I will die of it," she said simply. "I pray to God that he will release me from this pain and take me into his mercy."

"In his own time," the priest supplemented.

"No; now," she said. "Every day, Father, every day is such a misery for me. I keep my eyes shut in the morning in the hope that I have died in the night, but every morning I see daylight and know that it is another day I have to get through."

"You must put aside thoughts of your own death," he said firmly.

Surprisingly, Amy gave him the sweetest smile. "Father, it is my only comfort."

He felt, as he had felt before, that he could not advise a woman confronted with such a dilemma. "God must be your comfort and your refuge," he said, falling back on the familiar words.

She nodded, as if she were not much convinced. "Should I give my consent to a divorce?" she asked him. "Then he will be free to marry the queen, the scandal will die down in time, the country will be at peace, and I can be forgotten."

"No," the priest said decisively. He could not help himself; it was such a deep blasphemy against the church he still served in secret. "God joined you together, no man can put you asunder, even if he is your husband, even if she is the queen. She cannot pretend to be Pope."

"Then I have to live forever in torment, keeping him as my husband but without his love?"

He paused for a moment. "Yes."

"Even if it earns me his hatred and her enmity?"

"Yes."

"Father, she is Queen of England; what might she do to me?"

"God will protect and keep you," he said with a confidence he could not truly feel.

*   *   *

The queen had summoned Cecil to her privy chamber at Whitehall; Kat Ashley was in one window bay, Robert Dudley behind her desk, a few ladies-in-waiting seated at the fireside. Cecil bowed politely to them before approaching the queen.

"Your Majesty?" he said warily.

"Cecil, I have decided. I want you to sue for peace," she said rapidly.

His glance flickered to Sir Robert, who smiled wearily but offered no comment.

"The French ambassador tells me that they are sending a special commissioner for peace," she said. "I want you to meet with Monsieur Randan and find some way, some form of words that we can agree."

"Your Majesty . . ."

"We cannot fight a long war in Scotland, the Scots lords will never maintain a long campaign, and Leith Castle is practically impregnable."

"Your Majesty . . ."

"Our only hope would be for Mary of Guise to die, and though they say her health is poor, she is nowhere near death. And anyway, they say the same of me! They say that I am ground down by this war, and God knows, it is true!"

Cecil heard the familiar tone of hysteria in Elizabeth's voice and took a step back from her desk.

"Spirit, we must have peace. We cannot afford war, and we surely cannot afford defeat," she pleaded.

"Certainly I can meet with Monsieur Randan, and see if we can agree," he said smoothly. "I will draw up some terms and show them to you and then take them to him as he arrives."

Elizabeth was breathless with her anxiety. "Yes, and arrange a ceasefire as soon as possible."

"We have to have some sort of victory or they will think we are afraid," Cecil said. "If they think we are afraid they will advance. I can negotiate with them while we maintain the siege, but we have to continue the siege while we talk, the navy must maintain the blockade."

"No! Bring the men home!"

"Then we will have achieved nothing," he pointed out. "And they will not need to make an agreement with us, since they will be able to do as they wish."

She was out of her seat and striding round the room, restless with anxiety, rubbing at her fingernails. Robert Dudley went behind her and put his arm around her waist, drew her back to her chair, glanced at Cecil.

"The queen is much distressed at the risk to English life," he said smoothly.

"We are all deeply concerned, but we have to maintain the siege," Cecil said flatly.

"I am sure the queen would agree to maintain the siege if you were meeting with the French to discuss terms," Robert said. "I am sure she would see that you need to negotiate from a position of strength. The French need to see that we are in earnest."

Yes, Cecil thought. *But where are you in all of this? Soothing her, I see that, and thank God that someone can do it though I would give a fortune for it not to be you. But what game do you seek to play? There will be a Dudley interest in here, if only I could see it.*

"As long as the negotiations go speedily," the queen said. "This cannot drag on. The sickness alone is killing my troops as they wait before Leith Castle."

"If you were to go to Newcastle yourself," Dudley suggested to Cecil. "Take the French emissary with you and negotiate from there, at Norfolk's headquarters, so that we have them completely under our control."

"And far away from the Spanish representative, who still seeks to meddle," Cecil concurred.

"And close enough to Scotland so that they can take instruction from the queen regent, but be distanced from France," Dudley remarked.

And I shall be far from the queen so she cannot countermand me all the time, Cecil supplemented. Then the thought hit him: *Good God! He is sending me to Newcastle too! First her uncle, that he made commander of the Scottish border, and put in the front line of fighting, and now me. What does he think to do while I am gone? Supplant me? Appoint himself to the Privy*

Council and vote through his divorce? Murder me?

Aloud he said: "I would do it, but I would need an undertaking from Your Majesty."

Elizabeth looked up at him; he thought he had never seen her so drawn and tired, not even in her girlhood when she had faced death. "What do you want, Spirit?"

"That you promise me that you will be faithful to our long friendship while I am so far from you," he said steadily. "And that you will undertake no great decision, no alliance, no treaty"—he did not dare even to glance toward Dudley—"no partnership until I come home again."

She, at least, was innocent of any plot against him. She answered him quickly and honestly. "Of course. And you will try to bring us to peace, won't you Spirit?"

Cecil bowed. "I will do my very best for you and for England," he said.

She stretched out her hand for him to kiss. The fingernails were all ragged where she had been picking at them, when he kissed her fingers he felt the torn cuticles prickle his lips. "God bring Your Grace to peace of mind," he said gently. "I will serve you in Newcastle as I would serve you here. Do you keep faith with me too."

*   *   *

Cecil's horses and great train of soldiers, servants, and guards were drawn up before the doors of the palace, the queen herself and the court arrayed to see him off. It was as if she were signaling to him, and to everyone else who would take careful note, that he was not being bundled north to get him out of the way, but being sent off in state and would be badly missed.

He knelt before her on the stone step. "I wanted to speak to you before I left," he said, his voice very low. "When I came to your presence chamber last night they said you had retired and I could not see you."

"I was tired," she said evasively.

"It is about the coinage. And it is important."

She nodded and he rose to his feet, gave her his arm, and they walked down the palace steps together, out of earshot of his waiting train. "We need to revalue the coin of the realm," Cecil said quietly. "But it has to be done in utter secret or every beldame in the land will be trading coins away, knowing that they will be no good at the new value."

"I thought we could never afford it," Elizabeth said.

"We can't afford not to do it," Cecil said. "It has to be done. And I have found a way to borrow gold. We will mint new coins and in one move, overnight, call in the old, weigh them, and replace them with new."

She did not understand at first. "But people with stocks of coins will not have the fortune they thought they had."

"Yes," Cecil said. "It will hurt the people with treasuries, but not the common people. The people with treasuries will squeak but the common people will love us. And the people with treasuries are also merchants and sheep farmers and venturers, they will get good value for the new coins when they trade abroad. They won't squeak too loud."

"What about the royal treasury?" she asked, alert at once to her own diminished fortune.

"Your councillor Armagil Waad is dealing with it," he said. "You have been converting to gold since you came to the throne. We will make the coinage of this country solid once more, and they will call this a golden age."

Elizabeth smiled at that, as he knew she would.

"But it has to be an utter secret," he said. "If you tell one person," *and we both know which person it would be* "then he would speculate in coins and it would alert everyone who watches him. All his friends would speculate too, they would copy him, even if he did not warn them, and his rivals would want to know why and speculate also. This has to be an utter secret or we cannot do it."

She nodded.

"If you tell him you will be ruined."

She did not glance back up the steps at Dudley; she kept her eyes fixed on Cecil.

"Can you keep such a secret?" he asked.

Her dark Boleyn eyes gleamed up at him with all the bright cynicism of her merchant forebears. "Oh, Spirit, you of all people know that I can."

He bowed, kissed her hand, and turned to mount his horse. "When shall we do it?" she asked him.

"September," he said. "This year. Pray God we have peace then as well."

Summer 1560

It took Cecil and his entourage a week to reach Newcastle from London, riding most of the way on the Great North Road though fine early summer weather. He spent one night at Burghley, his new, beautiful half-built palace. His wife, Mildred, greeted him with her usual steady good humor, and his two children were well.

"Do we have much coin?" he asked her over dinner.

"No," she said. "When the queen came to the throne you told me that we should not save coin and since then it's easy to see that matters have got even worse. I keep as little as possible. I take rent in kind or in goods wherever I can, the coin is so bad."

"That's good," he said. He knew that he

need say no more. Mildred might live in a remote area but there was not much happening in the country and in the city that she did not know of. Her kin were the greatest Protestants in the land; she came from the formidably intelligent Protestant Cheke family, and constant letters of news, opinion, and theology passed from one great house to another.

"Is everything well here?" he asked. "I would give a king's ransom to stay and see the builders."

"Would it cost a royal ransom for you to be late in Scotland?" she asked shrewdly.

"Yes," he said. "I am on grave business, wife."

"Will we win?" she asked bluntly.

Cecil paused before replying. "I wish I could be sure," he said. "But there are too many players and I cannot know the cards they hold. We have good men on the border now; Lord Grey is reliable and Thomas Howard is as fiery as ever. But the Protestant lords are a mixed bunch and John Knox is a liability."

"A man of God," she said sharply.

"Certainly he acts as if divinely inspired," he said mischievously, and saw her smile.

"You have to stop the French?"

"Or we are lost," he concurred. "I'd take any ally."

Mildred poured him a glass of wine and said no more. "It's good to have you here," she remarked. "When all this is over perhaps you can come home?"

"Perhaps," he said. "Hers is not a light service."

The next morning, Cecil had broken his fast and was ready to leave at dawn. His wife was up to see him off.

"You take care in Scotland," she said as she kissed him farewell. "I know that there are Protestant rogues as well as Papist ones."

*   *   *

They made good time to Newcastle, arriving in the first week in June, and Cecil found Thomas Howard in good spirits, confident of the strength of the border castles, and determined that there should be no peace negotiations to cede what a battle might win.

"We are here with an army," he complained to Cecil. "Why would we bring an army if we are just going to make peace?"

"She thinks that Leith will never fall," Cecil said shrewdly. "She thinks this is a battle that the French will win."

"We can defeat them!" Norfolk exclaimed. "We can defeat them and then open negotiations for peace. They can ask us for terms when they are beaten."

Cecil settled down to the long process of negotiating with the French commissioner for peace, Monsieur Randan. At once Thomas Howard drew Cecil to one side to object to the French entourage.

"Cecil, half the so-called courtiers in his train are engineers," he said. "I don't want them looking over our dispositions and checking out the walls of the castle here and at Edinburgh. If you give them free rein they will see everything I have done here. The other half are spies. As they travel to Edinburgh and Leith, they will meet with their agents and their news will go straight back to France. Randan has to negotiate on his own word; he can't go galloping up to the queen regent at Leith and back every other day, seeing God knows what and talking to God knows who."

But Monsieur Randan was obdurate. He had to take instructions from Mary of Guise herself, and he could offer no peace proposals, nor answer the English proposals, without speaking with her. He had to go to Edinburgh, and he had to have safe conduct through the siege lines into Leith Castle.

"Might as well draw him a map," Thomas Howard said irritably. "Invite him to call in at every damned Papist house on the way."

"He has to see his master," Cecil remarked reasonably. "He has to put our proposals to her."

"Aye, and she is the one who is our greatest danger," Thomas Howard declared. "He is nothing more than her mouthpiece. She is a great politician. She will stay holed up in that castle forever if she can and prevent us from talking with the French. She will get between us and them. If we let Randan speak with her she will order him to ask for one thing and then another; she will agree and then withdraw, she will hold us here until the autumn, and then the weather will destroy us."

"Do you think so?" Cecil asked anxiously.

"I am sure of it. Already the Scots are slipping away, and every day we lose men to disease. When the hot weather comes we can expect the plague and when the cold weather comes we will be destroyed by the ague. We have to move now, Cecil, we cannot let them delay us with false offers of peace."

"Move how?"

"Move the siege. We have to break in. No matter what it costs. We have to shock them to the treaty."

Cecil nodded. *Yes, but I have seen your plans for the siege,* he said to himself. *It calls for phenomenal luck, extraordinary courage, and meticulous generalship, and the English army has none of these. You are right only in your fear: if Mary of Guise sits tight within Leith Castle we will be destroyed by time, and the French can occupy Scotland and the north of England at their leisure. You are right that the French have to be frightened into peace.*

*   *   *

Elizabeth was too weary to dress properly. Robert was admitted to her privy chamber as she sat with her women wearing a robe over her nightgown, with her hair in a careless plait down her back.

Kat Ashley, normally an anxious guardian of Elizabeth's reputation, admitted Robert without a word of complaint. Elizabeth's long-standing friend and advisor Thomas Parry was in the room already. Elizabeth settled herself in the window seat and gestured to Robert to sit beside her.

"Are you ill, my love?" he asked tenderly.

Her eyes were shadowed so darkly that she looked like a defeated bare-knuckle fighter. "Just tired," she said. Even her lips were pale.

"Here, drink this," Kat Ashley offered, pressing a cup of hot mead into her hand.

"Any news from Cecil?"

"None, yet. I am afraid they will attempt the castle again; my uncle is so hasty, and Lord Grey so determined. I wanted Cecil to promise me a cease-fire while the French commissioner was in the north, but he said that we must keep up the threat . . ." She broke off, her throat tight with anxiety.

"He is right," Thomas Parry said quietly.

Robert pressed her hand. "Drink it while it is hot," he said. "Go on, Elizabeth."

"It's worse than that," she said, obediently taking a sip. "We have no money. I can't pay the troops if they stay in the field another week. And then what will happen? If they mutiny we will be destroyed; if they try to make their own way home with no money in their pockets they will pillage from the border to London. And then the French will march freely behind them."

She broke off again. "Oh, Robert, it has all gone so terribly wrong. I have ruined everything that was left to me. Not even my half-sister Mary failed this country as I have done."

"Hush," he said, taking her hand and pressing it to his heart. "None of this is true. If you need money I will raise it for you; there are lenders we can go to, I promise it. We will pay the troops, and Howard and Grey will not attack without a chance of winning. If you want, I'll go north, and look for you, see what is happening."

At once she clutched his hand. "Don't leave me," she said. "I can't bear to wait without you at my side. Don't leave me, Robert; I can't live without you."

"My love," he said softly. "I am yours to command. I will go or stay as you wish. And I always love you."

She raised her head a little from the gold cup and gave him a fugitive smile.

"There," he said. "That's better. And in a moment you must go and put on a pretty gown and I will take you riding."

She shook her head. "I can't ride; my hands are too sore."

She held out her hands to show him. The cuticles all around the nails were red and bleeding, and the knuckles were fat and swollen. Robert took the hurt hands into his own and looked around at Kat Ashley.

"She has to rest," she said. "And not worry so. She is tearing herself apart."

"Well, you wash your hands and cream them, my love," Robert said, hiding his shock. "And then put on a pretty gown and come and sit with me by the fire, and we shall have some music and you can rest and I will talk to you about my horses."

She smiled, like a child being promised a treat. "Yes," she said. "And if there is a message from Scotland . . ."

Robert raised his hand. "Not one word about Scotland. If there is news, they will bring it to us as quickly as they can. We have to learn the art of patiently waiting. Come on, Elizabeth, you know all about waiting. I have seen you wait like a master. You must wait for news as you waited for the crown. Of all the women in the world you are the most elegant waiter."

She giggled at that, her whole face lighting up.

"Now that's true," Thomas Parry agreed. "Ever since she was a girl she could keep quiet and judge her moment."

"Good," Dudley said. "Now you go and get dressed, and be quick."

Elizabeth obeyed him, as if he were her husband to command, and she had never been Queen of England. Her ladies went past him with their eyes down, all except for Laetitia Knollys, who swept him a curtsy as she went past, a deep curtsy, one appropriate from a young lady-in-waiting to a king in waiting. There was not much that Laetitia ever missed about Lord Robert.

Newcastle,
June 7th 1560

1. *Assassination is a disagreeable tool of statecraft but there are occasions when it should be considered.*
2. *For instance when the death of one person is to the benefit of many lives.*
3. *The death of one enemy can be to the benefit of many friends.*

4. *In the case of a king or queen, a death which appears accidental is better than a defeat of that king or queen which might encourage others to think of rebellion in future.*

5. *She is, in any case, elderly and in poor health. Death will be a release for her.*

6. *I would advise you to discuss this with no one. There is no need to reply to this.*

Cecil sent the letter unsigned and unsealed by special messenger to be delivered to the queen's hand. There was no need to wait for any reply; he knew that Elizabeth would take any crime on her flexible conscience to get her army home.

*　　*　　*

The whole court, the whole world, waited for the news from Scotland, and still it only came in unrevealing snippets. Cecil's letters, arriving always at least three days old, told Elizabeth that he and the French envoy were planning to travel together to Edinburgh, as soon as the details of the French train could be agreed. He wrote that he was hopeful of agreement once Monsieur Randan, the French emissary for peace, could get instructions from Mary of Guise. He wrote that he knew Elizabeth would be anxious about the soldiers, and about the stores, about their arrears of pay, and about their conditions, but that he would report on all of that when he had met with Lord Grey in Edinburgh. She would have to wait for news.

They would all have to wait.

"Robert, I cannot bear this alone," Elizabeth whispered to him. "I am breaking down. I can feel myself breaking down."

He was walking with her in the long gallery, past the portraits of her father and her grandfather, and the other great monarchs of Europe. Mary of Guise's portrait glared down at them. Elizabeth had kept it in a place of honor in the hopes of confusing the French about her feelings toward the queen regent who had brought so much trouble to the kingdom and so much danger to Elizabeth.

"You need not bear it alone. You have me."

She paused in her stride and snatched

at his hand. "You swear it? You will never leave me?"

"You know how much I love you."

She gave an abrupt laugh. "Love! I saw my father love my cousin to desperation and then he ordered her execution. Thomas Seymour swore he loved me and I let him go to his death and never lifted a finger to save him. They came and asked me what I thought of him, and I said nothing in his favor. Not one word. I was an absolute traitor to my love for him. I need more than a promise of love, Robert. I have no reason to trust sweet promises."

He paused for a moment. "If I was free, I would marry you today."

"But you are not!" she cried out. "Again and again we come to this. You say that you love me and that you would marry but you cannot, and so I am alone and have to stay alone, and I cannot bear being alone anymore."

"Wait," he said, thinking furiously. "There is a way. There is. I could prove my love to you. We could be betrothed. We could make a betrothal *de futuro.*"

"A binding promise to wed in public when you are free," she breathed.

"An oath as binding as the marriage vow," he reminded her. "One that swears us to each other as surely as marriage. So when I am free, all we do is declare publicly what we have done in private."

"And you will be my husband, and be always at my side, and never leave me," she whispered hungrily, stretching out her hand to his. Without hesitation he took it and clasped it in his own.

"Let's do it now," Robert whispered. "Right now. In your chapel. With witnesses."

For a moment he thought he had gone too far and she would withdraw in fear. But she glanced around at the court that was languidly chattering, only half an eye on her strolling with her constant companion.

"Kat, I am going to pray for our troops in Scotland," she called to Mrs. Ashley. "None of you need come with me but Catherine and Sir Francis. I want to be alone."

The ladies curtsyed; the gentlemen bowed. Catherine and Francis Knollys followed Elizabeth and Robert as, arm in arm, they went quickly along the gallery together and down the broad flight of stone stairs to the Royal Chapel.

The place was in shadowy silence, empty

but for an altar boy polishing the chancel rail.

"You. Out," Elizabeth said briefly.

"Elizabeth?" Catherine queried.

Elizabeth turned to her cousin, her face alight with joy. "Will you witness our betrothal?" she asked her.

"Betrothal?" Sir Francis repeated, looking at Sir Robert.

"A *de futuro* betrothal, a pledge to publish our marriage later," Sir Robert said. "It is the queen's dearest wish and mine."

"And what of your wife?" Sir Francis said in a half whisper to Sir Robert.

"She will have a generous settlement," he replied. "But we want to do this now. Will you be our witnesses or not?"

Catherine and her husband looked at each other. "This is a binding vow," Catherine said uncertainly. She looked at her husband for guidance.

"We will be your witnesses," he said; and then he and Catherine silently stood on either side of the queen and her lover as the two of them turned to the altar.

Elizabeth's Papist candlesticks and crucifix twinkled in the lights of a dozen candle flames. Elizabeth sank to her knees, her eyes on the crucifix, and Robert knelt down beside her.

She turned to face him. "With this ring, I thee wed," she said. She took her signet ring, her Tudor rose signet ring, off her fourth finger, and held it out to him.

He took it and tried it on his little finger. To their delight it slid on as if it had been made for him. He took off his own ring, the one he used to seal his letters, his father's ring with the ragged staff and the bear of the Dudley family.

"With this ring I thee wed," he said. "From today and this day forth I am your betrothed husband."

Elizabeth took his ring and slid it on her wedding finger. It fitted perfectly. "From to-day and this day forth I am your betrothed wife," she whispered. "And I will be bonny and blithe at bed and board."

"And I will love no one but you till death us do part," he swore.

"Till death us do part," she repeated.

Her dark eyes were luminous with tears; when she leaned forward and kissed him on the lips they brimmed over. His memory of that afternoon would always be of the warmth of her lips and the saltiness of her tears.

*   *   *

They feasted that night, and called for music, danced and were merry for the first time in many days. No one knew why Elizabeth and Robert should suddenly be so filled with joy, no one but Catherine and Francis Knollys; and they had withdrawn to their private rooms. Despite the good cheer Elizabeth said she wanted to go early to bed, and she giggled as she said it.

Obediently, the court withdrew, the ladies escorted the queen to her privy chamber and the little traditions of the queen's bedding began: the ritual thrusting of the sword into her bed, the warming of her nightgown, the mulling of her ale.

There was a quiet tap at the door. Elizabeth nodded that Laetitia should open it.

Cecil's servant stood there. Mutely he showed a letter. When Laetitia reached for it he twitched it away from her hand. She raised her eyebrows in a fair mimicry of Elizabeth's impatience and stepped back.

Elizabeth came forward to take it. He bowed.

"How long did it take you to get here?" Elizabeth asked. "How old is this news?"

"Three days, Your Grace," the man said with another bow. "We have horses waiting down the Great North Road, and my lord has us riding in relays for speed. We've got it down to three days. You won't find anyone gets any news faster than you."

"Thank you," Elizabeth said and waved him away. Laetitia shut the door on him and went to stand at Elizabeth's shoulder.

"You, step back," Elizabeth said.

Laetitia retreated as Elizabeth broke the seal and spread the letter on her writing table. She had the code locked in a drawer. She started to decode Cecil's analysis of the use of assassination, then she sat back and smiled as she understood that he was telling her, in his oblique way, that the French were about to lose their outstanding political leader in Scotland.

"Good news?" Laetitia Knollys asked.

"Yes," Elizabeth said shortly. "I think so." *Bad news for the young Queen of Scots who will lose her mother,* she thought. *But some of us have had to live without a mother for all our lives. Let her know what it is like to be alone. Let her know that she has to fight for her kingdom as I have had to fight for mine. There will be no pity for the Queen of Scots from me.*

*   *   *

As soon as the women had withdrawn, and Elizabeth's companion was asleep, she rose up from the bed, combed out her hair, and unlocked the secret door between the adjoining rooms. Robert was waiting for her, the table laid for supper, the fire lit. He was struck at once that the color was back in her cheeks, the smile on her lips, and took all the credit for himself.

"You look better," he said, taking her in his arms and kissing her. "Marriage suits you."

"I feel better." She smiled. "I feel as if I am not alone anymore."

"You are not alone," he promised her. "You have a husband to take the burden for you. You will never be alone again."

She gave a little sigh of relief and let him draw her to a seat before the fire, and accepted a glass of wine that he poured for her. *I will not be alone,* she thought. *And Mary, Queen of Scots, will be an orphan.*

*

Cecil and Monsieur Randan could apparently agree on nothing, not even on the arrangements for their journey to Edinburgh from Newcastle. Thomas Howard demanded that Monsieur Randan's train be reduced before he travel through the borders, but the French emissary bore himself like a man who knew he was negotiating a victory for his country, and would compromise on nothing.

Although Mary of Guise was under siege in a largely hostile country, it was taking the might of the entire English army to hold her in Leith Castle, and the entire English navy was at anchor in the Firth of Forth supplying the troops. The French, however, had massive reserves and a massive treasury that could be deployed against England. The possibility of an attack on the southern ports while all the English manpower was tied up in Scotland woke Cecil most nights and sent him prowling around the battlements of Newcastle, certain that the siege must be ended, and ended soon.

For all his urbane calm in front of the French emissary, Cecil knew that he was playing for the very survival of England against near-impossible odds.

*

As soon as they were ready to leave for Edinburgh Monsieur Randan sent to Leith Castle to announce that they would call upon the regent for instructions within the week. The messenger reported back that Mary of Guise was ill with dropsy, but she would see the French commissioner, and she would give him his instructions as to the settlement.

"I think you will find that you have a hard negotiator to deal with," Monsieur Randan said, smiling at Cecil. "She is a Guise herself, you know, born and bred. She will not be disposed to hand over her daughter's kingdom to invaders."

"All we require is an agreement that French troops will not occupy Scotland," Cecil said levelly. "We are not the invaders here. On the contrary. We are defending the Scots against invasion."

Monsieur Randan shrugged his shoulders. "Ah, bah! What can I say? The Queen of Scotland is the Queen of France. I suppose she can send her servants wherever she wishes in her two kingdoms. France and Scotland are one and the same to our queen. Your queen commands her servants to do as she wishes, does she not?" He broke off with an affected laugh. "Oh! Except her Master of Horse, we hear, who seems to command her."

Cecil's pleasant smile did not falter at the insult. "We have to secure an agreement that the French troops will leave Scotland," he repeated quietly. "Or nothing can prevent the continuation of a war which will be damaging to both England and France."

"Whatever Her Majesty desires of me," Monsieur Randan declared. "I am commanded to see her tomorrow when we reach Edinburgh and she will tell me what is to be done, and I think you will find that you have to do it."

Cecil bowed his agreement as a man forced into a position that he could not defend, by an enemy with the upper hand.

But Monsieur Randan never met the regent, never received his instructions, never came back to Cecil with a refusal. For that night, Mary of Guise died.

*   *   *

In the middle of June came the news from Scotland that Elizabeth had been expecting for a sennight. Every day she had dressed in an ornate gown, seated herself under the cloth of estate, and waited for someone to tell her that a travel-stained messenger from Cecil had just now ridden into court. Finally, it happened. Robert Dudley escorted the man into her presence through a buzz of courtiers.

Elizabeth opened the letter and read it; casually, Dudley stood behind her, like a second monarch, and read it over her shoulder as of right.

"Good God," he said, when he reached the part where Cecil told the queen that Mary of Guise had suddenly died. "Good God, Elizabeth. You have the luck of the devil."

The color flooded into her face. She raised her head and smiled at her court. "See how we are blessed," she announced. "Mary of Guise has died of dropsy; the French are in disarray. Cecil writes to me that he has started work on a treaty to bring peace between our two nations."

There was a little scream from one of the ladies whose brother was serving with Lord Grey, and a ripple of applause that spread through the court. Elizabeth rose to her feet. "We have defeated the French," she announced. "God himself has struck down our enemy Mary of Guise. Let others be warned. God is on our side."

Aye, said Robert to himself, drawing close to the victorious queen and taking her hand so the two of them faced the court at this moment of triumph. *But who would have thought that God's chosen instrument would be a little weasel like William Cecil?*

Elizabeth turned to him, her eyes shining. "Is it not a miracle?" she whispered.

"I see the hand of man, I see the hand of an assassin, more than the hand of God," he said, narrowly watching her.

She did not flicker, and in that moment he understood that she had known everything. She had been waiting for the news of the regent's death, waiting with foreknowledge, probably since their wedding day when she had begun to look at peace again. And she could only have been prepared by Cecil.

"No, Robert," she said steadily. "Cecil writes to me that she died of her illness. It is a miracle indeed that her death should be so timely. God save her soul."

"Oh, amen," he said.

*   *   *

The warmer weather in July agreed with Amy and she made the effort to walk in the garden at Denchworth, every day. Still she did not hear from Robert as to where she should go next, still the puzzle as to what she should do continued to haunt her.

One of Alice Hyde's children had come back from the wet nurse and the toddler took a liking to her. He held up his little chubby arms to her to be lifted up, and shouted "Me-me!" whenever he saw her.

"Amy," she said with a little smile. "Can you say Amy?"

"Me-me," he repeated seriously.

Amy, childless and lonely, responded to the warmth of the boy, carried him on her hip, sang into his warm little ear, told him stories, and let him sleep on her bed during the day.

"She has taken to him," Alice said approvingly to her husband. "She would have been such a good mother if she had been blessed with children; it does seem a shame that she will never have a child of her own."

"Aye," he said dourly.

"And little Thomas likes her," she said. "He asks for her all the time. He prefers her to any other."

He nodded. "Then that child is the only person in England who does so."

*   *   *

"Now," Robert said with pleasure, walking with Elizabeth in the cool of the July morning beside the river. "I have some news for you. Better news from Scotland than you have heard for a long time."

"What news?" At once she was on the alert. *Cecil's man said that no one could get news quicker than me. What news can Robert have that I do not know?*

"I keep a couple of servants in Newcastle and Edinburgh," he said casually. "One of them came to my house this afternoon and told me that Cecil is confident of bringing the French to an agreement. His servant told my servant that Cecil wrote to his wife to expect him home in the middle of this month. Given that Cecil would never leave his work unfinished, we can be sure that he is confident of completing the treaty very soon."

"Why has he not written to me?" she demanded, instantly jealous.

Robert shrugged. "Perhaps he wants to be sure before he speaks to you? But, Elizabeth . . ."

"He wrote to his wife, before he wrote to me?"

Her lover smiled. "Elizabeth, not all men are as devoted as me. But this is such good news, I thought you would be delighted."

"You think he has made a settlement?"

"I am sure he has one in sight. My servant suggested that he will have it signed and sealed by the sixth."

"In three days' time?" she gasped. "So soon?"

"Why not? Once the queen was dead he had only servants to deal with."

"What d'you think he has achieved? He will not have settled for less than a French withdrawal."

"He must have a French withdrawal, and he should have gained the return of Calais."

She shook her head. "They will promise to talk about Calais; they would never return it just for the asking."

"I thought it was one of your demands?"

"Oh, I demanded it," she said. "But I didn't expect to win it."

"We should have it back," Robert said stubbornly. "I lost a brother at St. Quentin; I nearly lost my own life before the walls of Calais. The blood of good Englishmen went into that canal, the canal that we dug and fortified. It is as much an English town as Leicester. We should have it back."

"Oh, Robert . . ."

"We should," he insisted. "If he has settled for anything less, then he has done us a great disservice. And I shall tell him so. And, what is more, if we do not have Calais, then he has *not* secured a lasting peace, since we will have to go to war for it as soon as the men are home from Scotland."

"He knows that Calais matters to us," she said weakly. "But we would not go to war for it . . ."

"Matters!" Robert slammed his fist on the river wall. "Calais matters as much as Leith Castle, perhaps more. And your coat of arms, Elizabeth! The Queen of France has to give up quartering our arms on her shield. And they should pay us."

"Pay?" she asked, suddenly attending.

"Of course," he said. "They have been the aggressor. They should pay us for forcing us to defend Scotland. We have emptied the treasury of England to defend against them. They should compensate us for that."

"They never would. Would they?"

"Why not?" he demanded. "They know

that they are in the wrong. Cecil is bringing them to a settlement. He has them on the run. This is the time to hit them hard, while we have them at a disadvantage. He must gain us Scotland, Calais, our arms, and a fine."

Elizabeth caught his mood of certainty. "We could do this!"

"We must do this," he confirmed. "Why go to war if not to win? Why make peace if not to gain the spoils of war? Nobody goes to war just to defend, they go to make things better. Your father knew that, he never came away from a peace without a profit. You must do the same."

"I shall write to him tomorrow," she decided.

"Write now," Robert said. "He has to get the letter at once, before he signs away your rights."

For a moment she hesitated.

"Write now," he repeated. "It will take three days to get there at the fastest. You must get it to him before he completes the treaty. Write while it is fresh in our minds, and then the business of state is finished and we can be ourselves again."

"Ourselves?" she asked with a little smile.

"We are newly wed," he reminded her softly. "Write your proclamation, my queen, and then come to your husband."

She glowed with pleasure at his words and together they turned back to Whitehall Palace. He led her through the court to her rooms and stood behind her as she sat at her writing table, and raised her pen. "What should I write?"

She waits to write to my dictation, Robert rejoiced silently to himself. *The Queen of England writes my words, just as her brother took my father's dictation. Thank God this day has come, and come through love.*

"Write in your own words, as you would usually write to him," he recommended. *The last thing I want is for him to hear my voice in her letter.* "Just tell him that you demand that the French leave Scotland, you demand the return of Calais, the surrender of your coat of arms, and a fine."

She bowed her bronze head and wrote. "How much of a fine?"

"Five hundred thousand crowns," he said, picking the number at random.

Elizabeth's head jolted up. "They would never pay that!"

"Of course they won't. They will pay the first installment perhaps and then cheat on the rest. But it tells them the price we set on their interference with our kingdoms. It tells them that we value ourselves highly."

She nodded. "But what if they refuse?"

"Then tell him he is to break the negotiations off and go to war," Robert declared. "But they won't refuse. Cecil will win them to this agreement if he knows you are determined. This is a signal to him to come home with a great prize, and a signal to the French that they dare not meddle with our affairs again."

She nodded and signed it with a flourish. "I will send it this afternoon," she said.

"Send it now," he ordered. "Time is of the essence. He has to have this before he concedes any of our demands."

For a moment she hesitated. "As you wish."

She turned to Laetitia. "Send one of the maids for one of the Lord Secretary's messengers," she said. She turned back to Robert. "As soon as I have sent this, I should like to go riding."

"Is it not too hot for you?"

"Not if we go straightaway. I feel as if I

have been cooped up here in Whitehall for a lifetime."

"Shall I have them saddle the new mare?"

"Oh, yes!" she said, pleased. "I shall meet you at the stables, as soon as I have sent this."

He watched her sign and seal it and only then did he bow, kiss her hand, and saunter to the door. The courtiers parted before him, doffing their caps, many bowed. Robert walked like a king from the room and Elizabeth watched him leave.

The girl came down the gallery with the messenger following her, and brought him to Elizabeth, where she stood watching Robert stroll away. As he drew near, Elizabeth turned into a window bay, the sealed letter in her hand, and spoke to him so quietly that no one else could hear.

"I want you to take this letter to your master in Edinburgh," she said quietly. "But you are not to start today."

"No? Your Grace?"

"Nor tomorrow. But take it the day after. I want the letter delayed by at least three days. Do you understand?"

He bowed. "As you wish, Your Grace."

"You will tell everyone, very loudly and

clearly, that you are setting off at once with a message for Sir William Cecil, and that he should have it the day after tomorrow since you can now get letters to Edinburgh within three days."

He nodded; he had been in Cecil's service too long to be surprised at any double dealing. "Shall I leave London as if I were going at once, and hide on the road?"

"That's right."

"What day do you want him to have it?"

The queen thought for a moment. "What is today? The third? Put it into his hands on July the ninth."

The servant tucked the letter in his doublet and bowed. "Shall I tell my master that it was delayed?"

"You can do. It won't matter by then. I don't want him distracted from his work by this letter. His work will be completed by then, I hope."

Edinburgh
July 4th 1560

To the queen

The queen regent is dead but the siege is still holding, though the spirit has gone out of them.

I have found a form of words which

they can agree: it is that the French king and queen will grant freedom to the Scots as a gift, as a result of your intercession as a sister monarch, and remove their troops. So we have won everything we wanted at the very last moment and by the merciful intercession of God.

This will be the greatest victory of your reign and the foundation of the peace and strength of the united kingdoms of this island. It has broken the Auld Alliance between France and Scotland forever. It has identified you as the protector of Protestantism. I am more relieved and happy than I have ever been in my life.

God bless you and your seed, for neither peace nor war without this will profit us long, William Cecil, dated this day, the fourth of July, in Edinburgh Castle, 1560.

Cecil, having averted war, broken the alliance of the French with the Scots, and identified Elizabeth as Europe's newest and most daring power player, was walking in the cool of the evening in the little garden of

Edinburgh castle and admiring the planting of the small bay trees and the intricate patterns of the colored stones.

His servant hesitated at the top of the steps, trying to see his master in the dusk. Cecil raised his hand and the man came toward him.

"A letter from Her Majesty."

Cecil nodded and took it, but did not open it at once. She knew he was near to settlement, this would be a letter thanking him for his services, promising him her love and his reward. She knew, as no one else knew, that England had been on a knife edge of disaster with this war in Scotland. She knew, as no one else knew, that no one could have won them a peace but Cecil.

Cecil sat on the garden bench and looked up at the great gray walls of the castle, at the swooping bats, at the early stars coming out, and knew himself to be content. Then he opened his letter from the queen.

For a moment he sat quite still, reading the letter, and then rereading it over and over again. *She has run mad,* was his first thought. *She has run mad with the worry and distress of this war and now she has gone as war-hungry as she was fearful be-*

fore. Good God, how can a man make any sense of his life when he is working for a woman who can blow hot and cold in a second, never mind in a day.

Good God, how can a man make a lasting peace, an honorable peace, when the monarch can suddenly call for extra settlement after the treaty has been signed? The return of Calais? The coat of arms? And now a fine? Why not ask for the stars in the sky? Why not ask for the moon?

And what is this, at the end of the letter? To break off negotiations if these objects cannot be achieved? And, in God's name: do what? Make war with a bankrupt army, with the heat of summer coming? Let the French recall their troops to battle stations, who are even now packing to leave?

Cecil scrunched the queen's letter into a ball, dropped it to the ground, and kicked it as hard as he could, over the tiny ornamental hedge into the center of the knot garden.

Madwoman! he swore at it, though still he did not say a word out loud. *Feckless, vain, extravagant, willful woman. God help me that I ever thought you the savior of your country. God help me that I ever put my skills at your crazed service when I would have been better off planting my own garden at Burghley and never dancing attendance at your mad, vain court.*

He raged for a few moments more, walking backward and forward before the balled-up letter, discarded in the knot garden, then, because documents were both a treasure and a danger, he stepped over the little hedge and retrieved it, smoothed it out, and reread it.

Then he saw two things that he had missed at the first reading. Firstly the date. She had dated it the third of July but it had arrived five days after the treaty had been signed and peace proclaimed. It had taken far too long to arrive. It had taken double the journey time. It had come too late to influence events. Cecil turned for his messenger.

"Ho! Lud!"

"Yes, Sir William?"

"Why did this take six days to reach me? It is dated the third. It should have been here three days ago."

"It was the queen's own wish, sir. She said she did not want you troubled with the letter until your business had been done. She told me to leave London and go into hiding for three days, to give the impression to the court that I had set out at once. It was her order, sir. I hope I did right."

"Of course you did right in obeying the queen," Cecil growled.

"She said she did not want you distracted by this letter," the man volunteered. "She said she wanted it to arrive when your work was completed."

Thoughtfully, Cecil nodded the man away.

What? he demanded of the night sky. *What, in the devil's name, what?*

The night sky made no reply, a small cloud drifted by like a gray veil.

Think, Cecil commanded himself. *In the afternoon, say; in the evening, say; in a temper, she makes a great demand of me. She has done that before, God knows. She wants everything: Calais, her arms restored to her sole use, peace, and five hundred thousand crowns. Badly advised (by that idiot Dudley for example) she could think all that possible, all that her due. But she is no fool, she has a second thought, she knows she is in the wrong. But she has sworn before witnesses that she will ask for all these things. So she writes the letter she promises them, signs and seals it before them but se-*

cretly she delays it on the road, she makes sure that I do the business, that peace is achieved, before she lays an impossible demand upon me.

So she has made an unreasonable demand, and I have done a great piece of work and we have both done what we should do. Queen and servant, madam and man. And then, to make sure that her interfering gesture is nothing more than an interfering gesture, without issue: she says that if her letter arrives too late (and she has ensured that it will arrive too late) I may disregard her instructions.

He sighed. Well and good. And I have done my duty, and she has done her pleasure, and no harm is done to the peace except my joy in it, and my anticipation that she would be most glad, most grateful to me, is quite gone.

Cecil tucked her letter into the pocket inside his jacket. Not a generous mistress, he said quietly to himself. Or at any rate not to me, though clearly she will write a letter and delay it and lie about it to please another. There is not a king in Christendom or in the infidel lands who has a better servant than I *have been to her, and she rewards me with this . . . This trap.*

Not really like her, he grumbled quietly to himself, walking toward the steps to the castle doorway. *An ungenerous spirit, to distress me so at the moment of my triumph, and she is not usually ungenerous.* He paused. *But perhaps badly advised.*

He paused again. *Robert Dudley,* he remarked confidentially to the steps as he set his well-shined shoe on the first paving stone. *Robert Dudley, I would wager my life on it. Begrudging my success, and wishing to diminish it in her eyes. Wanting more, always more than can reasonably be granted. Ordering her to write a letter filled with impossible demand and then she writing it to please him but delaying it so as to save the peace.* He paused once more. *A foolish woman to take such a risk to please a man,* he concluded.

Then he paused in his progress again as the worst thought came to him. *But why would she let him go so far as to dictate her letters to me, on the greatest matter of policy we have ever faced? When he is not even a member of the Privy Council? When he is nothing but her Master of Horse?*

While I have been so far away, what advantages has he taken? What progress has he made? Dear God, what power does he have over her now?

*   *   *

Cecil's letter proclaiming the peace of Scotland was greeted by Elizabeth's court, led by Robert, with sour thanksgiving. It was good, but it was not good enough, Robert implied; and the court, with one eye on the queen and the other on her favorite, concurred.

The leading members of the Privy Council grumbled among themselves that Cecil had done a remarkable job and looked to have small thanks for it. "A month ago and she would have fallen on his neck if he could have got peace after only three months' war," Throckmorton said sourly. "She would have made him an earl for getting peace within six weeks. Now he has done it within a day of getting to Edinburgh and she has no thanks for him. That's women for you."

"It's not the woman who is ungrateful, it is her lover," Sir Nicholas Bacon said roundly. "But who will tell her? And who will challenge him?"

There was a complete silence.

"Not I, at any rate," Sir Nicholas said comfortably. "Cecil will have to find a solution to this when he comes home. For surely to God, matters cannot go on like this for very much longer. It is a scandal, which is bad enough, but it leaves her as something and nothing. Neither wife nor maid. How is she to get a son when the only man she sees is Robert Dudley?"

"Perhaps she'll get Dudley's son," someone said quietly at the back.

Someone swore at the suggestion; another man rose up abruptly and quitted the room.

"She will lose her throne," another man said firmly. "The country won't have him, the Lords won't have him, the Commons won't have him, and d'you know, my lords, *I* damned well won't have him."

There was a swift mutter of agreement, then someone said warningly, "This is near to treason."

"No, it isn't," Francis Bacon insisted. "All anyone has ever said is that they wouldn't accept Dudley as king. Well and good. There's no treason in that since he will never be king, there is no possibility of it in our minds. And Cecil will have to come home to see how to make sure there is no possibility of it in his mind too."

*   *   *

The man who knew himself to be King of England in all but name was in the stable yard inspecting the queen's hunter. She had ridden so little that the horse had been exercised by a groom and Dudley wanted to be sure that the lad was as gentle on the horse's valuable mouth as he would have been himself. While he softly pulled the horse's ears and felt the velvet of her mouth Thomas Blount came up behind him and quietly greeted him. "Good morning, sir."

"Good morning, Blount," Robert said quietly.

"Something odd I thought you should know."

"Yes?" Robert did not turn his head. No one looking at the two men would have thought they were concerned with anything but horse care.

"I came across a shipment of gold last night, smuggled in from the Spanish, shipped by Sir Thomas Gresham of Antwerp."

"Gresham?" Dudley asked, surprised.

"His servant on board, bristling with knives, sick with worry," Blount described.

"Gold for who?"

"For the treasury," Blount said. "Small coins, bullion, all shapes and sizes. My man, who helped unload, said there was word that it was for minting into new coin, to pay the troops. I thought you might like to know. It was about three thousand pounds' worth, and there has been more before and will be more next week."

"I do like to know," Robert confirmed. "Knowledge is coin."

"Then I hope the coin is Gresham's gold," Blount quipped. "And not the dross I have in my pocket."

Half a dozen thoughts snapped into Robert's head at once. He spoke none of them. "Thank you," he said. "And let me know when Cecil starts his journey home."

He left the horse with the groom and went to find Elizabeth. She was not yet dressed; she was seated at the window in her privy chamber with a wrap around her shoulders. When Robert came in Blanche Parry looked up at him with relief. "Her Grace won't dress though the Spanish envoy wants to see her," she said. "Says she is too tired."

"Leave us," Robert said shortly and waited while the women and the maids left the room.

Elizabeth turned and smiled at him and took his hand and held it to her cheek. "My Robert."

"Tell me, my pretty love," Robert said quietly. "Why are you bringing in boatloads of Spanish gold from Antwerp, and how are you paying for it all?"

She gave a little gasp and the color went from her face, the smile from her eyes. "Oh," she said. "That."

"Yes," he replied evenly. "That. Don't you think you had better tell me what is going on?"

"How did you find out? It is supposed to be a great secret."

"Never mind," he said. "But I am sorry to learn that you still keep secrets from me, after your promises, even though we are husband and wife."

"I was going to tell you," she said at once. "It is just that Scotland has driven everything from my mind."

"I am sure," he said coldly. "For if you had continued with your forgetfulness till the day that you called in the old coin and issued new, I would have been left with a small treasure room filled with dross, would I not? And left at a substantial loss, would I not? Was it your intention that I should suffer?"

Elizabeth flushed. "I didn't know you were storing small coin."

"I have lands; my tenants do not pay their rents in bullion, alas. I have trading debts which are paid in small coin. I have chests and chests of pennies and farthings. Do tell me what I may get for them?"

"A little more than their weight," she said in a very small voice.

"Not their face value?"

She shook her head in silence. "We are calling in the coins and issuing new," she said. "It is Gresham's plan—you know of it yourself. We have to make the coins anew."

Robert let go of her hand and walked to the center of the room while she sat and watched him, wondering what he would do. She realized that the sinking feeling in her belly was apprehension. For the first time in her life she was afraid what a man was thinking of her—not for policy, but for love.

"Robert, don't be angry with me. I didn't mean to disadvantage you," she said and heard the weakness in her own voice. "You

must know that I would not put you at a disadvantage, you of all people! I have poured
places and positions and lands upon you."

"I know," he said shortly. "It is partly that
which amazes me. That you should give
with one hand and cheat me with the other.
A whore's trick, in fact. Did you not think
that this would cost me money?"

She gasped. "I only thought it had to be a
secret, a tremendous secret, or everyone
will trade among themselves and the coins
will be worse and worse regarded," she said
quickly. "It is an awful thing, Robert, to
know that people think that your very coins
are next to worthless. We have to put it
right, and everyone blames me for it being
wrong."

"A secret you kept from me," he said.
"Your husband."

"We were not betrothed when the plan
started," she said humbly. "I see now that I
should have told you. It is just that Scotland
drove everything out—"

"Scotland is at peace now," he said firmly.
"And try and keep in your mind that we are
married and that you should have no secrets from me. Go and get dressed, Elizabeth, and when you come out you will tell

me every single thing that you and Cecil have agreed and planned together. I will not be made a fool of. You will not have secrets with another man behind my back. This is to cuckold me, and I will not wear horns for you."

For a moment he thought he had gone too far, but she rose to her feet and went toward her bedchamber. "I will send your maids to you," he said, taking advantage of her obedience. "And then we will have a long talk."

She paused in the doorway and looked back toward him. "Please don't be angry with me. I didn't mean to offend you. I would never offend you on purpose. You know how this summer has been. I will tell you everything."

It was the moment to reward her for her apology. He crossed the room and kissed her fingers and then her lips. "You are my love," he said. "You and I are true gold and there will be nothing mixed with that to spoil it. Between us there will always be an absolute honesty and openness. Then I can advise you and help you and you need turn to no other."

He felt her mouth turn up under his kiss as she smiled. "Oh, Robert, I do," she said.

*   *   *

Cecil allowed himself the indulgence of one night at home with his wife at Burghley before pressing on with his journey to London. Mildred greeted him with her usual calm affection but her gray eyes took in his lined face and the stoop of his shoulders. "You look tired," was all the she remarked.

"It was hot and dusty," he said, saying nothing about the several journeys he had been forced to make between Edinburgh and Newcastle to forge the peace and make it stick.

She nodded and gestured that he should go to his bedchamber, where in the palatial room there was hot water and a change of clothes waiting, a jug of cold ale and a warm fresh-baked loaf of bread. She had his favorite dinner ready for him when he came downstairs again, looking refreshed and wearing a clean dark suit.

"Thank you," he said warmly, and kissed her on the forehead. "Thank you for all this."

She smiled and led him to the head of the table where their family and servants waited for the master to say grace. Mildred was a staunch Protestant and her home was run on most godly lines.

Cecil said a few words of prayer and then sat down and applied himself to his dinner. His four-year-old daughter Anna was brought down from the nursery with her baby brother William, received an absent-minded blessing, and then the covers were cleared and Mildred and Cecil went to their privy chamber, where a fire was lit and a jug of ale was waiting.

"So it is peace," she confirmed, knowing that he would never have left Scotland with the task unfinished.

"Yes," he said shortly.

"You don't seem very joyous; are you not a blessed peacemaker?"

The look he shot at her was one she had never seen before. He looked hurt, as if he had taken a blow, not to his pride, nor to his ambition; but as if he had been betrayed by a friend.

"I am not," he said. "It is the greatest peace that we could have hoped for. The French army is to leave, England's interest in Scotland is acknowledged, and all barely without a shot being fired. This should be the very greatest event of my life, my triumph. To defeat the French would be a glorious victory at any time; to defeat them with a divided country, a bankrupt treasury, an unpaid army led by a woman is almost a miracle."

"And yet?" she asked, uncomprehending.

"Someone has set the queen against me," he said simply. "I have had a letter which would make me weep if I did not know that I had done the very best for her that could be done."

"A letter from her?"

"A letter asking me for the stars and the moon as well as peace in Scotland," he said. "And my guess is that she will not be pleased when I tell her that all I can give her is peace in Scotland."

"She is not a fool," Mildred pointed out. "If you tell her the truth she will hear it. She will know that you have done the best you can, and more than anyone else could have done."

"She is in love," he said shortly. "I doubt she can hear anything but the beating of her heart."

"Dudley?"

"Who else?"

"It goes on then," she said. "Even here,

we hear such scandal that you would not believe."

"I do believe it," he said. "Most of it is true."

"They say that the two are married and that she has his child in hiding."

"Now that is a lie," Cecil said. "But I don't doubt that she would marry him if he were free."

"And is it him who has poisoned her mind against you?"

He nodded. "I should think so. There can be only one favorite at court. I thought she could enjoy his company and take my advice; but when I have to go away then she has both his company and his advice; and he is a very reckless counselor."

Mildred rose from her chair and came to stand beside him and put her hand on his shoulder. "What will you do, William?"

"I shall go to court," he said. "I shall make my report. I am hundreds of pounds out of pocket and I expect no recompense or gratitude now. If she will not take my advice then I will have to leave her, as I once threatened to do before. She could not manage without me then; we shall see if she can manage without me now."

She was aghast. "William, you cannot leave her to that handsome young traitor. You cannot leave England to be ruled by the two of them. It is to throw our country into the hands of vain children. You cannot leave our church in their hands. They are not to be trusted with it. They are a pair of adulterers. You have to be in her counsel. You have to save her from herself."

Cecil, the queen's most senior and respected advisor, was always advised by his wife. "Mildred, to fight a man like Dudley I would have to use ways and means which are most underhand. I would have to treat him as an enemy of the country. I would have to deal with him as a loyal man turned traitor. I would have to deal with him as I would with . . ." He broke off to think of an example. "Mary of Guise."

"The queen who died so suddenly?" she asked him, her voice carefully neutral.

"The queen who died so suddenly."

She understood him at once but she met his gaze without flinching. "William, you have to do your duty for our country, our church, and our queen. It is God's work that you do, whatever means you have to use."

He looked back into her level gray eyes.

"Even if I had to commit a crime, a great sin?"

"Even so."

*   *   *

Cecil returned in the last days of July to find the court on a short progress along the southern shores of the Thames, staying at the best private houses that could be found and enjoying the hunting and the summer weather. He was warned not to expect a hero's welcome, and he did not receive one.

"How could you?" Elizabeth greeted him. "How could you throw away our victory? Were you bribed by the French? Have you gone over to their side? Were you sick? Were you too tired to do your task properly? Too old? How could you just forget your duty to me, and your duty to the country? We have spent a fortune in trying to make Scotland safe, and you just let the French go home without binding them to our will?"

"Your Grace," he began. He felt himself flush with anger and he looked around to see who was in earshot. Half the court was craning forward to see the confrontation, all of them openly listening. Elizabeth had chosen to meet him in the great hall of her host's house and there were people standing on the stairs to listen; there were courtiers leaning over the gallery. His scolding was as public as if she had done it at Smithfield market.

"To have the French at our mercy and to let them go without securing Calais!" she exclaimed. "This is worse than the loss of Calais in the first place. That was an act of war; we fought as hard as we could. This is an act of folly; you have thrown Calais away without making the slightest effort to regain it."

"Your Majesty—"

"And my coat of arms! Has she sworn never to use them again? No? How dare you come back to me with that woman still using my arms?"

There was nothing Cecil could do under this onslaught. He fell silent and let her rage at him.

"Elizabeth." The quiet voice was so filled with confidence that Cecil looked quickly up the grand staircase, to see who dared to address the queen by name. It was Dudley.

He shot a quick, sympathetic glance at Cecil. "My Lord Secretary has worked hard in your service and brought home the best peace that he could. We may be disappointed in what he has achieved, but I am sure there is no question of his loyalty to our cause and his devotion to our service."

Cecil saw how his words, his very tone quietened her temper. *He says "our" service?* he remarked to himself. *Am I serving him now?*

"Let us withdraw with the Lord Secretary," Dudley suggested. "And he can explain his decisions, and tell us how matters are in Scotland. He has had a long journey and an arduous task."

She bridled; Cecil braced himself for more abuse.

"Come," Dudley said simply, stretching out his hand to her. "Come, Elizabeth."

He commands her by name before the whole court? Cecil demanded of himself in stunned silence.

But Elizabeth went to him, like a well-trained hound running in to heel, put her hand in his, and let him lead her from the hall. Dudley glanced back to Cecil and allowed himself the smallest smile. *Yes,* the smile said. *Now you see how things are.*

*   *   *

William Hyde summoned his sister to his office, the room where he transacted the business of his estate, a signal to her that the matter was a serious one and not to be confused by emotions or the claims of family ties.

He was seated behind the great rent table, which was circular and sectioned with drawers, each bearing a letter of the alphabet. The table could turn on its axis toward the landlord and each drawer had the contracts and rent books of the tenant farmers, filed under the initial letter of their name.

Lizzie Oddingsell remarked idly that the drawer marked "Z" had never been used, and wondered that no one thought to make a table which was missing the "X" and the "Z," since these must be uncommon initial letters in English. *Zebidee,* she thought to herself. *Xerxes.*

"Sister, it is about Lady Dudley," William Hyde started without preamble.

She noticed at once his use of titles for her and for her friend. So they were to conduct this conversation on the most formal footing.

"Yes, brother?" she replied politely.

"This is a difficult matter," he said. "But to be blunt, I think it is time that you took her away."

"Away?" she repeated.

"Yes."

"Away to where?"

"To some other friends."

"His lordship has made no arrangements," she demurred.

"Have you heard from him at all?"

"Not since . . ." She broke off. "Not since he visited her in Norfolk."

He raised his eyebrows, and waited.

"In March," she added reluctantly.

"When she refused him a divorce and they parted in anger?"

"Yes," she admitted.

"And since then you have had no letter? And neither has she?"

"Not that I know of . . ." She met his accusing look. "No, she has not."

"Is her allowance being paid?"

Lizzie gave a little gasp of shock. "Yes, of course."

"And your wages?"

"I am not waged," she said with dignity. "I am a companion, not a servant."

"Yes; but he is paying your allowance."

"His steward sends it."

"He has not quite cut her off then," he said thoughtfully.

"He quite often fails to write," she said stoutly. "He quite often does not visit. In the past it has sometimes been months . . ."

"He never fails to send his men to escort her from one friend to another," he rejoined. "He never fails to arrange for her to stay at once place or another. And you say he has sent no one, and you have heard nothing since March."

She nodded.

"Sister, you must take her and move on," he said firmly.

"Why?"

"Because she is becoming an embarrassment to this house."

Lizzie was quite bewildered. "Why? What has she done?"

"Leaving aside her excessive piety, which makes one wonder as to her conscience—"

"For God's sake, brother, she is clinging to God as to life itself. She has no guilty conscience, she is just trying to find the will to live!"

He raised his hand. "Elizabeth, please. Let us stay calm."

"I don't know how to stay calm when you call this unhappy woman an embarrassment to you!"

He rose to his feet. "I will not have this conversation unless you promise me that you will stay calm."

She took a deep breath. "I know what you are doing."

"What?"

"You are trying not to be touched by her. But she is in the most unhappy position, and you would make it worse."

He moved toward the door as if to hold it open for her. Lizzie recognized the signs of her brother's determination. "All right," she said hastily. "All right, William. There is no need to be fierce with me. It is as bad for me as it is for you. Worse, actually."

He returned to his seat. "Leaving aside her piety, as I said, it is the position she puts us in with her husband that concerns me."

She waited.

"She has to go," he said simply. "While I thought we were doing him a favor by having her here, protecting her from slander and scorn, awaiting his instructions, she was an asset to us. I thought he would be glad that she had found safe haven. I thought he would be grateful to me. But now I think different."

She raised her head to look at him. He

was her younger brother and she was accustomed to seeing him in two contradictory lights: one as her junior, who knew less of the world than she did; and the other as her superior: the head of the family, a man of property, a step above her on the chain that led to God.

"And what do you think now, brother?"

"I think he has cast her off," he said simply. "I think she has refused his wish, and angered him, and she will not see him again. And, what is more important, whoever she stays with, will not see him again. We are not helping him with a knotty problem, we are aiding and abetting her rebellion against him. And I cannot be seen to do such a thing."

"She is his wife," Lizzie said flatly. "And she has done nothing wrong. She is not rebelling, she is just refusing to be cast aside."

"I can't help that," David said. "He is now living as husband in all but name to the Queen of England. Lady Dudley is an obstacle to their happiness. I will not be head of a household where the obstacle to the happiness of the Queen of England finds refuge."

There was nothing she could say to fault his logic and he had forbidden her to appeal to his heart. "But what is she to do?"

"She has to go to another house."

"And then what?"

"To another, and to another, and to another, until she can agree with Sir Robert and make some settlement, and find a permanent home."

"You mean until she is forced into a divorce and goes to some foreign convent, or until she dies of heartbreak."

He sighed. "Sister, there is no need to play a tragedy out of this."

She faced him. "I am not playing a tragedy. This *is* tragic."

"This is not my fault!" he exclaimed in sudden impatience. "There is no need to blame me for this. I am stuck with the difficulty but it is none of my making!"

"Whose fault is it then?" she demanded.

He said the cruelest thing: "Hers. And so she has to leave."

* * *

Cecil had three meetings with Elizabeth before she could be brought even to listen to him without interrupting and raging at him. The first two were with Dudley and a couple of other men in attendance, and Cecil had to bow his head while she tore into him, complained of his inattention to her business, of his neglect of his country, of his disregard for their pride, their rights, their finances. After the first meeting he did not try to defend himself, but wondered whose voice it was that came so shrill, from the queen's reproachful mouth.

He knew it was Robert Dudley's. Robert Dudley, of course; who stood back by the window, leaning against the shutter, looking down into the midsummer garden, and sniffed a pomander held to his nose with one slim white hand. Now and again he would shift his position, or breathe in lightly, or clear his throat, and at once the queen would break off and turn, as if to give way to him. If Robert Dudley had so much as a passing thought she assumed they would all be eager to hear it.

She adores him, Cecil thought, hardly hearing the detail of the queen's complaints. *She is in her first flush of love, and he is the first love of her womanhood. She thinks the sun shines from his eyes, his opinions are the only wisdom she can hear, his voice the only speech, his smile her only pleasure. It is pointless to complain, it is pointless to be angry with her folly. She is a young woman in the madness of first love and it is hopeless expecting her to exercise any kind of sensible judgment.*

The third meeting, Cecil found the queen alone but for Sir Nicholas Bacon and two ladies in attendance. "Sir Robert has been delayed," she said.

"Let us start without him," Sir Nicholas smoothly suggested. "Lord Secretary, you were going through the terms of the treaty, and the detail of the French withdrawal."

Cecil nodded and put his papers before them. For the first time the queen did not spring to her feet and stride away from the table, railing against him. She kept her seat and she looked carefully at the proposal for the French withdrawal.

Emboldened, Cecil ran through the terms of the treaty again, and then sat back in his chair.

"And do you really think it is a binding peace?" Elizabeth asked.

For a moment, it was as it had always been between the two of them. The young woman looked to the older man for his advice, trusting that he would serve her with absolute fidelity. The older man looked down into the little face of his pupil and saw her wisdom and her ability. Cecil had a sense of the world returning to its proper axis, of the stars recoiling to their courses, of the faint harmony of the spheres, of homecoming.

"I do," he said. "They were much alarmed by the Protestant uprising in Paris, they will not want to risk any other ventures for now. They fear the rise of the Huguenots, they fear your influence. They believe that you will defend Protestants wherever they are, as you did in Scotland, and they think that Protestants will look to you. They will want to keep the peace, I am sure. And Mary, Queen of Scots, will not take up her inheritance in Scotland while she can live in Paris. She will put in another regent and command him to deal fairly with the Scots lords, according to the terms of the peace contract. They will keep Scotland in name only."

"And Calais?" the queen demanded jealously.

"Calais is, and always has been, a separate issue," he said steadily. "As we have all always known. But I think we should demand it back under the terms of the treaty of Cateau-Cambrésis, when their lease falls due, as agreed. And they are more likely to honor the agreement now than before. They have learned to fear us. We have surprised them, Your Grace; they did not think we had the resolve. They will not laugh at us again. They certainly will not lightly make war on you again."

She nodded, and pushed the treaty toward him. "Good," she said shortly. "You swear it was the very best you could do?"

"I was pleased to get so much."

She nodded. "Thank God we are free from the threat of them. I wouldn't like to go through this past year again."

"Nor I," said Sir Nicholas fervently. "It was a great gamble when you took us into war, Your Majesty. A brilliant decision."

Elizabeth had the grace to smile at Cecil. "I was very brave and very determined," she said, twinkling at him. "Don't you think so, Spirit?"

"I am sure that if England ever again faces such an enemy, you will remember this time," he said. "You will have learned what to do for the next time. You have learned how to play the king."

"Mary never did so much," she reminded

him. "She never had to face an invasion from a foreign power."

"No, indeed," he agreed. "Her mettle was not tested as yours has been. And you were tested and not found wanting. You were your father's daughter and you have earned the peace."

She rose from the table. "I can't think what is keeping Sir Robert," she complained. "He promised me he would be here an hour ago. He has a new delivery of Barbary horses and he had to be there to see them arrive in case they had to be sent back. But he promised me he would come at once."

"Shall we walk down to the stables to meet him?" Cecil suggested.

"Yes," she said eagerly. She took his arm and they walked side by side, as they had walked so often before.

"Let's take a turn in the garden first," he suggested. "The roses have been wonderful this year. D'you know, Scotland is a full month behind in the garden?"

"Is it very cold and barbaric?" she asked. "I wish I could see it."

"You could go on progress to Newcastle one summer," he said. "They would be glad to see you there, and it would be good policy to visit the border castles."

"I should like to," Elizabeth said. "You must have ridden your horses into the ground. You went backward and forward from Edinburgh to Newcastle, didn't you?"

Cecil nodded. "I wanted to confer with your uncle, and I needed to keep an eye on Monsieur Randan. It was a hard ride and a poorly kept road, especially in Scotland."

She nodded.

"And what of you?" Cecil lowered his voice. The ladies walking behind them were out of earshot; Sir Nicholas was walking with Catherine Knollys. "How have things been with you these last two months, Princess?"

For a moment he thought she would turn the question aside with a laugh, but she checked herself. "I was very afraid," she said honestly. "Kat thought that my health would break under the strain."

"That was my fear," he said. "You bore up wonderfully."

"I couldn't have done it without Sir Robert," she said. "He can always calm me, Spirit. He has such a wonderful voice, and his hands . . . I think he has magic in his hands . . . it's why he can do anything with his horses. As soon as he lays his hand on my forehead I feel at peace."

"You are in love with him," he said gently.

Elizabeth looked quickly up at him to see if he was accusing her; but he met her eyes with steady sympathy.

"Yes," she said frankly, and it was a relief to her to be able to tell her counselor the truth at last. "Yes, I am."

"And he with you?"

She smiled. "Yes, oh yes. Think of the misery if he was not!"

He paused, then he asked her: "Princess, what will come of this? He is a married man."

"His wife is ill, and could die," Elizabeth said. "And anyway, they have been unhappy for years. He says that his marriage is no more. She will release him. I can grant them a divorce. Then he will marry me."

How to deal with this? She will not want wise counsel; she will want to be confirmed in this folly. But if I do not speak, who will? Cecil drew a breath. "My queen, Amy Dudley, Amy Robsart that was, is a young woman; there is no reason to think that she will die. You cannot delay your marriage waiting for a young woman to die. And you cannot possibly grant him a divorce; there are no grounds for a divorce. You danced at his wedding feast yourself, when they married for love with the blessing of their parents. And you cannot marry a commoner, a man whose family has been under the shadow of treason, a man with a living wife."

Elizabeth turned to him. "Cecil, I can, and I will. I have promised him."

Good God! What does she mean by that? What does she mean by that? What does she mean by that?

None of Cecil's horror showed in his face. "A private promise? Love talk? Whispered between the two of you?"

"A binding promise of marriage. "A *de futuro* betrothal before witnesses."

"Who witnessed?" he gasped out. "What witnesses?" *Perhaps they could be bribed into silence, or murdered. Perhaps they could be discredited, or exiled.*

"Catherine and Francis Knollys."

He was shocked into silence.

They walked, not saying a word. He found that his legs were weak beneath him at the horror of what she had told him. He had failed to guard her. She was entrapped, and the country with her.

"You are angry with me," she said in a small voice. "You think I have made a terrible mistake when you were not here to prevent me."

"I am horrified."

"Spirit, I could not help myself. You were not here, I thought that at any moment the French would invade. I thought I had lost my throne already. I had nothing left to lose. I wanted to know that at least I had him."

"Princess, this is a disaster worse than a French invasion," he said. "If the French had invaded, every man in the country would have laid down his life for you. But if they knew you were betrothed to marry Sir Robert, they would put Katherine Grey on the throne in your place."

They were approaching the stables. "Walk on," she said quickly. "I dare not meet him now. He will see I have told you."

"He told you not to confide in me?"

"He didn't have to! We all know you would advise me against him."

Cecil led her by another path into the garden. He could feel her trembling.

"The people of England would never turn against me just for falling in love."

"Princess, they will not accept him as your husband and your consort. I am sorry; but the best you can do now is to choose your successor. You will have to abdicate; you will have to give up your throne."

He felt her stagger as her knees gave way.

"Do you want to sit down?"

"No, let's walk, let's walk," Elizabeth said feverishly. "You don't mean it, Spirit, do you? You're just trying to frighten me."

He shook his head. "I tell you nothing but the truth."

"He is not so hated in the country? There are just a few who wish him ill at court—my uncle, of course, and the Duke of Arundel, those who are jealous of him and envy him his looks, those who want the favor that I show him, those who want his wealth, his position . . ."

"It's not that," Cecil said wearily. "Listen to me, Elizabeth, I am telling you the truth. It is not a little jealousy at court, it is an opinion which runs very deep in the country. It's his family and his position and his past. His father was executed for treason against your sister; his grandfather was executed for treason against your father. He has bad blood. Princess, his family has always been a traitor to yours. Everyone remembers that if the Dudleys rise high they abuse their power. No one would ever trust a Dudley with great position. And everyone knows that he is a married man, and no one has heard anything against his wife. He cannot just cast her aside; it would be an unbearable scandal. Already the courts of Europe laugh at you, and say that you are shamed by your adulterous love for your horse master."

He saw her flush at the thought of it.

"You should marry a king, Princess. Or an archduke at the very least, someone of good blood whose alliance will help the country. You cannot marry a common man with nothing more to recommend him than his good looks and his handling of his horse. The country will never accept him as your consort. I know it."

"You hate him too," she said fiercely. "You are as unkind to him as the rest of them."

Inveterately, he acknowledged to himself. But he smiled his gentle smile at her. "It would not matter how I felt about him, if he was the right man for you," he said gently. "I hope I would have the sense to advise you as to your best course, whatever my preferences. And, as it happens, I do not hate him; I rather like him. But I have long feared your particular favor to him. I have been afraid that it would come to a point. I never dreamed he would take it to this."

Elizabeth turned her head away; he saw her picking at her nails.

"It went further than I meant it to," she said, very low. "I was not thinking straight and I went further . . ."

"If you can escape from your promise of betrothal now, your reputation will have been stained, but you will recover, if you give him up and go on to marry someone else. But if you go through with it the people will throw you from your throne rather than bow the knee to him."

"Mary had Philip even though they hated him!" she burst out.

"He was an anointed king!" Cecil exclaimed. "They might hate him but they could not object to his breeding. And Philip had an army to support him; he was heir to the empire of Spain. What does Dudley have? Half a dozen retainers and the huntsmen! How will they serve him in the first riot that breaks out?"

"I have given my word," she whispered. "Before God and honorable witnesses."

"You will have to withdraw it," he said flatly. "Or this peace will be as nothing, for you will have won peace for England and Queen Katherine Grey."

"Queen Katherine?" she repeated, aghast. "Never!"

"Princess, there are at least two plots to put her on the throne instead of you. She is a Protestant like her sister Jane, she is well liked, she is of Tudor stock."

"She knows of this? She is plotting against me?"

He shook his head. "I would have had her arrested already if I thought there was the least question of her loyalty. I only mention her now so that you know there are people who would push you from your throne now—when they hear of this promise they will recruit many others."

"I will keep it secret," she said.

"It will have to be more than secret; it will have to be broken and hidden. You will have to withdraw it. You can never marry him and he knows it. You have to tell him that you have come to your senses and now you know it too. He has to release you."

*   *   *

"Shall I write to Mr. Forster?" Lizzie Oddingsell suggested to Amy, trying to keep her tone light and impersonal. "We could go and stay at Cumnor Place for a few weeks."

"Cumnor Place?" Amy looked surprised. She was seated in the window seat for the last of the light, sewing a little shirt for Tom Hyde.

"Yes," Lizzie said steadily. "We went to them this time last year, toward the end of the summer, before we went on to Chislehurst."

Amy's head came up very slowly. "You have not heard from my lord?" she asked, quite certain that the reply would be negative. "Mr. Hyde has not had a letter from my lord about me?"

"No," Lizzie said awkwardly. "I am sorry, Amy."

Amy bent her head back to her work. "Has your brother spoken to you? Does he want us to leave?"

"No, no," Lizzie said hastily. "I just thought that your other friends will be jealous if they do not see you. And then perhaps we could go on to the Scotts at Camberwell? You will want to shop in London, I suppose?"

"I thought he had been a little cool toward me," Amy said. "I was afraid that he wanted me to leave."

"Not at all!" Lizzie cried out, hearing her voice as overemphatic. "This is all my idea. I thought you might be tired of here and want to move on. That's all."

"Oh, no," Amy said with vacant little smile. "I'm not tired of being here, and I like it here, Lizzie. Let's stay for a while longer."

*   *   *

"What have you been doing all afternoon?" Sir Robert asked Elizabeth intimately as they dined in the privacy of her chamber. "I came to the council room as soon as I had seen the horses but you had not waited for me. They said you were walking with Cecil in the garden. But when I got to the garden you were nowhere to be found, and when I came back to your rooms they said you were not to be disturbed."

"I was tired," she said shortly. "I rested."

He scrutinized her pale face, taking in the shadows under her eyes, the pink eyelids. "He said something to upset you?"

She shook her head. "No."

"Were you angry with him about his failure in Scotland?"

"No. That's finished with. We can get nothing more than he has got."

"A great advantage thrown away," he prompted her.

"Yes," she said shortly. "Perhaps."

His smile was quite inscrutable. *He has persuaded her back under his influence,* he thought. *She really is quite hopelessly malleable.* Aloud he said, "I can tell that something is wrong, Elizabeth. What is it?"

She turned her dark eyes on him. "I can't talk now. She did not have to gesture to the small circle of courtiers who were dining with them and, as ever, constantly alert to everything they said and did. "I'll talk to you later, when we are alone."

"Of course," he said, smiling kindly at her. "Then let us set ourselves to amuse you. Shall we play cards? Or play a game? Or shall we dance?"

"Cards," she said. *At least a game of cards would prevent a conversation,* she thought.

*

Robert waited in his room for Elizabeth, Tamworth his valet on guard outside, the wine poured, the fire freshly heaped with sweet-scented apple wood. The door from her room opened and she came in, not with her usual eager stride, not with desire illuminating her face. Tonight she was a little hesitant, almost as if she wished herself elsewhere.

So, she has reconciled with Cecil, he thought. *And he has warned her off me. As I knew he would, once they were on good terms again. But we are as good as married. She is mine.* Aloud he said: "My dearest. This day has gone on forever," and took her into his arms.

Robert felt the slightest check before she moved close to him, and he stroked her back and murmured kisses into her hair. "My love," he said. "My one and only love."

He released her before she withdrew, and handed her into a chair at the fireside. "And here we are," he said. "Alone at last. Will you have a glass of wine, dearest?"

"Yes," she said.

He poured her the wine and touched her fingers as she took the wineglass from him.

He saw how she looked at the fire, and not at him.

"I am sure that there is something the matter," he said. "Is it something between us? Something that I have done to offend you?"

Elizabeth looked up at once. "No! Never! You are always . . ."

"Then what is it, my love? Tell me, and let us face whatever difficulty there is together."

She shook her head. "There is nothing. It is just that I love you so much; I have been thinking of how I could not bear to lose you."

Robert put down his glass and knelt at her feet. "You won't lose me," he said simply. "I am yours, heart and soul. I am promised to you."

"If we could not marry for a long time, you would still love me," she said. "You would wait for me?"

"Why should we not publish our betrothal at once?" he asked, going to the heart of it.

"Oh." She fluttered her hand. "You know, a thousand reasons. Perhaps none of them matter. But if we could not, would you wait for me? Would you be true to me? Would we always be like this?"

"I would wait for you. I would be true to you," he promised her. "But we could not always be like this. Someone would find out; someone would talk. And I couldn't go on always loving you and being at your side and yet never being able to help you when you are afraid or alone. I have to be able to take your hand before all the court and say that you are mine and I am yours, that your enemies are my enemies and that I will defeat them."

"But if we had to wait, we could," she pressed him.

"Why would we have to wait? Have we not earned our happiness? Both of us in the Tower, both of us thinking that we might face the block the next day? Have we not earned a little joy now?"

"Yes," she agreed hastily. "But Cecil says that there are many who speak against you, and plot against me, even now. We have to get the country to accept you. It may take a little time, that is all."

"Oh, what does Cecil know?" Robert demanded carelessly. "He's only just come back from Edinburgh. My intelligencers tell me that the people love you, and they will come to accept me in time."

"Yes," Elizabeth said. "In time. We will have to wait a little while."

He thought it was too dangerous to argue. "Forever, if you wish," he said, smiling. "For centuries if it is what you wish. You will tell me when you want to declare our betrothal, and it shall be our secret until then."

"I don't want to withdraw from it," she said hastily. "I don't want to break it."

"You cannot break it," he said simply. "And neither can I. It is indissoluble. It is a legally binding, sacred promise before God and witnesses. In the eyes of God we are man and wife and no one can part us."

*   *   *

A letter came for Amy from Robert's friend and client, Mr. Forster at Cumnor Place, inviting her to stay with him for the month of September. Lizzie Oddingsell read it aloud to Amy, who would not make the effort to puzzle it out herself.

"You had better reply and tell them that I shall be very pleased to stay with them," Amy said coldly. "Shall you come with me? Or stay here?"

"Why would I not come with you?" Lizzie demanded, shocked.

"If you wanted to leave my service," Amy said, looking away from her friend. "If you think, as your brother clearly does, that I am under a cloud, and that you would be better not associated with me."

"My brother has said no such thing," Lizzie lied firmly. "And I would never leave you."

"I am not what I was," Amy said, and the coldness went out of her voice in a rush and left only a thin thread of sound. "I do not enjoy my husband's favor anymore. Your brother is not improved by my visit, Cumnor Place will not be honored by having me. I see I shall have to find people who will have me, despite my lord's disfavor. I am no longer an asset."

Lizzie said nothing. This letter from Anthony Forster was a begrudging reply to her request that Amy might stay with them for the whole of the autumn. The Scotts of Camberwell, Amy's own cousins, had replied that they would unfortunately be away for all of November. It was clear that Amy's hosts, even Amy's own family, no longer wanted her in their houses.

"Anthony Forster has always admired you," Lizzie said. "And my brother and Alice were saying only the other day what a pleasure it was to see you playing with Tom. You are like one of the family here."

Amy wanted to believe her friend too much for skepticism. "Did they really?"

"Yes," Lizzie said. "They said that he had taken to you like no one else."

"Then can't I stay here?" she asked simply. "I would rather stay here than go on. I would rather stay here than go home to Stanfield at Christmas. I could pay for our keep, you know, if your brother would let us stay here."

Lizzie was silenced. "Surely, now that Mr. Forster has been so kind as to invite us we should go there," she said feebly. "You would not want to offend him."

"Oh, let's just go for a week or so then," Amy said. "And then come back here."

"Surely not," Lizzie hedged. "You would not want to seem ungracious. Let's go for the full month to Cumnor Place."

She thought for a moment that she had got away with the lie, but Amy paused, as if the whole conversation had been held in a foreign language, and she had suddenly understood it. "Oh. Your brother wants me to leave, doesn't he?" she said slowly. "They won't want me back here in October. They won't want me back here for a while, indeed, perhaps never. It is as I thought at first, and all this has been a lie. Your brother does not want me to stay. Nobody will want me to stay."

"Well, at any rate, Mr. Forster wants you," Lizzie said stoutly.

"Did you write to him and ask if we could go?"

Lizzie's gaze dropped to the ground. "Yes," she admitted. "I think it is either there, or Stanfield."

"We'll go there then," Amy said quietly. "Do you know, only a year ago he was honored by my company, and pressed me to stay longer than those few days. And now he will tolerate me for only a month."

*   *   *

Elizabeth, who had once snatched at every opportunity to see Robert alone, was now avoiding him, and finding ways to be with William Cecil. She cried off from a day's hunting at the last moment, saying that her head ached too much to ride, and watched the court, led by Robert, ride out. Laetitia

Knollys was at his side but Elizabeth let him go. Back in her rooms, Cecil was waiting for her.

"He says he will wait," she said, standing at the window of Windsor Castle to catch a last glimpse of him as the hunt wound down the steep hill to the town and the marshes beside the river. "He says it will make no difference if we do not announce our betrothal. We can wait until the time is right."

"You have to withdraw," Cecil said.

She turned toward him. "Spirit, I cannot. I dare not lose him. It would be worse than death to me, to lose him."

"Would you leave your throne for him?"

"No!" she exclaimed passionately. "Not for any man. Not for anything. Never."

"Then you have to give him up," he said.

"I cannot break my word to him. I cannot have him think of me as faithless."

"Then he will have to release you," Cecil said. "He must know that he should never have entered into such a promise. He was not free to enter into it. He was already married. He is a bigamist."

"He'll never let me go," she said.

"Not if he thought there was any chance of winning you," Cecil agreed. "But what if he thought it was hopeless? And if he thought he might lose his place at court? If it was a choice between never seeing you again and living disgraced in exile; or giving you up and being as he was before the promise?"

"Then he might," Elizabeth conceded reluctantly. "But I can't threaten him with that, Spirit. I don't even have the courage to ask him to release me. I can't bear to hurt him. Don't you know what love is? I cannot reject him. I would rather cut off my own right hand than hurt him."

"Yes," he said, unimpressed. "I see that it has to be done by him, as if by his free choice."

"He feels the same about me!" she exclaimed. "He would never leave me."

"He would not cut off his right hand for you," Cecil said knowingly.

She paused. "Do you have a plan? Are you planning a way that I can be free?"

"Of course," he said simply. "You will lose your throne if any word of this mad betrothal gets out. I have to think of a way to save you, and then we have to do it, Elizabeth. Whatever it costs."

"I will not betray my love for him," she

said. "He must not hear it from me. Anything but that. I would rather die than he thought me faithless."

"I know," Cecil said, worried. "I know. Somehow, it has to be his decision and his choice."

*   *   *

Amy and Lizzie Oddingsell rode across the broad, open Oxfordshire countryside from Denchworth to Cumnor. The high ground was wild and open, pretty on a summer's day with flocks of sheep shepherded by absentminded children who shouted at the travelers and came leaping like goats themselves to see the ladies ride by.

Amy did not smile and wave at them, nor scatter groats from her purse. She did not seem to see them. For the first time in her life she rode without an escort of liveried menservants around her, for the first time in many years she rode without the Dudley standard of the bear and ragged staff carried before her. She rode on a slack rein, looking around her, but seeing nothing. And her horse drooped its head and went along dully, as if Amy's light weight was a heavy burden.

"At least the fields look in good heart," Lizzie said cheerfully.

Amy looked blankly around her. "Oh, yes," she said.

"Should be a good harvest?"

"Yes."

Lizzie had written to Sir Robert to tell him that his wife was moving from Abingdon to Cumnor and received no reply. His steward sent no money for the settlement of their debts, nor for tipping the Abingdon staff, and did not tell Lizzie that an escort would be provided for her. In the end, they were attended by Lizzie's brother's men, and a small cart came behind them with their goods. When Amy had come out on the doorstep into the bright morning sunlight, pulling on her riding gloves, she saw the little cavalcade and realized that from now on she would travel as a private citizen. The Dudley standard would not proclaim her as a wife of a great lord, the Dudley livery would not warn people to clear the road, to doff their caps, to bend their knees. Amy had become no more than Miss Amy Robsart—less than Miss Amy Robsart, for she was not even a single woman who might marry anyone, a woman with prospects;

now she was that lowest form of female life, a woman who had married the wrong man.

Little Tom clung to her skirt and asked to be lifted up.

"Me-me!" he reminded her.

Amy looked down at him. "I have to say good-bye to you," she said. "I don't think they will let me see you again."

He did not understand the words but he felt her sadness like a shadow.

"Me-me!"

She bent down swiftly and kissed his warm, silky head, smelled the sweet little boy scent of him, and then she rose to her feet and went quickly out to her horse before he could cry.

It was a beautiful summer day and a wonderful ride through the heart of England, but Amy did not see it. A lark went up from the cornfield on her right, higher and higher, its wings beating with each rippling note, and she did not hear. Slowly up the green slope of the sides of hills they labored, and then slipped down to the wooded valleys and the fertile fields on the valley floor and still Amy saw nothing, and remarked on nothing.

"Are you in pain?" Lizzie asked, catching

a glimpse of Amy's white face as she lifted the veil from her riding hat for a sip of water when they stopped by a stream.

"Yes," Amy said shortly.

"Are you ill? Can you ride?" Lizzie asked, alarmed.

"No, it is just the same as always." Amy said. "I shall have to grow accustomed to it."

Slowly, the little procession wound past the fields on the outskirts of Cumnor and then entered the village, scattering hens and setting the dogs barking. They went past the church with the handsome square stone tower standing tall on its own little hill, skirted by fat trees of dark yew. Amy rode by, without a glance at Elizabeth's flag which fluttered from the pole at the head of the tower, through the muddy village streets which wound around the low-browed thatched cottages.

Cumnor Place was set alongside the churchyard but the little cavalcade went around the high wall of pale limestone blocks to approach the house through the archway. The drive led them through an avenue of yew trees, and Amy shivered as their gloom fell over the sunlit path.

"Nearly there," Lizzie Oddingsell said cheerfully, thinking that Amy might be tired.

"I know."

Another soaring archway set into the thick stone walls took them into the courtyard and the very heart of the house. Mrs. Forster, hearing the horses, came out from the great hall on the right-hand side to greet them.

"Here you are!" she cried out. "And in what good time! You must have had a very easy ride."

"It was easy," Lizzie said, when Amy did not reply, but merely sat on her horse. "But I am afraid Lady Dudley is very tired."

"Are you, your ladyship?" Mrs. Forster inquired with concern.

Amy lifted the veil from her hat.

"Oh! You do look pale. Come down and you shall rest," Mrs. Forster said.

A groom came forward and Amy slid down the horse's side in a clumsy jump. Mrs. Forster took her hand and led her into the great hall where a fire was burning in the large stone hearth.

"Will you take a cup of ale?" she asked solicitously.

"Thank you," Amy said.

Mrs. Forster pressed her into a great wooden chair by the fireside and sent a page running for ale and cups. Lizzie Oddingsell came into the room and took a seat beside Amy.

"Well, here we are!" Mrs. Forster remarked. She was conscious of the difficulty of her position. She could hardly ask for news of court, when the only news was that the queen's behavior with this white-faced young woman's husband was becoming more blatant every day. The whole country knew now that Robert Dudley was carrying himself like a king-to-be, and Elizabeth could hardly see anyone else for the glamour that was her dark-headed Master of Horse.

"The weather seems set very fair," Mrs. Forster said, for lack of anything else.

"Indeed, yes. It's hot," Lizzie agreed. "But the wheat looks very well in the fields."

"Oh, I know nothing about it," Mrs. Forster said quickly, emphasizing her position as the wealthy tenant of a beautiful house. "You know, I know nothing about farming."

"It should be a very good crop," Amy ob

served. "And I imagine we shall all be glad of the bread to eat."

"Indeed, yes."

The arrival of the page broke the embarrassed silence. "Mrs. Owen is also staying with us," Mrs. Forster told them. "She is the mother of our landlord, Mr. William Owen. I think your husband . . ." She broke off in confusion. "I think Mr. William Owen is well known at court," she said clumsily. "Perhaps you know him, Lady Dudley?"

"My husband knows him well," Amy said without embarrassment. "And thinks highly of him, I know."

"Well, his mother is honoring us with a long visit," Mrs. Forster continued, recovering. "You will meet her at dinner, and Mr. Forster will be home for dinner. He rode out today to see some neighbors of ours. And he told me to take particular good care of you both."

"How kind," Amy said vaguely. "I think I should like to rest now."

"Certainly." Mrs. Forster rose to her feet. "Your room is just above the hall, overlooking the drive."

Amy hesitated, she had been going

toward the best bedroom on the other end of the building.

"Let me show you," Mrs. Forster said, and led the way out of the great hall, through the double archway, through the stone-flagged buttery to the circular stone stairs.

"Here you are, and Mrs. Oddingsell is nearby," she said, gesturing to the two wooden doors.

"It seems so odd that this should have been a monastery only fifty years ago," Amy said, pausing by one of the wooden corbels which showed a little cherub, polished from dark wood to blond by constant touching. "This little angel may have helped someone to pray."

"Thank God that we have been freed from Popish superstition," Mrs. Forster said fervently.

"Amen," Lizzie said smartly.

Amy said nothing at all; but touched the cheek of the little angel, and opened the heavy wooden door to her chamber and went in.

They waited until the door had closed behind her.

"She is so pale, is she ill?" Mrs. Forster demanded.

They turned and went to Lizzie Oddingsell's chamber. "She is very tired," Lizzie said. "And she hardly eats. She complains of a pain in her breast but she says it is heartache. She is taking it all very badly."

"I heard she had a canker of the breast?"

"She is always in pain but there is no growth. That is another London rumor, like all the others."

Mrs. Forster pursed her lips and shook her head at London rumors, which were wilder and more detailed every day. "Well, God protect her," Mrs. Forster said. "I had the devil's own job to persuade my husband to have her here at all. Of all the men in the world I would have thought him the most likely to pity her, but he said to my face that it was more than his life was worth to offend Sir Robert now, and more important than anything in the world to him to be in his lordship's good books if he is going to rise as everyone says."

"And what do they say?" Lizzie prompted. "How much higher can he go?"

"They say he will be king-consort," Mrs. Forster said simply. They say he is married to the queen already in secret, and will be crowned at Christmas. And she, poor lady, will be forgotten."

"Yes, but forgotten where?" Lizzie demanded. "My brother will not have her back, and she cannot live at Stanfield Hall all the year round; it is little more than a farm. Besides, I do not know that their doors are open to her. If her family refuse her, where is she to go? What is she to do?"

"She looks as if she will not survive it," Mrs. Forster said flatly. "And there will be the solution to his lordship's difficulty. Should we get a doctor for her?"

"Yes," Lizzie said. "There's no doubt in my mind that she is sick of grief, but perhaps a doctor could give her something so that at least she could eat and sleep and stop this continual weeping."

"She cries?"

Lizzie's own voice trembled. "She swallows it down during the day, but if you ever listen to her chamber door at night you will hear her. She cries in her sleep. All night long the tears run down her cheeks and she cries for him. She whispers his name in her sleep. Over and over she asks him: 'My lord?' "

*

Cecil and Elizabeth were in the rose garden at Windsor with the ladies of the court when Robert Dudley came to join them, the Spanish ambassador with him.

Elizabeth smiled and gave de Quadra her hand to kiss. "And is this visit one of pleasure or one of business?" she asked.

"Now I am dedicated to pleasure," he said in his strong accent. "I have conducted my business with Sir Robert and I can spend the rest of my time taking pleasure in your company."

Elizabeth raised her penciled eyebrows. "Business?" she asked Robert.

He nodded. "All done. I was telling the Spanish ambassador that we are to have a tennis tournament this evening, and he would be most interested to watch."

"It is only a little game," Elizabeth said. She did not dare glance toward Cecil. "Some of the young men of the court have formed themselves into teams, the Queen's Men and the Gypsy Boys." There was a ripple of laughter from the ladies at the two names.

The Spanish ambassador smiled, looking

from one to another. "And who are the Gypsy Boys?" he asked.

"It is an impertinence to Sir Robert," the queen said. "It is a nickname they call him."

"Never to my face," Sir Robert said.

"An insult?" the more formal Spaniard asked.

"A jest," Robert said. "Not everyone admires my coloring. I am thought too dark for an Englishman."

Elizabeth took a little breath of desire; it was unmistakable. Everyone heard it and Dudley turned to her with a most intimate smile. "Fortunately, not everyone despises me for my dark skin and black eyes," he said.

"They are practicing now." Elizabeth was unable to take her eyes from the curve of his mouth.

"Shall we go and see?" Cecil intervened. He led the ambassador away and the rest of the court followed. Slowly, Dudley offered Elizabeth his arm and she slid her hand on his sleeve.

"You look entranced," he said quietly to her.

"I am," she said. "You know."

"I know."

They walked for a few paces in silence. "What did the ambassador want?" she asked.

"He was complaining about Spanish gold being shipped out of the Netherlands by our merchants," Dudley said. "It is illegal to take their bullion out of the country."

"I know that," she said. "I don't know who would do such a thing."

Blandly, he ignored the quickness of her lie. "Some eager inspector searched one of our ships and found that the cargo manifest was forged. They have confiscated the gold and let the ship go, and the Spanish ambassador was to make a formal complaint."

"Is he to come before the Privy Council?" she asked, alarmed. "If they discover we are shipping gold they will know it is to mint new coins. There will be a run against the old coins. I will have to speak to Cecil; we have to keep this secret." She started forward but Robert retained her hand and kept her back.

"No, of course he can't see the Privy Council," Robert said decisively. "It has to be kept private."

"Have you given him a time to see me and Cecil?"

"I have dealt with it," Robert said simply.

Elizabeth paused on the path, the sun very hot on the back of her neck. "You've done what?"

"I dealt with it," he repeated. "Told him that there must have been a mistake, I condemned smuggling as a general rule, I agreed that smuggling bullion from one country to another is most dangerous for trade. I promised him it would not happen again and said that I would look into it personally. He believed half of it, at the most, but will send his despatch to the Spanish emperor, and we are all satisfied."

She hesitated, suddenly cold despite the heat of the day. "Robert, on what basis did he speak to you?"

He pretended not to understand her. "As I have said."

"Why did he speak to you? Why not take this complaint to Cecil? Or come direct to me? Or ask to meet with the Privy Council?"

Robert slid his arm around her waist, though anyone of the court glancing back could have seen him holding her. "Because I want to take trouble from your shoulders, my love. Because I know as much about kingship as you, or Cecil, and to tell the truth, probably more. Because I was born to do this, just as much as you, or Cecil; probably more. Because his complaint was about your agent Thomas Gresham, who now reports directly to me. This is my business as much as yours. Your business is my business. Your currency is my currency. We do everything together."

Elizabeth could not make herself move from his touch, but she did not melt into him, as she usually did. "De Quadra should have come to me," she insisted.

"Oh, why?" Robert demanded. "Don't you think he knows that I shall be your declared husband within the year? Don't you think everyone knows that we are betrothed and will soon announce it? Don't you think he already deals with me as if I were your husband?"

"He should speak with me or Cecil," she persisted. She rubbed at the cuticles of her fingernails, to push them back from the polished nails.

Dudley took her hand. "Of course," he said. "When it is something that I cannot deal with for you."

"And when would that be?" she demanded sharply.

He chuckled in his self-confidence. "D'you know, I cannot think of a single thing that you or Cecil could do better than me," he admitted.

*   *   *

Cecil was seated next to Elizabeth at the tennis tournament but neither of them followed the play.

"He only met with de Quadra to spare me trouble," she whispered to him in a rapid monotone.

"He has no authority, unless you give it to him," Cecil said steadily.

"Cecil, he says that everyone knows that we are betrothed, that de Quadra thinks of him as my husband and so my representative."

"This has to stop," Cecil said. "You have to stop this . . . usurpation."

"He is not disloyal," she said fiercely. "Everything he does is for love of me."

Yes, he is the most loyal traitor who ever threw down a queen for love of her, Cecil thought bitterly. Aloud he said: "Your Grace, it may be for your good, but don't you know that his power over you will be reported to the Spanish emperor and be seen as weakness? Don't you think the English Catholics will know that you plan to marry a divorced man? You, of all women: the daughter of a divorced queen, a queen executed for adultery?"

Nobody ever spoke to the queen of her mother, except in tones of the most unctuous deference. Elizabeth went white with shock. "I beg your pardon," she said icily.

Cecil was not frightened into silence. "Your reputation has to be of the purest," he said adamantly. "Because your mother, God rest her soul, died with her reputation most foully slandered. Your father divorced a good woman to marry her and then blamed his decision on witchcraft and lust. No one must revive that libel and apply it to you."

"Be very careful, Cecil," she said coldly. "You are repeating treasonous slander."

"You be careful," he said roundly, and rose from his seat. "Tell de Quadra to meet with us both tomorrow morning to make his formal complaint. Sir Robert does not transact business for the Crown."

Elizabeth looked up at him and then, very slightly, she shook her head. "I cannot," she said.

"What?"

"I cannot undermine Sir Robert. The business is done, and he has said only what we would have said. We'll leave it."

"He is indeed king-consort then, in everything but name? You are content to give him your power?"

When she said nothing, Cecil bowed. "I will leave you," he said quietly. "I have no humor to watch the match. I think the Gypsy's Men are certain to win."

*   *   *

Anthony Forster, returning home with a new scroll of madrigals under his arm, was in merry mood and not best pleased to be greeted by his wife with a domestic crisis before he had even entered the great hall.

"Lady Dudley is here and is very ill," she said urgently. "They arrived this morning, and she has been sick since then. She cannot keep down food, the poor thing cannot even keep down drink, and she complains of a pain in her breast which she says is heartbreak, but I think may be a canker. She won't let anyone see it."

"Let me in, wife," he said, and walked past her into his hall. "I'll take a glass of ale," he said sternly. "It was hot work riding home in this heat."

"I am sorry," she said briefly. She poured

him the ale and bit her tongue while he settled himself in his own chair and took a long draught.

"That's better," he said. "Is dinner ready?"

"Of course," she said respectfully. "We were just awaiting your return."

She made herself stand in silence until he took another swig of ale and then turned and looked at her.

"Now then," he said. "What's all this?"

"It's Lady Dudley," she said. "Very ill. Sick, and with a pain in her breast."

"Better send for a physician," he said. "Dr. Bayly."

Mrs. Forster nodded. "I'll send someone for him at once."

He rose from his seat. "I'll wash my hands before dinner." He paused. "Is she fit to see me? Will she come down for dinner?"

"No," she said. "I think not."

He nodded. "This is very inconvenient, wife," he said. "To have her in our house at all is to share in her disgrace. She cannot enjoy a long illness here."

"I don't think she's enjoying anything," she said acidly.

"I daresay not," he said with brief sympathy. "But she cannot stay here for longer than the appointed time, sick or not."

"Has his lordship forbidden you to offer hospitality to her?"

Mr. Forster shook his head. "He doesn't have to," he said. "You don't have to get wet to learn it's raining. I know which way the wind is blowing, and it's not me that will catch cold."

"I'll send for the doctor," his wife said. "Perhaps he will say it was just riding in the heat that made her sick."

*   *   *

The Cumnor stable lad made good time and reached Oxford as Dr. Bayly, the queen's Professor of Physic at Oxford, was sitting down to his dinner. "I can come at once," he said, rising to his feet and reaching for his hat and his cape. "Who is ill at Cumnor Place? Not Mr. Forster, I trust?"

"No," the lad said, proffering his letter. "A visitor, just arrived from Abingdon. Lady Dudley."

The doctor froze, hat halfway to his head, his cape, arrested in mid-swing, flapping to fall at one shoulder like a broken wing. "Lady Dudley," he repeated. "Wife of Sir Robert Dudley?"

"The same," said the lad.

"Sir Robert that is the queen's Master of Horse?"

"The queen's Master of Horse is what they call him," repeated the lad with a broad wink, since he had heard the rumors as well as everyone else.

Dr. Bayly slowly put his hat back down on the wooden settle. "I think I cannot come," he said. He swung his cape from his shoulder and draped it on the high back of the bench. "I think I dare not come, indeed."

"It's not said to be the plague, nor the sweat, sir," the boy said. "She's the only one sick in the house, and there's no plague in Abingdon that I've heard of."

"No, lad, no," the doctor said thoughtfully. "There are things more dangerous than the plague. I don't think I should be engaged."

"She's said to be in pain," the lad went on. "One of the housemaids said she was crying, heard her through the door. Said she heard her ask God to release her."

"I dare not," the doctor told him frankly. "I dare not see her. I could not prescribe physic for her, even if I knew what was wrong with her."

"Why not? If the lady is ill?"

"Because if she dies they will think she has been poisoned and they will accuse me of doing it," the physician said flatly. "And if, in her despair, she has taken a poison already and it is working its way through her body, then they will blame the physic that I give her. If she dies I will get the blame and perhaps have to face trial for her murder. And if someone has poisoned her already, or someone is glad to know that she is sick, then they will not thank me for saving her."

The lad gaped. "I was sent to fetch you to help her. What am I to tell Mrs. Forster?"

The doctor dropped his hand on the lad's shoulder. "Tell them that it was more than my license is worth to meddle in such a case," he said. "It may be that she is taking physic already and that it has been prescribed to her by a greater man than I."

The lad scowled, trying to comprehend the physician's meaning. "I don't understand," he said.

"I mean that if her husband is trying to poison her then I don't dare to meddle," the doctor said bluntly. "And if she is sick unto death then I doubt that he would thank me for saving her."

*

Elizabeth was in Robert's arms; he was covering her face, her shoulders with kisses, licking her neck, overwhelming her as she laughed and pushed him away and pulled him back all at the same time.

"Hush, hush, someone will hear," she said.

"It is you making all the noise with your screaming."

"I'm as quiet as a mouse. I'm not screaming," she protested.

"Not yet, but you will be," he promised, making her laugh again and clap a hand over her mouth.

"You are mad!"

"I am mad with love," he agreed. "And I like winning. D'you know how much I took off de Quadra?"

"You were betting with the Spanish ambassador?"

"Only on a certainty."

"How much?"

"Five hundred crowns," he exulted. "And d'you know what I said?"

"What?"

"I said he could pay me in Spanish gold."

She tried to laugh but he saw at once the

snap of anxiety in her eyes. "Ah, Elizabeth, don't spoil this; the Spanish ambassador is easy enough to manage. I understand him, he understands me. It was a jest only. He laughed and so did I. I can manage affairs of state; God knows, I was born and bred to them."

"I was born to be queen," she flashed at him.

"No one denies it," he said. "Least of all me. Because I was born to be your lover and your husband and your king."

She hesitated. "Robert, even if we declare our betrothal you would not take the title of king."

"Even if?"

She flushed. "I mean: when."

"*When* we declare our betrothal I shall be your husband and King of England," he said simply. "What else would you call me?"

Elizabeth was stunned into silence, but at once she tried to manage him. "Now Robert," she said mildly. "You'll hardly want to be king. Philip of Spain was only ever known as king-consort. Not king."

"Philip of Spain had other titles," he said. "He was emperor in his lands. It didn't matter to him what he was in England; he was hardly ever here. Would you have me seated at a lower place, and eating off silver when you eat off gold, as Philip did with Mary? Would you want to so humble me before others? Every day of my life?"

"No," she said hastily. "Never."

"D'you think me not worthy of the crown? Good enough for your bed but not good enough for the throne?"

"No," she said. "No, of course not. Robert, my love, don't twist and turn my words. You know I love you; you know I love no one but you, and I need you."

"Then we have to complete what we have started," he said. "Grant me a divorce from Amy, and publish our betrothal. Then I can be your partner and helpmeet in everything. And I will be called king."

She was about to object but he drew her toward him again and started to kiss her neck. Helplessly, Elizabeth melted into his embrace. "Robert . . ."

"My love," he said. "You taste so good that I could eat you."

"Robert," she sighed, "My love, my only love."

Gently he scooped her up into his arms and took her to the bed. She lay on her back as he slipped off his gown and came naked toward her. She smiled, waiting for him to put on the sheath that he always used in their lovemaking. When he did not have the ribboned skin in his hand, nor reach to the table by the bed, she was surprised.

"Robert? Have you not a guardian?"

His smile was very dark and seductive. He crawled up the bed toward her, pressing his naked body against every inch of her, overwhelming her with the faint musky smell of him, the warmth of his skin, the soft, prickly mat of hair at his chest, and the rising column of his flesh.

"We have no need of it," he said. "The sooner we make a son for England's cradle the better."

"No!" she said, shocked, and started to pull away. "Not until we are known to be married."

"Yes," he whispered in her ear. "Feel it, Elizabeth, you have never felt it properly. You have never felt it like my wife has felt it. Amy loves me naked and you don't even know what it is like. You've never had half of the pleasure I have given her."

She gave a little moan of jealousy and at once reached down, took hold of him, and guided him into her wetness. As their bodies came together and she felt his naked flesh with her own, her eyes fluttered shut with pleasure. Robert Dudley smiled.

*   *   *

In the morning the queen declared that she was ill and could see no one. When Cecil came to her door she sent out word that she could see him very briefly, and only if it was a matter of urgency.

"I am afraid so," he said solemnly, gesturing at the document in his hand. The sentries stood to one side and let him into her bedchamber.

"I told them I needed you to sign for the return of French prisoners," Cecil said, coming in and bowing. "Your note said to come at once with an excuse to see you."

"Yes," she said.

"Because of Sir Robert?"

"Yes."

"This is ridiculous," he said baldly.

"I know it."

Something in the flatness of her voice alerted him. "What has he done?"

"He has made . . . a demand of me."

Cecil waited.

Elizabeth glanced at the faithful Mrs. Ashley. "Kat, go and stand outside the door and see that there is no one listening."

The woman left the room.

"What demand?"

"One I cannot meet."

He waited.

"He wants us to declare our betrothal, for me to grant him and that woman a divorce, and for him to be called king."

"King?"

Her head bowed down, she nodded, not meeting his eyes.

"King-consort was good enough for the Emperor of Spain."

"I know. I said. But it is what he wants."

"You have to refuse."

"Spirit, I cannot refuse him. I cannot let him think me false to him. I have no words of refusal for him."

"Elizabeth, this madness will cost you the throne of England, and all the danger and all the waiting, and the peace of Edinburgh, will be for nothing. They will push you from the throne and put in your cousin as queen. Or worse. I cannot save you from this; you are finished if you put him on the throne."

"Have you thought of nothing?" she demanded. "You always know what to do.

Spirit, you must help me. I have to break with him and before God, I cannot."

Cecil looked at her suspiciously. "Is that all? That he wants a divorce and to be called king? He has not hurt you, or threatened you? You remember that would be treason, even if done in love? Even if done by a betrothed lover?"

Elizabeth shook her head. "No, he is always . . ." She broke off, thinking what intense pleasure he gave her. "He is always . . . But what if I have a child?"

His look of horror was as dark as her own. "Are you with child?"

She shook her head. "No. Well, I don't know . . ."

"I assumed that he took care . . ."

"Until last night."

"You should have refused."

"I cannot!" she suddenly shouted. "Do you not hear me, Cecil, though I tell you over and over again? I cannot refuse him. I cannot help but love him. I cannot say no to him. You have to find a way for me to marry him, or you have to find a way for me to escape his demands, because I *cannot* say no to him. You have to protect me from my desire for him, from his demands; it is your duty. I cannot protect myself. You have to save me from him."

"Banish him!"

"No. You have to save me from him without him ever knowing that I have said one word against him."

Cecil was silent for a long moment, then he remembered that they had only a short time together: the queen and her own Secretary of State were forced to meet in secret, in snatched moments, because of her folly. "There is a way," he said slowly. "But it is a very dark path."

"Would it teach him his place?" she demanded. "That his place is not mine?"

"It would put him in fear of his life and humble him to dust."

Elizabeth flared up at that. "He never fears," she blazed. "And his spirit did not break even when his whole family was brought low."

"I am sure he is indefatigable," Cecil said acidly. "But this would shake him so low that he would give up all thought of the throne."

"And he would never know that I had ordered it," she whispered.

"No."

She paused. "And it would not fail."

"I don't think so." He hesitated. "It requires the death of an innocent person."

"Just one?"

He nodded. "Just one."

"No one that I love?"

"No."

She did not pause for a moment. "Do it then."

Cecil allowed himself a smile. So often when he thought Elizabeth the weakest of women he saw that she was the most powerful of queens.

"I will need a token of his," he said. "Do you have anything with his seal?"

Almost she said "no." He saw the thought of the lie go through her mind.

"You do?"

Slowly, from the neck of her gown she drew out a gold chain bearing Dudley's signet ring that he had given her when they had plighted their troth. "His own ring," she whispered. "He put it on my finger when we were betrothed."

Cecil hesitated. "Will you give it to me for his undoing? His token of love to you? His own signet ring?"

"Yes," she said simply. "Since it is him, or

me." Slowly, she unclipped the chain and held it up so that the ring fell down into her palm. She kissed it, as if it were a sacred relic, and then reluctantly handed it to him.

"I must have it back," she said.

He nodded.

"And he must never see it in your hands," she said. "He would know at once that it had come from me."

Cecil nodded again.

"When will you do it?" she asked.

"At once," he replied.

"Not on my birthday," she specified like a child. "Let me be happy with him on my birthday. He has planned a lovely day for me; don't spoil it."

"The day after then," Cecil said.

"Sunday?"

He nodded. "But you must not risk conceiving a child."

"I will make an excuse."

"I will need you to play a part," Cecil warned her.

"He knows me too well; he sees through me in a moment."

"Not play a part to him. You will have to make some remarks to others. You have to set a hare running. I will tell you what to say."

She wrung her hands. "It will not hurt him?"

"He has to learn," Cecil said. "You want this done?"

"It must be done."

Would to God I could just have him murdered and be done with it, Cecil thought as he bowed and left the room. Kat Ashley was waiting outside the queen's chamber as Cecil came out and they exchanged one brief, appalled glance at the mess in which this new queen was entrapped in only the second year of her reign.

But though not dead I shall bring him down so low that he knows he can never be king, Cecil thought. *Another Dudley generation and another disgrace. Will they ever learn?* He stalked along the gallery past the queen's forebears, her handsome father, the gaunt portrait of her grandfather. *A woman cannot rule,* Cecil thought, looking at the kings. *A woman, even a very clever woman like this one, has no temperament for rule. She seeks a master and God help us, she chose a Dudley. Well, once he is cut down

*like a weed and the path is clear she can
seek a proper master for England.*

*   *   *

The page, reporting that the doctor would
not attend Lady Dudley, was summoned
before Mrs. Forster.

"Did you tell him she was ill? Did you say
Lady Dudley needed his help?"

The lad, wide-eyed with anxiety, nodded
his head. "He knew," he said. "It was because she is who she is that he wouldn't
come."

Mrs. Forster shook her head and went to
find Mrs. Oddingsell.

"Our own physician will not attend her, for
fear of being unable to cure her," she said,
putting the best appearance on the matter
as she could.

Mrs. Oddingsell paused at this fresh bad
news. "Did he know who his patient would
be?"

"Yes."

"He refused to come in order to avoid
her?"

Mrs. Forster hesitated. "Yes."

"So now she has nowhere to go, and no
physician will heal her?" she demanded in-

credulously. "What is she to do? What am I to do with her?"

"She will have to come to terms with her husband," Mrs. Forster said. "She should never have quarreled with him. He is too great a man to offend."

"Mrs. Forster, you know as well as I, she has no quarrel with him but his adultery and his desire for a divorce. How is a good wife to meet such a request?"

"When the man is Robert Dudley, his wife had better agree," Mrs. Forster said bluntly. "For look at the strait she finds herself in now."

*   *   *

Amy, a little better after a rest of two days, walked down the narrow circular stair from her room to the buttery below, and then through the great hall into the courtyard, her hat swinging in her hand. She walked across the cobbled courtyard, putting her hat on her head and tying the ribbons under her chin. Although it was September the sun was still very hot. Amy went through the great archway and turned left to walk on the thickly planted terrace before the house. The monks had walked here in their times of quiet prayer and reading, and she could still trace the paving stones of their circular walk in the rough-cut grass.

She thought that they must have struggled with greater difficulties than hers, that they must have wrestled with their souls and not worried about mere mortal things like whether a husband would ever come home again, and how to survive if he did not. *But they were very holy men,* she said to herself. *And learned. And I am neither holy nor learned, and in fact I think I am a very foolish sinner. For God must have forgotten me as much as Robert has done if they could both leave me here alone, and in such despair.*

She gave a little gulp of a sob and then rubbed the tears from her cheek with her gloved hand. *No point in crying,* she whispered miserably to herself.

She took the steps down from the terrace to walk through the orchard toward the garden wall, the gate, and the church beyond.

The gate was stuck when she pulled at it, and then a man stepped forward from the other side of the wall, and pushed it free for her.

"Thank you," she said, startled.

"Lady Amy Dudley?" he asked.

"Yes?"

"I have a message for you from your husband."

She gave a little gasp and her cheeks suddenly blushed red. "Is he here?"

"No. A letter for you."

He handed it over and waited while she examined the seal. Then she did an odd thing. "Have you a knife?"

"What for, my lady?"

"To lift off the seal. I don't break them."

He took a little dagger, sharp as a razor, from its sheath in his boot. "Take care."

She inserted the blade between the dried shiny wax and the thick paper and lifted the seal from the fold. She tucked it into the pocket of her gown, returned the knife to him, and then unfolded the letter.

He saw that her hands were shaking as she held the letter to read it, and that she read very slowly, her lips spelling out the words. She looked at him. "Are you in his confidence?"

"I am his servant and his liegeman."

Amy held out the letter to him. "Please," she said. "I don't read very well. Does that say that he is coming to see me tomorrow at midday, and that he wants to see me alone in the house? That I must clear the house of everyone and wait for him alone?"

Awkwardly, he took the letter and read it quickly. "Yes," he said. "At midday tomorrow, and it says to dismiss your servants for the day and sit alone in your chamber."

"Do I know you?" she said suddenly. "Are you new in his service?"

"I am his confidential servant," he said. "I had business in Oxford and so he asked me to take this letter. He said there would be no need of any reply."

"Did he send me a token?" she asked. "Since I don't know you?"

The man gave her a thin smile. "I am Johann Worth, your ladyship. And he gave me this for you." He reached into his pocket and gave her the ring, the Dudley signet ring with the ragged staff and the bear.

Solemnly she took it from him and at once slipped it on her fourth finger, snugly it fitted above her wedding ring, and she smiled as she put her fingertip on the engraving of the Dudley crest.

"Of course I shall do exactly as he asks," she said.

*

The Spanish ambassador, de Quadra, staying at Windsor for the weekend of Elizabeth's birthday, found himself opposite Cecil to watch an archery tournament on the upper green before the palace gardens on Friday evening. He noticed at once that the Lord Secretary was looking as grave as he had done since his return from Scotland, and was wearing his customary black unrelieved by any slashing, color, or jewelry, as if it were an ordinary day and not the eve of the queen's birthday.

Carefully he worked his way round so that he was near the Lord Secretary as the party dispersed.

"And so all is prepared for the queen's birthday tomorrow," the Spanish ambassador observed. "Sir Robert swears he will give her a merry day."

"Merry for her, but little joy in it for me," Cecil said incautiously, his tongue loosened by wine.

"Oh?"

"I tell you, I cannot tolerate much more of it," Cecil continued in a tone of muted anger. "Everything I try to do, everything I say has to be confirmed by that cub."

"Sir Robert Dudley?"

"I've had enough of it," Cecil said. "I left her service once before, when she would not take my advice over Scotland, and I can do it again. I have a beautiful house and a fine young family, and I never have time to see them, and the thanks I get for my service is shameful."

"You are not serious," the Spaniard said. "You would not really leave?"

"It is a wise sailor who makes for port when a storm is coming," Cecil said. "And the day that Dudley steps up to the throne is the day that I step out into my garden at Burghley House and never see London again. Unless he arrests me the moment I resign, and throws me into the Tower."

The ambassador recoiled from Cecil's anger. "Sir William! I have never seen you so distressed!"

"I have never felt such distress!" Cecil said bluntly. "I tell you, she will be ruined by him and the country with her."

"She could never marry him?" de Quadra asked, scandalized.

"She thinks of nothing else and I cannot make her see reason. I tell you, she has surrendered all affairs to him and she means to marry him."

"But what of his wife? What of Lady Dudley?"

"I don't think she will live very long if she stands in Dudley's way, do you?" Cecil asked bitterly. "He is not a man to stop at much with a throne in his sights. He is his father's son, after all."

"This is most shocking!" the ambassador exclaimed, his voice hushed to a whisper.

"I am certain he is thinking of killing his wife by poison. Why else would he put it about that she is ill? Though I hear that she is quite well and has now employed a taster for her food. What do you think of that? She herself thinks he will murder her."

"Surely the people would never accept him as king? Especially if his wife died suddenly and suspiciously?"

"You tell her," Cecil urged him. "For she will hear not one word against him from me. I have spoken to her, Kat Ashley has spoken to her. In God's name, you tell her what will come from her misconduct, for she may listen to you when she is deaf to all of us."

"I hardly dare," de Quadra stammered. "I am not in her confidence."

"But you have the authority of the Spanish king," Cecil insisted. "Tell her, for God's sake, or she will have Dudley and lose the throne."

*   *   *

De Quadra was an experienced ambassador, but he thought that no one had ever before been entrusted with such a wild mission as to tell a twenty-seven-year-old queen on the very morning of her birthday that her most senior advisor was in despair, and that everyone thought she would lose her throne if she did not give up her love affair.

Her birthday morning started with a stag hunt and Robert had all the huntsmen dressed in the Tudor colors of green and white and the entire court dressed in silver, white, and gold. Elizabeth's own horse, a big white gelding, had a new saddle of red Spanish leather and new bridle, a gift from Dudley.

The Spanish ambassador held back as the queen and her lover rode at their usual breakneck speed, but when they had killed, and had drunk a glass of wine over the stag's head to celebrate, and were riding home, he eased his horse beside hers and wished her a happy birthday.

"Thank you," Elizabeth gleamed.

"I have a small gift for you from the

emperor back at the castle," the ambassador said. "But I could not contain my good wishes a moment longer. I have never seen you in such health and happiness."

She turned her head and smiled at him.

"And Sir Robert looks so well. He is a happy man to have your favor," he started carefully.

"Of all the men in the world he has earned it," she said. "Whether in war or peace he is my most trusted and faithful advisor. And in days of pleasure he is the best of companions!"

"And he loves you so dearly," de Quadra remarked.

She drew her horse a little closer to him. "May I tell you a secret?" she asked.

"Yes," he swiftly assured her.

"Sir Robert will soon be a widower and free to marry," she said, keeping her voice very low.

"No!"

She nodded. "His wife is dead of an illness, or very nearly so. But you must tell no one about it until we announce it."

"I promise I shall keep your secret," he stumbled. "Poor lady, has she been ill very long?"

"Oh, yes," Elizabeth said carelessly. "So he assures me. Poor thing. Are you coming to the banquet tonight, sir?"

"I am," he said, he tightened his grip on the horse's reins and fell back from her side. As they rode up the winding road to the castle he saw Cecil, waiting for the return of the hunt, on the little battlements above the entrance. The ambassador shook his head toward Elizabeth's advisor as if to say that he could make sense of nothing, that it was as if they were all trapped in a nightmare, that something very bad was happening, but no one could know quite what.

*   *   *

Elizabeth's birthday celebrations, which had started with a roar of guns, ended in a blaze of fireworks that she viewed from a barge in the Thames, heaped with late roses, with her closest friends and her lover at her side. When the fireworks died down the barges rowed slowly up and then down the river so that the people of London, lining the banks to admire the show, could call out their blessings on the twenty-seven-year-old queen.

"She will have to marry soon," Laetitia

observed to her mother in a muted whisper. "Or she'll have left it too late."

Catherine glanced toward the profile of her friend and the darker shadow behind her which was Robert Dudley. "It would break her heart to marry another man," she predicted. "And she'll lose her throne if she marries him. What a dilemma for a woman to face. Pray God you never love unwisely, Lettice."

"Well, you've seen to that," Laetitia said smartly enough. "For being betrothed without love I am unlikely to find it now."

"For most women it is better to marry well than to marry for love," Catherine said, unruffled. "Love may follow."

"It didn't follow for Amy Dudley," Laetitia observed.

"A man like Robert Dudley would bring trouble for his lover or his wife," her mother told her. As they watched, the barge rocked and Elizabeth stumbled a little. At once Robert's arm was around her waist and, careless of the watching crowds, she let him hold her, and leaned back against him so that she could feel the warmth of his body at her back.

"Come to my room tonight," he whispered in her ear.

She turned to smile up at him. "You'll break my heart," she whispered. But I cannot. It is my time of the month. Next week I shall come back to you."

He gave a little growl of disappointment. "It had better be soon," he warned her. "Or I shall come to your bedchamber before the whole court."

"Would you dare to do that?"

"Try me," he recommended. "See how much I would dare."

*　　　*　　　*

Amy dined with her hosts on Saturday night and ate a good dinner. They drank the health of the queen on this, her birthday night, as did every loyal household in the land, and Amy raised her glass and touched it to her lips without flinching.

"You are looking better, Lady Dudley," Mr. Forster said kindly. "I am glad to see you well again."

She smiled and he was struck with her prettiness, which he had forgotten while thinking of her as a burden.

"You have been a kind host indeed," she

said. "And I am sorry to come to your house and immediately take to my bed."

"It was a hot day and a long ride," he said. "I was out that day and I felt the heat myself."

"Well, it will be cold soon enough," Mrs. Forster said. "How quickly time passes. It's Abingdon fair tomorrow, think of that already?"

"I am riding over to Didcot," Mr. Forster said. "There's some trouble with the tithes for the church. I said I would listen to the vicar's sermon and then meet him and the churchwarden. I'll dine with him and come home in the evening, my dear."

"I'll let the servants go to the fair then," Mrs. Forster said. "They usually have a holiday on fair Sunday."

"Will you go?" Amy asked with sudden interest.

"Not on the Sunday," Mrs. Forster said. "All the common folk go on the Sunday. We could ride over on Monday if you wish to see it."

"Oh, let's go tomorrow," Amy said, suddenly animated. "Please say we can. I like the fair all busy and filled with people. I like to see the servants all dressed up in their best and buying ribbons. It's always best on the first day."

"Oh, my dear, I don't think so," Mrs. Forster said doubtfully. "It can be very rough."

"Oh, go," her husband recommended. "A little bustle won't hurt you. It'll lift Lady Dudley's spirits. And if you want any ribbons or anything you will know that they have not sold out."

"What time shall we go?" Mrs. Oddingsell asked.

"We could leave at about midday," Mrs. Forster suggested, "and take our dinner at Abingdon. There's a good enough inn, if you wish to dine there."

"Yes," Amy said. "I should love to do that."

"Well, I am glad to see you so restored to health that you want to go out," Mr. Forster said kindly.

*   *   *

On Sunday morning, the day they were all to go to the fair, Amy came down to breakfast looking pale and ill again.

"I slept so badly, I am too ill to go," she said.

"I am sorry," Mrs. Forster said. "Do you need anything?"

"I think I will just rest," Amy said. "If I could sleep I am sure I would be well again."

"The servants have all gone to the fair already, so the house will be quiet," Mrs. Forster promised. "And I will make you a tisane myself, and you shall take your dinner in your room, in your bed if you wish."

"No," Amy said. "You go to the fair as you planned. I wouldn't want you to delay for me."

"I wouldn't dream of it," Mrs. Forster said. "We won't leave you all on your own."

"I insist," Amy said. "You were looking forward to it, and as Mr. Forster said yesterday, if you want some ribbons or something, the first day is always best."

"We can all go tomorrow, when you are better," Lizzie put in.

Amy rounded on her. "No!" she said. "Didn't you hear me? I just said. I want you all to go, as you planned. I shall stay behind. But I want you all to go. Please! My head throbs so, I cannot stand an argument about it! Just go!"

"But will you dine alone?" Mrs. Forster asked. "If we all go?"

"I shall dine with Mrs. Owen," Amy said.

"If I feel well enough. And I shall see you all when you come home again. But you must go!"

"Very well," Lizzie said, throwing a warning glance at Mrs. Forster. "Don't get so distressed, Amy dear. We'll all go and we'll tell you all about it tonight, when you have had a good sleep and are feeling better."

At once the irritability left Amy, and she smiled. "Thank you, Lizzie," she said. "I shall be able to rest if I know you are all having a good time at the fair. Don't come back till after dinner."

"No," Lizzie Oddingsell said. "And if I see some nice blue ribbons that would match your riding hat I will buy them for you."

*   *   *

The queen went to the Royal Chapel in Windsor Castle and walked in the garden on Sunday morning. Laetitia Knollys walked demurely behind her, carrying her shawl and a book of devotional poems in case the queen chose to sit and read.

Robert Dudley walked to meet her as she stood, looking toward the river where a few little wherry boats plied up and down to London and back.

He bowed in greeting. "Good morning,"

he said. "Are you not tired after your celebrations yesterday?"

"No," Elizabeth said. "I am never tired by dancing."

"I thought you might come to me, even though you had said you wouldn't. I couldn't sleep without you."

She put her hand out to him. "It is still my time," she said sweetly. "It will only be another day or two."

He covered her hand with his own. "Of course," he said. "You know I would never press you. And when we declare our marriage and we sleep in the same bed every night you shall order it just as you please. Don't be afraid of that."

Elizabeth, who had thought that she would always order everything just as she pleased by right, and not by another's permission, kept her face perfectly calm. "Thank you, my love," she said sweetly.

"Shall we walk?" he asked her.

She shook her head. "I am going to sit and read."

"I will leave you then," he said. "I have an errand to run but I shall be back by dinner time."

"Where are you going?"

"Just to look at some horses in Oxford-shire," he said vaguely. "I doubt they will be worth buying but I promised to go and see them."

"On a Sunday?" she said, faintly disapproving.

"I'll just look," he said. "There is no sin in looking at a horse on a Sunday, surely. Or shall you be a very strict Pope?"

"I shall be a strict supreme governor of the church," she said with a smile.

He leaned toward her as if he would kiss her cheek. "Then give me a divorce," he whispered in her ear.

*   *   *

Amy, seated in the silent house, waited for Robert's arrival, as he had promised in his letter. The house was quite empty except for old Mrs. Owen, who had gone to sleep in her room after an early dinner. Amy had walked in the garden, and then, obedient to the instructions in Robert's letter, gone to wait in her room in the empty house.

The window overlooked the drive and she sat in the window seat and watched for the Dudley standard and the cavalcade of riders.

"Perhaps he has quarreled with her," she

whispered to herself. "Perhaps she is tired of him. Or perhaps she has finally agreed to marry the archduke and they know that they have to part."

She thought for a moment. *Whatever the reason, I have to take him back without reproach. That would be my duty to him as his wife.* She paused. She could not stop her heart from lifting. *And, in any case, whatever the reason, I would take him back without reproach. He is my husband, he is my love, the only love of my life. If he comes back to me*—She broke off from the thought. *I can't even imagine how happy I would be if he were to come back to me.*

She heard the sound of a single horse and she looked out of the window. It was not one of Robert's high-bred horses, and not Robert, riding high and proud on the horse, one hand on the taut reins, one hand on his hip. It was another man, bowed low over the neck of the horse, his hat pulled down over his face.

Amy waited for the sound of the peal of the bell, but there was silence. She thought perhaps he had gone to the stable yard and would find it empty since all the lads had gone to the fair. She rose to her feet, thinking that she had better go and greet this stranger herself, since no servants were at home. But as she did so, her bedroom door silently opened, and a tall stranger came in quietly and shut the door behind him.

Amy gasped. "Who are you?"

She could not see his face, he still had his hat pulled low over his eyes. His cape was of dark blue wool, without a badge of rank. She did not recognize his height nor his broad build.

"Who are you?" she asked again, her voice sharp with fear. "Answer me! And how dare you come into my room!"

"Lady Amy Dudley?" he asked, his voice low and quiet.

"Yes."

"Sir Robert Dudley's wife?"

"Yes. And you are?"

"He said for me to come to you. He wants you to come to him. He loves you once more. Look out of the window, he is waiting for you."

With a little cry, Amy turned to the window and at once the man stepped behind her. In one swift motion he took her jaw in his hands and quickly twisted her neck sideways and upward. It broke with a crack, and she slumped in his hands without even a cry.

He lowered her to the floor, listening intently. There was no sound in the house at all. She had sent everyone away, as she had been told to do. He picked her up, she was as light as a child, her cheeks still flushed pink from the moment that she thought that Robert had come to love her. The man held her in his arms and carried her carefully from the room, down the little winding stone stair, a short flight of half a dozen steps, and laid her at the foot, as if she had fallen.

He paused and listened again. Still, the house was silent. Amy's hood was slipping back off her head, and her gown was crumpled, showing her legs. He did not feel he could leave her uncovered. Gently, he pulled down the skirts of the gown and put the hood straight on her head. Her forehead was still warm, her skin soft to his touch. It was like leaving a sleeping child.

Quietly, he went out through the outer door. His horse was tethered outside. It raised its head when it saw him but it did not whinny. He closed the door behind him, mounted his horse, and turned its head away from Cumnor Place to Windsor.

*   *   *

Amy's body was found by two servants who had come home from the fair, a little ahead of the others. They were courting and had hoped to steal an hour alone together. When they came into the house they saw her, lying at the foot of the stairs, her skirts pulled down, her hood set tidily on her head. The girl screamed and fainted, but the young man gently picked up Amy, and laid her on her bed. When Mrs. Forster came home they met her at the gate and told her that Lady Dudley was dead from falling down the stairs.

"Amy!" Lizzie Oddingsell breathed her name and flung herself from her horse and raced up the stairs to Amy's bedroom.

She was laid on her bed, her neck turned horridly so that her face was twisted toward the door, though her shoulders lay flat. Her expression was the blankness of death, her skin was chill as stone.

"Oh, Amy, what have you done?" Lizzie mourned. "What have you done? We'd have found a way round things, we'd have found somewhere to go. He still cared for you, he would never have neglected you. He might have come back. Oh, Amy, dearest Amy, what have you done?"

*   *   *

A message must be sent to Sir Robert. "What shall I say?" Mrs. Forster demanded of Lizzie Oddingsell. "What should I write? What can I tell him?"

"Just say she's dead," Lizzie said furiously. "He can come down himself if he wants to know why or how."

Mrs. Forster wrote a brief note and sent it to Windsor by her servant John Bowes. "Make sure you give it to Sir Robert, into his own hand, and to no one else," she cautioned him, uncomfortably aware that they all were in the very center of a massive breaking scandal. "And tell no one else of this business, and come straight home without talking to anyone but him."

*   *   *

At nine o'clock on Monday morning Robert Dudley strode to the queen's apartments and walked in without glancing to any of his friends and adherents who were talking and standing around.

He marched up to the throne and bowed. "I have to speak with you alone," he said without any preamble. Laetitia Knollys noticed that his hand was gripping his hat so tightly that the knuckles were gleaming white.

Elizabeth took in the tension in his face, and got to her feet at once. "Of course," she said. "Shall we walk?"

"In your chamber," he said tautly.

Her eyes widened at the sharpness of his tone but she took his arm and the two of them went through the doors into her privy chamber.

"Well!" one of her ladies-in-waiting remarked softly. "He is more like a husband every day. Soon he will be ordering us as he orders her."

"Something's happened," guessed Laetitia.

"Nonsense," said Mary Sidney. "It will be a new horse or something. He rode to Oxfordshire to look at a horse only yesterday."

*   *   *

As soon as the door was shut behind them, Robert thrust his hand into his doublet and pulled out a letter. "I've just had this," he said shortly. "It is from Cumnor Place where Amy has been staying with my friends. Amy, my wife, is dead."

"Dead?" Elizabeth said, too loud. She clapped her hand over her mouth and looked at Robert. "How dead?"

He shook his head. "It doesn't say," he said. "It is from Mrs. Forster and the damn fool of a woman just says that she is sorry to inform me that Amy died today. The letter is dated Sunday. My servant is on his way to find out what has happened."

"Dead?" she repeated.

"Yes," he said. "And so I am free."

She gave a little gasp and staggered. "Free. Of course you are."

"God knows I would not have had her die," he said hastily. "But her death sets us free, Elizabeth. We can declare our betrothal. I shall be king."

"I'm speechless," she said. She could hardly take her breath.

"I too," he said. "Such a sudden change, and so unexpected."

She shook her head. "It's unbelievable. I knew she was in poor health . . ."

"I thought she was well enough," he said. "She never complained of anything more than a little pain. I don't know what it can be. Perhaps she fell from her horse?"

"We had better go out," Elizabeth said.

"Someone will bring the news to court. We had better not hear it together. Everyone will look at us and wonder what we are thinking."

"Yes," he said. "But I had to tell you at once."

"Of course, I understand. But we had better go out now."

Suddenly he snatched her to him and took a deep, hungry kiss. "Soon they will all know that you are my wife," he promised her. "We will rule England together. I am free; our life together starts right now!"

"Yes," she said, pulling away from him. "But we had better go out."

Again he checked her at the door. "It is as if it were God's will," he said wonderingly. "That she should die and set me free at this very moment, when we are ready to marry, when we have the country at peace, when we have so much to do. 'This is the Lord's doing; it is marvelous in our eyes.'"

Elizabeth recognized the words she had said at her own accession to the throne. "You think that this death will make you king," she said, testing him. "As Mary's death made me queen."

Robert nodded, his face bright and glad.

"We shall be King and Queen of England to-gether," he said. "And we will make an England as glorious as Camelot."

"Yes," she said, her lips cold. "But we should go out now."

*   *   *

In the presence chamber Elizabeth looked around for Cecil and when he came in, she beckoned him to her. Sir Robert was in a window embrasure talking casually to Sir Francis Knollys about trade with the Spanish Netherlands.

"Sir Robert has just told me that his wife is dead," she said, half covering her mouth with her hand.

"Indeed," Cecil said steadily, his face a mask to the watching courtiers.

"He says he does not know the cause."

Cecil nodded.

"Cecil, what the devil is happening? I told the Spanish ambassador that she was ill, as you told me to do. But this is so sudden. Has he murdered her? He will claim me as his own and I shall not be able to say no."

"I should wait and see if I were you," Cecil said.

"But what shall I do?" she demanded urgently. "He says that he will be King of England."

"Do nothing for the time being," Cecil said. "Wait and see."

Abruptly she turned into the bay of the window and dragged him in beside her. "You shall tell me more," she demanded fiercely.

Cecil put his mouth to her ear and whispered quietly. Elizabeth kept her face turned away from the court to look out of the window. "Very well," she said to Cecil, and turned back to the court.

"Now," she announced. "I see Sir Nielson there. Good day, Sir Nielson. And how is business in Somerset?"

*   *   *

Laetitia Knollys stood before Sir William Cecil's desk while the rest of the court was waiting to be called to dinner.

"Yes?"

"They are saying that Robert Dudley is going to murder his wife and that the queen knows all about it."

"Are they? And why are they saying such a slanderous lie?"

"Is it because you started it?"

Sir William smiled at her and thought again what a thorough Boleyn girl she was: the quickness of the Boleyn wit and the enchanting Howard indiscretion.

"I?"

"Someone overheard you telling the Spanish ambassador that the queen would be ruined if she marries Dudley and you can't stop her, she's determined." Laetitia ticked off the first point on her slim fingers.

"And?"

"Then the queen tells the Spanish ambassador, in my own hearing, that Amy Dudley is dead."

"Does she?" Cecil looked surprised.

"She said 'dead or nearly so,'" Laetitia quoted. "So everyone thinks that we are being prepared for the news of her death by some mystery illness, that when it comes they will announce their marriage and the widower Robert Dudley will be the next king."

"And what does everyone think will happen then?" Cecil asked politely.

"Now that, no one dare say very loud, but some men would give you a wager that her uncle will come marching down from Newcastle at the head of the English army and kill him."

"Really?"

"And others think there will be an uprising which the French would pay for to put Mary, Queen of Scots, on the throne."

"Indeed."

"And others think there would be an uprising which the Spanish would pay for, to put Katherine Grey on the throne, and keep Mary out."

"These are very wild predictions," Cecil complained. "But they seem to cover all possibilities. And what do you think, my lady?"

"I think that you will have a plan up your sleeve which allows for these dangers to the realm," she said and gave him a roguish little smile.

"We should hope I do," he said. "For these are very grave dangers."

"D'you think he's worth it?" Laetitia asked him suddenly. "She is risking her throne to be with him, and she is the most cold-hearted woman I know. Don't you think he must be the most extraordinary lover for her to risk so much?"

"I don't know," Cecil said dampeningly.

"Neither I nor any man in England seems to find him very irresistible. On the contrary."

"Just us silly girls then." She smiled.

*   *   *

Elizabeth feigned illness in the afternoon; she could not tolerate being in private with Robert, whose exultation was hard to conceal, and she was waiting all the time for a message from Cumnor Place which would bring the news of Amy's death to court. She gave out that she would dine alone in her room and go early to bed. "You can sleep in my room, Kat," she said. "I want your company."

Kat Ashley looked at her mistress's pallor and at the redness of the skin where she was picking at her nails. "What's happened now?" she demanded.

"Nothing," Elizabeth said abruptly. "Nothing. I just want to rest."

But she could not rest. She was awake by dawn, seated at her desk with her Latin grammar before her, translating an essay on the vanity of fame. "What are you doing that for?" Kat asked sleepily, rising from her bed.

"To stop myself thinking of anything else," Elizabeth said grimly.

"What is the matter?" asked Kat. "What has happened?"

"I can't say," Elizabeth replied. "It's so bad that I can't tell even you."

She went to chapel in the morning and then back to her rooms. Robert walked beside her as they came back from her chapel. "My servant has written me a long letter to tell me what happened," he said quietly. "It seems that Amy fell down a flight of stairs and broke her neck."

Elizabeth went white for a moment, then she recovered. "At least it was quick," she said.

A man bowed before her and Elizabeth paused and gave him her hand; Robert stepped back and she went on alone.

In her dressing room, Elizabeth changed into her riding clothes, wondering if they would indeed all be going hunting. The ladies of her court were waiting with her when, at last, Kat came into the room and said, "Sir Robert Dudley is outside in the presence chamber. He says he has something to tell you."

Elizabeth rose to her feet. "We will go out to him." The court was mostly dressed to go hunting; there was a murmur of surprise as people noticed that Robert Dudley was not in riding clothes but in the most somber black. As the queen came in with her ladies he bowed to her, raised himself up, and said, perfectly composed, "Your Grace, I have to report the death of my wife. She died on Sunday at Cumnor Place, God rest her soul."

"Good God!" the Spanish ambassador exclaimed.

Elizabeth glanced toward him with eyes that were as blank as polished jet. She raised her hand. At once, the room quietened as everyone crowded closer to hear what she would say.

"I am very sorry to announce the death of Lady Amy Dudley, on Sunday, at Cumnor Place in Oxfordshire," Elizabeth said steadily, as if the matter were not much to do with her.

She waited. The court was stunned into silence, everyone waiting to see if she would say more. "We will go into mourning for Lady Dudley," Elizabeth said abruptly, and turned to one side to speak to Kat Ashley.

Irresistibly, the Spanish ambassador, de Quadra, found himself moving toward her.

"What tragic news," he said, bowing over her hand. "And so sudden."

"An accident," Elizabeth said, trying to remain serene. "Tragic. Most regrettable. She must have fallen down the stairs. She had a broken neck."

"Indeed," he said. "What a strange mischance."

*　　　*　　　*

It was afternoon before Robert came to Elizabeth again. He found her in the garden, walking with her ladies before dinner.

"I shall have to withdraw from court for mourning," he said, his face grave. "I thought I should go to the Dairy House at Kew. You can come and see me easily there, and I can come to see you."

She slid her hand on his arm. "Very well. Why do you look so odd, Robert? You are not sad, are you? You don't mind, do you?"

He looked down at her pretty face as if she were suddenly a stranger to him. "Elizabeth, she was my wife of eleven years. Of course I grieve for her."

She made a little pout. "But you were desperate to put her aside. You would have divorced her for me."

"Yes, indeed, I would have done, and this

is better for us than the scandal of a divorce. But I would never have wished her dead."

"The country has thought her half dead any time in the last two years," she said. "Everyone said she was terribly ill."

He shrugged. "People talk. I don't know why they all thought she was ill. She traveled; she rode out. She was not ill, but in the last two years she was very unhappy; and that was all my fault."

She was irritated and let him see it. "Saints' sake, Robert! You will never choose to fall in love with her now that she is dead!" she teased him. "You will never now find great virtues in her that you didn't appreciate before?"

"I loved her when she was a young woman and I was a boy," he said passionately. "She was my first love. And she stood by me through all the years of my troubles and she never once complained of the danger and difficulty I led her into. And when you came to the throne and I came into my own again she never said one word of complaint about you."

"Why would she complain of me?" Elizabeth exclaimed. "How would she dare complain?"

"She was jealous," he said fairly. "And she knew she had cause. And she did not receive very fair or generous treatment from me. I wanted her to grant me a divorce and I was unkind to her."

"And now she is dead you are sorry, though you would have gone on being unkind to her in life," she taunted him.

"Yes," he said honestly. "I suppose all poor husbands would say the same: that they know they should be better than they are. But I feel wretched for her, today. I am glad to be a single man, of course. But I would not have wanted her dead. Poor innocent! No one would have wanted her dead."

"You do not recommend yourself very well," Elizabeth said archly, turning his attention to their courtship once more. "You do not sound like a good husband at all!"

For once Robert did not respond to her. He looked away, upriver to Cumnor, and his gaze was somber. "No," he said. "I was not a good husband to her, and God knows, she was the sweetest and best wife a man could have had."

There was a little stir among the waiting court, a messenger in the Dudley livery had entered the garden and paused at the fringe of the court. Dudley turned and saw the man and went toward him, his hand out for the proffered letter.

The watching courtiers saw Dudley take the letter, break the seal, open it, and saw him pale as he read the words.

Elizabeth went swiftly toward him and they parted to let her through. "What is it?" she demanded urgently. "Have a care! Everyone is watching you!"

"There is to be an inquest," he said, his lips hardly moving, his voice no more than a breath. "Everyone is saying that it was no accident. They all think that Amy was murdered."

*   *   *

Thomas Blount, Robert Dudley's man, arrived at Cumnor Place the very day after Amy's death, and examined all the servants one by one. Meticulously, he reported back to Robert Dudley that Amy had been known as a woman of erratic temper, sending everyone off to the fair on Sunday morning, though her companion Mrs. Oddingsell and Mrs. Forster had been unwilling to go.

"No need to mention that again," Robert Dudley wrote back to him, thinking that he did not want his wife's sanity questioned, when he knew he had driven her to despair.

Obediently, Thomas Blount never mentioned the matter of Amy's odd behavior again. But he did say that Amy's maid Mrs. Pirto had remarked that Amy had been in very great despair, praying for her own death on some occasions.

"No need to mention this, either," Robert Dudley wrote back. "Is there to be an inquest? Can the men of Abingdon be trusted with such a sensitive matter?"

Thomas Blount, reading his master's anxious scrawl well enough, replied that they were not prejudiced against the Dudleys in this part of the world, and that Mr. Forster's reputation was good. There would be no jumping to any conclusion of murder; but of course, it must be what everyone thought. A woman does not die by falling down six stone steps, she does not die from a fall which does not disturb her hood or ruffle her skirts. Everyone thought that someone had broken her neck and left her on the floor. The facts pointed to murder.

*

"I am innocent," Dudley said flatly to the queen in the Privy Council chamber at Windsor Castle, a daunting place to speak of such private things. "Good God, would I be such a sinner as to do such a deed to a virtuous wife? And if I did, would I be such a fool as to do it so clumsily? There must be a thousand better ways to kill a woman and make it appear an accident than break her neck and leave her at the foot of half a dozen stairs. I know those stairs; there is nothing to them. No one could break their neck falling down them. You could not even break your ankle. You would barely bruise. Would I tidy the skirts of a murdered woman? Would I pin her hood back on her head? Am I supposed to be an idiot as well as a criminal?"

Cecil was standing beside the queen. The two of them looked in silence at Dudley like unfriendly judges.

"I am sure the inquest will find out who did it," Elizabeth said. "And your name will be cleared. But in the meantime, you will have to withdraw from court."

"I will be ruined," Dudley said blankly. "If you make me go, it looks as if you suspect me."

"Of course I do not," Elizabeth said. She glanced at Cecil. He nodded sympathetically. "*We* do not. But it is tradition that anyone accused of a crime has to withdraw from court. You know that as well as I."

"I am not accused!" he said fiercely. "They are holding an inquest; they have not returned a verdict of murder. No one suggests that I murdered her!"

"Actually, everyone suggests that you murdered her," Cecil helpfully pointed out.

"But if you send me from court you are showing that you think me guilty too!" Dudley spoke directly to Elizabeth. "I must stay at court, at your side, and then it will look as if I am innocent, and that you believe in my innocence."

Cecil stepped forward half a step. "No," he said gently. "There is going to be a most dreadful scandal, whatever verdict the inquest brings in. There is going to be a scandal which will rock Christendom, let alone this country. There is going to be a scandal which, if one breath of it touched the throne, would be enough to destroy the queen. You cannot be at her side. She cannot brazen out your innocence. The best thing we can all do is to behave as usual. You go to the

Dairy House, withdraw into mourning, and await the verdict, and we will try to live down the gossip here."

"There is always gossip!" Robert said despairingly. "We always ignored it before!"

"There has never been gossip like this," Cecil said in very truth. "They are saying that you murdered your wife in cold blood, that you and the queen have a secret betrothal, and that you will announce it at your wife's funeral. If the inquest finds you guilty of murder then many will think the queen your accomplice. Pray God you are not ruined, Sir Robert, and the queen destroyed with you."

He was as white as the linen of his ruff. "I cannot be ruined by something I would never do," he said through cold lips. "Whatever the temptation, I would never have done such a thing as to hurt Amy."

"Then surely you have nothing to fear," Cecil said smoothly. "And when they find her murderer, and he confesses, your name is cleared."

"Walk with me," Robert commanded his lover. "I must talk with you alone."

"She cannot," Cecil ruled. "She looks too guilty already. She can't be seen whispering

with a man suspected of murdering an innocent wife."

Abruptly, Robert bowed to Elizabeth and
left the room.

"Good God, Cecil, they won't blame me,
will they?" she demanded.

"Not if you are seen to distance yourself
from him."

"And if they find that she was murdered,
and think that he did it?"

"Then he will have to stand trial, and if
guilty, face execution."

"He cannot die!" she exclaimed. "I cannot
live without him. You know I cannot live
without him! All this will be a disaster if it
comes to that."

"You could always give him a pardon," he
said calmly. "If it comes to that. But it won't.
I can assure you, they will not find him
guilty. I doubt that there is any evidence to
link him to the crime, except his own indiscretion and the general belief that he
wanted his wife dead."

"He looked heartbroken," she said pitifully.

"He did indeed. He will take it hard; he is
a very proud man."

"I cannot bear that he should be so distressed."

"It cannot be helped," Cecil said cheerfully. "Whatever happens next, whatever the inquest rules, his pride will be thrown down and he will always be known as the man who broke his wife's neck in the vain attempt to be king."

* * *

At Abingdon the jury was sworn in and started to hear the evidence about the death of Lady Amy Dudley. They heard that she insisted on everyone going to the fair so that she was left alone in the house. They heard that she was found dead at the foot of the small flight of stairs. The servants attested that her hood was tidy on her head, and her skirts pulled down, before they had picked her up and carried her to her bed.

In the pretty Dairy House at Kew, Robert ordered his mourning clothes but could hardly bear to stand still as the man fitted them.

"Where is Jones?" he demanded. "He is much quicker than this."

"Mr. Jones couldn't come." The man sat back on his heels and spoke, his mouth full of pins. "He said to send you his apologies. I am his assistant."

"My tailor did not come when I sent for him?" Robert repeated, as if he could not believe the words. "My own tailor refused to serve me?" *Dear God, they must think me halfway to the Tower again; if not even my tailor is troubled for my custom, then they must think me halfway to the scaffold for murder.*

"Sir, please let me pin this," the man said.

"Leave it," Robert said irritably. "Take another coat, an old coat, and make it to the same pattern. I cannot bear to stand and have you pin that damned crow color all over me. And you can tell Jones that when I next need a dozen new suits I shall remember that he did not attend me today."

Impatiently, he threw off the half-fitted jacket and strode across the little room in two strides.

Two days and not a word from her, he thought. *She must think I did it. She must think me so wicked as to do such a thing. She must think me a man who would murder an innocent wife. Why would she want to marry such a man? And all the time there will be those very quick to assure her that it is just the sort of man I am.*

He broke off.

But if she were accused, I would go to her side, he thought. *I would not care whether she were guilty or no. I couldn't bear knowing that she was alone and frightened and feeling that she had not a friend in the world.*

And she knows that of me too. She knows that I have been accused before. She knows that I have faced a death verdict without a friend in the world. We promised each other that we would neither of us ever be so alone again.

He paused by the window; the cold glass under his fingers sent a deep shiver through him, though he did not remember why it should be such a dreadful sensation.

"Dear God," he said aloud. "Much more of this and I shall be carving my crest into the chimney piece as I did with my brothers in the Tower. I have come so low again. So low, again."

He leaned his forehead against the glass when a movement on the river caught his eye. He shaded his face against the thick glass to see more clearly. It was a barge with the drummer beating to keep the rowers in time. He squinted his eyes, he made out the flag, the royal standard. It was the royal barge.

"Oh, God, she has come!" he said. At once he could feel his heart pounding. *I knew she would come. I knew she would never leave me, whatever it cost her, whatever the danger, we would face it down together. I knew she would be at my side, always. I knew she would be faithful. I knew she would love me. I never doubted her for a moment.*

He tore open the door and ran from the room, through the river entrance and into the pretty orchard where he had given Elizabeth her May Day breakfast only sixteen months ago.

"Elizabeth!" he shouted, and ran through the orchard toward the landing stage.

It was the royal barge; but it was not Elizabeth getting out of the barge to the landing stage. Dudley halted, suddenly sick with disappointment.

"Oh, Cecil," he said.

William Cecil came down the wooden steps toward him and held out his hand. "There," he said kindly. "Never mind. She sent her best wishes."

"You have not come to arrest me?"

"Good God, no," Cecil said. "This is a courtesy visit, to bring you the queen's best wishes."

"Her best wishes?" Robert said brokenly. "Is that all?"

Cecil nodded. "She can't say more; you know that."

The two men turned and walked to the house.

"You are the only man to come to see me from the court," Robert said as they entered the house, their boots ringing on the wooden floor in the silence. "Think of that! Of all my hundreds of friends and admirers that flocked around me every day when I was at the very center of the court, of all the thousands of them who were proud to call me their friend, who claimed my acquaintanceship even when I hardly knew them . . . and you are the only visitor I have had here."

"It's a fickle world," Cecil agreed. "And true friends are few and far between."

"Far between? Not for me, since I have no true friends at all, I see. You are my only friend, as it turns out," Dudley said wryly.

"And I would not have given you good odds a mere month ago."

Cecil smiled. "Well, I am sorry to see you brought so low," he said frankly. "And sorry to find you with such a heavy heart fitting your mourning clothes. Do you have any news from Abingdon?"

"I daresay you know more than me," Robert said, conscious of Cecil's formidable spy network. "But I have written to Amy's half-brother and asked him to go and make sure the jury do their best to discover the facts, and I have written to the foreman of the jury and begged him to name whoever did it, whoever it may be, without fear or favor. I want the truth to come out of this."

"You insist on knowing?"

"Cecil, it is not me, so who? It's easy enough for everyone else to think it murder and me with blood on my hands. But I know, as no one else can know, that I did not do it. So if I did not do it, who would do such a thing? Whose interest would be served by her death?"

"You don't think it was an accident?" Cecil inquired.

Robert gave a brief laugh. "Good God, I wish I could think that, but how could it be?

Such a short flight of stairs, and her sending everyone out for the day? My worst, my constant fear is that she harmed herself, that she took some poison or a sleeping draft and then threw herself down the stairs headfirst, to make it look like an accident."

"Do you think she was so unhappy that she would have killed herself? I thought her more pious than that? Surely she would never imperil her immortal soul, even if she were heartbroken?"

Robert dropped his head. "God forgive me, it was I who broke her heart," he said quietly. "And if she did herself to death then her love of me cost her a place in heaven as well as happiness in this life. I was unkind to her, Cecil, but before God I never thought it would end like this."

"You really think you drove her to take her own life?"

"I can think of nothing else."

Gently, Cecil touched the younger man's shoulder. "It is a heavy burden you carry, Dudley," he said. "I cannot think of a heavier burden of shame."

Robert nodded. "It has brought me very low," he said softly. "So low that I cannot think how to rise again. I think of her, and I remember her when I first met her, and first loved her, and I know I am the sort of fool who picks a flower to put in his buttonhole and then drops it and leaves it to die from mere wanton carelessness. I took her up like a primrose, as my mother called her, and then I tired of her, and I dropped her as if I was a selfish child; and now she is dead and I can never ask her forgiveness."

There was a silence.

"And the worst thing," Dudley said heavily, "is that I cannot ever tell her that I am sorry that I hurt her so badly. I was always thinking of myself; I was always thinking of the queen; I was chasing my own damned ambition and I did not think what I was doing to her. God forgive me, I put the thought of her away from me, and now she has taken me at my word, and gone away from me, and I will never see her again, and never touch her, and never see her smile. I told her I did not want her anymore, and now I do not have her."

"I will leave you," Cecil said quietly. "I did not come to intrude on your grief; but just to tell you that in all the world, at least you have one friend."

Dudley raised his head and reached out his hand for Cecil.

The older man gripped it hard. "Courage," he said.

"I cannot tell you how thankful I am that you came," Robert said. "Will you remember me to the queen? Urge her to let me come back to court as soon as the verdict is known. I won't be dancing for a while, God knows, but I am very lonely here, Cecil. It is exile as well as mourning."

"I'll speak to her for you," Cecil assured him. "And I will pray for you, and for Amy's soul. You know, I remember her on her wedding day. She just shone with happiness; she loved you so much. She thought you the finest man in the world."

Dudley nodded. "God forgive me for teaching her differently."

Windsor Castle
Memorandum to the queen
Saturday 14th September 1560
1. The jury has delivered a verdict of accidental death on Amy Dudley and so Sir Robert may return to court to his usual duties, if you wish.

2. *The scandal of his wife's death will always cling to his name; he knows this, and so do we all. You must never, by word or deed, indicate to him that this shame could ever be overcome.*

3. *And so you will be safe from any further proposals of marriage from him. If you must continue your love affair it must be with the utmost discretion. He will now understand this.*

4. *The matter of your marriage must be urgently addressed: without a son and heir we are all working for nothing.*

5. *I shall bring to you tomorrow a new proposal from the archduke that I think will be much to our advantage. Sir Robert cannot oppose such a marriage now.*

*　　　*　　　*

Thomas Blount, Dudley's man, stood at the back of the church of St. Mary the Virgin at Oxford and watched the Dudley standard of the ragged staff and bear ride past him at slow march, followed by the elaborate black-draped coffin that was all that was left of little Amy Robsart.

It was all done just as it should be. The queen was represented, and Sir Robert was not there, as was the custom. Amy's half-brothers and the Forsters were there to show Lady Dudley every respect in death that she had lacked in the last days of her life. Lizzie Oddingsell did not attend; she had gone back to her brother's house, filled with such anger and grief that she would speak to no one of her friend except to say once, "She was no match for him," which Alice Hyde gleefully fell on as proof of murder, and which William saw as a fair description of a marriage that had been ill-starred from start to finish.

Thomas Blount waited to see the body interred and the earth shoveled in the ground. He was a thorough man, and he worked for a meticulous master. Then he went back to Cumnor Place.

Amy's maid, Mrs. Pirto, had everything ready for him, as he had ordered. Amy's box of jewels, locked with their key, Amy's best gowns, folded neatly and wrapped with bags of lavender heads, the linen from her bed, the furniture that traveled with her wherever she went, her box of personal goods: her sewing, her rosary, her purse, her gloves, her little collection of wax seals cut from the letters that Robert had sent her over the eleven years of their marriage, and all his letters, tied with a ribbon and arranged by date, worn by constant handling.

"I'll take the jewel box and the personal things," Blount decided. "You shall take the rest back to Stanfield and leave them there. Then you can go."

Mrs. Pirto bowed her head and whispered something about wages. "From the bailiff at Stanfield when you deliver the goods," Thomas Blount said. He ignored the woman's red eyes. All women wept easily, he knew. It meant nothing, and as a man, he had important business to transact.

Mrs. Pirto murmured something about a keepsake.

"Nothing worth remembering," Thomas Blount said roundly, thinking of the trouble that Amy had caused his master in life and in death. "Now you get on, as I must."

He tucked the two boxes under his arm and went out to his waiting horse. The jewel box slid easily into his saddlebag, the box of personal effects he handed to his groom to strap on his back. Then he heaved himself up into the saddle and turned his horse's head for Windsor.

* * *

Robert, returning to court wearing dark mourning clothes, held his head high and looked scornfully around him as if daring anyone to speak. The Earl of Arundel hid a smile behind his hand, Sir Francis Knollys bowed from a distance, Sir Nicholas Bacon all but ignored him. Robert felt as if a chill circle of suspicion and dislike was wrapped around him like a wide black cape.

"What the devil is amiss?" he asked his sister. She came toward him and presented her cold cheek to be kissed.

"I assume that they think you murdered Amy," she said flatly.

"The inquest cleared me. The verdict was accidental death."

"They think you bribed the jury."

"And what do you think?" He raised his voice and then abruptly spoke more quietly as he saw the court glance round at the two of them.

"I think you have taken this family to the very brink of ruin again," she said. "I am sick of disgrace; I am sick of being pointed at. I have been known as the daughter of a traitor, as the sister of a traitor, and now I am known as the sister of a wife murderer."

"Good God, you have not much sympathy to spare for me!" Robert recoiled from the blank hostility of her face.

"I have none at all," she said. "You nearly brought down the queen herself with this scandal. Think of it! You nearly ended the Tudor line. You nearly destroyed the reformed church! Certainly, you have ruined yourself and everyone who bears your name. I am withdrawing from court. I can't stand another day of it."

"Mary, don't go," he said urgently. "You have always stood by me before. You have always been my sister and friend. Don't let everyone see that we are divided. Don't you abandon me, as everyone else has."

He reached out to her, but she stepped away and whipped her hands behind her back so that he could not touch her. At that childish gesture which recalled her in the schoolroom so vividly to him, he nearly cried out. "Mary, you would never abandon me when I am so low, and I have been so wrongly accused!"

"But I think you are rightly accused," she said quietly, and her voice was like ice in his ears. "I think you killed her because you thought in your pride that the queen would stand by you, and everyone else would wink at it. That they would all agree it was an accident and you would go into mourning a widower and come out the queen's betrothed."

"That could still happen," he whispered. "I did not kill her, I swear it. I could still marry the queen."

"Never," she said. "You are finished. The best you can hope for is that she keeps you on as Master of Horse and as her little disgraced favorite."

She turned from him. Robert, conscious of the eyes of everyone upon him, could not call her back. For a moment, he made a move to catch the hem of her gown and jerk her round, before she got away; but then he remembered that everyone watching believed him to be a man who was violent to women, a man who had killed his wife, and his hands felt heavy.

There was a stir at the door of the privy chamber and Elizabeth came out. She was very pale. She had not been out riding nor walking in the garden since the day of her birthday, when she had told the Spanish ambassador that Amy was dead or nearly so—three days before anyone knew that Amy had been found dead. There were many who thought that her opinion, three whole days before the announcement of the death, that Amy was dead "or nearly so," was more than a lucky guess. There were many who thought that Robert had been executioner, and Elizabeth the judge. But none of them would dare say such a thing when she could come out of her room, as now, flick her eye around the presence chamber, and count on the support of every great man in the country.

She looked past Robert and on to Sir Nicholas; she nodded at Sir Francis, and turned to speak to his wife, Catherine, who was behind her. She smiled at Cecil and she beckoned the Hapsburg ambassador to her side.

"Good day, Sir Robert," she said, as the ambassador moved toward her. "I give you my condolences on the sad and sudden death of your wife."

He bowed and felt his anger and his grief swell up so strongly that he thought he

THE VIRGIN'S LOVER 787

might vomit. He came up, his face betraying nothing. "I thank you for your sympathy," he said. He let his angry look rake them all. "I thank all of you for your sympathy which has been such a support to me," he said, and then he stepped to a window bay, out of the way, and stood all alone.

*　　　*　　　*

Thomas Blount found Sir Robert in the stable. There was a hunt planned for the next day and Sir Robert was checking the horses for fitness, and inspecting the tack. Forty-two saddles of gleaming supple leather were arranged in long rows on saddle horses in the yard, and Sir Robert was walking slowly between the rows looking carefully at each saddle, each girth, each stirrup leather. The stable lads, standing alongside their work, were as rigid as soldiers on parade.

Behind them the horses were standing, shifting restlessly, a groom at each nodding head, their coats gleaming, their hooves oiled, their manes pulled and combed flat.

Sir Robert took his time but could find little wrong with the horses, the tack, or the stable yard. "Good," he said finally. "You can give them their evening feed and water, and put them to bed."

Then he turned and saw Thomas Blount. "Go into my office," he said shortly, pausing to pat the neck of his own horse. "Yes," he said softly to her. "You don't change, do you, sweetheart?"

Blount was waiting by the window. Robert threw his gloves and whip on the table and dropped into the chair before his desk.

"All done?" he asked.

"All done quite correctly," Blount said. "A small slip in the sermon."

"What was it?"

"The stupid rector said that she was a lady 'tragically slain' instead of 'tragically died.' He corrected himself, but it jarred."

Sir Robert raised one dark eyebrow. "A slip?"

Blount shrugged. "I think so. A nuisance, but it's not strong enough to be an accusation."

"It adds grist to the mill," Robert observed.

Blount nodded.

"And you dismissed her staff, and you

have her things?" Deliberately Robert kept his voice light and cold.

"Mrs. Oddingsell had gone already. Apparently she had taken it very hard," Blount said. "Mrs. Pirto I sent back to Stanfield with the goods and she will be paid there. I sent a note. I saw Mr. and Mrs. Forster; they have a sense that a great scandal has been brought to their door." He smiled wryly.

"They will be compensated for their trouble," Dudley said shortly. "Any gossip in the village?"

"No more than you would expect," Blount said. "Half the village accept the verdict of accidental death. Half think she was murdered. They'll talk about it forever. But it makes no difference to you."

"Nor to her," Robert said quietly.

Blount fell silent.

"So," Robert said, rousing himself. "Your work is done. She is dead and buried and whatever anyone thinks, no one can say anything that can hurt me more."

"It's finished," Blount agreed.

Robert gestured for him to put the boxes on the table. Blount put down the keepsake box and then the little box of jewels with the key beside it. He bowed and waited.

"You can go," Robert said.

He had forgotten the box. It was his gift to Amy when they had been courting; he had bought it for her at a fair in Norfolk. She had never had many jewels for the small box. He felt the familiar irritation that even when she had been Lady Dudley, and commanded his fortune, still she had nothing more than a small jewel box, a couple of silver-gilt necklaces, some earrings and a ring or two.

He turned the key in the box and opened it up. On the very top lay Amy's wedding ring, and his signet ring with his crest, the bear and ragged staff.

For a moment, he could not believe what he was seeing. Slowly, he put his hand into the box and lifted out the two gold circles. Mrs. Pirto had taken them from Amy's cold fingers and put them in her jewel box and locked it up, as a good servant should do.

Robert looked at them both. The wedding ring he had slipped on Amy's finger that summer day eleven years ago, and the signet ring had never left his own hand until he had put it on Elizabeth's finger to seal their betrothal, just four months ago.

Robert slipped his signet ring back on his finger, and sat at his desk while the room grew dark and cold, wondering how his ring had got from the chain around his mistress's neck to the finger of his dead wife.

*   *   *

He walked by the river, a question beating at his brain. *Who killed Amy?* He sat on the pier like a boy, boots dangling over the water, looking down into the green depths where little fishes nibbled at the weed on the beams of the jetty, and heard in his head the second question: *Who gave Amy my ring?*

He rose up as he grew chilled, and strolled along the tow path, westward toward the sun which slowly dropped in the sky and went from burning gold to embers as Robert walked, looking at the river but not seeing it, looking at the sky but not seeing it.

Who killed Amy?

Who gave her my ring?

The sun set and the sky grew palely gray; still Robert walked onward as if he did not own a stable full of horses, a stud of Barbary courses, a training program of young stallions, he walked like a poor man, like a man whose wife would give him a horse to ride.

Who killed Amy?
Who gave her my ring?

He tried not to remember the last time he had seen her, when he had left her with a curse, and turned her family against her. He tried not to remember that he had taken her in his arms and she in her folly had heard, and he in his folly had said: "I love you."

He tried not to remember her at all because it seemed to him that if he remembered her he would sit down on the riverbank and weep like a child for the loss of her.

Who killed Amy?
Who gave her my ring?

If he thought, rather than remembered, he could avoid the wave of pain which was towering over him, ready to break. If he treated her death as a puzzle rather than a tragedy he could ask a question rather than accuse himself.

Two questions: *Who killed Amy? Who gave her my ring?*

When he stumbled and slipped and jolted himself to consciousness he realized that it had grown dark and he was walking blindly beside the steep bank of the deep, fast-flowing river. He turned then, a survivor from a family of survivors who had been wrong to marry a woman who did not share his inveterate lust for life.

Who killed Amy?

Who gave her my ring?

He started to walk back. It was only when he opened the iron gate to the walled garden that the coldness of his hand on the latch made him pause, made him realize that there were two questions: *Who killed Amy? Who gave her my ring?* but only one answer.

Whoever had the ring owned the symbol that Amy would trust. Amy would clear the house for a messenger who showed her that ring. Whoever had the ring was the person who killed her. There was only one person who could have done it, only one person who would have done it:

Elizabeth.

*   *   *

Robert's first instinct was to go to her at once, to rage at her for the madness of her power. He could not blame her for wishing Amy gone; but the thought that his mistress could murder his wife, the girl he had married for love, filled him with anger. He wanted to take Elizabeth and shake the arrogance, the wicked, power-sated confidence out of her. That she should use her power as queen, her spy network, her remorseless will, against a target as vulnerable and as innocent as Amy, made him tremble like an angry boy at the strength of his feelings.

Robert did not sleep that night. He lay down on the bed and stared at the ceiling but over and over again he saw in his mind's eye Amy receiving his ring, and running out to meet him, with his signet ring clenched in her little fist as her passport to the happiness she deserved. And then some man, one of Cecil's hired killers no doubt, greeting her in his place, breaking her neck with one blow, a clenched fist to her ear, a rabbit chop to her neck, and catching her as she fell, carrying her back into the house.

Robert tortured himself with the thought of her suffering, of her moment of fear, perhaps of a moment of horror when she thought the killer came from him and the queen. That thought made him groan and turn over, burying his face in the pillow. If Amy had died thinking that he had sent an assassin against her then he did not see how he could bear to live.

The bedroom window lightened at last; it was dawn. Robert, as haggard as a man ten years his senior, rose to the window and looked out, his linen sheet wrapped around his naked body. It was going to be a beautiful day. The mist was curling slowly off the river and somewhere a woodpecker was drilling. Slowly the liquid melody of a song thrush started up like a benediction, like a reminder that life goes on.

I suppose I can forgive her, Robert thought. *In her place, I might have done the same thing. I might have thought that our love came first, that our desire must be satisfied, come what may. If I had been her, I might have thought that we have to have a child, that the throne has to have an heir, and we dare not delay. If I had absolute power as she does I would probably have used it, as she has.*

My father would have done it. My father would have forgiven her for doing it. Actually, he would have admired her decisiveness.

He sighed. "She did it for love of me," he said aloud. "No other reason but to set me free so that she could love me openly. No other reason but that she could marry me, and I could be king. And she knows that we both want that more than anything in the world. I could accept this terrible sorrow and this terrible crime as a gift of love. I can forgive her. I can love her. I can draw some happiness out of this misery."

The sky grew paler and then slowly the sun rose, pale primrose, over the silver of the river. "God forgive me and God forgive Elizabeth," Robert prayed quietly. "And God bring Amy the peace in heaven which I denied her on earth. And God grant that I am a better husband this time."

There was a tap at his chamber door. "It's dawn, my lord!" the servant called out. "Do you want your hot water?"

"Yes!" Robert shouted back. He went to the door, trailing the sheet, and shot back the bolt from the inside. "Put it down there, lad. And tell them in the kitchen that I am hungry, and warn the stable that I will be there within the hour; I am leading out the hunt today."

*   *   *

He was in the stable an hour before the court was ready to ride, making sure that everything was perfect: horses, hounds, tack, and hunt servants. The whole court was riding out today in merry mood. Robert stood on a vantage point of the steps above the stable and watched the courtiers mounting up, the ladies being helped into their saddles. His sister was not there. She had gone back to Penshurst.

Elizabeth was riding, in fine spirits. Robert went to help her into the saddle but then delayed, and let another man go. Over the courtier's head she shot him a little tentative smile and he smiled back at her. She could be assured that things would be all right between them. She could be forgiven. The Spanish ambassador saw them off; the Hapsburg ambassador rode beside her.

They had a good morning's hunting. The scent was strong and the hounds went well. Cecil rode out to meet them at dinner time when they were served with a picnic of hot soup and mulled ale and hot pasties under the trees which were a blaze of turning color: gold and red and yellow.

Robert stood away from the intimate circle around Elizabeth, even when she turned and gave him a shy little smile to invite him to her side. He bowed, but did not go closer. He wanted to wait until he could see her alone, when he could tell her that he knew what she had done, he knew that it had been for love of him, and that he could forgive her.

After they had dined and went to remount their horses, Sir Francis Knollys found his horse had been tied beside Robert's mare.

"I must offer you my condolences on the death of your wife," Sir Francis said stiffly.

"I thank you," Robert replied, as coldly as the queen's best friend had spoken to him.

Sir Francis turned his horse away.

"Do you remember an afternoon in the queen's chapel?" Robert suddenly said. "The queen was there, me, you, and Lady Catherine. It was a binding service, remember? It was a promise that cannot be broken."

The older man looked at him, almost with pity. "I don't remember any such thing," he said simply. "Either I did not witness it, or it did not happen. But I do not remember it."

Robert felt himself flush with the heat of temper. "I remember it well enough; it happened," he insisted.

"I think you will find you are the only one," Sir Francis replied quietly and spurred on his horse.

Robert checked the horses over, and glanced at the hounds. One horse was limping slightly and he snapped his fingers for a groom to lead it back to the castle. He supervised the mounting of the court; but he hardly saw them. His head was pounding with the duplicity of Sir Francis, who would deny that Robert and the queen had sworn to marry, who was suggesting that the queen would deny it too. *As if she would betray me,* Robert swore to himself. *After what she has done to be with me! What man could have more proof that a woman loves him than she would do such a thing to set me free? She loves me, as I love her, more than life itself! We were born for each other, born to be together. As if we could ever be apart! As if she did not do this terrible, this unbearable crime for love of me! To set me free!*

"Are you glad to be back at court?" Cecil asked in a friendly tone, bringing his horse alongside Robert's.

Robert, recalled to the present, looked at him. "I cannot say I am merry," he said quietly. "I cannot say that my welcome has been warm."

The secretary's eyes were kind. "People will forget, you know," he said gently. "It will never be the same again for you, but people forget."

"And I am free to marry," Dudley said. "When people have forgotten my wife, and her death, I will be free to marry again."

Cecil nodded. "Indeed, yes. But not the queen."

Dudley looked at him. "What?"

"It is the scandal," Cecil confided in him in his friendly tone. "As I told you when you left court. She could not have her name linked with yours. Your sons could never take the throne of England. You are infamed by the death of your wife. You are ruined as a royal suitor. She will never be able to marry you now."

"What are you saying? That she will never marry me now?"

"Exactly," Cecil replied, almost regretfully. "You are right. She can never marry you now."

"Then why did she do it?" Dudley demanded, his whisper as soft as falling snow. "Why kill Amy, my wife, if not to set me free? Amy, the only innocent among us, Amy who had done nothing wrong but hold faith. What was the benefit if not to release me for marriage with the queen? You will have been in her counsel; you will have made this plan together. It will have been your villains who did it. Why murder little Amy if not to set me free to marry the queen?"

Cecil did not pretend to misunderstand him. "You are not released for marriage with the queen," he said. "You are prevented forever. Any other way and you would always have been eligible. You would always have been her first choice. Now she cannot choose you. You are forever disbarred."

"You have destroyed me, Cecil," Dudley's voice broke. "You killed Amy and fixed the blame on me, and destroyed me."

"I am her servant," Cecil said, as gentle as a father to a grieving son. "As you know."

"She ordered the death of my wife? Amy died by Elizabeth's order so that I should be shamed to the ground and never, never rise again?"

"No, no, it was an accidental death," Cecil reminded the younger man. "The inquest ruled it so, the twelve good men of Abingdon, even when you wrote to them and pressed them to investigate most closely. They had their verdict; they brought it in. It was accidental death. Better for all of us if we leave it so, perhaps."

AUTHOR'S NOTE

The mystery of how Amy Robsart died is still unsolved four centuries after her death. Several culprits have been suggested: malignant cancer of the breast which would account for reports of breast pain, and could result in the thinning of the bones of her neck; Robert Dudley's agents; Elizabeth's agents; Cecil's agents; or, suicide.

Also fascinating are the incriminating and indiscreet remarks from Cecil and Elizabeth to the Spanish ambassador in the days before Amy's death, which he recorded for his master, just as I present them in this fictional account.

It seems to me that Cecil and Elizabeth knew that Amy would die on Sunday, September 8, and were deliberately planting evidence with the ambassador to incriminate

Robert Dudley. Elizabeth incriminates herself as an accessory by predicting Amy's death before the event, and by saying that she died of a broken neck, before the detailed news reaches the court.

Why Elizabeth and Cecil should do such a thing we cannot know. I don't believe that either of them blurted out the truth by accident, to the man most likely to circulate such scandal. I suggest that it was Elizabeth and Cecil's plan to smear Dudley with the crime of wife-murder.

Certainly the shadow of guilt was effective in preventing Robert from attaining the throne. In 1566 William Cecil wrote a six-point memorandum to the Privy Council listing the reasons that Robert Dudley could not marry the queen: "IV. He is infamed by the death of his wife."

Were Elizabeth and Robert full lovers? Perhaps in these more permissive days we can say that it hardly matters. What does matter is that she loved him all her life, and despite his later marriage to Laetitia Knollys (another Boleyn redhead) he undoubtedly loved her. His last letter was to Elizabeth, telling her of his love, and when she died it was with his letter by her bedside.

This is a short list of the books that helped my research for this novel.

Adlard, George. *Amye Robsart and the Earl of Leicester,* 1870

Bartlett, A. D. *An Historical Account of Cumnor Place,* 1850

Brigden, Susan. *New Worlds, Lost Worlds: The Rule of the Tudors: 1485–1603,* 2000

Clarke, John. *Palaces and Parks of Richmond and Kew,* 1995.

Cressy, David. *Birth, Marriage and Death: Ritual, Religions and the Life Cycle in Tudor and Stuart England,* 1977.

Darby, H. C. *A New Historical Geography of England Before 1600,* 1976.

Doran, Susan. *Monarchy and Matrimony: The Courtships of Elizabeth I,* 1996.

Dovey, Zillah. *An Elizabethan Progress,* 1996.

Dunn, Jane. *Elizabeth and Mary: Cousins, Rivals, Queens,* 2003.

Dunlop, Ian. *Palaces and Progresses of Elizabeth I,* 1962.

Evans, R. J. W. *St. Michael's Church, Cumnor: A Guide,* 2003

Frere, Sir Bartle. *Amy Robsart of Wymondham,* 1937.

Grierson, Francis. "An Elizabethan Enigma," *Contemporary Review,* August 1960.

Guy, John. *Tudor England,* 1988.

Haynes, Alan. *The White Bear: Robert Dudley, the Elizabethan Earl of Leicester,* 1987.

———. *Invisible Power: The Elizabethan Secret Services 1570–1603,* 1992.

———. *Sex in Elizabethan England,* 1997.

Hibbert, Christopher. *The Virgin Queen,* 1992.

Hume, Martin A. S. *The Courtships of Queen Elizabeth,* 1898.

Jackson, Revd. Canon. "Amye Robsart," *The Nineteenth Century, A Monthly Review,* ed. James Knowles, March 1882, no 61.

Jenkins, Elizabeth. *Elizabeth and Leicester,* 1961.

Loades, David. *The Tudor Court,* 1986.

Milton, Giles. *Big Chief Elizabeth,* 2000.

Neale, J. E. *Queen Elizabeth,* 1934.

Picard, Liza. *Elizabeth's London,* 2003.

Pettigrew, T. J. *An Inquiry Concerning the Death of Amy Robsart,* 1859.

Plowden, Alison. *The Young Elizabeth,* 1999.

———. *Elizabeth: Marriage with My Kingdom,* 1999.

———. *Tudor Women: Queens and Commoners,* 1998.

Read, Conyers. *Mr. Secretary Cecil and Queen Elizabeth,* 1955.

Ridley, Jasper. *Elizabeth I,* 1987.

Rye, Walter. *The Murder of Amy Robsart, A Brief for the Prosecution,* 1885.

Sidney, Philip. *Who Killed Amy Robsart?* 1901.

Somerset, Anne. *Elizabeth I,* 1997.

Starkey, David. *Elizabeth,* 2001.

Strong, Roy. *The Cult of Elizabeth,* 1999.

Turner, Robert. *Elizabethan Magic: The Art and the Magus,* 1989.

Waldman, Milton. *Elizabeth and Leicester,* 1944.

Walker, Julia M., ed. *Dissing Elizabeth: Negative Representations of Gloriana,* 1998.

Weir, Alison. *Children of England,* 1997.

———. *Elizabeth the Queen,* 1999.

Wilson, Derek A. *Sweet Robin: A Biography of Robert Dudley, Earl of Leicester, 1533–1588,* 1981.

Yaxley, Susan. *Amy Robsart, Wife of Robert Dudley, 1532–1560,* 1996.

ABOUT THE AUTHOR

PHILIPPA GREGORY is the author of several novels, including *The Other Boleyn Girl* and *The Queen's Fool*. *Wideacre,* her debut, was a *New York Times* bestseller and the first in a trilogy that included *The Favored Child* and *Meridon*. A writer and broadcaster for radio and television, she lives in England.

For further information about this and any of Philippa Gregory's other books, and on forthcoming appearances, reviews, and unpublished material, please visit her website at www.philippagregory.com.